Joanna Cannon graduated from Leicester Medical School and worked as a hospital doctor, before specialising in psychiatry. Her first novel, *The Trouble with Goats and Sheep*, was a top ten bestseller in both hardback and paperback, and was a Richard and Judy pick. She lives in the Peak District with her family and her dog.

# THREE THINGS ABOUT ELSIE

*There are three things you should know about Elsie. The first thing is that she's my best friend. The second is that she always knows what to say to make me feel better. And the third thing . . . might take a little bit more explaining.* Eighty-four-year-old Florence has fallen in her flat at Cherry Tree Home for the Elderly. As she waits to be rescued, she wonders if a terrible secret from her past is about to come to light. And if the charming new resident is who he claims to be, why does he look exactly like a man who died sixty years ago?

*Books by Joanna Cannon*
*Published by Ulverscroft:*

**THE TROUBLE WITH GOATS AND SHEEP**

JOANNA CANNON

# THREE THINGS ABOUT ELSIE

*Complete and Unabridged*

# CHARNWOOD
*Leicester*

First published in Great Britain in 2018 by
The Borough Press
An imprint of Harper Collins*Publishers*
London

First Charnwood Edition
published 2018
by arrangement with
Harper Collins*Publishers*
London

A catalogue record for this book is available
from the British Library.

ISBN 978–1–4448–3768–1

Published by
F. A. Thorpe (Publishing)
Anstey, Leicestershire

Set by Words & Graphics Ltd.
Anstey, Leicestershire
Printed and bound in Great Britain by
T. J. International Ltd., Padstow, Cornwall

This book is printed on acid-free paper

*To George and Florrie*

# 4.48 p.m.

'How did you fall, Flo?' they'll ask when they find me. 'Did you feel dizzy? Were you wearing your glasses? Did you trip?'

They'll work as they talk. Putting a cuff around my arm and fastening a plastic clip on my finger, and unwrapping all the leads from one of their machines. Someone will shine a light in my eyes, and someone else will rummage through all my tablets and put them in one of their carrier bags.

'Did you feel faint? Can you smile for me? Can you squeeze my hand?'

They'll carry me out of my front room, and they will struggle, because it's barely big enough for me, let alone these two men and their uniforms. They will put me in the back of their ambulance, in the bright-white, blanketed world they inhabit, and I will blink and crease my eyes and try to make sense of their faces.

'It's all right, Flo,' they will say. 'Everything is going to be fine, Flo.'

Even though they don't know me. Even though I have never said they can call me Flo. Even though the only person who has ever called me that is Elsie.

One of them will sit with me, as we move along the streets, under the spin of a blue light. The light will turn across his face as we travel, and he will smile at me from time to time, and

1

his hand will somehow find mine in the darkness.

When we get to the hospital, I will be rattled across A&E and taken through red double doors, to people with the same questions and the same bright lights, and they will wheel me down blank corridors and put me through their machinery. A girl at a desk will look up as I pass by, and then she will turn away, because I am just another old person on a trolley, wrapped up in blankets and trying to hold on to the world.

They will find me a ward, and a nurse with quiet hands. She will move very slowly, but everything will be done in a moment, and the nurse with quiet hands will be the first person to listen with her eyes. The bed will be warm and smooth, and I won't worry even when the lights are switched off.

Everything I've just told you is yet to happen. None of it is real. Because right at this very moment, I'm lying on the sitting-room floor, waiting to be found. Waiting for someone to notice I'm not here any more.

I have all this time before they arrive, to work out what I'm going to say. All this time to remember everything that happened, right from the beginning, and turn it into something they'll understand. Something they'll accept. You'd think the silence would help, but it doesn't. The only thing I can hear is my own breath, arguing its way backwards and forwards, and just when I'm sure I have an idea all ironed out, it slides away from me and I have to start from the beginning again.

'Do try to focus, Florence,' Elsie always says. 'Concentrate on one word at a time.'

But Elsie isn't here to help me, and so I'll have to search through the words all by myself, because buried amongst them, I need to find a place for the silence. Everyone's life has a secret, something they never talk about. Everyone has words they keep to themselves. It's what you do with your secret that really matters. Do you drag it behind you forever, like a difficult suitcase, or do you find someone to tell? I said to myself I would never tell anyone. It would be a secret I'd keep forever. Except now that I'm lying here, waiting to be found, I can't help worrying that this is my lot. Perhaps the closing words of my chapter will be spoken in a room filled with beige and forgetfulness, and no one was ever meant to hear them. You never really know it's the final page, do you, until you get there?

I wonder if I've already reached the end of the story.

I wonder if my forever is now.

# Florence

It was a month ago when it all started. A Friday morning. I was glancing around the room, wondering what I'd done with my television magazine, when I noticed.

It was facing the wrong way. The elephant on the mantelpiece. It always points towards the window, because I read somewhere it brings you luck. Of course, I know it doesn't. It's like putting new shoes on a table, though, or crossing on the stairs. There's a corner of your head that feels uncomfortable if you don't follow the rules. Normally, I would have blamed one of the uniforms, but I always go over everything with a duster after they've gone. There's usually a need for it and it helps to pass the time. So I would have spotted it straight away. I notice everything.

'Do you notice anything?'

Miss Ambrose had arrived for our weekly chat. Fidgety. Smells of hairspray. A cousin in Truro. I decided to test her. She scanned the room, but any fool could tell she wasn't concentrating.

'Look properly,' I said. 'Give it your full attention.'

She unwound her scarf. 'I am,' she said. 'I am.'

I waited.

'The elephant. The elephant on the mantel-piece.' I prodded my finger. 'It's facing towards the television. It always faces towards the window. It's moved.'

4

She said, did I fancy a change? A change! I prodded my finger again and said, 'I didn't do it.'

She didn't take me seriously. She never does. 'It must have been one of the cleaners,' she said.

'It wasn't the cleaners. When I went to bed last night, it was facing the right way. When I got up this morning, it was back to front.'

'You haven't been dusting again, have you, Florence? Dusting is our department.'

I wouldn't let her find my eyes. I chose to look at the radiator instead. 'I wouldn't dream of it,' I said.

She sat on the armchair next to the fireplace and let out a little sigh. 'Perhaps it fell?'

'And climbed back up all by itself?'

'We don't always remember, do we? Some things we do automatically, without thinking. You must have put it back the wrong way round.'

I went over to the mantelpiece and turned the elephant to face the window again. I stared at her the whole time I was doing it.

'It's only an ornament, Florence. No harm done. Shall I put the kettle on?'

I watched the elephant while she rummaged around in the kitchen, trying to locate a ginger nut.

'They're in the pantry on the top shelf,' I shouted. 'You can't miss them.'

Miss Ambrose reappeared with a tray. 'They were on the first shelf, actually. We don't always know what we're doing, do we?'

I studied her jumper. It had little pom-poms

5

all around the bottom, in every colour you could possibly wish for. 'No,' I said. 'We probably don't.'

Miss Ambrose sat on the very edge of the armchair. She always wore cheerful clothes, it was just a shame her face never went along with it. Elsie and I once had a discussion about how old Miss Ambrose might be. Elsie plumped for late thirties, but I think that particular ship sailed a long time ago. She always looked like someone who hadn't had quite enough sleep, but had put on another coat of lipstick and enthusiasm, in an effort to make sure the rest of the world didn't ever find her out. I watched the radiator again, because Miss Ambrose had a habit of finding things in your eyes you didn't think anyone else would ever notice.

'So, how have you been, Florence?'

There are twenty-five grooves on that radiator.

'I'm fine, thank you.'

'What did you get up to this week?'

They're quite difficult to count, because if you stare at them for any length of time, your eyes start to play tricks on you.

'I've been quite busy.'

'We've not seen you in the day room very much. There are lots of activities going on — did you not fancy card-making yesterday?'

I've got a drawer full of those cards. I could congratulate half a dozen people on the birth of their beautiful daughter with one pull of a handle.

'Perhaps next week,' I said.

I heard Miss Ambrose take a deep breath. I

knew this meant trouble, because she only ever does it when she needs the extra oxygen for a debate about something.

'Florence,' she said.

I didn't answer.

'Florence. I just want to be sure that you're happy at Cherry Tree?'

Miss Ambrose was one of those people whose sentences always went up at the end. As though the world appeared so uncertain to her that it needed constant interrogation. I glanced out of the window. Everything was brick and concrete, straight lines and sharp corners, and tiny windows into small lives. There was no horizon. I never thought I would lose the horizon along with everything else, but it's only when you get old that you realise whichever direction you choose to face, you find yourself confronted with a landscape filled up with loss.

'Perhaps we should have a little rethink about whether Cherry Tree is still the right place for you?' she said. 'Perhaps there's somewhere else you'd enjoy more?'

I turned to her. 'You're not sending me to Greenbank.'

'Greenbank has a far higher staff-to-resident ratio.' Miss Ambrose tilted her head. I could see all the little lines in her neck helping it along. 'You'd have much more one-to-one attention.'

'I don't want one-to-one attention. I don't want any attention. I just want to be left in peace.'

'Florence, as we get older, we lose the ability to judge what's best for us. It happens to

7

everyone. You might enjoy Greenbank. It might be fun.'

'It's not much fun when no one listens to what you say,' I spoke to the radiator.

'Pardon?'

'I'm not going. You can't make me.'

Miss Ambrose started to say something, but she swallowed it back instead. 'Why don't we try for a compromise? Shall we see how things go over the next . . . month, say? Then we can reassess.'

'A month?'

'A re-evaluation. For all of us. A probationary period.'

'Probation? What crime did I commit?'

'It's a figure of speech, Florence. That's all.' Miss Ambrose's shoes tapped out a little beige tune on the carpet. She pulled out a silence, like they always do, hoping you'll fill it up with something they can get their teeth into, but I was wise to it now.

'It's *Gone with the Wind* tomorrow afternoon,' she said eventually, when the silence didn't work out for her.

'I've seen it,' I said.

'The whole world's seen it. That's not the point.'

'I was never very big on Clark Gable.'

I was still looking at the radiator, but I could hear Miss Ambrose lean forward. 'You can't just bury yourself in here, Florence. A month's probation, remember? You've got to meet me halfway.'

I wanted to say, 'Why have I got to meet

8

anybody halfway to anywhere?' but I didn't. I concentrated on the radiator instead, and I didn't stop concentrating on it until I heard the front door shut to.

'He had bad breath, you know, Clark Gable,' I shouted. 'I read about it. In a magazine.'

★  ★  ★

There are three things you should know about Elsie, and the first thing is that she's my best friend.

People chop and change best friends, first one and then another depending what kind of mood they happen to find themselves in and who they're talking to, but mine has always been Elsie and it always will be. That's what a best friend is all about, isn't it? Someone who stands by you, no matter what. I can't say we haven't had our arguments over the years, but that's because we're so opposite. We even look opposite. Elsie's short and I'm tall. Elsie's tiny and I have big feet. Size eight. I tell everybody. Because Elsie says there comes a point when feet are so large, the only thing really left to do is to boast about them.

We spend most of our time with each other, me and Elsie. We even opted to eat our meals together, because it makes it easier for the uniforms. It's nice to have a bit of company, because nothing in this world sounds more lonely than one knife and fork rattling on a dinner plate.

It was later that day, the day Miss Ambrose

gave me my ultimatum, and Elsie and I were sitting by the window in my flat, having our lunch.

'They've still not shown their face,' I said.

I knew she'd heard me, the woman in the pink uniform. She was dishing up my meal on a wheel three feet away, and I'm a clear speaker, even at the worst of times. Elsie says I shout, but I don't shout. I just like to make sure people have understood. I even tapped on the glass to be certain.

'Number twelve.' I tapped. 'I said they've still not shown their face. They've been in there a few days now, because I've seen lights go on and off.'

The woman in the pink uniform spooned out a puddle of baked beans. She didn't even flinch.

Elsie looked up.

'Don't shout, Flo,' she said.

'I'm not shouting,' I said. 'I'm making a point. I'm not allowed to do very much any more, but I'm still allowed to make a point. And that skip hasn't been collected yet. They need a letter.'

'So why don't you write one?' said Elsie.

I looked at her and looked away again. 'I can't write a letter, because I've been given an ultimatum.'

'What do you mean?'

'Miss Ambrose has put me on probation.' I spoke into the glass.

'What crime did you commit?'

'It's a figure of speech,' I said. 'That's all.'

'They'll clear the skip away soon, Miss Claybourne,' said the woman.

I turned to her. 'They shouldn't be allowed to

sweep a person away like that. Someone ought to be told.'

'They can do whatever they want when you're dead,' said Elsie. 'Your world is their oyster, Florence.'

In the courtyard, a tumble of leaves gathered at the edge of the grass, and oranges and reds turned over and over on the concrete. 'I only saw her last week. Walking along that path with a shopping bag.'

The woman in the pink uniform looked up. 'It should make a difference,' I said. 'That I saw her. Now everything she ever was is lying in that skip.'

'They had to clear the flat,' she said, 'for the next person.'

We both watched her. She gave nothing away.

'I wonder who that is,' I said.

Still nothing.

'I wonder as well,' said Elsie.

The woman in the pink uniform frowned at herself. 'I've been off. And anyway, Miss Bissell deals with all of that.'

I raised my eyebrow at Elsie, but Elsie went back to her fish finger. Elsie gave up far too easily, in my opinion. There was a badge on the front of the woman's uniform that said 'Here to Help'.

'It would be quite helpful,' I said to the badge, 'to share any rumours you might have heard.'

The words hovered for a while in mid-air.

'All I know is, it's a man,' she said.

'A man?' I said.

Elsie looked up. 'A man?'

'Are you certain?' I said.

Yes, she said; yes, she was quite certain.

Elsie and I exchanged a glance over the tablecloth. There were very few men at Cherry Tree. You spotted them from time to time, planted in the corner of the communal lounge or wandering the grounds, along paths that led nowhere except back to where they'd started. But most of the residents were women. Women who had long since lost their men. Although I always thought the word 'lost' sounded quite peculiar, as though they had left their husbands on a railway platform by mistake.

'I wonder how many people went to her funeral,' I said. 'The woman from number twelve. Perhaps we should have made the effort.'

'There's never a particularly good turnout these days.'

Elsie pulled her cardigan a little tighter. It was the colour of mahogany. It did her no favours. 'That's the trouble with a funeral when you're old. Most of the guest list have already pipped you to the post.'

'She wasn't here very long,' I said.

Elsie pushed mashed potato on to her fork. 'What was her name again?'

'Brenda, I think. Or it might have been Barbara. Or perhaps Betty.'

The skip was filled with her life — Brenda's, or Barbara's, or perhaps Betty's. There were ornaments she had loved and paintings she had chosen. Books she'd read, or would never finish; photographs that had smashed from their frames as they'd hit against the metal. Photographs she

12

had dusted and cared for, of people who were clearly no longer here to claim themselves from the debris. It was so quickly disposed of, so easily dismantled. A small existence, disappeared. There was nothing left to say she'd even been there. Everything remained exactly as it was before. As if someone had put a bookmark in her life and slammed it shut.

'I wonder who'll dust my photograph after I'm gone,' I said.

I heard Elsie rest her cutlery on the edge of the plate. 'How do you mean?'

I studied the pavement. 'I wonder if I made any difference to the world at all.'

'Does it matter, Flo?' she said.

My thoughts escaped in a whisper. 'Oh yes, it matters. It matters very much.'

When I turned around, Elsie was smiling at me.

★   ★   ★

'Which one was that, then?' I said.

The pink uniform had left us with a Tunnock's Tea Cake and the Light Programme. Elsie insisted it was called Radio 2 now, but perhaps she'd given up correcting me.

'The one with a boyfriend called Daryl and acid reflux,' said Elsie. We watched the uniform make its way up the stairwell of the flats opposite, flashes of pink against a beige landscape. 'Enjoys making mountains out of molehills.'

'Is she the one with a wise head on her shoulders?' I said.

13

'No.' Elsie stirred her tea. 'That's Saturday. Blue uniform. Small ears. You must try to remember. It's important.'

'Why is it important?'

'It just is, Florence. It just is. I might not always be here to remind you, and you'll need to remember for yourself.'

'I always get them mixed up,' I said. 'There are so many of them.'

There *were* so many of them. Miss Bissell's 'army of helpers'. They marched through Cherry Tree, feeding and bathing and shuffling old people around like playing cards. Some residents needed more help than others, but Elsie and I were lucky. We were level ones. We were fed and watered, but apart from that, they usually left us to our own devices. Miss Bissell said she kept her north eye on the level ones, which made it sound like she had a wide range of other eyes she could choose from, to keep everybody else in line. After level three, you were moved on, an unwanted audience to other people's lives. Most residents were sent to Greenbank when they had outstayed their welcome, which was neither green, nor on a bank, but a place where people waited for God in numbered rooms, shouting out for the past, as if the past might somehow reappear and rescue them.

'I wonder what level he's on.' I peered out at number twelve. 'The new chap.'

'Oh, at least a two,' Elsie said. 'Probably a three. You know how men are. They're not especially resilient.'

'I hope he's not a three, we'll never see him.'

'Why in heaven's name would you want to see him, Florence?' Elsie sat back, and her cardigan blended in with the sideboard.

'It helps to pass the time,' I said. 'Like the Light Programme.'

★ ★ ★

We sat by the window in my flat, because Elsie says it has a much better view, and the afternoon wandered past in front of us. More often than not, there's something happening in that courtyard. Whenever I'm at a loose end, I always look out of the window. It's the best thing since sliced bread. Much more entertaining than the television. Gardeners and cleaners, and postmen. No one ever taking any notice whatsoever of anyone else. All those separate little lives, and everyone hurrying through them to get to the other side, although I'm not entirely sure they'll like what they find when they get here. I doubt it was anything to do with the woman who dished up our baked beans, but a short while later, they arrived to collect the skip. I watched them. They loaded someone's whole life into a lorry and drove it away. There wasn't even a mark on the pavement to say where it had been.

I watched someone walk through the space where it had stood. Everything carried on as it always did. People rushed from place to place to keep out of the rain, uniforms travelled along stairwells, pigeons measured out their time along the lengths of guttering and waited for the right moment to fly away to somewhere else. It felt as though the impression this woman had made on the world was so unimportant, so insignificant, it dissolved away the very minute she left.

'You're very maudlin this afternoon, Florence.'

'I'm just commenting,' I said. 'I'm not allowed to do very much any more, but I'm still allowed to comment.'

I was fairly sure she was smiling, but I couldn't tell you for definite, because I wouldn't give in to looking.

$$\star \quad \star \quad \star$$

I kept my eye on number twelve, but nothing happened of any interest. About three o'clock, Miss Bissell marched up the communal stairwell with a clipboard and an air of urgency.

'Miss Bissell,' I said, pointing.

'Indeed,' Elsie said.

'She has a clipboard, Elsie. She must be doing his levels.'

'So it would seem,' she said.

We measured out our afternoon with pots of tea, but the rinse of a September light seemed to push at the hours, spreading the day to its very edges. I always thought September was an odd month. All you were really doing was waiting for the cold weather to arrive, the back end, and we seemed to waste most of our time just staring at the sky, waiting to be reassured it was happening. The stretch of summer had long since disappeared, but we hadn't quite reached the frost yet, the skate of icy pavements and the prickly breath of a winter's morning. Instead, we

16

were paused in a pavement-grey life with porridge skies. Each afternoon was the same. Around four o'clock, one of us would say the nights were drawing in, and we would nod and agree with each other. Between us, we would work out how many days it was until Christmas, and we would say how quickly the time passes, and saying how quickly the time passes would help to pass the time a little more.

The winters at Cherry Tree always took longer, and this would be my fifth. It was called sheltered accommodation, but I'd never quite been able to work out what it was we were being sheltered from. The world was still out there. It crept in through the newspapers and the television. It slid between the cracks of other people's conversation and sang out from their mobile telephones. We were the ones hidden away, collected up and ushered out of sight, and I often wondered if it was actually the world that was being sheltered from us.

'The nights are drawing in, aren't they?' said Elsie.

We watched the lights begin to switch on in the flats opposite. Rows of windows. A jigsaw of people, whose evenings leaked out into a September dusk. It was the time of day when you could see into different lives, a slice of someone else, before their world became curtained and secretive.

'Someone's in,' I said.

Most of the uniforms had gone home, and Miss Bissell and her Mini Metro had long since sped through the lights at the bottom of the road and vanished up the bypass, but a bulb had been switched on in the lounge of number twelve. It faltered, like the reel of a cine film, and I watched, frame by frame, as a man walked across the room. Middle-aged, I thought, but the faulty light made it difficult to be sure.

I felt a catch of breath in my throat.

'How many days is it until Christmas?' said Elsie. 'Do you want to count them with me?'

'No,' I said. 'I don't, especially.'

'It's ninety-eight,' she said. 'Ninety-eight!'

'Is it?'

I watched the man. He wore a hat and an overcoat, and he had his back to us, but every so often he showed the edge of his face, and my mind tried to make sense out of my eyes.

'How very strange,' I whispered.

'I know.' Elsie smoothed tea cake crumbs from the tablecloth. 'Last Christmas only seems like yesterday.'

The man paced the room. There was something about the way he lifted his collar, the shrug of his shoulders, and it made the world turn in my stomach. 'It does. But it can't be.'

'It is. Ninety-eight. I've counted them whilst you've been wasting your time staring out of that window.'

I frowned at Elsie. 'Ninety-eight what?'

'Days until Christmas.'

'I didn't mean — ' I looked back, but the lightbulb had given up, and the man with the collar and the shrug of the shoulders had vanished. 'I thought I recognised someone.'

Elsie peered into the darkness. 'Perhaps it was

18

one of the gardeners?'

'No, at number twelve.' I looked at her. I changed my mind and turned back. 'I must be wrong.'

'It's dark, Florence. It's easy to make a mistake.'

'Yes, that's what happened,' I said. 'I made a mistake.'

Elsie went back to sweeping crumbs, and I pulled the sleeves down on my cardigan.

'Shall we have another bar on the fire?' I said. 'It's gone a bit cold, hasn't it?'

'Florence, it's like an oven in here.'

I stared into the shadows and the window of number twelve stared back at me. 'I feel as though someone just walked over my grave.'

'Your grave?'

I definitely must have made a mistake.

Because anything else was impossible.

'It's just a figure of speech,' I said. 'That's all.'

*  *  *

We were halfway through Tuesday before I saw him again.

Elsie was having her toenails seen to, and it always takes a while, because she's difficult to clip. One of the uniforms was dusting the flat, and I was keeping my eye on her, because I've found people do a much more thorough job if they're supervised. They seem to appreciate it when I point out something they've missed.

'How would we manage without you, Miss Claybourne?' they say.

19

This particular one was especially slapdash. Flat feet. Small wrists. Earrings in her nose, her lips, her eyebrows — everywhere except her ears.

There was a mist. The kind of mist that hammers the sky to the horizon to stop any of the daylight getting in, but I saw him straight away, as soon as I turned to the window. He sat on one of the benches in the middle of the courtyard, staring up at number twelve. He was wearing the same hat and the same grey overcoat, but that wasn't why I recognised him. It was because of the way he pulled at his collar. The way he wore his trilby. The very look of him. You can spot someone you know, even in a strange place or a crowd of people. There's something about a person that fits into your eyes.

I wanted to point him out to the girl with the earrings. I wanted to make sure she could see him as well. You hear about it, don't you? Old people's minds conjuring things up from nowhere and inventing all sorts of nonsense to fill the empty space, but the girl was in the middle of having a conversation with herself, and pushing a duster around the mantelpiece. And I was on probation. Miss Ambrose hadn't gone into detail, but I was fairly certain hallucinations wouldn't go down particularly well.

When I looked again, the man was still sitting there, but his elbows were resting on the back of the seat, just like they always used to. As I watched, I felt the colour leave my face. I wanted to knock on the glass, make him turn around, but I couldn't.

20

'Miss Claybourne?'

Because if I did, I might never be able to look away.

'Miss Claybourne? Is everything all right?'

I didn't move from the window. 'No it isn't,' I said. 'It's about as far from all right as it can get.'

'But I've been over the mantelpiece twice. If I dust it again, it'll make me late for the next one.'

The girl stood in front of the television with a can of Pledge. The earrings covered her face like punctuation marks.

'Not the mantelpiece,' I said. 'Out there. Ronnie Butler. On a bench. Do you see him?'

Sometimes, words just fall out of your mouth. Even as they leave, you know they really shouldn't, but by then it's too late and all you can do is listen to yourself. The girl said, 'Who's Ronnie Butler?' and curiosity made all the earrings rearrange themselves on her face.

'Someone from the past. Someone I used to know.'

I pulled at the edge of the curtain, even though it was perfectly straight.

The girl began collecting up her cans and cloths, and dusters, and arranging them in a little pink basket. 'That's good, then, isn't it? You'll be able to have a lovely catch-up.'

I looked back at the courtyard. He was standing now, and as I watched, he made his way along the path that led back to the main gates. 'No,' I said. 'It isn't good. It isn't good at all.'

'Why ever not?'

I waited before I answered. I waited until the basket had been filled, until I'd heard the click of the front door, and the drag of the girl's feet along the corridor outside. I waited for all of that before I answered her question. And when I did, the words still came out in a whisper.

'Because Ronnie Butler drowned in 1953.'

★ ★ ★

'Do you ever imagine you see things?'

Elsie had returned from the chiropodist, and she was admiring his craftsmanship through her tights. 'Oh, all the time,' she said.

'You do?'

'Oh yes.' Elsie wriggled her toes and they crackled in their 30-denier prison. 'I imagine it's raining, but when I get outside, I find that it isn't. And I often imagine I've got more milk in the fridge than I actually have.'

'No, I mean people. Do you ever imagine people?'

Elsie stopped wriggling and looked up. 'What a strange question. I don't think so,' she said. 'But then again, I wouldn't know, would I?'

I hadn't moved from the window since I saw him. Or thought I saw him. I had watched staff disappear into buildings, and visitors forced to shuffle around the grounds with faded relatives, but I hadn't seen the man again. Number twelve was quiet and dark, and the bench was deserted. Perhaps I'd invented him. Perhaps this was the start of my mind crossing over the bridge between the present and the past, and not bothering to come back.

Elsie was watching me now. 'Who do you

22

think you saw?' she said.

'No one.' I started straightening the ornaments on the sideboard. 'I need to visit Boots Opticians. I need to get my glasses changed.'

'You've only just changed them,' she said. 'And why do you keep picking things up and putting them back again exactly where they were?'

I let go of Brighton seafront and looked at her. You could fit Elsie's worries into a matchbox. 'Did you see anyone?' I said. 'On the way over?'

She frowned. 'No one in particular,' she said. 'Why, who have you seen?'

'Miss Bissell,' I said. 'A man delivering letters.'

'The postman?'

I nodded. 'And that strange little woman from number four. Round face. Never speaks. Not very good with stairs.'

'Mrs Honeyman?'

'I think so,' I said. 'And I saw Dora Dunlop as well. She wasn't in her nightdress either. Fully dressed, she was.'

Elsie raised her eyebrows. 'They're sending her to Greenbank, you know. I overheard.'

I felt all the space behind my eyes fill up. 'She'll never cope,' I whispered.

Elsie didn't reply, but I thought I saw her shoulders give a little shrug.

'You haven't seen anyone interesting, then?' I said.

'No, no one.'

I drank some tea.

'I wish you'd just spit it out, Florence.'

'I just thought I saw someone we used to

23

know,' I said, into the china. 'Can't remember his name.'

'Oh, I wonder who it might be. Someone from school? From the factory?'

I swallowed another mouthful of tea. 'Not sure. Can't place him.'

'I'm sure I'll be able to.' Elsie inspected the empty courtyard through the glass. 'I've always been better at faces than you.'

She was the only one left. The only one who would know if my mind had finally wandered away and left me all to my own devices. But sixty years ago, we'd packed up the past, and parcelled it away, and promised ourselves we'd never speak of it again. Now we were old. Now we were different people, and it felt as though everything we went through had happened to someone else, and we had just stood and watched it all from the future.

She tried to see a little further into the darkness. 'I do hope I spot him as well.'

'Me too,' I said, into the cup.

# 5.06 p.m.

There's all manner of nonsense under that sideboard.

It's amazing what falls behind furniture when your back is turned. I'd never have noticed if I hadn't been lying here, but now I have, I can't stop staring. They don't make a job of it, the cleaners. They're all headphones and aerosol cans. Some of them even switch the television on while they're working. Never ask. I watch from a corner of the room and point things out, and they glance sideways and hoover around my feet. 'Let them get on with it,' Elsie says. 'Enjoy being a lady of leisure, Florence.' It's not in my nature to be leisurely, though. Elsie's more of a sitter, and I've always been a doer. It's why we get on so well.

Occasionally, you see the same one twice. There's a girl comes on a Thursday. Or it might be a Tuesday. I know it's a day beginning with a T. Dark hair, blue eyes. One hand on the vacuum cleaner, the other pressing a mobile telephone to her ear. She's always laughing down that telephone. Pretty laugh. The kind of laugh that makes you want to join in, except I can't understand a word she's saying. I think she might be German. When I went to the shop near the main gates, they had a box of shortbread. *Made in Germany*, it said on the back, and so I bought it, because I thought it might remind her

25

of home. We could have it with a cup of tea, I thought; break the ice a bit. Get to know each other. I mentioned it, but she was so busy talking down that telephone and the front door banged shut when I was halfway through a sentence. I expect she was in a rush. That's the trouble, isn't it, everyone is in a rush. We can have them another time, when I get over this fall. No harm done, because they're still in the packet.

She might be the one to find me. The German girl. She'll forget about her telephone as soon as she realises. It will fall to the floor, but she'll ignore it and kneel down on the carpet next to me. As she leans forward, her hair will fall into her face, and she'll have to brush it back behind her ear. Her hands will be warm and kind, and her fingers will wrap around mine.

'Are you all right, Florence? What have you done to yourself?'

'Not to worry, I'll be fine,' I'll say. 'I don't want you fretting.'

We will wait for the ambulance, and while we are waiting, she'll ask me how I fell, how it all happened, and I will hesitate and look away. I'm not even sure what I'll tell her. I remember the newsreader smiling at me and shuffling her papers, and I remember the silence when I switched off the television. There is a special kind of silence when you live alone. It hangs around, waiting for you to find it. You try to cover it up with all sorts of other noises, but it's always there, at the end of everything else, expecting you. Or perhaps you just listen to it with different ears. I heard a noise, perhaps. Or a

26

voice? I'm trying to decide what made me fall to begin with, but the only thing I remember is opening my eyes and being somewhere I knew I shouldn't be.

The ambulance men will get here, and the German girl will be relieved, and all the worry will empty out of her eyes, because you always assume once a uniform arrives, everything will be fine. It isn't always the way, of course. I know that more than anybody. One of the men will push back the furniture, and the other will put a little mask on my face. The pieces of elastic won't stay behind my ears, and there'll be such a fuss made. They'll strap me into a chair, one of those with a seatbelt on it, and they'll put a blue blanket over me, and the German girl will make a big point about making sure it's straight.

'Are you all right, Florence? Is there anything else you need?'

When we get outside, the cold will pinch at my nose and my ears, and my eyes will start to water.

'Soon have you there, Flo. You hang tight, Flo,' the ambulance men will say, and I won't mind that they call me Flo, because they have kind eyes.

They will lift me up and carry me down the outside steps, and as they do, I will look out over the town, at the liquid ink of the night and the lights that shine from other people's lives, and it will seem as though I'm flying.

And I will feel as light as air.

27

# Florence

Friday was bingo. Elsie forced me to go on the pretext of it being good for me, but I knew it was only because it was a rollover week.

'You've only got a month to prove yourself,' she pointed out to me, quite unnecessarily. 'So you might as well start now.'

And so we found ourselves in the corner of the residents' lounge, watching everyone mishear all the numbers. People sat with their feet suspended on pouffes, and their mouths wide open, staring at pieces of cardboard and wondering what they were meant to be doing with them. Miss Bissell was nowhere to be seen, and her second in command had been left to pull out the ping-pongs.

Miss Ambrose held up a ball. 'Twenty-two,' she shouted.

Everyone started quacking.

'Pardon?' she said.

'Two little ducks,' someone shouted.

Miss Ambrose held up another ball. 'Number eleven.'

Of course, everyone whistled.

'Legs eleven,' shouted someone else.

Miss Ambrose looked at the ball. 'It's like a different language.'

'It's the language of growing old,' I said. 'Like pantry and wireless.'

'How am I supposed to speak it?' Miss

28

Ambrose played with the back of an earring. 'I'm only in my late thirties.'

We all stared at Miss Ambrose. I was just on the verge of saying something when Elsie gave me one of her eyebrows.

'You'll be there soon enough,' I said instead. 'It's like waking up in a different country.'

Miss Ambrose pulled out another ping-pong. It was a two.

'I suppose this is one little duck, then?' she said.

'See. You're fluent already.'

Miss Ambrose stopped fiddling with her earring, and coughed.

★  ★  ★

We'd only been there ten minutes and my mind started to wander. It can't help itself. It very often goes for a walk without me, and before I've realised what's going on, it's miles away. I'm not even sure when that started to happen. Elsie says to think of them as butterfly thoughts, but I can't help worrying. I never used to be like this, and if you're not in charge of the inside of your own head, what are you in charge of? Miss Ambrose says it doesn't just happen to old people. It can happen when people are depressed as well. Perhaps there are times when your life is so unbearably miserable, but the only part of you that can run away from it and leave, is your mind.

It always happens to me in that blasted day room. I was staring out of the window into the car park, and wondering why silver cars are so popular when they show up all the dirt, when I saw her. Dora Dunlop. Fully dressed. There was a uniform either side of her, and she had a suitcase and three carrier bags at her feet. I could see pieces of her life peeping out of the top. Knitting and a pair of slippers, and the folded edge of a magazine.

'You can't make me,' she was shouting, and her voice slid into the room through an open window. 'I don't have to do what you say!'

The uniforms concentrated on the ground and the sky, and anything else within their eyes' reach that didn't involve Dora Dunlop.

'YOU CAN'T MAKE ME.'

A few people looked up from their bingo cards, and Miss Ambrose reached across and closed the window. After she'd dropped the catch, I thought I saw her glance over at me.

Dora was silenced now. A tiny, grey figure, standing in the middle of a car park, still packed with shouting and despair, except no one could hear any more.

I nudged Elsie. 'They're taking her to Greenbank,' I said. 'Look. Out in the car park.'

'I'm concentrating on the numbers. We only need one more for a line.'

'But she's frightened. We should go and help. Stick up for her.'

I turned to the window, but the car park was empty. Dora Dunlop and her carrier bags had vanished.

'She's gone,' I said.

I looked back at Elsie.

She was staring at me.

When we were finished with the bingo (which no one ever won), everybody took it in turns to go to the toilet, and one of the uniforms passed around a plate of egg sandwiches. Room temperature. Too much cress. Not enough mayonnaise. Elsie disappeared to the ladies', and I was just considering whether I should eat her sandwich and spare her the disappointment, when Miss Ambrose stood up in the middle of the room and clapped her hands very loudly — and rather unnecessarily, if you want my opinion, as the only thing you could hear at that point was the push of dentures into buttered bread.

'Some news,' she said, and a flush crept from underneath her flowered shirt and wandered on to her face. 'We've had a new resident join us this week.'

At that very moment, a mouthful of egg sandwich had been making its way down my throat, and her words brought it to a standstill. People looked up from their plates, and in the far corner, two residents instigated a small round of applause. The only person who didn't react was Mrs Honeyman, who continued to snore very gently into a side plate.

'As you know, here at Cherry Tree, we like to make our guests feel especially welcome.' Miss Ambrose clasped her hands to her bosom in a welcoming way. 'So I'm sure you'll all join me in saying a very big hello to our latest friend and neighbour.'

I didn't realise he was there, standing by the bulletin board, until he stepped forward.

Over the years, I've found my eyesight to be less and less trustworthy. Even with glasses, I'm reluctant to believe a word it says, but this time, there was no doubt. This time, it couldn't have been more accurate.

It was him.

Ronnie Butler.

I knew straight away. There aren't many things remaining in the world that I'm sure of, but this was one of them. He was older, of course. Less definite. More worn. Those things don't really alter a person at the end of the day, though. It's just the small print. What really matters is the eyes. The smile. The way someone looks across a room as though they had never left.

I have felt fear many times in my life. I feel it each time I sit alone in darkness, and dare to peel away a corner of the past. I've felt it over the years in an unexpected mention of his name, or a casual remark. It was strange, because up until that day, it had been the very absence of him which frightened me, but now he was here, standing not ten feet in front of me, I finally knew what real terror was, and there was nothing quite like it. It felt as though it could pull my heart right out of my chest.

Because he was back.

And I had been found.

'A happy, contented community . . . ' I could hear Miss Ambrose's voice somewhere outside my own thoughts. Ronnie looked exactly the same. Some faces disappear into old age, and their past self and present self are two completely different people, but the lines on Ronnie's face had only made more of who he was. Even the scar was there. A tiny mark at the corner of his mouth, which disappeared each time he smiled.

'A safe harbour in those twilight years,' said Miss Ambrose.

Twilight was a ridiculous word to use. It means dim and confusing, and stumbling about. I couldn't swear to it, but I was almost certain he expected me to be there. It was the look more than anything. The same look he had in the factory yard and on the bus, and across a kitchen table. When you've seen that look you don't ever forget it. Even a lifetime later.

'So please join me in welcoming the new occupant of number twelve, Mr Gabriel Price.'

There was a beat of silence before I heard my own voice.

'Gabriel Price?'

All the breath I'd been holding escaped along with the shout, and there was the scrape of a chair leg, as someone leaned forward to look. Miss Ambrose tilted her head to one side, and she stared at me.

'At your service.' Ronnie Butler touched the edge of his trilby. He stepped forward, and I felt the back of the chair push into my bones. I could almost smell the night he died. I could almost reach out across the years and take it in my hands, and carry it with me out of the room. A pulse drilled into my throat with such violence, I couldn't understand how the whole room hadn't heard.

Ronnie looked straight into my eyes and smiled, and when he did, the little scar at the corner of his mouth disappeared.

Like magic.

★ ★ ★

'We're off then, are we?'

I'd waited for Elsie outside the ladies'. I took hold of her elbow as soon as she came out.

'We are,' I said.

'Can't it wait? I had my mind especially set on mandarin segments.'

'I'll open a tin when we get home.'

'And what about the raffle? It's a rollover week.'

'There's a box of shortbread in the bottom cupboard. You can have that.'

'It's not the winning, Florence. It's the anticipation,' she said. 'The thrill of the chase.'

'I just want to get out of here.' We stopped halfway along the path that led behind the blocks of flats, and I let go of her elbow. Not many people used this path. There were leaves collected around its edges, and the grass there seemed to have forgotten it needed to grow. Most people liked the front path, with its handkerchief borders and opportunities to pass the time of day, because people always seem to like to walk the same way everyone else walks. But I preferred this one. It was a forgotten path. A path that could sort out a problem.

I saw the tick of confusion in Elsie's eyes. 'What on earth's the matter, Flo?'

34

'Nothing. Nothing's the matter. Whatever makes you think that?'

She looked down. 'Because your hands are shaking,' she said.

# Miss Ambrose

'Off her rocker, if you ask me.'

No one had. However, to Handy Simon, questions were only ever optional. To Handy Simon, the world was a place in need of a running commentary, and he seemed to have volunteered himself to provide an explanation, just in case anyone might find themselves in need of one.

'Hmmm?' Anthea Ambrose peered into her compact mirror. She had bought it because everything was magnified by the power of ten. This was something she was now beginning to regret, but she found herself unable to look away. It was like watching a car accident on the opposite side of the motorway.

'Leaping up and shouting like that.' Handy Simon dragged a table back to its rightful place, and the sound of an abandoned plate of egg sandwiches rattled across the empty room. 'Whatshername.'

Miss Ambrose shut the mirror, and all her worries hid themselves behind the click of a compact. 'Florence,' she said. 'Miss Claybourne. I suspect it's only a matter of time before she goes to Greenbank.'

'I don't know how you tell them all apart.'

Miss Ambrose returned the mirror to her handbag. 'It's my job.'

Handy Simon took an egg sandwich, and

launched it into his mouth. 'There's so many of them, and they all look the same,' he said, without giving the sandwich an opportunity to leave. 'I'll pop outside now, if that's all right with you. Clean some of the mess out of the guttering. Or we'll have a blockage to deal with.'

There was a time when Anthea Ambrose had briefly considered the merits of Handy Simon. After all, trainers can be cleaned. Hair can be trimmed. You see it on television programmes. People buy a whole new wardrobe from John Lewis and part their hair on the opposite side, and all of a sudden they're completely different people. It was a time when Miss Ambrose had scanned the horizon for a possible husband, like a castaway searching for the arrival of a distant ship.

'Preventing the efficient flow of rainwater.' He took another sandwich. 'Which could eventually lead to permanent damage.'

Although some ships were perhaps best left unboarded.

'And potential structural problems, if the situation isn't addressed promptly.'

For fear of having the entire rest of your life explained to you.

★ ★ ★

Anthea Ambrose walked back to her flat at the far edge of the grounds. It was separate from the residents' apartments, but she trod on an identical beige carpet ('Universal beige,' said Miss Bissell, 'goes with everyone,') and the doors

37

closed with the same faint click of apology. Her flat also offered a similar view, through windows that opened only a fraction of an inch, because the fear of residents slipping through and defenestrating also seemed to extend to the staff. When Anthea Ambrose looked out from her kitchen window, a concertina of old age unfolded before her, beckoning into the future. The flat came with the job (a job she had only planned to stay in for twelve months). She'd applied for others, she'd even got an interview for one, but it was on the day that a new resident had decided to escape en route at the traffic lights, and she was so busy trying to calm the poor woman down, she didn't make it. They hadn't ever called her back.

Miss Ambrose never walked quickly, although she wasn't sure if it was because she felt ashamed at being able to manage it (against a backdrop of walking sticks and Zimmer frames), or whether old age had somehow leaked into her bones and persuaded her to join in. She'd never meant to work with the elderly. She'd meant to be an air hostess or something in publishing. Something glamorous. Something where she could walk quickly. But it was as though life had an undercurrent, and no matter how hard she tried to swim in the other direction, it was determined to pull her away. It would be so much easier, she thought, if you knew what the world's intentions were in the first place. It would save such a lot of energy. Instead of paddling around aimlessly, you could swim with confidence towards your target, ignoring the temptation and the distraction, and all the other swimmers, who battled and argued with the tide.

The grounds were silent, and she passed vacant benches and a deserted gazebo. She glanced over at the Japanese Garden. It had taken an age to persuade Miss Bissell it was a worthwhile idea. She'd read about Japanese gardens in a magazine. They were supposed to promote inner peace and reflection, but Miss Bissell said it was perhaps unwise to encourage the residents to reflect too rigorously on anything at their time of life.

Actually, Miss Bissell just said, 'I don't think so, Anthea,' and Miss Ambrose had offered up the rest in an effort to instigate a discussion. Miss Ambrose rarely stood up to Miss Bissell, but on this occasion she had persisted for several months, and eventually, Miss Bissell had given in. Although a line was drawn at lanterns, because of the moth issue. Miss Ambrose wondered if anyone ever used the garden, or whether it just stood as a giant Japanese monument to a time when she thought she could perhaps make a difference. There was no one in there now, of course, because the whole of Cherry Tree was deserted at this time of day. Residents tended to doze off in front of radios and cold cups of tea, and it was perfectly acceptable to fall asleep, as long as one remained vertical. It was very tempting to join them. Each afternoon was a battle for Miss Ambrose. A battle between denial and acceptance. Acceptance of the fact that, although there were no hand rails in her own apartment, there still remained a space on the wall for them to be attached.

As Miss Ambrose turned the corner, she spotted Gabriel Price. He sat on the very last bench before her front door, under a grey, paper-thin sky, his elbows resting on the back of the seat. Miss Ambrose was so surprised to see another human being this deep into the afternoon, a small sound broke free from the bottom of her throat. As she grew closer, she thought she saw him smile, but she had begun to realise that with Gabriel Price you could never quite be certain.

'Miss Ambrose.'

'Do call me Anthea, Mr Price.'

He didn't.

She decided to plough on, nevertheless.

'I'm surprised to see you out and about,' she said. 'Most of our residents are resting at this time of the day.'

'I don't believe in resting, Miss Ambrose. The devil makes work for idle hands, don't you think?'

Miss Ambrose fiddled with the back of an earring.

'Although you wouldn't know anything about that, of course. Running this place is a twenty-four-hour marathon, I should imagine.'

'Well, I wouldn't say I — '

'But of course you do. Look how you dealt with that debacle in the day room.'

'Miss Claybourne? Well, I suppose . . . '

He smiled again. It was a full stop in disguise.

'They get very muddled, the elderly.' He spoke

as though they were a tribe of people he observed from afar. 'Easily confused.'

Miss Ambrose tried to summon up one of her understanding head-tilts, but she was distracted by the way he stretched his arms across the back of the bench. The way the light seemed to disappear the lines on his skin and fade the grey in his hair.

'How old did you say you were again, Mr Price?'

'I didn't, Miss Ambrose.' He replaced his trilby and stood so effortlessly, it looked as though the bench had somehow helped him on his way. 'But I'm not quite ready for the dying of the light just yet.'

'Well, no. Quite. Of course not.'

'But a young woman such as yourself wouldn't know anything at all about that.'

Miss Ambrose felt a flush on her skin. A jumble of words appeared in her mouth, but by the time she'd organised them into a sentence, he'd already disappeared around the corner.

'How very extraordinary,' she said.

Miss Ambrose walked the rest of the way to her flat. It was only when she turned the key, when she heard the door's click of apology and felt the beige carpet under her feet, that she realised she had arrived there slightly faster than usual, and with a little more purpose.

# Florence

I waited. I waited until coats had been hung up and kettles had been switched on, and tins of fruit had been emptied into bowls and drowned in Ideal Milk. I even waited whilst Elsie ate spoonfuls of oranges with a look of deep concentration. I waited until all of this was done with before I spoke.

'I need to discuss someone with you,' I said. 'Someone from the past.'

Her chewing slowed a little.

There are times when sharing a problem only seems to make it grow. Hearing the words out loud gives them a strength they never seem to have inside your own head, and it's easier sometimes to let them stay there, unnoticed. If you lock something away for long enough, if you can manage to keep it from escaping, eventually it feels as though it never really happened in the first place. But I knew as soon as I told Elsie, as soon as I allowed the problem to leave, I'd lose ownership of my worrying and I'd never be able to silence it again.

'Someone I've seen,' I said.

'Who?' Elsie placed the spoon at the edge of the bowl, and she became very still.

I had to force the words from my mouth. I had to push them away.

'Ronnie,' I said, eventually.

I watched her face. There wasn't a jot of reaction.

42

'Ronnie Butler,' I said.

She looked at me for a moment, and she smiled. 'You daft bugger. You can't have. Dead as a doornail, Ronnie. They buried him, don't you remember?' She reached for the spoon again, but I held on to her wrist.

'No,' I said. 'He's out there right now. I've seen him.'

'How can you possibly have seen someone who's been dead sixty years? You're just getting confused.'

'It's him.' I slammed my hand on the table, and Elsie rattled along with the dessert bowl. 'He's come back for me.'

When Elsie spoke again, her words were wrapped up in a whisper. 'He's dead, Florence. No one has come back for anyone.'

'Then who have I seen?'

'It must be someone who looks like him. They say everyone has a double, don't they? You've just made a mistake, that's all.'

I went over to the window and listened to the leafy quietness of the courtyard. 'I must be getting confused. It can't be him, can it? Not after all this time?'

She always undoes the stitches of other people's worrying and makes them disappear. That's the second thing you should know about Elsie. She always knows what to say to make me feel better. 'Of course it can't, Florence. People just don't do that, do they? They don't come back from the dead.'

'You're right. Of course they don't. Let's forget I ever spoke.'

43

'Good. Because if Miss Ambrose hears you talking like that, you'll be lucky to get a fortnight, let alone a month.'

I reached over for the *Radio Times*, and that's when I looked at the mantelpiece. That's when I noticed.

The elephant.

It was facing the wrong way again.

★   ★   ★

'Stop getting yourself in a twist,' Elsie said. 'You've made another mistake, that's all.'

It's Elsie all over. Forever telling me I'm worrying over nothing, forever telling me not to tie myself in a knot. I've known her since we were at school. We met on a bus. A bus! I wonder how many people meet on public transport these days. A stab in the dark, but I'd hazard a guess and say not many. People seem to put all their energy into ignoring each other instead.

She didn't believe me about the elephant any more than she believed me about Ronnie. I could tell.

'You're off on one of your tangents again,' she said. 'Stop hurrying into the future, hunting down catastrophes.'

I pretended to agree with her, just for the sake of peace. I even stopped looking for Ronnie and moved away from the window, but I couldn't help glancing over there from time to time. She caught me at it on a few occasions and gave me one of her looks.

'You were exactly the same at school,' she said.

44

''Do you think that girl looks unwell? What should we do?' or 'I've heard Norman's father beats him. Who do you think we should tell?''

I didn't answer. I just shuffled a bit closer to the window, to make a point.

'You shouldn't witter on about people so much,' she said. 'Norman could look after himself.'

'But he couldn't,' I turned to her. 'Norman was short and skinny, and he hadn't got anyone else to stand up for him. He said he was going to run away to London. London would have swallowed him up.'

'It was a long time ago.'

'It feels like yesterday,' I said. 'Sometimes, I think there must be a shortcut between the past and the present, but no one bothers to tell you about it until you get old.'

'You spent so long in and out of other people's lives back then, you barely had time for your own.'

I carried on looking through the window, but I could hear her fingers, tapping out her thoughts on the tablecloth.

'Do you remember? It's how we first met. You were trying to do the right thing.' She leaned forward and interrupted my viewing.

'I've got too much on my mind to be concerned with that,' I said.

'The girl on the school bus with the twisted ankle?' She leaned a little more. 'You gave up your seat, didn't you?'

I noticed her glance at my hands. They were folding backwards and forwards in my lap.

45

Sometimes, I don't even know I'm doing these things until someone points it out to me. 'No, I didn't,' I said. 'I don't remember any girl with a twisted ankle. You're getting me mixed up with somebody else.'

'It was you, Florence. She hobbled on to the school bus and no one stood up. No one except you. That's how you found yourself sitting next to me a few stops later. That's how we met.'

'You're making it up.' My lips closed very tightly, and I could feel all the little lines stitch them together.

'I'm not making it up. It was a long second, don't you remember?'

I stopped turning my hands. 'What's a long second?' I said.

She explained it to me. Even though she said she'd explained it very many times before. I always seem to forget. It's when you catch the clock, holding on to a second so it lasts just a fraction longer than it should. When the world gives you just a little bit more time to make the right decision. There are long seconds all over the place. We just don't always notice them. 'But you noticed this one, Florence. You made your decision. You gave up your seat. And that's how we met.'

'I don't remember my life without you in it,' I said.

'We were just at the age when you start to notice other children. When you pick out who you might be friends with. I chose you long before you chose me.' She smiled. 'There was a kindness about you, even then. As if someone

46

took all the kindness other people discard and ignore, and leave lying about, and stuffed it into you for safekeeping.'

I tried to find the memory and pull it back in, but it felt very far away, and the elastic was too loose.

She found my eyes with hers. 'Try to think. There are things in the past you need to find again, Florence. It's important.'

'Is it?'

'We laughed, because the seat you gave up was the one next to that boy who was in the scouts, and he did nothing but talk the girl's ear off about first aid. She hung on his every word. I can't remember her name. Tall. Dark hair. Her parents owned the little shoe shop on the high street.'

I felt the elastic tighten. 'They emigrated, that family, all of them.' I let the words go very slowly, just in case they were the wrong ones. 'To Australia.'

'Yes, they did.' Elsie was pleased with me. I can always tell when she's pleased with me, because she gets a glitter about her eyes. 'But the girl stayed here. She didn't go with them.'

'Men for the land, women for the home. Guaranteed employment. Ten pounds, it cost. Ten pounds for a brand new life.'

I turned back to the window.

'Ronnie Butler was on that bus,' I said.

47

# Handy Simon

Handy Simon wore a St Christopher around his neck, although he'd never travelled further than Sutton Coldfield. His father gave it to him when Simon turned eighteen, and the only time he'd removed it was when they took his appendix out in 1995. 'Keep you safe,' his father said. 'Out of harm's way.' Generally, it had. Although whether the last twenty-five years was the work of St Christopher, or because Simon was naturally cautious, remained to be seen. He touched the medallion and stared at the guttering. He might only be travelling up a ladder, but surely the principle remained the same.

Handy Simon was not a fan of heights. All of life's bad experiences had occurred when his feet were off the ground. Even his mother died on an aeroplane. A heart attack at thirty thousand feet on the way back from Spain ('At least it was on the way home,' his father had said, over the ham tea). It was their first foreign holiday. Simon often wondered whether, if they'd chosen Margate over Malaga, she might still be alive now. Although she was very fond of sweet sherry and never held back at a buffet table, so quite possibly not. That was the problem when your parents were so much older than everyone else's. You ran the risk of losing them before you'd really got to know each other.

'Was I planned?' he once asked his mother.

48

'You were a surprise,' she told him. 'A miracle.'

'Like Jesus?'

'Not quite like Jesus,' she said.

He tested out the first rung with the heel of his boot. Life at Cherry Tree involved a more than reasonable amount of ladder work. He'd once mentioned the words 'health and safety' to Miss Bissell in the staff room, but she had arched an eyebrow in silence and returned to her Sudoku. Simon found this was the main problem with people. They never listened. They were too busy enjoying the sound of their own voices to take any notice of him, and because of that, they missed out on a wealth of information. Not anecdotes or stories, but statistics and proof. Facts. Facts were the important things. Facts stood the test of time. Without facts, the world would become a giant mess of rumour and hearsay, and everything would fall apart.

He turned his collar against the wind. North-easterly. Bitter. Becoming cloudier as the day progressed. Once the wind found its way into Cherry Tree, it never seemed to be able to find its way out. It was the architecture. The wind took the path of least resistance, it rushed down from the buildings and hid around corners. People thought corners were the best places to escape the wind, but often, they were the most dangerous. Simple physics. He'd tried to explain this to Miss Ambrose one day, but her eyes had glazed over in a most unattractive fashion. He hadn't given up, mind. It wasn't in his nature. Instead, he'd printed out a page on the subject from the internet for her. Some people are visual learners, after all. Actually, forty-three per cent of people are visual learners.

Simon knew he'd made a mistake as soon as he got to the seventh rung. He felt the push of air against the ladder, and heard the creak of metal on the tiles. He wondered if his life might flash before him, or at least the parts with a degree of significance, but all he saw was a cracked roof tile and a pigeon, looking down on him with clockwork curiosity. Perhaps he didn't have any significant parts. Perhaps his significant parts were yet to come, and would now never arrive, due to a north-easterly wind and his decision to have one more egg sandwich. He'd just begun to feel the inevitability of the slide, an unexpected journey back to earth, when a voice said, 'Steady on there, young man,' and the ladder righted itself and the world became vertical again.

When Simon looked down (which took a surprisingly large amount of courage), he saw the top of a trilby and an overcoated forearm holding up the ladder. The new chap. From the day room. Whatshisname again.

'Price,' said the man, and shook hands when Simon reached the protection of solid ground. He nodded at the ladder. 'Health and safety issue, if you ask me.'

'Exactly.' Simon tried to swallow, but he couldn't find anything to do it with. 'I've told them as much.'

'That's the problem with people today. They never listen.'

'Exactly,' said Simon. He said it a few more times, just for good measure. 'I need some ties for the ladder. Secure it to the wall.'

'I'll help, if you like.' Mr Price straightened his trilby. 'Give you a hand.'

Simon wasn't entirely sure of the average age of a Cherry Tree resident, but he felt it was one more suited to holding up supermarket queues than ladders. The man in the trilby looked more than capable, mind you. As though age had tightened his springs, rather than unwound them.

'Don't look so worried, Simon,' he said. 'I'm not quite ready for the knacker's yard just yet.'

A string of 'no's came out of Simon's mouth in a little dance. 'Oscar Swahn won an Olympic medal in his seventies,' he said. 'Fauja Singh ran the London Marathon at ninety-two. History is littered with people who achieved great things in old age.'

The man lifted the ladder away from the guttering. 'Those are very interesting facts, Simon. Why don't you tell me some more?'

And so he did.

# Florence

I could tell Elsie thought it was a completely ridiculous suggestion, but she still went along with it. It's one of the best things about her.

'Of course I'll come with you. That's what friends are for,' she said.

'You don't want to argue about it?'

'Sometimes it's easier,' she said, 'just to agree. Or I'll spend the entire rest of the day listening to you talk me into it.'

The potting shed, I told her. If we sit in the potting shed, we're bound to spot him sooner or later, and you can see for yourself. I wanted to prove I wasn't hallucinating, that I hadn't lost my mind.

'Of course you haven't lost your mind,' she said.

I wasn't so sure. Although it's such a silly turn of phrase. It implies it's somehow your fault. It suggests you were being careless, or became distracted along the way and mislaid it somewhere, like a set of house keys, or a Jack Russell terrier. Or a husband, perhaps. Although I suppose losing your mind can prove quite helpful sometimes, because it does hint there is a possibility, however slim, that you may find it again.

★　★　★

52

It smelled of creosote, the potting shed. Creosote and soil. We were surprised it was unlocked, but there are times Cherry Tree seems stuck somewhere in the 1950s, when the whole world was unlocked but no one had yet thought to steal from it. It was dark too. There was a feathery light, but it didn't quite meet up with the corners. There were shelves at the back, with all manner of bottles and jars stretched along them — many of which, I suspected, did not contain what they claimed to. Below the shelving, a row of gardening equipment rested against the wood, and made odd shadows on the walls. I didn't know all their names, but there was a giant spade, still holding on to lumps of earth. Elsie asked me what each of the tools was called, because she said she was always looking for an opportunity to stretch my mind. I told her my mind wasn't in the mood for being stretched. I told her, if she wanted to know the names for all the different tools, she could find them out for herself, and I pulled out some old deckchairs for us to sit on instead. As soon as I opened them up, I could tell they weren't safe, but she said they'd be perfectly fine if we stayed put and didn't move around too much, and so we rested on decayed canvas and peered through a window smeared with last year's gardening.

'We could be at home instead of sitting here,' she said. 'With a full pot of tea and Radio 4.'

I ignored her. She was used to it by now. Whilst I ignored her, I listened to a blackbird singing outside the shed window. You wouldn't think something so small would have such a lot to say for itself.

She spoke a bit louder. 'We could be at home,' she said, 'instead of sitting here.'

I turned, and the glass in my spectacles found the light. 'You need to see him for yourself, Elsie.'

We sat in silence for a moment. Even the blackbird.

'I know the name,' I said, after a while. 'Gabriel Price. I've seen it before.'

'You always say you know people, Florence. It's one of your habits.'

I sat back, and the deckchair creaked at me.

'Here's the best place to get a good look at him,' I said. 'And I have seen the name before. It isn't one of my habits. It's the truth.'

The potting shed does have a useful view. Cherry Tree consists of four blocks of flats, called (rather unimaginatively) A, B, C and D. Miss Ambrose once spearheaded a campaign to have them renamed a little more romantically, but, like many of Miss Ambrose's ideas, it never really took off. The main buildings crouch in the middle, and on either side are two courtyards. From where we sat, we could see both of them: a patchwork of perennials and ceramic planters, and gravel paths with no real purpose, like an elaborate board game. We watched old people shuffle from bench to bench, passing parcels of conversation between themselves and trimming their afternoons. We saw Miss Ambrose, dawdling back to her flat as usual, with the world pressing down on her shoulders, and Gloria, from the kitchens, having a smoke in the back yard of the canteen. But no sign of Ronnie Butler.

'Or whoever it was you think you saw,' said Elsie.

'He'll be along in a minute,' I told her, 'and then we'll be well away.'

'We should have brought some sandwiches,' she said.

I started to stretch my legs out, but then I remembered the deckchair and put a stop to myself.

'And a flask,' she said. 'We always did that when we went anywhere, do you remember?'

I said yes, but I had half a mind on the window and I wasn't really concentrating. I could feel a seed of worry begin fidgeting inside my head.

'What if one of the gardeners finds us first?' I said. 'Or that handyman. I can't remember his name.'

'Simon,' she said. 'You know full well he's called Simon. You would have remembered if you'd thought about it for long enough. You need to think about things for longer before you give up, Florence.'

I didn't answer, and we were stuck in a wordless argument for a while.

'Do you remember taking sandwiches on holiday, when we were children?' she said eventually. 'Do you remember going to Whitby?'

I said I remembered, but I wasn't sure. She could tell straight away, because nothing much gets past Elsie.

55

'Think, Florence,' she said. 'Think.'

I tried. Sometimes, you feel a memory before you see it. Even though your eyes can't quite find it, you can smell it and taste it, and hear it shouting to you from the back of your mind.

'Ham and tomato,' I said. 'With boiled eggs!'

'Yes,' she said. 'Yes! We ate them on the beach at Saltwick Bay, when we went looking for fossils.'

I thought for a moment. 'We never found any fossils, though, did we?'

'No,' she said. 'You're right. We didn't find any fossils.'

There was a silence again, before I spoke.

'Why is it,' I said, 'I can remember what was in my sandwiches at Saltwick Bay, but I can't remember the name of the handyman?'

There was a tremor in her voice, and she had to speak a bit louder to make a way through it. 'If we knew that, we wouldn't be sitting here talking about it now, would we?' she said.

'I don't suppose we would,' I said back.

'Now tell me his name again, Florence. The handyman. Don't give up so easily. What is he called?'

I didn't answer.

★   ★   ★

It was another ten minutes before we saw him. I spotted the handyman first, marching through the grass, holding on to a ladder, but I couldn't tell who was at the other end with all the darkness and the dirt.

I started tapping on Elsie's arm. 'Look. Do you see him? Do you see him?'

She said, 'Give me a chance,' and she got her glasses out and peered through the window. 'I can't make anyone out from here except Simon; they need to be a bit closer.'

'They will be in a minute,' I said.

And they were.

Very close.

So close, they couldn't have been heading anywhere else.

She still didn't see him. I know she didn't. Not until the door was pulled open, and the shed was flooded with light. She saw him perfectly then, even though he was standing behind Simon. He seemed to fill the entire doorway, and he showed not even the smallest indication of surprise, but looked as though he fully expected us both to be there. Simon didn't say anything at all. I knew he was still looking at us when he reached for a piece of rope on one of the shelves, but I was more concerned about the man in the doorway.

When Simon left, the inside of the shed was a box of ink again and I could hear my own breath, needling the air. 'Well?' I said.

We stared at the space where they had stood. We stared for a very long time, and eventually Elsie said, 'But it makes no sense.'

I stopped staring and turned to her. 'It's him, though, isn't it? It's Ronnie?'

She told me she wasn't sure. She said it looked like him, but how could it be? I'm not certain what I said next, but I know I ended up shouting, because sometimes you have so much fear, you don't know where to put it and shouting is the only way for it all to escape from you. Elsie waited patiently for everything to come out, and when it had, she reached for my hand in the darkness.

'Yours was the first hand I ever held,' she said.

I was still angry, and my words came out in a snap. 'Not your mother's?'

'My mother's hands were always far too busy waiting for my father to come back. I suppose I must have held my sisters' hands at some point,' she said. 'But yours are the first I remember.'

She was right. We held hands as we climbed hills, as we waited on pavements, and as we ran through fields, and we held hands as we faced all the things in life we didn't think we could manage alone.

'Are you there, Elsie?' I said.

Her hand was older now. The skin was livered and loosened, and the bones pressed into my flesh, but it still fitted into mine, just like it always had. I needed to feel its strength, and she squeezed my hand, so I could be sure it was there.

'I'm here,' she said.

Neither of us spoke for a long time.

'What do you think he wants?' I said, eventually.

'We don't know that it's him.'

'But if it is?'

'I don't know.'

'What do you think we should do?'

'I don't know,' she said again. 'But I don't

58

think we should do anything at all right at this moment.'

'Whyever not?' I could just make out the shift of her silhouette in the darkness. 'We've got to tell someone.'

'But what?' she said. 'What are we going to tell them? That Ronnie has come back from the dead? No, there isn't any proof, you'll just have to take our word for it. You're on probation, Florence. You've got to be careful.'

There was a silence again.

'They'll send me to Greenbank,' I said.

I heard her whisper back to me in the dark. 'Perhaps that's just what he wants.'

# Handy Simon

'The potting shed?'

Anthea Ambrose put down her calculator and folded her arms so tightly they disappeared into her jacket. 'What on earth would anybody be doing sitting in the potting shed?'

Handy Simon tried to find something in the room to stare at, other than Miss Ambrose's eyes, even though they seemed to take up most of the space.

'I couldn't really say,' he said.

'And what were you doing in the potting shed?'

'We were getting some rope for the ladder.'

'We?'

'Mr Price was with me.' Simon's shoes began to shuffle. Whenever he was worried, his anxiety always seemed to make a beeline for his feet.

'You were having quite the party in there, weren't you?'

'Yes, Miss Ambrose.'

He'd known this was a mistake as soon as he'd seen Miss Ambrose was doing the accounts. The monthly accounts always made Miss Bissell irritable, and any emotion experienced by Miss Bissell was eventually passed around amongst everyone else. It was in his contract to report these events: a duty of care, it said. He was told at his annual appraisal that everyone's opinion mattered. Just because he was a handyman, didn't mean what he had to say wasn't valuable. Everyone was valuable at Cherry Tree. No one was defined by their job.

'What a load of bollocks,' his dad had said.

'Is it?' They had been sitting on the patio, just over five years ago, when Simon first started working at Cherry Tree. The breeze caught the edges of the fly screen, and a row of multi-coloured ribbons applauded against the door frame. 'Do you think our jobs make us who we are?'

'Of course they bloody do,' said his father, who had been known as Fireman John for his entire adult life. 'Jobs are our identity, aren't they? Where do you think surnames come from?'

Simon didn't answer.

'Wheeler.' His dad squinted into the sunshine. 'Mason, Potter, Taylor?'

'Right,' said Simon. 'But that won't happen to me. I'll never be defined by my job. Cherry Tree isn't like that.'

'What a load of bollocks,' said his dad.

Handy Simon watched Miss Ambrose, who had picked up her calculator again. He was never really sure when he should leave. Some people didn't make it clear. He could hear the calculator keys again, and so he shuffled his feet just a little, just to remind Miss Ambrose they existed.

'You can go now, Simon,' she said.

'Right you are.'

He was just about to close the door when she shouted him back.

'Simon, what exactly was Mr Price doing with you this afternoon?'

'Moving a ladder, Miss Ambrose.' He saw the surprise in her eyebrows. 'He's very capable for his age.'

'And what age would that be?' she said.

'I'm not exactly sure, Miss Ambrose.'

'No,' she said. 'Neither am I.'

As he closed the door, he noticed she had put the calculator down again, and was staring very hard at the line of filing cabinets on the far wall.

*   *   *

Simon turned his collar and punched his fists deep into his pockets. Sometimes, Cherry Tree had that effect. It made him want to push himself into his clothes and disappear. When he was little, he'd wanted to be a fireman, like his dad, but by the time he reached his teens, he realised he wasn't brave enough. His father had saved almost a whole family once, before Simon was even born. Pulled them out of a burning building one by one, like teeth. He was eighteen and a local hero. Strangers shook his hand and bought him drinks, and made a big fuss of him wherever he went. Even, years later, it was a conversation that was lifted out of a drawer every now and then, and passed around so they could all admire it. His father always left the room when that happened. He said it reminded him of the one he missed, the one who wasn't saved. Even so, it became the whole of who his father was. Everything else he had done, or would ever do, disappeared in the moment he decided to run towards the flames. As though he shook the

62

rest of himself away, like a second skin. Everyone expected Simon to follow in his father's footsteps, to travel some strange, imaginary line drawn by genetics, but he couldn't do it. He knew he was someone who would run away from a disaster, rather than towards it, and the only person he'd ever think about saving was himself.

'Not everyone can be brave. No one thinks any less of you,' his mother had said.

She told all her friends it was because of his asthma.

'I don't even have asthma.'

'Best if we just keep that to ourselves,' she said.

Simon glanced at the day room as he walked past, his hands still pocketed away. There was a scattering of residents in there already, planted in their armchairs, waiting for the evening shift. A television shouted out gardening advice, and a tape of subtitles ran across the bottom of the screen, because there was more than a handful of residents for whom the shouting would never be loud enough. Everything at Cherry Tree was set at a high volume. The radios, the televisions, even the people. Shouting became acceptable, almost expected. The staff even shouted when there were no residents about, as though everyone who worked there had been recalibrated. It was only in the muteness of his flat, where he wallpapered his evenings with tea and silence, and where the only song was the hum of a refrigerator, that Simon discovered just how loud the rest of the world could be.

# 5.49 p.m.

I have never done anything remarkable. I've never climbed a mountain or won a medal. I've never stood on a stage and been listened to, or crossed a finishing line before anyone else. When I look back, I have led quite an ordinary life. I sometimes wonder what the point of me was. 'Does God have a plan, and where does he see me fitting into it?' I asked the vicar once. He came to Cherry Tree with his leaflets, handing them around and trying to persuade us all into being religious.

'We each have a role to play, Miss Claybourne,' he said. 'Jesus loves everyone.'

'I'm sure he does,' I said. 'But love isn't enough, is it? You need to have some kind of purpose. I was wondering what mine might have been?'

I looked at him. I thought he might give me an interesting answer. Something comfortable and reassuring. But he just checked his watch and started talking to Mrs Honeyman about harvest festivals.

So even the vicar doesn't know why I'm here.

Elsie says I shouldn't dwell on things so much, but when you get to this age, it passes the time.

'There has to be a reason, though, doesn't there?' I said to her once. 'Or have I spent the last eighty-four years just sitting in the audience?'

64

'Of course you haven't been sitting in the audience. No one sits in the audience. Even the seats in a theatre are still a stage.'

I've no idea what she meant. Times like that I just nod, because it's less time-consuming and it makes life easier for both of us. She just comes out with these things. Like the girl with the twisted ankle. I'm sure she makes half of it up. It makes you wonder, though. It makes you wonder if you did have a purpose, but it floated past you one day, and you just didn't think to flag it down.

Lying here, there's not really very much else to do except wonder. Of course, I've wondered about Ronnie more than anyone. He was right under Elsie's nose in that potting shed, but she wasn't having any of it. She was exactly the same, even when we were at school. She'd tell me to stop worrying, before I'd even given her all my evidence. Before she'd heard the full story. The only difference is, no one will ever hear the full story this time. I never thought it would come to this. You always think a secret will only be a secret for so long, that one day you will turn to someone else and say, 'I've never told anyone this . . . ' and the secret will vanish and become something else. It's only when you get to the end of your life, when you're lying on a wipe-clean carpet with only yourself for company, you realise that you never did manage to find the right someone to tell.

# Florence

'Justin's bringing his accordion this afternoon.'

She stood in the middle of my sitting room, although it's too small to really warrant having a middle.

'Perhaps next week,' I said.

Miss Ambrose took a deep breath. 'Just five minutes, Florence. We'll walk over together.'

'It won't be worth taking my coat off.'

'That's fine,' she said. 'However you want to do it.'

'His eyes are very close together.'

'Pardon?'

'Justin's,' I said. 'It's an indication of criminal tendencies. You can tell a lot by how far apart people's eyes are. I read about it. In a magazine.'

I stared into her face.

'Florence, I'm quite certain that Justin — '

'And he doesn't get any thinner, does he?'

'Florence!'

Whilst she wound all her layers back on, my gaze travelled the room. The dining chairs were pushed tight against the table, and the newspaper was read and folded in the corner. The vase was in the middle of the sideboard. Perhaps slightly off-centre, looking at it. Perhaps just an inch to the left. The newspaper was in the right-hand corner. The vase was an inch to the left. Or was it the other way around?

'I've changed my mind,' I said. 'I'm staying here. I'm busy.'

'Florence. I thought we agreed?'

'You did all the agreeing,' I said. 'I didn't do any of it.'

'Socialising is just as important as eating and drinking properly. You need to mix with people. If you don't . . . ' Her sentence couldn't find its ending.

'If I don't, what?' I said.

She smiled a frown. 'If you don't, perhaps Greenbank really is the right decision for you.'

I closed my mouth as tightly as I could, because I was worried about what might fall out of it.

'Ready?' Miss Ambrose tucked her scarf inside her jacket.

I nodded.

The last thing I thought of, as she pulled the door to, was the elephant. Staring at the window. Waiting for me to get back.

★ ★ ★

I looked for him as soon as I walked in the room.

I went through all the faces. I did it more than once, because people kept moving around, and I was worried I'd miss somebody out. I even had a walk up and down. Once or twice, someone tried to speak to me, but I refused to involve myself, because if you're not careful, you find yourself caught and you have to spend the next two hours sitting with someone and inventing things to say. In the end, I found a chair at the back on my

67

own. I was given a cup of tea, that must have been Miss Ambrose, and I balanced the saucer on my knee.

The room started to fill with residents, with walking sticks and overcoats, and after a few minutes, there was a wall of conversation around me. I couldn't tell what anyone was talking about, because they were all standing up and their voices wandered away, but every so often, a word would escape and find me. Gardening, I think. And the television. Perhaps the weather. I had used up my conversation on all these subjects a long time ago, and so I stayed in my seat and lived in the middle distance.

I'd been there a few minutes before I realised Elsie had sat next to me.

'You came, then?' she said. 'After all?'

I held on to the saucer. 'I didn't have much choice. Miss Ambrose was in one of her moods. The kind where she doesn't hear the word no.'

'You'll enjoy it, Florence. He's very good, is Justin. He gets everyone singing. Even Mrs Honeyman.'

'He won't get me,' I said. 'He isn't here yet, I've had a look.'

Elsie glanced across the room. 'He's over there, by the weeping fig. He's just getting his accordion out.'

'Not Justin.' I looked around before I whispered, 'Ronnie.'

Elsie shook her head. 'I thought we had an agreement that there was no point in worrying until we could be certain.'

'No,' I said. 'I didn't agree with any of that.

68

You made that agreement with yourself. How can you say we shouldn't worry, when you saw him with your own set of eyes?'

'Even if it is Ronnie, and it may very well just be someone who looks like him — '

'Exactly like him,' I said.

' — then perhaps we just need to sit tight and batten down the hatches. He may not want anything at all. It might just be a coincidence.'

'He's been inside my flat.'

'How do you know?'

'Because he's moved things around. I've a good mind to go over there right now and catch him at it.'

A pool of quiet spread around us, and a few people looked across.

'Florence, stop shouting. If Miss Ambrose notices — '

'I'm not shouting. I'm making a point,' I said. 'I'm not letting him get away with it.'

Elsie shook her head again. 'You made a mistake. Forgot where you put something.'

'I didn't forget. It was the elephant.'

'But it can't have been the elephant, because elephants never forget.'

General Jack. Ex-military. Stumbles over his words. Forever wears the same tired grey raincoat. When I looked up, he was leaning on his walking stick and smiling, although his smile always shook a little at the edges. If he hadn't got a conversation of his own, he had a habit of inviting himself into the middle of other people's. I always thought of him as general Jack, with a small g, but he said he didn't even mind

69

that so much, because general Jack made him sound as if he was still a little bit useful.

'It's not often we see you over here, Florence. I was beginning to forget what you look like.'

'You saw me on Tuesday. I was at Healthy Hearts.'

'No,' he said. 'I kept an eye out for you, but you stayed in your flat.'

Elsie sighed. 'You told Miss Ambrose to stuff it.'

'Did I? I don't remember that.' I looked around the room. 'Perhaps I should apologise.'

'I'm certain she's heard worse,' said Elsie.

I was still searching for Miss Ambrose when I spotted him. Ronnie. He was at the edge of the room, leaning into the wallpaper, learning about other people's lives. His arms were folded across his chest and he had the same expression he wore in the yard at the factory all those years ago. He'd always stand alone to eat. When he'd finished, he'd pull a match from his shoe and light up a cigarette. Even then he had the kind of expression that cut a conversation before it had even begun, one that made people look for another face to speak to.

'He's over there.' I thought I'd whispered, but people turned again and Elsie closed her eyes and shook her head.

Jack looked over his shoulder. 'The new chap?'

'He's not that new,' I said.

'Florence.' Elsie took my arm. 'I thought we decided to keep things to ourselves for a while. Haven't we learned from experience that blurting things out isn't always the best way forward?'

'How do you mean?' Jack leaned in a little more.

'I know him,' I said. 'I know him from years ago.'

'Then let's invite him over.' Jack started waving his stick around, but I managed to reach out and put a stop to it.

Jack sat on the chair opposite, and he searched my face for an answer. I don't know what made me tell him. It might have been the concern waiting in his eyes, looking for a home. It might have been because Elsie let go of everything so easily, and I needed someone to hold my worrying for me. Or it might have been that he reminded me of my father, with a reassurance that waited for me on old shoulders. Whichever it was, it made me explain about the elephant, and the scar in the corner of Ronnie's mouth. Although I didn't tell him everything. There are some things that sit in your mind for so many years, gathering weight, there is no longer an explanation left to fit them.

He looked at me.

'Well?' I said.

'I hate to see you distressed like this, Florence.'

'That's not an opinion,' I said.

One of the uniforms appeared with a tray. It wasn't the German girl, it was the one with a thick plait that runs the whole length of her back. Red face. A watch too big for her wrist. I wasn't in a mind for eating, but I didn't want to offend her, so I put some sandwiches in a serviette and slipped them inside my handbag.

'Well?' I said again, after she'd left.

'I think . . . ' The words took a while to find their way out. 'I think, if you're concerned, then we should all be concerned as well.'

I let out a lot of air and folded my arms. 'See,' I said to Elsie. 'Jack doesn't think I'm being stupid.'

'No one has even remotely suggested you're being stupid,' she said.

'We should tell someone.' I folded my arms a little more tightly. 'Miss Bissell. The police. The government.'

'You're on a trial period,' Elsie said. 'What on earth will it look like if we go running to Miss Bissell?'

'I'm on probation,' I said to Jack. 'I've only got a month to prove to Miss Ambrose that I'm not losing my mind.'

Jack looked at us both and reached out his hand. 'I tell you what, Florence. Why don't we try the thing my doctor always tells me to do?'

I wouldn't unfold my arms. 'What's that?' I said.

He patted my knee. 'Why don't we watch, and wait?'

*   *   *

I did another circuit. Whilst they were all singing about drunken sailors, I could hear Jack and Elsie, even though I was right at the far end of the room. The end where Ronnie was standing. Or where he had been standing, because he wasn't there any more. I could see the trolley

72

and the noticeboard, and Mrs Honeyman cushioned in an armchair, but the space where Ronnie Butler had been standing was empty.

'Where did he go?' I whispered.

No one answered.

I went into the corridor. The only person I saw was the German girl, who disappeared into one of the rooms. 'Are you looking for me?' I shouted, but the double doors swung their goodbye long after she'd vanished. Even reception was empty. Just a telephone that rang to itself, until it was answered by Miss Bissell's voice, although Miss Bissell was nowhere to be seen.

*Thank you for calling Cherry Tree Accommodation for the Elderly. All calls are recorded for training and monitoring purposes.*

I walked back down the corridor. I followed the singing, until I found Jack and Elsie's voices again, and as I walked, I looked through the little windows in each of the doors. It wasn't until I got to the kitchens that I found him. He was standing by one of the trays of sandwiches, taking something out of his pocket.

★ ★ ★

'He's trying to poison us.'

Jack walked us back to my flat. I told him it wasn't necessary. I was so sure it wasn't necessary, I told him before he'd even offered, but he would insist.

'Why on earth would he do that?' Elsie took off her coat and commandeered her usual seat by

73

the fireplace. 'What possible reason would Ronnie have to poison anybody? You're going off on one of your tangents again.'

'What was he doing in there, then, tampering with the food?' I went straight to the window and pulled the curtains to. 'Why was he in the kitchens?'

'He was probably helping himself to another sandwich,' she said. 'Or looking for extra milk. They never give you enough, do they? They skimp on everything.'

'We're not allowed in the kitchens.' I sat in the other armchair and glanced back at the curtains. There was a slice of daylight pushing through a gap in the material. 'It says so on the door. It says staff only. Everything is recorded for training and monitoring purposes. Perhaps they recorded him in the kitchens. They might have monitored him. Perhaps we should ask.'

Elsie pinched the little space between her eyes and I glanced at the window again.

Jack reached across and pulled the curtains tighter. 'Is that better?' he said, and I nodded. 'Now, let's take a step back and think about the best thing to do.'

'A light might be an idea,' said Elsie. 'I can't see a thing in here now.'

I only realised when I switched the lamp on, when the glow from the bulb stretched into the corners of the room. I'd been too busy worrying about the sandwiches to notice.

'The elephant,' I said.

We all looked at the mantelpiece.

The elephant had disappeared.

# Handy Simon

'Ninety-seven?' Handy Simon looked for a chair to lower himself into, but there wasn't one available. 'Ninety-seven?' he said again.

'Ninety-seven.' Miss Ambrose stabbed at the manila folder with her index finger. 'He doesn't look ninety-seven. Can you believe it?'

Simon screwed his face up into thinking. He thought about his grandfather, who had been in the St John's Ambulance until well into his eighties, and the woman from the corner shop who fought off a gang of hooligans with just a walking stick and a phrase she'd heard on the television.

'I'm not sure,' he said.

Miss Ambrose repeated, 'Can you believe it?' and Simon realised it was the sort of question people ask when they're not actually looking for a well-reasoned answer, but they just want someone else in the room to agree with them.

'No,' he said, and unscrewed his face again. 'No, I can't.'

Simon looked out into the day room. Miss Ambrose's office had glass partitions, but they were the kind with a grid all the way across, and it always felt as though you were viewing life through a chessboard. After Justin had packed away his accordion, most of the residents had drifted into the television room, and Gabriel

Price sat with his back to them, on one of the hard chairs usually reserved for the staff. He was facing the screen, but from the angle of his head, it was obvious he was looking somewhere else.

'There's something fishy going on,' Miss Ambrose was saying. 'Something I can't quite put my finger on.'

Miss Ambrose and her finger weren't particularly reliable, it had to be said. Miss Bissell, on the other hand, could put her finger on anything, day or night, with the most breathtaking accuracy.

'Perhaps we should ask Miss Bissell.'

As soon as Simon heard the words, he realised they were the wrong ones. It sometimes felt as though there was a giant hole between his brain and his mouth, and there was nothing in place to stop all his thoughts falling through it.

'We don't need to bother Miss Bissell with everything, do we, Simon?'

Simon thought about answering, but decided it was safer to opt for shaking his head instead.

'Keep an eye on him.' She nodded through the chessboard. 'And while you're at it, keep an eye on everyone else as well. Florence Claybourne has been acting most peculiarly in recent days. Perhaps it's about time we had her assessed for Greenbank.'

And so Handy Simon became a Mata Hari. Which filled him with both self-importance and self-loathing, all in the same moment.

★ ★ ★

76

Simon had never been a big fan of responsibility. He had spent most of his life ducking around corners to get out of its way, even though there had been times over the years when it had chased him across the horizon for all he was worth.

He walked across the courtyard towards the car park, and his trainers pushed a path through the gravel. The engine started just as the clock clicked to half past, and a weather forecast sprang from the radio and tumbled around the car. Grey. Overcast. Becoming colder. When he drove out of the main gates, he knew the woman with the Patterdale terrier would be watching the traffic on the pedestrian crossing, and the man in the four-by-four would be lighting his cigarette as he waited. At the bottom of the road, the butcher would be pulling trays from a window, and the woman from the fruit and veg shop would be carrying an A-board before she disappeared it through a doorway. If the first set of lights was green, it meant Simon would only be able to glance at the windows of the car showroom and not stare for a full three minutes. But if he managed to get into second gear by the time he reached the florist, he would get through the second set of lights without them changing back to red. He would remember to swerve to avoid the pothole just after the park gates, and if he was lucky, he would pull into a space right outside the takeaway. The man behind the counter would say, 'Good evening, Mr Simon,' and hand him a white plastic bag, and neither of them would say another word to each other until the following week. Simon would eat his food on the settee that evening. His mother was no longer there to stop him, and although the novelty had long since worn away, he still remembered her each time he did it. Afterwards, he would put the white plastic bag and the empty cartons in the pedal bin, and switch out the lights in the kitchen. For a moment, he would stare at the clock on the microwave, and listen to the fridge humming to itself in a linoleum quietness. It never took Simon very long to get to sleep, but that night he would lie in bed and think about the theatre of strangers who made up his days, and he would wonder, perhaps, if they sometimes thought about him too. Because it somehow feels as though everyone is connected to everyone else, even though they perhaps don't realise it, and he finds the idea strangely reassuring, but Simon would be asleep before he could really work out why.

# Florence

I saw Elsie look at Jack. There was less doubt in her eyes now. There was no apology, and I didn't ask for one, because I'd rather it appeared in its own good time.

'I told you he'd been in here. Didn't I tell you?' I said.

Jack walked over to the mantelpiece. 'I wonder why he chose the elephant.'

'Because elephants never forget,' I said. 'He's making a point. He's telling us he's got a long memory.'

Elsie shot me a look from the corner.

'I'm only telling the truth,' I shouted.

'I just wish you'd tell it a little more quietly,' she said. 'We need to stay calm, Florence. We need to think.'

'I'm making it clear,' I shouted. 'I'm not allowed to do many things any more, but I'm still allowed to make things clear.'

'If he really didn't drown, and it really is Ronnie,' she said, 'why do you think he's doing this now? After all these years?'

'I don't know.' The words left my mouth too quickly and she frowned at me.

Jack was still studying the mantelpiece. 'It's breaking and entering, although there's no sign of him doing either.'

'That might be because he's still in here.' I stood, but my legs felt as though they hadn't

79

agreed to go along with it, and so I lowered myself back again. 'Perhaps he hasn't left yet. Check the other rooms. Make sure.'

I could hear Jack walking around the flat and opening doors.

Elsie was watching me. I tried to find something in her eyes, something my fear could lean on. The second thing about Elsie is that she always knows the right thing to say, and I waited for her to say it. 'Everything's going to be fine, Florence,' she said. 'If it is him, then at least he's made his first move. We've been through worse, haven't we?'

I nodded. We had. Much, much worse.

'But if it is him,' I said, 'there's one thing that really bothers me.'

'What's that?'

I waited for a moment before I answered. 'Who on earth did they bury in 1953?'

My question still sat between us when Jack reappeared. He said, 'All clear,' and pulled out one of the dining chairs.

'Perhaps you'll believe all the other things now,' I said. 'Perhaps instead of doubting me, you'll help me find some evidence before they send me off to Greenbank.'

'No one has ever doubted you.' Elsie reached out, but I held my hands on my knee.

'The sandwiches!' I'd only just remembered. 'Do you believe me about the sandwiches now? There are some in my bag,' I said. 'Get rid of them. Wrap them in something and put them in the dustbin, before they hurt someone.'

Jack reached over for my bag, which sat at the

far end of the dining table. 'This?' he said.

'Yes,' I said. 'You do it. Just get them out of there. I don't want to touch them.'

He opened the bag and stared inside.

'Well, go on then,' I said.

He still stared. When he finally did reach in, he didn't pull out any sandwiches. I knew what it was going to be; I knew what it was going to be before I even saw it.

It was the elephant.

★ ★ ★

I sat in the armchair with a cup of sweet tea Jack made before he left, and which had almost certainly grown cold, because I could see slivers of brown clinging to the sides and trying to escape the china. There was a brush of sweat on my forehead, and I knew there was the ladder in my tights from catching my leg against the sideboard, because I could feel it grow each time I moved. There was still an energy in the flat, though, wandering around and looking for somewhere to land. We were alone, Elsie and me, and the room had grown dark around us. My eyes struggled to find the edges of the furniture amongst all the shadows, and the shapes changed as the day disappeared.

'Shall I put the light back on?' I heard her say.

I didn't reply. I'd switched the lamp off the minute Jack went. I've no idea why, it just felt safer somehow. Less obvious.

'How about the wireless, then?' she said. 'Do you fancy a bit of company?'

81

I couldn't turn my mouth into an answer.

'You used to love music. The first time you came round for tea, we had a conversation about music. My mother was there, do you remember?'

I looked at her.

'My other sisters were with us, too. You remember Dot and Gwen?'

'I remember their faces,' I said.

She smiled at me, and I smiled back.

'That's all that matters, Florence. Why don't we try three things? Why don't we start with Gwen?'

After a little while of trying, I could feel my mind untether itself and drift back.

'Spent all her time in the kitchen,' I said. 'Always knitting. She knitted you a scarf, didn't she? And Gwen was the only one who could get through to your mother, most of the time.'

'She was, she was. Now what about Dot?'

'Never stopped moving. Always busy. Always involving herself in something. Didn't she get married and move away?'

'She did,' Elsie said. 'You're doing really well, Florence.'

'It's the names.' I frowned into my hands.

'Names don't really matter, do they?'

'I don't suppose so. I've just never been very good at them.'

I haven't. My mind has never enjoyed holding on to them. Even when I was younger, I would be told a name and straight away it would slip through the gaps and disappear. Elsie had so many sisters, it confused me right from the outset.

Elsie, Gwen, Beryl and Dot.

It sounded like Elsie's mother had been working her way through a piano keyboard.

Every Good Boy Deserves Favour.

Perhaps there would have been an F next, but Elsie's father left for the war and returned as a telegram on the mantelpiece. Her mother was convinced they'd made a mistake, and she would roll her eyes and tut at the telegram, as though it was deliberately trying to trick her into early widowhood.

'How can they be sure it's him?' she said to her sister, and to us, and more often than not to an empty room. 'How do they know?'

No one had the answer, even though they looked very hard for it in the ceiling and the floor, and in each other's eyes. No one ever looked straight at Elsie's mother. It was too dangerous. It was like spinning a wheel and not knowing quite what you were going to get. And all the time, the telegram sat in the letter rack on the mantelpiece and watched. But whether Elsie's father was dead or not, there would now only ever be four of them and they all had to accept the fact there was never going to be an F. At least, not until Elsie found me on the bus. The first time she brought me home for tea, we all sat around the kitchen table and she shouted, 'We have an F! We have a Favour!'

Everyone was silent. Even her mother.

'We're a keyboard now, don't you see? Every good boy deserves favour.' She pointed to each of us in turn.

'What about me?' said her mother. 'Where do I fit in?'

Her name was Isabel.

'I don't know,' Elsie said. Beryl glared across the table. Even Gwen shook her head very slightly.

'And Charlie. What about your father? What will he say when he hears about all this?'

We all looked at the letter rack in silence. I didn't dare swallow, because I knew the noise it made would be loud enough to wake the dead. Even her father (if her father was, in fact, actually dead).

Instead, I pushed away the piece of Victoria sponge I was eating, dabbed at my mouth with a napkin and said, 'Well, Mrs Colecliffe. Charlie is a C, and Middle C is the most important note on a keyboard. Without it, none of the other notes would even exist.'

Her mother beamed across the kitchen table. And from that moment on, everyone was nice to me.

I watched Elsie, now, as my mind told me the story.

'Every good boy deserves favour,' I said. 'Your mother liked me, didn't she?'

'Of course she did. We all did.'

'Dot and Gwen?' I said. 'They liked me?'

'You know they did.'

'Even Beryl?'

There was a pause, and she knew I'd heard it. 'As much as Beryl ever liked anyone,' she said.

I traced the pattern on the armchair with my finger. Backwards and forwards along the lines, always trying to find the place I started from. 'I think about Beryl a lot,' I said. 'All the living we've done since. All that life she never got to have.'

The air left Elsie's chest, but no words left with it.

My finger still followed the pattern, and I found my way back to the beginning.

'We can't let him get away with it,' I said. 'We've got to prove who he is, before it's too late.'

# 6.39 p.m.

They need a letter, the council. There's a new Basildon Bond in the sideboard, and as soon as I'm back on my feet, I'm going to pull it out and write one.

It's the rubbish. There's too much of it. People are getting tired of things and throwing them away, and we're running out of space to put it all in. I read about it. In a magazine. When we've finished with something, we shouldn't be putting it in the bin, we should be reusing it. The magazine said so. I've told enough people, but none of them listens.

'Don't you worry about the rubbish, Miss Claybourne. Worrying about the rubbish is our department,' they say.

Someone has to worry though, don't they? No one else seems to. There are great skips of rubbish at the back of the kitchens. I've seen them. Full of waste. Food people would be grateful for. Clothes as well. All they need is a darn, but people won't get a needle and thread out these days. I'd got quite a collection together before Gloria found me.

'Don't you go bothering yourself with all this, Florence,' she said, and she lifted it out of my hands and put everything back.

I didn't kick up a fuss, because what she didn't realise was that it was my second trip. I've already sewn up the anorak. And the socks. I've saved all the old newspapers for when the nights start drawing in, and I'm going to use the egg cartons for my bits and pieces. Elsie says they smell, but she's always been over-particular. We get fed up of things too easily, I said to her. We shouldn't be so quick to throw things away. There's always a use for something if you look hard enough.

I'm going to ask Gloria to help me write that letter. She's a pleasant girl, Gloria. Always smiling. Kind eyes. And you couldn't wish for nicer teeth. Everyone has bad days, don't they, and I just met her in the middle of one. Gloria might be the one to find me, and if she does, I'm going to explain all about the rubbish again. When she knocks at the door, I'll give her a shout. I don't want to cause any alarm, so I'll probably say something like, 'I hate to be a bother, but I've got myself in a bit of a situation, Gloria.' I won't want her to ring for an ambulance, but she'll insist, because she's that kind of girl. When it gets here, she'll sit in the back with me, and even though the ambulance sways along all the roads, and all the leads and the little boxes of equipment will sway along with it, she will never let go of my hand. Not once.

'Don't you worry, Florence. I'm not going to leave your side.'

The ambulance man will sit on the opposite seat. He will rest his hands on his knees, and I will look down at his boots and think how tired the leather looks, and I will ask him if his shift is nearly over.

He'll say, 'Not long to go now,' and he'll wink

at me, and I will try to think of the last time someone winked at me, and I won't be able to come up with anything.

'That's so typical of you, Florence. Always thinking about other people,' Gloria will say, and she'll squeeze my hand.

And I'll tell her she can call me Flo, if she'd like.

I'm not sure when Gloria finishes work. Five, I think. It might be gone that by now, but there must be times when she stays late. Everybody does these days, don't they?

# Florence

On Tuesday afternoons, I always go to the hairdresser, and Cheryl washes my hair and messes around with a comb for a while, until she finds me an entire head of it again. Not Cheryl with a cherry, but Cheryl with a shhhh. Although I'm always forgetting and I don't see why it makes that much difference.

It's not a real hairdresser's, it's a room at the back of the residents' lounge, but they do their best, and put posters up of people no one could ever look like, and arrange the cans of hairspray on a little coffee table next to the door. She's an odd girl, Cheryl. Short blonde hair. Always frowning. A tattoo on the inside of her wrist. It's her little girl's name, apparently, but no one ever mentions it. The last time I went, I didn't realise Ronnie was in there as well until I closed the door, and by that time, I couldn't find a way to get out again.

He was sitting in the other chair, and he smiled at me. But it wasn't enough of a smile that you could give one back, even if you'd wanted to.

'Miss Claybourne.' Cheryl lifted herself off one of the counters and pulled out a seat. 'What will it be today?'

She always said the same thing. What will it be today? I thought one week I might surprise her. I might say Rita Hayworth red or a fringe like

Veronica Lake, but I knew it would only make Cheryl-with-a-shhhh frown even more than she does already, and so I said what I always said as well. Just the usual, Cheryl. And she got out her comb and put a little cape around my shoulders.

Another girl was cutting Ronnie's hair. No one knew what her name was, and as there were only two of them, everybody always called her Not-Cheryl. 'Who did your set and blow dry?' and people would reply, 'Not-Cheryl,' and we all knew where we were because that's who she was. She knew we did it, and she didn't seem to mind. Not-Cheryl was taking pieces of Ronnie's hair between her fingers and snipping at the ends. I watched through the mirrors.

'You settling in all right, Mr Price?' said Not-Cheryl.

'Perfectly grand,' he said. 'I feel as though I've been here all my life.'

His voice. It hadn't changed at all. I tried to close my ears to the sound, but it still crept in, and each word turned my stomach over. For someone so full of violence, his voice was almost soft and whispery, like a woman's. If you listened very carefully, there was even a lisp.

'Where did you say you were from originally?' The girl took another pair of scissors from her pocket.

He didn't answer for a moment, then he said, 'Here and there,' and I could hear the smiling. His words were still full of themselves, even after all these years.

'That's nice,' she said.

Cheryl combed my hair out, and I looked in

the mirror and wondered how long I'd looked this old. 'There's lots of activities go on in the day room, Mr Price,' she said, 'if you want to meet some more people,' and I thought, I'm sitting in your seat and you should be talking to me, you shouldn't be talking to him.

I heard Ronnie shift in his chair, and all the pretend leather creaked with his weight. 'I've been rather too busy for that,' he said, 'of late.'

'What have you been up to, then?' said Not-Cheryl, who was young enough to fall into traps.

I heard the chair again. 'I've been tracing my family tree, as it happens.'

I was sure his reflection was staring at me, but Cheryl and her overall kept getting in the way.

'I've always wanted to do that.' Cheryl pulled the ends of my hair over my ears. 'It must be really fascinating.'

'Oh, it is,' said Ronnie. 'Fascinating.'

'How far back did you go?' Cheryl gave up on my ears and searched for a parting instead.

Ronnie took a while to answer. He always did. It was as though he needed to enjoy the taste of his own opinion for a while, before he was willing to let it go. 'As far back as I needed to,' he said.

'I wouldn't know where to start.' Not-Cheryl spoke to the mirror. 'I know my great-grandma used to live in Prestatyn, but everyone lost touch.'

I was certain Ronnie moved again, because when I looked up, his reflection seemed closer. 'It's amazing what you can find out with a little research. You can trace anyone you like if you're determined enough.' He smiled. 'Even great-grandmas who used to live in Prestatyn.'

'Do you think so?' said the girl.

'Anyone is traceable.' He stood and brushed down his jacket. 'I think you'll find there are no hiding places left in this world any more.'

As he spoke, he looked at me. I was worried they could hear me breathing. I was worried Cheryl would ask if I was all right, and why I'd gone so pale, and if I'd like a glass of water. But no one said anything. Ronnie slipped through the door and back into the lounge, the girl swept away all traces of him from the floor, and Cheryl pulled a towel from a shelf and wrapped it around my shoulders and said, 'Shall we get you sorted out, then?'

I didn't say anything. I sat there and tried to concentrate on the radio, but it wasn't playing a song I wanted to hear. I listened to Not-Cheryl talking about her great-grandma in Prestatyn, and Cheryl pretending to be interested. I listened to the click of the scissors and the whir of the hairdryer, and the sound of water running in a sink. I tried to make these noises cover up my thinking, but all they did was make it louder.

When I went to pay, I tried to take my mind off things, and I looked at the tattoo on Cheryl's wrist whilst she was searching for change in the till.

'It's a lovely name,' I said. 'Alice. I had an aunt called Alice a long time ago.'

When I spoke, she dropped the coins on the floor. It took her an age to collect them all, but when she had, she stood back up again and looked me right in the eye for the first time.

'Thank you so much, Miss Claybourne,' she said.

'You're very welcome, Cheryl,' I said back. Although I wasn't even sure what it was she was welcome to.

★ ★ ★

After I'd left the hairdresser's, I went to the little shop near the main gates. I thought I might have a look around. Treat myself. I knew Ronnie wouldn't be in there, because Miss Bissell allowed him to go to the supermarket all by himself. I'd seen him. Walking across the courtyard, weighed down by carrier bags. Although what he finds to buy in there, I couldn't tell you. I thought perhaps Jack or Elsie might be around, though, and we'd all be able to walk back to my flat together.

It was empty, as it happened. Just the man behind the counter, who doesn't look up when he's serving you, let alone when you walk in. I used to try and pass the time of day, but then I noticed he wears those little headphones in his ears, and half the time he isn't even listening.

'I'm just having a browse,' I shouted, when I walked in. 'Don't mind me.'

And he didn't.

I did my best, but it's difficult to browse in a shop that small. There's only so long you can stare at a loaf of bread. Qwick Stop, it's called. I've had it out with Miss Bissell on many an

93

occasion, but she says it's out of her remit. I don't really know what a remit is exactly, but you can guarantee if Miss Bissell has one, it stretches as far as she damn well wants it to. The shop is all primary colours and bright lights, although it still looks tired, like it needs a good bottoming. It sells basics. Aisles full of milk and bread, and lavatory paper. They have a freezer packed with ready meals and ice cream, and a little display of cakes and biscuits. I studied the display for as long as I could, before the man started peering round the till. In the end, I plumped for the Battenberg. It's nice to have a bit of cake in, just in case you have an unexpected visitor, and you can't go wrong with a Battenberg. Although I did think I might still have one unopened in a tin somewhere.

When I went to pay, the man had taken his earphones out, but he still shouted, 'One pound seventy-four pence.' I shouted, 'Thank you,' back again. I was putting the change in my purse when I said, 'Would you like me to go round and give everything the once-over?' He stared at me.

'Would you like me to give the shelves a clean?' I said.

'We have a cleaner, thank you.'

'You don't have to pay me,' I said. 'I'm free now, as luck would have it. I could soon get started.'

'That won't be necessary,' he said.

I was about to point out a few things to him, and explain how necessary it actually was, when the girl with the plait came in. She wasn't wearing her uniform, but she was wrapped into a scarf and wearing a coat that was at least two sizes too big for her.

'Are you looking for me?' I said.

She frowned and shook her head, and put three bars of chocolate on the counter.

'Hungry?' said the man. He didn't shout this time.

'I just fancied something sweet,' she said.

I smiled at her. 'I've just bought a lovely Battenberg. Why don't you come over. I could put the kettle on. Cut you a slice?'

She looked at me over the scarf. 'No thank you, Miss Claybourne,' she said.

'You'd better hurry,' I said, 'before it all goes.' I gave a little laugh, but she didn't answer.

I waited a bit, but they started talking about something they both watch on the television, and I couldn't really join in, so I left them to it. I took the long way around the courtyards. I sat on one of the benches for a while, and looked up at the windows of my flat. I'd left the lights on, but you still couldn't really see much from the outside, even when you stood and craned your neck. I was going to go up there, but then I thought I should call in at the residents' lounge. Check the noticeboard. I hadn't looked at it since I'd had my hair done, and they might have pinned up something important.

When I walked in, Jack was laughing at some television programme he had on at full volume, and Elsie was sitting in the corner and watching the birds through the French windows. I went over to the noticeboard, although nothing had changed, but neither of them spotted me. They wouldn't have seen me at all if I hadn't gone to the coffee table to find a magazine I wanted to take home.

'Florence!' Jack shouted over all the canned laughter. 'What have you been doing with yourself?'

I didn't bother looking up. 'I've had my hair done.'

'Of course you have,' he said. 'Of course you have. Very fetching.'

'I just wanted a magazine. I've got lots to do, I need to be on my way.'

'Why don't you take your coat off? Stay here a bit?' he said.

'No, you're busy.' I nodded at the television.

I'd got as far as the door when he shouted to me. 'Florence,' he said. 'You've forgotten your magazine.'

When I went back, he reached for the remote control and turned off the television programme. 'Do me a favour and keep me company for a bit?'

'I thought you were watching that,' I said.

'Only until someone better came along.' He pointed to the other armchair.

Elsie shouted from the corner, 'For heaven's sake sit down, you're making the room look untidy.' And she shook her head and laughed.

'Just for a bit then,' I said. 'But I can't stay for many minutes.'

★  ★  ★

I told them both as I was taking my coat off.

'He found out where I was,' I said, as I pulled

at one of the sleeves. 'He researched me.'

'He was probably just talking about tracing his family tree.' Elsie looked at me over the top of a cup. 'It's easy to get the wrong end of the stick in a hairdresser's. All those strong smells and running water.'

'No,' I said, 'he came looking. He wanted to find me.'

'And why would he want to do that?' Jack said.

I thought I saw Elsie shake her head very slightly.

'Because of what happened,' I said. 'Because of what happened to Beryl.'

Elsie was definitely shaking her head now, but I decided I wasn't forced to take any notice.

Elsie says I can't help myself. She says I've always been the same. She says my mouth runs away with me, and before anyone realises, I've said everything there is to say.

'Some things are better left in the past,' she says, 'but all you want to do is dig them up again and show everybody.'

'Beryl was Elsie's sister,' I said to Jack. 'Something happened to her. Something terrible.'

'Jack doesn't want to hear about that,' Elsie said. 'Why don't you tell him about the factory instead? We had some good times there, didn't we? Despite everything?'

'I never wanted to work in the factory,' I said. 'Neither of us did.'

It was true. We didn't. But sometimes life takes you along a path you only intended to glance down on your way to somewhere else, and when you look back, you realise the past wasn't the straight line you thought it might be. If you're lucky, you eventually move forward, but most of us cross from side to side, tripping up over our second thoughts as we walk through life. I never used to be like that. I always knew exactly what I wanted to be, even when I was a child.

'Did Beryl work at the factory?' Jack said.

I shook my head. 'Apparently we mustn't talk about Beryl.'

Jack frowned. 'What about the factory, then? If you didn't want to work there, what did you want to do?'

'I wanted to be a scientist,' I told him. 'I wanted to make a difference with my life.'

I did. The first time I announced it to the world, we were sitting at my kitchen table. The house smelled of warmth and pastry, and my dog, Seth, lay at our feet, his tail beating a tune into the carpet. Elsie said she sometimes borrowed my family, just to taste what it was like for a while. She said it was the only time she ever saw cutlery arranged around a placemat.

'I'm going to invent something.' I moved my schoolbooks from the path of a dessert spoon. 'Something that will change the world.'

'And what about you, Elsie?' my mother said.

Elsie reached down and stroked Seth's head. 'Beryl says we'll both end up working at the factory, and I'm not sure you can really change the world from there.'

'Beryl doesn't know anything,' I said. 'Beryl talks too much.'

98

It was true. Beryl did talk too much, and talking too much would eventually be her downfall, but of course none of us knew that then.

'You can change the world from this kitchen table if you want to.' My mother reached down into the dresser and lifted out an armful of dinner plates. 'All you have to do is make wise decisions.'

Jack is listening to the story. 'She was right,' he said. 'Your mother was right.'

My mother was always right. My mother looked like the kind of woman who had made wise decisions her entire life. Her hair was always pinned, her clothes always ironed. Whenever I walked through the front door, she would appear from a corner of the house, wiping her hands or carrying something interesting. It was as though she was a template for motherhood, cut from one of the dressmaking patterns Elsie's sister always left on their dining-room table. I think a mother was all she'd ever wanted to be. Florence's mother. It was how she always introduced herself to people, and it made me feel as though by being born, I'd accidentally swallowed up everything else she used to be.

I turned to Jack. 'I wanted us to go to university,' I said. 'I had it all planned, but Elsie wouldn't come with me.'

There was a softness at the edges of Jack's voice. 'She wouldn't?'

'It's not that I didn't want to,' Elsie said. 'You know how things were. You knew exactly why I couldn't go.'

We had sat on the lawn later that evening, watching Seth chase moths. He could never quite manage to catch one, and so he barked at them in a temper fit instead. A lopsided bark. A sound filled with a strange sense of urgency that dogs always feel when no one else is able to. Not ready to give up on the summer, Elsie and I had wrapped ourselves up into cardigans and curled into abandoned deckchairs. The evenings had grown cold and inevitable, and I could feel the seasons turn in the air.

I sat up straight in my deckchair. 'How do you know you're not the university type?' I said. 'We're only fourteen. We don't even know who we are yet.'

In the far corners of the garden, an autumn evening had stolen away the light. We might only have been fourteen, but I knew Elsie had more than managed to discover herself already. In her mother. The violent rages. The way she refused to eat for days at a time. The way she had to be coaxed from her bed like a child. Elsie had discovered herself when she found her mother cleaning the house in the early hours of the morning, and when her mother gave away her father's clothes, only to stand on doorsteps and beg them back a few hours later. In the way Elsie's sisters, one by one, seemed to be escaping. Gwen was training to be a teacher. Beryl had started looking at wedding dresses without even the slightest hint of a man in her life, and Dot had moved to the Midlands and married an obnoxious little fool called Harold, who put all his energy into telling other people what they should be thinking. Elsie's mother said she did it to spite them all.

'There's always a choice, isn't there?' I said. 'Every situation has an alternative waiting for you by the side of it.'

She didn't reply.

'Don't you think,' I said, 'we can change everything, just with the small decisions we make?'

She still didn't reply. I knew for Elsie, looking into the future must have felt like re-reading a book she'd never very much enjoyed in the first place.

'You never know what life has in store, do you?' I said. Seth settled down between the deckchairs and looked up at us both.

Elsie stared at the trees, where autumn rested on the branches, waiting for its turn. 'No,' she said. 'I don't suppose you do.'

\*    \*    \*

My mother died the following January.

'Lungs,' Elsie's mother said. 'They run in your family.'

I wanted to say that lungs ran in everyone's families, along with kidneys and livers, and hearts, but after Elsie's father was killed, her mother became strangely fixated with death. The more violent the end of someone's life, the better. She once walked three miles in the pouring rain to stare at a tree where a motorcyclist had been decapitated. 'It's important,' she said. 'To look.' At first, I couldn't understand why she would want to do something so intensely morbid, but then I realised it was a comfort to her. She liked to remind herself that God hadn't just singled her out for tragedy alone. It happened to other people, too. It somehow helped her to think we were all hurtling towards our destiny without having any choice in the matter. When I tried to explain it, Beryl said, 'She needs her head read, if you ask me,' without even looking up from her magazine. Elsie's mother probably did need her head read, but no one ever managed it. There were so many stories in there, I doubt even she could find all the words.

We started at the factory that summer.

'It's just temporary,' I said, as I slid on to the chair next to Elsie's. 'Until my father gets back on his feet.'

It was a chair I would sit on for the next forty years.

⋆   ⋆   ⋆

'So neither of you went to university?' said Jack.

I shook my head. 'We worked at the factory instead, for that horrible little man. The one who marched up and down, and shouted at everybody.'

'Mr Beckett,' Elsie said. 'The supervisor.'

'Mr Beckett. You don't give me enough time to think. You rush me too much. I would have got there myself if I'd had a minute.'

Elsie arched her eyebrow, but I chose to ignore it.

102

Jack reached over for his tea. 'What did you make at the factory?'

I laughed. 'Corsets.' He laughed along with me. 'They were all bones and panels,' I said. 'When you tried to sew one, it was like holding on to a hostage.'

'You were very good,' Elsie said. 'Mr Beckett's star pupil.'

I looked across the lounge, and into the past. It was more useful than the present. There were times when the present felt so unimportant, so unnecessary. Just somewhere I had to dip into from time to time, out of politeness. When I came back, Jack was waiting for me. 'There was a girl,' I said. 'Sat next to me and Elsie. She couldn't get the hang of it at all. Shook every time she tried to thread a needle.'

'You mean Clara?' Elsie said.

I nodded. 'Said Beckett was just like her father. She was terrified of him.'

'What happened to Clara?' said Jack.

I whispered, 'She hanged herself.'

'She did not!' Elsie put down her cup, and it argued with its saucer. 'Wherever has that come from?'

I ignored her and turned to Jack. 'Elsie's mother said Clara was still swinging when they found her.'

'No one hanged themselves.' Elsie hadn't got anything else to put down, so she raised her voice instead. 'You're getting all mixed up again. Why on earth would she do that?'

'She was afraid,' I said. 'Mr Beckett used to bully her.'

'Surely they did something about him, after that?' said Jack.

Elsie leaned forward and tried to find my eyes. 'But you helped her, Florence. Don't you remember? You taught her how to thread and how to stretch the corset. She got really good at it.'

I stared at her. 'I don't remember.'

'You spent hours teaching her. She started coming to the dance with us on a Saturday night. Married the boy who worked in the fishmonger's. Moved to Wales, I think.'

I began to say something and swallowed it back.

'Try to remember, Florence. The long second. What did you do with it?'

'Take your time,' Jack said. 'Don't worry about it. We all get in a muddle.'

I turned over thoughts like a game of cards, trying to decide on the ones that matched. The coat still rested on my knees, and I felt the material twist between my fingers. After a while, I said, 'I can't find a memory I trust.'

'I'll bet you can.' Jack reached for my hands. 'Tell me something clear. Tell me something you're absolutely sure of.'

I stopped twisting the material, and looked him straight in the eye. 'Ronnie Butler worked in the factory,' I said.

\* \* \*

'When did you last see it?'

It was the girl in the tangerine overall. Of all

104

the pointless questions you could ask a person who has lost something, this has to be the one to win a prize.

'If I knew that,' I said, 'I'd know where to find it, wouldn't I?'

She was an unusual-looking girl. Small eyes. Small ears. Wears a crucifix. Although if she's ever seen the inside of a church, I'll go to the foot of our stairs.

'What does it look like?' she said.

'It's a book.' I closed my eyes. 'It's book shaped. It has words in it.'

'But what colour is it?'

'I don't know. Blue. Green, perhaps. I don't remember. I don't take any notice of the outside, it's the inside I'm interested in.'

'My mum says things are always where you least expect them to be,' said the girl. 'Why don't we try looking there?'

'The refrigerator, then? Or maybe the lavatory cistern?'

The girl smiled. 'Yes, exactly!'

I closed my eyes again.

The book should have been exactly where I left it. On the little table next to my armchair. Each night I leave it there when I go to bed, and each morning I pick it up from where I left it, and read until Elsie comes over.

'You must have put it somewhere else last night.' The girl poked around behind the cushions. 'Perhaps you were a bit absent-minded.'

'My mind isn't absent,' I said. 'It's very much present and correct, thank you. It's just old.'

The girl stood with her hands on her hips in the middle of the room. 'Well, it'll turn up,' she said. 'When you least expect it.'

Which, I believe, means 'I'm tired of looking.'

'It's not the first thing, either.' I sat in the armchair whilst she unpacked her little basket of dusters. 'Last week, a pint of milk vanished from the fridge — and I know it was there, because I'd only started it that morning — and the week before, I found the *Radio Times* underneath my pillow.'

The girl didn't say anything.

'It was one of you, wasn't it? It must have been. I'd rather you told me you'd done it, then I can stop worrying.'

Still nothing.

'If this carries on,' I said, 'I'm going to have to have a word with Miss Ambrose.'

The girl carried on rubbing Pledge into the sideboard.

'Or even Miss Bissell.'

The girl's duster became very still. 'Why don't we make you a nice pot of tea, Miss Claybourne, and we'll have another look.'

I knew the mention of Miss Bissell would rouse the troops. I have my routines. I read my *Radio Times* by the window, and my book in the armchair. I buy one pint of milk on a Monday, and it lasts me five days. I live my life around habits. When your days are small, routine is the only scaffolding that holds you together.

I could hear the girl filling the kettle and rummaging around in a drawer.

'Put everything back where you found it,' I

106

shouted. 'I know where it's all supposed to be.'

I heard her open the fridge.

'There's three quarters of a pint left in there.' I could hear my voice tremble, even though where it came from felt firm. 'And don't think I don't know it.'

The refrigerator door didn't close.

'And shut the door properly,' I said. 'Or we'll have an operation on our hands.'

The door still didn't close, and after a few minutes, the girl walked back into the sitting room.

'Is this your book, Miss Claybourne?' she said very quietly.

I took it from her. It felt cold.

*   *   *

I made them change the locks. There was such a performance. They were two hours trying to talk me out of it, but I wouldn't be budged.

I just said, 'Security,' when they asked why. I didn't mention Ronnie, but only because Elsie spent the whole morning explaining to me why I shouldn't.

'I'm as frightened as you are,' she said, 'but I'm also frightened he's going to get us sent to Greenbank. One of us has got to stay calm.'

'You don't care. You don't care what he's doing.' I must have pulled the cushions off the settee, because when I looked, they were all across the floor. 'No one ever cares about me,' I said.

'It was my sister, remember? It was my sister, not yours.'

107

Elsie shouted. Elsie never shouts. I stopped worrying about the cushions and looked at her instead, and then I began to shake. When she held me, I felt smaller somehow. As though all her kindness made me shrink.

'Let's just leave, Elsie,' I whispered into her cardigan. It smelled of wool and reassurance. 'Let's go. Let's go somewhere he'll never find us.'

We stood together, and our beige life slotted around us. It was a holding place. A waiting room. 'Where would we go, Florence?' she said. 'We have nowhere to run to.'

'Then what are we going to do?' It was me who shouted then, but the room was so small, there was nowhere for the shouting to go.

She stepped back, and took hold of my shoulders. 'We're going to do what we have always done, and we are going to stand firm,' she said. 'Don't let him win. It's a game.'

'I'm not sure I even know how to play.'

Her grip tightened, until she held the very bones of me. 'Don't let him know you're afraid. Don't give him the satisfaction.'

'But I am,' I said. 'And I don't care who knows it.'

She looked right into my eyes. 'Why do you think he's doing this to you, Florence? What happened that you're not telling me?'

I started to answer, but the words fell into a thought, and disappeared.

Jack arrived, and all of us waited together for the locksmith. When Jack was in the room, it seemed to help, even if he didn't say a word. He drew the curtains and switched on the lamp, and he put a cup of tea on the table next to me. Every so often, he looked over and reminded me to drink it.

'They'll be here soon,' he said. 'The locksmiths. We won't have to wait long.'

'I wish we could all be as calm as you, Jack,' Elsie said.

I looked over at him. 'It must be the army. Old soldiers are always unflustered.'

He looked back. 'I expect so. Although I had my moments.'

'At least you returned,' I said.

'I almost didn't.'

We both heard the full stop.

'You could see it at the town-hall dance,' I said. 'All the missing men. We used to have to partner each other, me and Elsie.'

Elsie looked over at me. It was true. Like Elsie's father, young men were disappeared by the war, and instead of choosing between a foxtrot and a tango, they were carved into cool stone in a park memorial, and serenaded by the music of other people's lives. I wondered how many stopped to read their names.

We walked through the park one day, Elsie and I. It was not long after the war, and we stood in front of the memorial in a faded light. 'Do you think they felt brave?' I said.

'Bravery means you have a choice, doesn't it?' she said. 'It means you could have turned away but you chose not to.'

I looked at the names. There were so many, we had to lift our heads to see the people at the top.

'I don't think any of these men had a choice,' she said.

'No.' I read their ages as I spoke. 'I don't think they did either.'

'Brave is just a word we use about them to make ourselves feel better,' she said.

There were holes in everyone's lives after the war. There were gaps in the landscape long after it had ended, gaps where young men should have been. We did our best to close the gaps, to rearrange ourselves and shuffle along, and become different people, but the space stretched beside us as a constant reminder. It was never more obvious than on a Saturday night. A town hall filled with women, dancing amongst themselves, searching for a mend-and-make-do partner in a world everyone was trying to adjust to. They didn't realise in old age they would mirror their younger selves, and waltz out their lives together again, thieved of their husbands, and searching once more to make sense of it all.

'You used to dance?' said Jack.

'We did,' I said. 'Elsie liked the foxtrot, but I preferred the tango. You know where you are with a tango. Foxtrots can end up all over the place.'

'That's half the fun.' Elsie sat back, and sunlight from the window marched on to her face and found all the wrinkles. 'Although you wouldn't always dance with me. Sometimes, you refused point blank.'

Jack tapped his stick on the carpet. 'I used to do a mean foxtrot,' he said, 'before this got in the way.'

'It's important, to know when to sit a dance out,' I said.

* * *

The locksmith arrived. Elsie said I asked him too many questions. Jack made another cup of tea and tried to draw me away. I knew what he was up to. I'm not daft. There were things I needed to know, though. Where the locks come from, how many keys there were, and if the locksmith people kept a copy. The locksmith stopped answering after a while, and when he drank his tea, he stared at the same page in the newspaper without ever moving his eyes.

'I wasn't overly fond of him,' I said, as soon as the front door closed.

Jack watched the man make his way down the steps. 'He had all the right paperwork. I checked.'

'He'll hear you!' Elsie said.

'I don't much care if he does,' I said. 'And he's made a mess of the carpet.'

He hadn't, but I couldn't think of anything else to pick on. Jack gave it a brush anyway, and started a conversation about how there are no craftsmen left in the world any more, so at least we all had something to agree with.

The three of us sat back down and watched the key, which waited in the middle of the dining table, not realising the huge amount of trouble it had caused.

Miss Ambrose arrived at a quarter to. She peered at the new lock for a good few minutes before she spoke.

'Are you happy now?' she said. 'All this effort to convince you, when no one is actually getting into your flat in the first place.'

I didn't shift my eyes from the radiator.

'This isn't helping your case, you know. I hope this will be an end to it?'

The words curved into a question, but I decided not to reply, and Jack just stared at his hands.

Miss Ambrose left, and I looked up from the radiator just as the door clicked shut.

'It won't make any bloody difference,' I shouted.

Elsie pressed the palms of her hands against her eyes.

'You know what he's like,' I said. 'When he was younger, he could pick a lock and get in anywhere he wanted to. He had a talent for it. Failing that, he'll just get a copy made. Of the new key.'

'And how is he going to manage that?' Elsie said, without shifting her hands. 'He can't magic one up from thin air.'

'Miss Ambrose keeps them all in her office. In a little tin cupboard on the wall,' I said.

Jack frowned. 'She does?'

'Next to the filing cabinets.'

He sat forward. 'What's in the filing cabinets?'

'Us,' I said.

★   ★   ★

We were sitting in the day room, eyeing up Miss Ambrose's office.

112

'I've never been a criminal before,' I said.

Elsie glanced over. 'Try to sit normally, Florence.'

'I am sitting normally.'

I knew I wasn't. I sat on the very edge of my seat, and when I looked down at my hands, my knuckles were bone white. I could hear the rain, hammering against the French windows, asking to be let in. It was the kind of rain that joins everything together and makes it difficult to see a way out.

'Perhaps she'll be in there all day,' I said. 'Perhaps we won't get a chance.'

I straightened one of the cushions and looked back towards the office. Miss Ambrose sat at her desk, and she studied the wall in front of her, as though the answer to all of life's problems lay within its plaster.

'She has to move at some point,' Elsie said. 'Everyone does.'

The day room was empty, apart from Mrs Honeyman, who was dozing off against the trelliswork where Miss Ambrose was attempting to grow ivy up the walls. No one really knew why this was, except Miss Ambrose. Jack waited on the seat by the noticeboard, and we all looked at a television screen without watching. It was a gardening programme. Someone was standing on a patio in clean wellington boots, explaining how to plant seeds.

Jack pointed at the screen with his walking stick. 'At our age, it's an act of optimism, planting seeds.'

I went back to whitening my knuckles.

'It'll go off in a minute,' Elsie said. 'It's antiques next. *What's It Worth?* Everyone likes antiques.'

'Perhaps if I was a roll-top table, I might get more visitors,' I said, and everyone stared.

Even Mrs Honeyman.

# Miss Ambrose

Anthea Ambrose peered out into the day room. General Jack was laying down the foundations of an opinion, and Florence Claybourne had spent the last twenty minutes staring at her. Now Jack was joining in, turning in his chair and frowning.

Miss Ambrose took out her notebook. She was writing down things of her own, because she wasn't convinced Handy Simon was to be relied upon. Plus, it wasn't something you could necessarily put down in words. Words were not always adequate. This was more of a feeling. A sense that things were not quite as they should be, and it troubled her.

'I wonder if I might trouble you?'

A voice sent the pencil flying from her hand, and she scrambled around on the floor to retrieve it.

'Mr Price. Not a problem. What can I do for you?'

Gabriel Price didn't reply until she had found the pencil, repositioned herself on the seat, and brushed a stray piece of hair from her top lip.

'It's a delicate matter, I'm afraid.' He glanced into the day room through the chequered glass. 'May I speak with you privately?'

She hesitated for a moment and said, 'Of course,' and he reached back to close the office door.

Miss Ambrose felt the day room disappear. It

115

was strange how just a click sent everyone else an ocean away, rather than just the other side of a pane of glass. The television threw out images of antique furniture, Mrs Honeyman still dozed in the corner, and Jack waved his walking stick around at no one in particular. Even the rain had stopped, and the silence made it seem as if the world was a very elaborate play, written and performed for her entertainment, and yet one in which she was only ever going to be part of the audience.

'Miss Ambrose?'

'Sorry, I drifted off for a moment. What were you saying?'

'The tall woman.' He nodded at the day room. 'You must excuse me, I've not quite got to grips with everyone's names yet.'

'Miss Claybourne?'

He nodded. 'Yes, that would be the one.' He checked the door again. 'The thing is, I think she might be having a few problems.'

'Problems?'

'With the old upstairs.' He tapped a finger against his temple. 'Short on the marbles.'

'I'm sorry?'

He sighed and put his hands on the desk. 'I think she might be getting a bit confused.'

'Really?' Miss Ambrose looked over at her notebook. 'Whatever gives you that idea?'

'You know I'm not one to complain.'

'Of course not.'

'But she's been — how can I put this nicely — spying on people.'

'People?'

116

'Me, actually,' he said. 'With binoculars.'

Miss Ambrose sat back.

'I wasn't going to mention it. I don't want to get Florence into trouble, and I've got no objection to being spied upon.' He laughed, but Miss Ambrose had noticed that laughter never quite climbed as far as his eyes. 'But I thought I'd better say something. Vulnerable, the elderly, aren't they? When they get to that stage?'

'They certainly are.' Miss Ambrose frowned.

'I'll leave it with you,' he said.

She expected him to go, but he didn't. Instead, he stood, just for a moment, the not-quite-smile resting on his mouth, the not-quite-stare held in his eyes. Eventually, the door unclicked and he disappeared, and Miss Ambrose found that she could breathe again.

She needed to think, but any thoughts she had were eaten away by the tap of Jack's walking stick and Mrs Honeyman's snoring, and the sound of Florence Claybourne making one of her points, and so she took her notepad and her pencil, and a lipstick for good measure, and decided to go for a walk.

# Florence

'She's off,' I said.

Elsie watched Miss Ambrose's retreating back. 'So she is.'

Jack took up his position in the corridor.

Miss Ambrose's office reminded me of a jumble sale. Everything was on display. Drawers not quite closed, cupboards slightly ajar, all her belongings spread out on the desk like a shop counter.

'Wherever do we start?' I picked up a stapler, and its jaw hung open to reveal a set of silver teeth.

'I wonder how she manages to work,' Elsie said. 'You'd think she'd be too distracted.'

I examined a collection of pen tops and paperclips, which leaked from a plastic box at the corner of her desk. 'Perhaps it represents her mind?'

'Busy?'

'A bloody mess,' I said, and Elsie laughed.

Through the glass, I could see the top of Jack's cap wandering up and down the corridor. Elsie saw it too. 'Let's get a move on,' she said.

We searched. Strangely, it is more difficult to search in a place that's disorganised, because you can never quite be sure how familiar someone is with their own particular mess. It might be very personal, exactly where on the floor litter has fallen and how many inches a drawer lies open. We had to work carefully, but despite our best efforts, all we found were half a dozen Sainsbury's receipts and last year's staff Christmas card.

'Doesn't Miss Bissell look lovely?' I said. 'She really suits an elf costume.'

'Don't get distracted, Florence. Try to concentrate.'

'It's just a shame she's not smiling.'

'Florence! We're supposed to be looking for evidence, remember? Something we can use to stop them sending you away. We're running out of time.'

I put down the Christmas card. 'Those are the filing cabinets I meant.' I looked over at the far wall. 'There'll be something in there.'

The filing cabinets were in the corner of the room. Giant silver monsters. The kind of filing cabinet no one owns any more, with drawers you are only allowed to open one at a time, for fear of the entire thing crashing down and murdering an innocent bystander.

And they were locked.

'All the best drawers are,' I said, because I knew she didn't have time to question me. We studied the room instead. There were so many hiding places for a key, the thought of looking for one was paralysing.

'Imagine you're Miss Ambrose,' Elsie said. 'What would you do?'

I looked around. 'I'd probably tidy up a bit.'

Elsie put her hands to her face. 'With the key,' she said.

'The key?' I had to wait for my eyes to remember and then I said, 'It could be anywhere.'

'It'll be stuck underneath the desk with a bit of BluTack.' Jack appeared in the doorway.

I felt underneath the desktop.

Elsie lifted her eyebrows. 'How did you know that?' she said.

'War makes a man of you.' He winked at us both.

Elsie took the key over to the filing cabinet. 'Let's just see if it fits.'

It did. The first drawer groaned on its runners, as though we had woken it from a heavy sleep, and there we all were in our manila folders, rows of silent people with silent pasts, waiting to be listened to.

'Shall we read about ourselves?' I reached into the C tab and pulled myself out.

'No we will not.' Elsie put me back inside again. 'We're not going to read about anyone other than him, not even ourselves. You know everything there is to know about yourself; you don't need to go reading about it.'

'I thought it might be nice to be reminded,' I said.

I closed the top drawer and pulled out the second one. I reached in. 'P, Price, Gabriel.'

We began to read.

\* \* \*

'Ninety-seven?'

We didn't get further than 'date of birth'.

'Isn't Ronnie the same age Beryl would have been?' I said.

It was the unexpectedness of it, I suppose, but Elsie's eyes reddened at the sound of her sister's name. People need to be spoken about, I think. Their names need to be brought into conversations and mentioned in passing. Sometimes, a name is the only thing we can leave behind, and if people are afraid to use it, to hear it spoken out loud, we eventually fade away and become lost forever, just because no one ever talks about us any more.

'Don't people usually lie the other way?' I said.

Elsie opened the file, and a newspaper clipping tumbled to the floor.

'I knew I'd heard the name,' I said. 'I told you, didn't I?'

### Have-A-Go Hero Rescues
### Mugging Victim (97)

*Dan Carter (18) became a hero yesterday as he caught an attacker who mugged pensioner Gabriel Price (97) in broad daylight (both pictured below).*

*Mr Price had just collected his pension when he was pushed to the pavement. His cries alerted Mr Carter, who raced to his aid, and managed to restrain the attacker until police arrived. The story has appeared in the national press, and Mr Carter has even been interviewed by the BBC. 'I just did what anyone would have done,' he said.*

*Mr Price was unavailable for comment.*

'Anyone wouldn't though, would they?' I said. 'It was a headline in one of my old newspapers, and it was on the radio. They had a whole programme on acts of kindness.'

There was very little else. A doctor's letter about cholesterol. A dentist's letter about having false teeth fitted. A brief note from social services. Inability to cope. Difficulties with activities of daily living. Poor self-care.

'He looks like he can cope to me,' I said.

We looked down the page.

'Ronnie Butler wasn't born in Whitby,' Elsie said.

'No, but perhaps Gabriel Price was. If Gabriel Price even exists.'

We looked again at the photograph in the clipping. It had been taken a few weeks earlier, but despite the grainy ink of the newspaper, there was no question that it was Ronnie who stared back at us from the page.

'It's a wonder no one spotted him,' Elsie said. 'Being in all the newspapers.'

I stared at the photograph. 'Perhaps they did,' I said.

# 7.10 p.m.

Funny things, photographs. They trap you in a moment forever, and you can never leave. There's one on that little table in the corner. I don't have many photographs, because no one ever bothered taking them of me, but this is from school. All of us in a row, staring down a camera lens into the future. There's me on one end and Elsie on the other. Whenever I see an old photograph, I always look for myself.

'There I am,' I say. 'I'm there, look!' as though I've bumped into an old friend.

We're all in our uniforms, and everyone is saying cheese. Everyone except little Eileen Everest. It was as though she knew she wouldn't have a future to look into. Run over by a tram on Llandudno seafront when she was seven. I often look at Eileen, imprisoned behind wood and glass, watching us all grow old without her. She never really belonged, even in that photograph. There's always one child in a class. One who doesn't fit in. A little soul at the edge of the playground, not knowing where they should stand. You can spot them a mile off. That was Eileen Everest. She was sickly, too. Bad chest. That's why she went to Llandudno in the first place. We were standing on the town-hall steps, hiding behind our mothers' coats whilst they had a conversation about how they were planning to go. I was going to tell her all about Whitby and say, 'Why don't you visit there instead?' but I didn't. Because no one ever spoke to Eileen Everest. It was just something we didn't do.

It was the last I ever saw of her.

Next to the photograph, there's a telephone, although it never gets used from one week to the next. If I ever need to give my number to someone, I have to look it up on a piece of paper.

'All our residents have access to a telephone.' I hear Miss Bissell say this sometimes, when she's giving one of her guided tours. I don't have access now, not from where I'm lying. I never used it even when I did. I don't care what they all thought.

'If you continue to misuse the telephone, Florence,' said Miss Ambrose, 'we're going to have to take it away.'

I didn't misuse anything. I didn't ring for any taxis. What would I need with half a dozen taxis, all going to different places? She paid for the pizzas as well, out of the petty cash. She had to, because the man in the red apron wouldn't leave. I knew it was Ronnie. Ringing up in that soft, whispery voice of his. Pretending to be anyone he wanted to.

'Don't look at me,' I said, but she did anyway. She never took her eyes off me when she was handing them round. 'There's no point in anything going to waste,' she said.

I didn't have any. I've never eaten pizza in my life, I said, and I'm not going to start now. She didn't even answer me. That's the problem with

Cherry Tree. People sometimes forget that you're waiting for a reply.

Another problem with Cherry Tree is there are no cherry trees. I've had this out with Miss Bissell on more than one occasion, but she won't be told. 'One of them must be,' is all she can come up with, but none of them is. It's the kind of name you give to these places, though. Woodlands, Oak Court, Pine Lodge. They're often named after trees, for some reason. It's the same with mental health units. Forests full of forgotten people, waiting to be found again. The last time I spoke to Miss Bissell about it, she said we could grow a cherry tree and have a planting ceremony. Invite a celebrity to come and hold the spade, that type of nonsense. Nothing will come of it, of course. It feels like you can call a thing whatever you want to, in an attempt to turn it into something else. Everyone knows it doesn't change what it is, but it alters people's view of it, which is perhaps the only thing that really matters. You can't trust anything to be what it calls itself any more.

It's like the day room. It isn't a day room, it's an All The Bloody Time Room. Everybody will be in there now and it isn't daytime. They'll all be sitting on Dralon settees, living a soap-opera life through a television screen. Someone will lose the remote control in a jumble of cushions, and Miss Ambrose will have to appear from behind her glass and dig down the side of chairs until it's found. People will doze off and wander off, and have muddled-up arguments about imaginary things, and no one will notice I'm not

125

there. Because I am never there.

Elsie was forever telling me to join in. She always said, 'You might enjoy it, if you try.'

Elsie found it easy, talking to people. If anyone new started at work, she was drawn across that factory floor like an iron filing. I couldn't do it. You can't just slip on a different coat and become someone else. So I would leave it to her, and spend my time listening to the leftovers of other people's conversations. The only problem is, I've spent so long standing at the edge that when I finally turn away, I doubt there is anyone in this world who will even notice.

I do wish that gas fire was on.

# Florence

It was Tuesday. Tuesday was Healthy Hearts. Fitness Pete had a T-shirt with 'Just Do It' on the front, and a talent for making an hour pass very slowly, and so I walked back to the flat before anyone realised I wasn't there. Thinking filled up my ears, and I almost didn't hear Miss Ambrose calling my name.

'Florence?'

And doing a strange little trot on the path behind me.

'I'm giving it a miss,' I shouted back. 'I'm not allowed to do many things any more, but I'm still allowed to give things a miss.'

'Florence, I wondered if I might have a little word?'

I rearranged my face before I turned.

The trot eventually brought her level. 'Shall we go to your flat?' She nodded across the courtyard. 'To have our little chat?'

'Let's start now,' I said. 'If it's that little, we might even finish it before we get there.'

'The thing is . . . ' Her voice slowed along with her pace. 'I've had a complaint.'

I looked up at the rooftops. A bird sat on the guttering of the day room, and followed us with marbled eyes. It was black, but it wasn't a blackbird.

'Well, not a complaint as such. More of an observation.'

127

It was much bigger. Bigger than a pigeon.

The bird sidestepped, shifting its weight and listening to us, and hammering out its curiosity on the plastic. What do we call you? Bigger Than A Pigeon.

'I suppose observation isn't really accurate either. Perhaps concern. Yes, that's it. Someone has expressed concern.' Miss Ambrose nodded at her final choice.

I frowned at the bird. 'Which someone?' I said.

Miss Ambrose cleared her throat. 'Well, it's Mr Price, to be honest.'

'Mr Price?' The bird fired itself into the sky, and I could hear its laughter scatter across the courtyard. 'What has Mr Price got to be concerned about?'

I held the key to the front door and hoped she wouldn't notice the tremor at its tip.

'Well, it's you, actually,' she said.

'Me?' I tried to remember what my normal face looked like. 'Why is he concerned about me?'

Miss Ambrose winced, as though she'd pulled a hamstring. 'He says you've been watching him, Florence.'

'I watch a lot of things.' The key stayed in mid-air. 'The news, the weather forecast, the world pass by.'

'Yes, I'm sure.' Miss Ambrose paused, her eye on the key. 'But none of them with binoculars.'

The key fell to the floor. 'Binoculars? He says I've been watching him with binoculars? I don't even own a pair of binoculars. I wouldn't know where to start with a pair of binoculars.'

Miss Ambrose gave me the kind of smile you give to a dog who can't quite manage to catch its ball. 'Shall we?' she said, and nodded at the front door.

'I've never heard such nonsense in my life.' I pulled at my raincoat. I couldn't find a way out of it.

Miss Ambrose wandered ahead into the sitting room.

'It's slander.' I finally escaped from the coat. 'I want to speak to Miss Bissell. Get her on the telephone.'

When I walked into the sitting room, Miss Ambrose was poised by the door, with her mouth ever so slightly open. Her fingers still rested on the handle.

I followed her gaze.

They were on the windowsill, their strap hanging against the radiator. Next to them was a brown leather case. Hand-stitched by the look of it. There was a small cloth, too. For cleaning the lenses, I would think.

Miss Ambrose spoke, but her gaze remained fixed. 'Shall we put the kettle on?' she said.

★　★　★

'No one is sending anyone to Greenbank,' said Jack.

We sat on one of the benches, the three of us, in a row of thinking. As we watched, leaves broke free from tired branches, and an autumn cemetery lay at our feet. Even the bench felt graveyard cold. An early frost had crept into the

129

wood, and it had left its hiding place and found its way into my bones.

'They're probably coming for me right now,' I said. 'They're probably on their way.' Panic abandoned my stomach and climbed towards my throat.

Elsie said, 'You're not doing yourself any favours, Florence, getting in a state. You're on probation, remember?'

'I didn't do anything wrong,' I said.

She sighed. 'It's a figure of speech, that's all.'

'A crow!' I shouted. I knew I'd shouted, but sometimes it happens before I can put a stop to it. 'It was a crow. They can't send me to Greenbank, because I've remembered it was a crow.'

Jack looked up. 'What are you talking about?'

'I couldn't remember what that bird was called. Now I remember. It's a crow. There's another one there, look.'

'Does it matter what it's called? What would you like to call it?' he said.

I stared at the crow. 'Black, Not A Pigeon,' I said.

Elsie raised her eyebrows.

'Does it look any different, now you've given it a name?' said Jack.

I shook my head at Black, Not A Pigeon.

'You're still here to see it and listen to it, and watch it fly. So does it really matter if you can't remember what it's called?' he said.

'I don't suppose it does,' I said.

'So why don't you sit down, and we'll try to work out this problem.'

130

I didn't realise I had stood.

Jack sighed. The breath left his body, and clouds of white thinking drifted across the courtyard. 'I think you need to tell me about Beryl,' he said.

They met at the dance, Beryl and Ronnie.

I never know where to begin, so I began with that. I told Jack about how, whichever band was playing that week, they would conjure up Al Bowlly and send him spinning across the room. About how we all travelled across a Saturday-night dance floor without a backward glance, before old age arrived and kept us in our seats.

'Elsie and I always danced together,' I said, 'before she met her Albert.'

'Who's Alb — ' said Jack.

'The love of my life,' Elsie answered before he'd even finished the question.

'She had her head turned by a young man,' I said. 'Most of them did.'

'But not you, Florence?' Jack leaned a little further forward in his seat.

'No. Not me.' Before I explained, I looked at Elsie for reassurance, for confirmation that my mind hadn't embroidered on to the memories, because I knew she hadn't forgotten any of it. 'Beryl did, though,' I said.

Whenever you dance, you see a showreel spin of people as you move around the floor. The stop-start of conversation. Glances across the room. That night, I remember Beryl standing in the far corner, trying her utmost to have nothing to do with us. There were machinists from the factory as well, elbowing attention away from each other by the door, and for all his dislike of conversation, Ronnie Butler was leaning against the stage. Feeding his eyes. Each time Elsie and I turned, the room had moved. People shifted, drinks changed hands, but Ronnie never altered. Some people are watchers. Observers. They stand just a fraction further away from everyone else, but those inches separate them from the rest of the world like an ocean.

We sat the next dance out. I could see Beryl across the crowd, snatches of her between the dancers. I saw Ronnie walk towards her. She looked up at him, and played with the necklace around her throat, moving the beads between her fingers. The floor turned and I lost them. Even when I lifted myself up and tried to see over the top of people, they had both disappeared. I didn't realise, until she spoke, that Elsie had been watching them too.

'I know we work with him, but I've never liked Ronnie Butler,' she said. 'Do you think Beryl will be all right?'

We both leaned against the wall, finding our breath.

'She's a grown woman. Of course she'll be all right.'

I don't think it was what I said that made her worry. I think it was the beat of silence before I answered.

'And was she all right?' said Jack.

'At first,' I told him. 'But isn't everybody?'

I looked for the next piece of the story, but I couldn't find it.

132

Elsie tapped my arm. 'You always stayed over at our house on a Saturday night, Florence. You can remember. If you're going to tell it, at least tell it properly.'

★   ★   ★

On the Sunday, Beryl was late to breakfast. When she did get there, she snapped her way through it, fighting with the porridge bowl and the teapot, and anything else that came within an inch of her.

'What's got your goat?' Gwen poked at the fire and it replied with thick clouds of smoke.

Beryl waved her hands around. 'Can't you do that when the back door's open?'

'It needs mending. There'll be such a song and dance if the fire's out.'

'Is she awake yet?' Beryl stopped waving and looked up at the ceiling. We all did.

'Not yet,' I said. 'Did you enjoy yourself last night?'

I hid the question in another sentence.

'What's it to you?'

But she found it.

'We saw you talking to Ronnie Butler,' Elsie said.

Gwen stopped poking the fire and looked at us both.

'I can talk to who I want,' Beryl spoke to the whole room.

'Florence says he's a bad sort.' Elsie looked over at where I sat at the other end of the table. 'She doesn't like him.'

Beryl forced porridge into her throat and stared across at me. 'Florence doesn't like anyone. I don't think Florence even likes herself most of the time.'

★   ★   ★

The following week, Beryl brought Ronnie round to meet everyone. He was presented as an achievement. For an achievement, he didn't speak much. In fact, he got through an entire pot of tea without saying a single word. Beryl did all the talking for him. She asked him a question and answered it herself within a few seconds to save him the trouble, and when she looked across, he only nodded back.

Even their mother tried to get a conversation out of him.

'Do you know my Charlie?' she said.

Ronnie leaned back and shook his head.

'He'll be as pleased as punch when he finds out our Beryl's got herself a young man.'

Ronnie looked over at the mantelpiece.

Their mother reached for the teapot. 'He's away at the moment. Government business.' She stood and blocked Ronnie's view of the telegram. 'He'll be back. Any day now.'

We all watched her disappear into the kitchen, and Ronnie leaned further back in his chair. 'She's soft in the head, isn't she?' he said. 'Your mam.'

'He's just shy,' Beryl said afterwards as she cleared the table. 'You'll like him when you get to know him.'

Neither Elsie nor I had any intention whatsoever of getting to know him, but as it happened, he didn't give us the chance. Whenever he paid a visit, he moved wordlessly around the house. He watched everyone over the tops of newspapers and fattened himself in silence with someone else's food. We once caught him in the kitchen, with his feet on the table, shoes pressing into a linen cloth. Before Elsie had a chance to say anything, he removed them. Slowly. Silently. Kicked his boots across the floor.

'Can't have your father coming back and seeing another man's feet on his table, can we?' and he tapped the side of his head and laughed.

Elsie and I looked at the telegram on the mantelpiece, and just for a moment, I saw things through her mother's eyes.

After a while, we stopped going downstairs when Ronnie was in the house. We sat in Elsie's room instead, and listened. Because all of Ronnie's conversation seemed to find its way out when he was alone with Beryl. We could hear an army of words, marching through the floor-boards. He'd pick at what she was wearing or how she spoke. Any little detail he'd decided was getting on his nerves that day. Beryl's voice danced around the edges, but every so often, the snap of his was louder and Beryl became very silent.

One morning, she came to the kitchen table with a black eye.

Everyone fussed around her. They poked and

prodded, and tried to prise the lid off a conversation, but the only thing she would say was, 'I tripped.'

And for someone who never stopped talking, she started to say nothing at all.

\* \* \*

Jack watched the floor, the whole time I was talking. His gaze didn't leave. I wondered how many sadnesses he'd witnessed, yet there was still room in his eyes for a little more.

'He made their mother worse as well,' I said and glanced at Elsie. 'Feeding her mind about all sorts. He said the government were listening in on people, encouraged her to tear at the wallpaper to look for microphones. I caught him once, pointing out which walls she hadn't checked.'

Once I found the first story, I realised there were so many more, and I couldn't stop them spilling out. Ronnie hit Beryl all the time. It became a routine. And like most routines, she eventually seemed to accept it. She would appear most days with a black eye or a bloodied lip, and fold her face into her sleeve to make it unseen.

So many women at the factory arrived at work exactly the same. No one thought anything of it. The bruises drifted from black to purple, green to yellow, without a word being said. It was like wearing a different headscarf or a new pair of gloves. Then one morning, ownership would be renewed, and they changed back to black.

'The bruises weren't the worst thing,' I said.

'The worst thing was waiting for them to happen.'

We all tried to talk to Beryl. Even Dot came up for the day and did her very best, but love paper-aeroplanes where it pleases. I have found that it settles in the most unlikely of places, and once it has, you're left with the burden of where it has landed for the rest of your life.

'It went on for months,' I said. 'No one could stop it.'

Even their mother tried. Their mother, whose world had become so small, it rarely reached further than the corners of her eiderdown. Ronnie walked through the door one evening, a cigarette fashioned to his bottom lip, and Elsie's mother took the letter rack and threw it at his face. The telegram twisted and turned on its journey to the floor.

'She needs locking up, your mother,' said Ronnie. He wiped the blood from his mouth afterwards. 'She needs to be in a funny farm. I've a good mind to report her.'

'You wouldn't dare,' Elsie said, but he just smiled at her.

His face wouldn't stop bleeding, and his mouth gaped at the corner, the flesh hanging by a thread.

'He needs to go to hospital,' I said. 'He needs an X-ray. And stitches.'

I could hear the clock eat away at the seconds. No one spoke.

'My father will take him,' I said.

When they returned, my father said Ronnie was 'an unusual young man', which was

137

probably the closest he ever came to a direct criticism.

Ronnie lost a tooth. And gained a scar. Right in the corner of his mouth, where it disappeared each time he smiled.

\* \* \*

Jack still gazed at the floor.

I started to fold a newspaper someone had left on the seat, because all of a sudden, it felt as though I had a lot of energy and nowhere to put it.

Elsie said, 'We all tried our best, Florence. Everyone did. She just wouldn't listen.'

Backwards and forwards the newspaper went, trying to find sense in my thoughts. 'We should have done more to stop him.'

'It wasn't your job, Florence,' Elsie said. 'It wasn't your job to stop him.'

'If something upsets you, it upsets me. Even Beryl. I was part of your piano keyboard, remember? I was Favour. You said so.'

I think I must have been shouting again, because Jack and Elsie both made a very big thing of looking around to see if anyone had heard.

'That night never should have happened. It never should have been allowed to happen.' My voice filled the courtyard.

'What night?' said Jack. 'What happened?'

My hands stopped turning.

It felt like reaching for something that had rolled under a settee. Something that brushed at your fingertips, but was always just out of reach.

I stared at him.

'I can't remember,' I whispered. 'It's gone.'

I turned to Elsie and she looked back at me.

'Where do they go,' I said, 'the words? What happens to them?'

'I don't know,' she said.

The newspaper was still in my hands. All those headlines. Weather forecasts. Adverts. People telling you this and that, and the other. All those words.

I looked back at Elsie. I needed her to find the story for me.

'It's not my story to tell, Flo,' she said. 'I wasn't there.'

'Can you remember anything? About this night you mentioned?' Jack said.

I studied the newspaper. There was a photograph on the front page. A group of people standing around a trestle table, laughing at nothing in particular. From the way they were standing, it was obvious they didn't know each other and the photographer had just put them all there for convenience's sake.

'I remember there were other people,' I said to the picture. 'I wasn't on my own.'

'Who else?' Jack says. 'Do you know?'

Elsie looked at me.

'Clara was there,' I said. 'She didn't hang herself, did she? She can't have done, because she was there that night. I remember her now.'

Elsie searched beyond me to somewhere I couldn't see. I wasn't sure if she was looking at a point in the future, or a point in the past, and from her eyes, it was obvious she couldn't decide either.

'Yes, Clara,' she said eventually. 'Clara was there.'

'Well then,' he said. 'Why don't we try asking her, see what she remembers? Do you know where she is now?'

I didn't need to ask Elsie. It came to me like switching on a light.

I took a breath before I answered. 'She's in Greenbank,' I said.

# Handy Simon

Handy Simon tucked the pen into his clipboard. Since the potting-shed incident Miss Bissell had insisted on regular head counts, and he appeared to be the man for the job.

'You're dependable, Simon,' she'd said. 'You're someone who can be relied upon to count.'

Simon was a big fan of quantifying things, but he couldn't understand the purpose of measuring old people.

'So we know where they are,' Miss Bissell had said, 'so we can keep track of them. Otherwise no one knows what they're up to. They do head counts everywhere these days.'

'They do?'

'Oh yes. The House of Lords. Tesco. They're all at it.'

Miss Ambrose had provided him with a clipboard and a large pen, which wrote in different-coloured ink, depending on which button you pressed. Red for names, green for location, she'd said, but Simon kept forgetting to press the buttons, so everyone was documented in a light brown. Twice a day, he had to go round, locating people, and when he found them, he could never remember who was who, and he had to ask everyone their name.

Miss Ambrose pointed to his list. 'I think some of them might be having you on,' she said.

'You do?'

'Well, as far as I'm aware, we don't have a Roy Rogers living here.' She scanned the page. 'Or a Desmond Tutu. We've got to take this seriously, Simon. Greenbank won't take a referral without hard evidence.'

They gave him a sheet of photographs, for ID purposes. The only problem was, the residents spent so long trying to find themselves, the whole escapade took twice as long as it had before. In the meantime, all the other jobs piled up.

'I shan't be responsible for the grouting,' he said to Miss Bissell, as they met in the corridor, but she just sailed past in a cloud of indifference.

He was getting the hang of it, though. They were creatures of habit, the elderly. They frequented the same rooms, and ate the same meals at the same times. They watched the world from an identical view each day, and had the same conversations in the same corridors, with the same people. He knew exactly where to find them. Some, however, were trickier than others. Florence Claybourne, for example, busied about so much, you never knew quite where she'd be.

'I don't know why you waste your time,' she said, when he found her. 'There are people missing off that photographic sheet, and my picture isn't anything remotely like me at all.' She jabbed at the ID page. 'I look like someone dug me up.'

Simon stayed quiet. He had learned, with Florence, that it was much easier to let

142

everything come out in its own time, like drawing a boil.

'There are leaves gathering in that guttering,' she was saying, 'and if someone doesn't top up the lavatory paper in the ladies', we'll have a mutiny on our hands.'

'I'll see to it later, Florence.'

'Why don't you see to it now? Instead of standing here gossiping with me?'

'It's one o'clock,' Simon said. 'I always go to the staff room and sit by the window at one o'clock, and eat my Pot Noodle.'

\* \* \*

The staff room wasn't the best place to find sanctuary. It was an afterthought at the end of the main corridor and, like a giant fruit bowl, it had become a magnet for all the things nobody knew what to do with. There were piles of empty folders and coats people had stopped caring about enough to wear, and in the corner was a tower of back issues of *Dementia Now!* because no one knew how to cancel the subscription. Even the furniture was confused. It was a melting pot of leftover chairs and tired sofas, and Miss Ambrose had swathed everything in crocheted blankets, which various residents had constructed, usually on their deathbeds.

'Heart failure,' Miss Ambrose would say, as she held up a mixture of pinks and purples. And another. 'Cellulitis of the left leg.'

Simon sat back on a nasty case of pneumonia and waited for his Pot Noodle to take. The only other person in there was Gloria from the kitchens. She was perched on the sill blowing Lambert & Butler out of a narrow gap in the window.

'Aren't you a bit too old to be smoking behind the bike sheds?' he said. He stirred his chicken and mushroom. 'You'll cop it if Miss Bissell catches you. She'll have you on a disciplinary.'

'I'm fifty-two, old enough to make decisions for myself, and she won't catch me.' Gloria flicked the end of the cigarette on to the gravel, where it joined its friends. 'She's halfway through tai chi in the car park.'

'I don't know where all that nonsense comes from.' Simon prodded at his Pot Noodle.

Gloria sank into one of the chairs. 'China, mainly.'

'No, I mean why do it here?'

'Because it flushes your mind of toxins, Simon. It unburdens your soul. Does your soul not need unburdening?'

'Not currently,' he said. 'Not that I'm aware of.'

She tutted. 'Everyone's soul is clogged up with something. We collect it as we travel through life.'

'It's the residents who should be doing it then, not the staff. Most of them have got eighty-odd years' worth of clogging.'

'Health and safety, Simon. She's worried someone will twist their knee warding off a monkey. You've got to be careful with energy flows. They're not a laughing matter.'

'So why aren't you out there, keeping yourself young and unburdened?'

'I was gagging for a smoke,' she said, 'and besides, my dad says ageing is all in the mind. We only age because we expect to.'

'Your dad's a proper loony tune.' Simon brushed at his trousers, started to say something else, changed his mind and had another brush at his trousers instead.

'Don't go asking me out again, Simon. I've said it before: I'm too old for you.'

'Only ten years, and I thought ageing was all in the mind.'

'That's not the point. There's plenty of young ladies out there, why don't you ask one of them instead?'

Simon wandered Cherry Tree in his mind. There were lots of women, but they all seemed to be collected by husbands at the end of each shift, or drove themselves away to semi-detached houses and semi-detached lives. 'There's Denise on reception, I suppose,' he said.

'Oh, I wouldn't go there.' Gloria heaved herself up, went over to the sink and rinsed her coffee cup. 'Her back bedroom's full of real-life dolls and her mother took a day off work to give them all a bath.'

Simon gazed at the ceiling. 'What about Lorraine in housekeeping?'

Gloria turned from the sink with her mouth open. 'You can't ask Lorraine.'

'Why not?'

'Because chances are she's a lesbian. And I can say that, Simon, because I used to be one.'

He stared at her.

'Don't look so shocked. It's a big world out

there. You want to get yourself inside it and have a look around.'

The thing is, he would. If only he could find the way in.

'Do you fancy a drink after work?' he said. 'I mean as friends. People. People having a drink together after work?'

'Can't.' She pulled the tabard over her head and the static pulled at her hair. 'I've got to go round to my dad's. He's re-enacting the Civil War on Saturday afternoon and I promised I'd sew his doublet.'

'He's eighty-two, Gloria.'

'All in the mind,' she mouthed, and tapped the top of his head as she squeezed past. 'And your Pot Noodle's going cold.'

The door slammed behind her and Simon looked out into the gardens. One of the residents sat alone on a bench in the courtyard, and he watched as they had a small conversation with themselves. And Simon wondered where his life ended and their life began, and how we could all be stitched so tightly together, yet the threads between everybody still go unnoticed.

146

# Florence

'It hasn't changed, has it?' I said. 'It looks just as unpleasant as it always has.'

I hadn't seen Greenbank for years, and yet as we turned into the driveway, it felt as though I'd just looked back at it after glancing away. It's the kind of stout, Georgian house that never seems to change. Whilst the rest of the world decays and rebuilds and reinvents itself, places like Greenbank watch and wait, and gather up memories.

There were four of us. Me, Elsie, General Jack and Jack's son, Chris, who'd been persuaded by his father to chauffeur us on our little outing. Chris underwent deep interrogation by Miss Bissell. She walked around him a full three hundred and sixty degrees with her clipboard, and asked enough questions to satisfy two sides of A4. We watched through the chessboard glass, Jack leaning on his walking stick as though we were at a sheepdog trial.

Chris was the only hope we had. Miss Bissell would never let us escape into the world on our own.

When he left the office, Chris had acquired a layer of sweat and a new set of creases in his forehead, but he gave us a sideways thumbs-up and bobbed his knees.

'He's a maths teacher,' said Jack.

★ ★ ★

147

We sat in the back of the car, Elsie and I. Chris was driving and Jack shouted instructions from the passenger seat at the top of his voice. I became a child on a seaside holiday, and read out all the road signs as we passed by.

'Give way, two hundred yards,' I said. 'It's a red triangle.'

'Shall we just let Chris do the driving?' Elsie pointed through the gap between the front seats. 'I'm sure he's more than capable.'

'Toilets, two hundred metres. Ladies and gentlemen.'

She lowered her voice. 'Do you want the toilet?'

'Not especially, thank you,' I shouted.

We passed retail parks, sprouting like broccoli at the edge of towns. Empty high streets with injured shops, boarded and bruised, shouting their red messages at no one in particular. People who pulled their world behind them in a trolley, and waited whilst pelican crossings counted down their lives in orange seconds. Groups of teenagers, who stretched their afternoons out on street corners. All those small lives, acting out their purpose in a strange solitude. I passed the time by describing everything in detail, and Elsie stopped ignoring me after a while and joined in. Every so often, Chris looked at us in the rear-view mirror and frowned.

We passed a sports shop. Plastic people in green and orange stared out from the window. 'I don't recognise anything,' I said. 'Where's the little place that sells sweets in paper bags?'

Elsie looked over. 'I'm not sure people buy

sweets in paper bags any more.'

'And every other shop is a hairdresser's. I never realised people had so much hair.'

We stopped at a set of traffic lights and I craned around Elsie to see the churchyard. The gravestones waited in rows, and they watched Marks & Spencer through a gap between a bank and a building society.

'I'll end up in there,' I said. 'As sure as eggs is eggs.'

'Have another sucky sweet and don't be so morbid.'

I reached into the bag. 'I'm only being realistic.'

She took the empty wrapper and put it in her pocket. 'Well if you want to be completely realistic, you won't end up in there at all. You'll end up in the cemetery at the other end of town.'

'They've built a cemetery?'

'They have,' she said. 'Too many old people, so they had to make an overspill. Like a car park.'

'That's a shame.' I looked out of the back window as we drove away.

'It is,' she said. 'I was hoping we could both have a corner spot, near the chancel.'

I took another sweet for later. 'Now we'll end up in the middle of a field, overlooking the bypass.'

★  ★  ★

We reached Greenbank. There was low cloud, a cliff-top of a sky, and it started to spit down at

149

us. The building waited for us through a windscreen crowded with rain, and the edges of it blurred against the clouds until the chalk white of the bricks vanished into nothing.

'We're here,' said Chris, quite unnecessarily.

No one moved.

I reached for the door handle, but then I changed my mind and put my hand back on my lap.

'Shall we head inside?' Jack nodded towards the rain. 'Are you coming, Chris?'

Chris took a CD and a Boots meal deal out of the glove compartment. 'I think I'll wait here. Listen to a bit of ABBA. Pass the time.'

'It's warmer inside,' Jack said.

Chris looked up at the glass mouths of the Georgian windows and shook his head.

'I'm going in,' Jack said. 'I'd rather face Greenbank than sit here and watch you eat a prawn sandwich.'

★ ★ ★

The woman who opened the main door was dressed in varying shades of beige, as if her wardrobe had been selected entirely from a row on a paint chart. Small eyes. Thin lips. Elephant's Breath.

She made an 'o' without a sound to go with it, and stepped back to allow us inside, where we fell into a world of beige carpets and beige wallpaper, and weighted velvet curtains. It was the air you noticed first, though. Still and polished with age, like walking into a room that is only used at

150

Christmas, and each time you breathed in, your lungs filled up with the past.

'You'll find Clara in our west wing,' said the woman, and she turned down a long corridor. It was less than a minute before she launched into the brochure.

'And on the left, we have our secondary day room, with a forty-eight-inch plasma television screen and a constant staff presence.'

I glanced in. The television was switched off. All forty-eight inches of it.

'And on the right, our award-winning gardens can be enjoyed through the French windows.'

'Award-winning?' I whispered to Elsie and tried the handle.

'Which are locked at all times, for health and safety purposes.' The woman turned and smiled at us, and I smiled back and lifted my fingers away from the glass.

I looked into each room as we passed. They were silent and empty, except for the occasional glimpse of a distant uniform. 'Everyone must be on a trip,' I said.

We arrived in another hallway, which drifted with lavender and old age. 'Visitors are not usually permitted in residents' rooms,' said the beige woman, 'but Clara is — ' She consulted her notes. ' — not comfortable in communal areas.'

'She never was,' I said. 'She was terrified of people, especially her father.'

'It took us ages to persuade her to come to the dance,' said Elsie.

'The dance?' I pushed my thoughts into a frown.

151

'Florence, that's why we're seeing her. To ask about the dance,' Elsie said.

The woman looked at her notes. 'Dance? It doesn't say anything about a dance in here.'

'No,' I said. 'I don't suppose it does.'

'We're on the third floor.' The woman looked at Jack. 'Would you like to use the lift?'

The lift waited for customers in the corner of the hall. It had an iron gate and a very complicated pulley system, which appeared to be suspended from the ceiling.

'I think I'll go with the stairs,' said Jack.

'Don't mind the stick,' I said. 'He only uses it to boss people about.'

Jack was still laughing when we reached the first landing.

As we climbed, the scent of lavender disappeared, and was replaced with the wipe-clean fragrance of a waiting room. Its aroma was rather like a doctor's surgery or how you would imagine an operating theatre to smell. The furnishings altered, too. Vases of flowers were exchanged for cages of bedsheets, and the oil paintings became health and safety notices, drilled into the plaster and yellowed with age. Even the carpet turned to lino beneath our feet, as though gravity had pulled all the soft furnishings to the ground floor.

The woman turned right down another corridor. The doors became numbered, and the brochure descriptions disappeared along with the dried flowers. Within each room was a small piece of torment. Eyes were glazed with vacancy. Mouths gaped. Limbs rested on angry, twisted sheets, although perhaps worse were the ones who lay silent in perfectly made beds. The ones who had run out of arguing. I stared into each room, and a parcel of life stared back. Outside each door was a photograph, and the corridor looked as though a giant family album had been unfolded along its walls. People posed in gardens and on seafronts. They lifted children on to their hips and looked out at us from beneath Christmas trees. The woman saw us staring.

'It shows the staff who they used to be,' she said.

I tried to match the people in the rooms with the people under the Christmas trees. The ice-cream people on promenades, creasing their eyes in the sunshine, the people smiling at me from their black-and-white lives. But they had all disappeared.

'Here we are.' The woman waited outside a door numbered forty-seven. Further down the corridor, I heard singing.

' 'Onward, Christian Soldiers',' I said.

'Onward indeed,' said Elsie.

The woman coughed. 'Shall we?'

Room forty-seven was filled with light. As we'd walked through Greenbank, the clouds had hurried across a September sky, exchanging the rain for a watery sunlight. The harsh lines, the sharp edges of a windowsill, the white stare of a pictureless wall, were all diluted with a butterscotch kindness. On the bedside table were a box of tissues and a beaker of water. The room had an echo.

The woman said, 'She has everything she

needs,' before all of us were even inside.

I looked up at the ceiling, and it looked back at me with a magnolia indifference.

'We couldn't trace any family.' The woman ran a finger down a page in her notes. 'She used to live in Wales. Husband died years ago.'

'Husband?' I said.

'She married Fred. From the dance,' said Elsie.

'The one who always smelled of fish?'

'He worked in the fishmonger's, Florence. I keep telling you, but you don't take it in.'

The woman looked through her notes. 'Fish? It doesn't say anything about fish in here.'

'No,' I said. 'I don't suppose it does.'

'We went to his funeral, don't you remember?' said Elsie. 'Clara stood by the grave in the pouring rain, because she couldn't bear to leave him behind. You persuaded her to get in the car. No one else could.'

'She was still swinging when they found her,' I said.

'No.' Elsie took hold of my coat sleeve. 'Don't you remember? Measure twice, cut once. Trim the thread at an angle.'

She waited for a few minutes.

'I helped her?' I said.

We both looked at the clock on the wall, measuring out the seconds. 'You did.'

A door opened and a girl in a brown uniform armed an old woman back to a seat. It took me a moment to realise the old woman was Clara. Her shoulders were too small. Her eyes were too quiet. Her hands were worn and shot through

154

with veins. All I could see were the crumbs of a person, the leftovers of a life, but then she smiled, and I wondered how I could have failed to recognise her in the first place.

'Here's Clara,' Elsie said. 'Talk to her, Florence. She knew you best of all.'

The old woman frowned at us. 'Who is it?'

I looked at Elsie, and I looked at the old woman and I took a step forward. My shoe leather squeaked on a mopped floor and I folded the belt on my raincoat.

'It's Florence,' I said. 'Florence. From the factory. Do you remember?'

I watched the woman's eyes, milky with too much seeing. I watched the question tread through her mind, and the confusion steal away her answer.

I said, 'Florence,' again, then I took another step and said, 'Flo.'

There was a touchpaper silence.

Clara clapped her hands and a happiness filled all the spaces in the room. 'Flo!' she said. 'Have you come to take me home? I've been waiting ever such a long time.'

* * *

Clara moved between the past and the present, like slipping a coat on and off. We struggled to follow her. Jack was completely lost. She stole between the two, taking what she needed from each. Cherry-picking the past, until it became one that kept her warm and secure, in the room with a blank ceiling and pictureless walls. We

155

tried to manage a conversation. We tried to guide it past anything dark and unsafe.

The woman in beige looked at her watch.

'Do you remember Beryl?' I said.

Clara repeated the name.

'Elsie's sister.' I searched for an explanation. I looked at Elsie and said, 'How would you describe her?'

'Try three things,' Elsie said. 'You're good at three things.'

'Dark hair.' I hesitated. 'Bit of a temper. Always looked like she'd rather be somewhere else. She died, do you remember?'

Clara looked up at us, and her eyes began to fill. 'Beryl died?' she said.

'She did,' I said, 'but it was a very long time ago. She used to dance with Ronnie. Do you remember him?'

We waited. A search was clearly being conducted in the corners of Clara's mind.

'Drowned,' she said eventually. 'Washed up on Langley Beach. The fish ate most of him.' She smiled. 'My Fred would have been so proud.'

'Do you remember the night Beryl died?'

My words fell into a silence, and in the silence, I could hear my own breathing. The shift of Jack's walking stick. The woman in beige turning a page in her folder.

'At the dance?' Clara said.

I nodded, and held on to my breath.

'I'd love to hear Al Bowlly again.' Clara looked up at the ceiling, as though Al Bowlly himself were floating right above her head.

I turned back to Elsie and Jack.

156

'I don't suppose you remember anyone called Gabriel Price?' said Jack. 'Was he at the dance with you?'

Clara thought for a moment, and then she began to sing.

*Midnight, with the stars and you . . .*

'The night Beryl died,' I said. 'Can you remember anything?'

*Midnight, and a rendezvous . . .*

The woman in beige closed the folder. 'You've lost her now. Once she starts singing, she can go on for days.'

But as we turned to leave, Clara stopped singing and she called out: 'What did you say your name was again?'

'It's Florence, Clara. From the factory. Flo.'

When we reached the door, she shouted, 'You'll come back for me, won't you, Flo? You won't forget?'

Her words followed us all the way down the corridor.

★　★　★

We returned in silence. Just the shuffle of Elsie's shoes and the tap of Jack's walking stick on linoleum. When we reached the ground floor, the feel of carpet beneath her feet seemed to give the woman in beige a newly found optimism, and she began to hum.

'What's the difference between humming and singing?' I asked Elsie, but she didn't have an answer.

The woman in beige opened the front door

157

and stepped on to the porch. 'Well, that went splendidly,' she said.

'Did it?' I took a bodyful of September air.

'Much better than the last visitor. She was very calm this time.'

I'd just reached the last step when I heard Jack's voice. 'The last visitor? Who was that, then?'

I waited.

'Elderly chap. Healthcare assistant said he whispered something in Clara's ear and Clara became quite hysterical. No idea what it was, although it never needs much. Took us days to calm her down.'

'What did he look like, this elderly chap?' said Jack.

I turned to listen. Although I don't know why, because I already knew what she was going to say.

⋆   ⋆   ⋆

We walked back to the car in a knot of thinking. When we got inside, Chris wiped mayonnaise from his mouth with the back of a hand.

'Get what you want, then?'

Jack looked straight ahead, somewhere into the distance. 'Oh, I think we got a little more than that,' he said.

I pushed at the condensation on the window with the sleeve of my coat.

'Let's just get back home,' Elsie said.

I spoke through the smear of breath on the glass. 'Wherever that may be.'

The journey was quiet. I'd given up reading road signs, and Jack decided Chris was trustworthy enough to drive the car all by himself. The rain started again, but it was slight and indecisive, and every so often, the windscreen wipers shouted out in frustration, as they ran out of things to wipe.

# Handy Simon

Handy Simon chewed the end of his pen and frowned at the form. Miss Bissell had handed it to him right at the end of his lunch break. He'd frowned at it then, and his eyebrows hadn't really had a minute to themselves since.

'Everyone has one, Simon,' she'd said, when she saw his expression. 'I'm not just singling you out.'

*Personal Development Plan*, it said at the top of the first sheet. There were several pages, but he hadn't ventured further than the first for now.

*Where am I now? Where do I want to be? How am I going to get there?* it said across the top. Simon gave an enormous sigh and started to write.

'That's not what they mean, Simon.' Miss Ambrose looked over his shoulder.

'It says here there are no wrong answers.' He tapped the page with the top of his pen.

'They say that, but there always are,' said Miss Ambrose. 'And that's definitely one of them.'

Simon crossed it out.

'Perhaps come back to it.' Miss Ambrose pointed to further down the page. 'There's an easier one. Why not answer that instead?'

*What are my best qualities?*

Simon chewed the end of his pen again.

'I can't think of any,' he said.

'There must be something? What are you good at?'

'Crosswords,' said Simon. 'And I can always get the top off a jar of marmalade when no one else can.'

'Write that, then,' she said. 'Only put 'problem-solving' and 'kindness'. Miss Bissell loves that sort of thing.'

'Should I not mention the marmalade?'

'No,' said Miss Ambrose. 'Best not.'

*What are my weaknesses?*

'Prawn cocktail crisps?' Simon looked up at Miss Ambrose, who shook her head.

'Try and be a little less specific,' she said.

He smoothed at the creases on the page. 'It's too difficult to think of weaknesses.'

'It's easy when you put your mind to it.' Miss Ambrose lifted her coat from the back of a chair. 'I needed an extra side of A4.'

After she'd left, Simon flicked through the rest of the form. Miss Bissell said Personal Development Planning was all the rage. 'It helps us to be more aware,' she said. 'More in tune with our minds.'

Simon wasn't sure his mind played a tune he especially wanted to listen to. He looked at the other sections. There was a whole page devoted to goals. Short-term, medium-term and long-term.

*Replace roof tiles on day room*, he wrote in the short-term section, then he crossed it out and moved it to medium. It was better to be realistic.

*Being realistic*, he wrote in the strengths

section. He smiled. Perhaps it wasn't as difficult as he'd thought it was going to be. He had a look at the last page.

*How do you make a difference to those around you?*

Simon scratched his head with the end of the pen.

*How do you measure your success?*

How did anyone measure their success? It was all right for his dad. His dad had a medal to show how successful he was, how many lives he'd pulled out of that building, although he never got his medal out of the drawer, because in his own eyes, he was a failure. Other people had certificates and letters after their name. Even his Auntie Jean's dog had a rosette. He had an O-level in woodwork and a Blue Peter badge, and he'd bought the Blue Peter badge from a car-boot sale. For all his love of measuring things, Simon realised he didn't really have any way of measuring himself.

He was still thinking about it when the door went. It was Gloria, and Cheryl from the salon. Simon smoothed down the back of his head, because he was always worried his hair was being judged.

'Have you filled one of these things out?' he said.

Gloria looked over his shoulder. 'My dad did mine. Spent a whole weekend on it. Quite enjoyed himself.'

Simon thought his own dad could have filled one out in a matter of minutes.

Cheryl didn't answer. Cheryl very often didn't

answer and everyone was used to it. She would sit in corners and stare into coffee cups, or rub the inside of her wrist. Like some people twisted their wedding rings, or played with their hair.

'Are you stuck?' Gloria said.

Simon tapped on the page with his pen. 'How do you make a difference to those around you?'

'Well?'

'I'm not sure that I do,' he said.

Gloria sat on the arm of the sofa. 'Of course you do. Everybody does.'

Simon waited for her to elaborate, but she went to the window instead, and perched herself on the ledge. Then again, Simon very often thought there was more to a sentence than anyone else seemed to.

'She's off again,' said Gloria. 'Florence.'

Simon tried to look, but he couldn't see over the top of a filing system someone started and never got around to finishing. 'What's she up to?'

'Wandering around the courtyard. Staring up at windows. Having a bit of a shout. She'll be Greenbanked soon, at this rate. I heard them talking about her when I was restocking the fridges.'

'She's worse since the new bloke arrived,' said Simon. 'Whatshisname.'

'Gabriel.' Gloria flicked ash out of the gap. 'I like Gabriel. He gave me a brilliant curry recipe.'

'He helped me with the ladders.'

'I might try it on the residents,' Gloria said. 'Although I'd have to call it something else.'

'How do you mean?'

'If I say it's curry, no one will eat it. If I call it

163

'Spicy Somerset Stew', they'll come back for seconds.' She tapped the side of her head.

Simon looked back at the form.

'You've got all weekend to fill that out,' Gloria said. 'Unless you've got other plans?'

Simon thought this was the worst thing about Fridays. People's sudden interest in what you did with your free time. He knew what his plans were, because they were exactly the same plans he had every weekend. He would watch football on the television, and perhaps a film, if he could find one he hadn't seen before. He would go to McDonald's Drive-Thru on Sunday and eat his meal watching all the cars on the bypass through his windscreen, and he'd lick his fingers, and gather up the empty sachets of barbecue sauce and the salty cardboard, and push everything into the litter bin before it got on his upholstery. Then he might sit in the park for a bit. Think about getting a dog (although he knew he never would). Perhaps have a wander round Morrisons. Complain about the Christmas stuff being out so early, and then buy himself a box of mince pies.

'Usual,' he said. 'Bit of sport; out for Sunday lunch. Go for a hike somewhere and see something of the countryside.'

Simon was quite shocked he'd managed to make himself sound slightly interesting, so he decided to ride the wave.

'I was thinking of going to the pictures,' he said. 'If either of you are interested. As friends. People going to the pictures together. Work colleagues.'

164

Gloria shook her head. 'I can't, Simon. I'm on a yoga retreat, quietening my chakras.'

Simon looked at Cheryl. Cheryl said a very faint, 'No, thanks,' without even offering up any kind of excuse. She just carried on staring at her wrist.

Gloria threw her cigarette end towards the gravel and pulled down the window.

'She's still out there. I wonder if we should tell somebody.'

'Leave her be,' said Cheryl. 'I like Florence.'

Simon and Gloria stared.

'There's a kindness about her,' Cheryl said. 'It pops out when she thinks no one's looking.'

Simon looked back at the questions. The blank spaces hadn't got any smaller.

'Stop fretting over it.' Gloria fished a lanyard from her cleavage. 'It's only a bloody form.'

He thought of saying something, but he chewed his words into a pen top instead. When they left, he turned back to the first page, but he found the questions hadn't got any smaller either, and so he went over to the ledge where Gloria had sat, and he watched Florence instead. And all the time he did, the only thing he could hear was the ticking of a clock.

# Florence

I couldn't decide which bench to sit on. The one on the far end was near the flat, but it was the furthest away from any of the main buildings, and the one near the day room had bird nonsense all over it. I changed my mind quite a few times. I saw Gloria staring at me from the staff-room window, but it's a free country, and I could change my mind as many times as I wanted to.

I wish I'd never offered her a piece of cake. I was only being civil. It was the girl with pink hair. Green tabard. Tiny feet. Chews her fingernails right down to the skin. You look tired, I said to her. She was changing the bedsheets. Spending far too long on the corners. Why don't I make you a cup of tea? Take the edge off things.

'We're not allowed to, Miss Claybourne,' she said. 'Miss Bissell doesn't let us take anything from the residents. Not even cups of tea.'

'Well, what she doesn't know won't hurt her,' I said.

I put the kettle on and I decided she could have my best cup. The one with Princess Diana on it. I bought it after she died. To remember her by. I don't even let Elsie have that cup, because she's too clumsy.

'I'll put two sugars in,' I shouted. 'Give you a bit of a boost.'

I was stirring when she came in. Yawning. No

effort to put her hand over her mouth. No one seems to bother these days.

'Why don't we have a bit of cake?' I said. 'Push the boat out?'

'I couldn't, Florence. Really.'

'Oh go on, I'm not going to tell anyone. I've got a lovely Battenberg. Just in that cupboard above your head.'

She looked up and reached for the handle. It all seemed to happen in slow motion. I couldn't work out what was going on at first, where it was all coming from. They fell all over the worktop and a few of them spilled on to the floor.

The girl stood in silence.

'I didn't buy all those,' I said. 'I only bought one. Who put all those in there? Was it you?'

She didn't say anything. She just carried on staring.

There were twenty-three. She counted them. I wanted her to take them away, but she said she wasn't allowed to, that she'd have to tell Miss Bissell and someone would come over.

No one did.

I waited.

In the end, I had to go outside, because I couldn't stand it any longer. It was the smell. The marzipan. It's funny, because I used to love the smell of marzipan. It reminded me of Christmas and mixing bowls, and my mother, dusted in flour and smiling. Now the smell filled the whole flat, and it made me feel sick. I even sat in the bathroom with the door shut to get away from it, but it crept in somehow. I could taste it. Jack had gone off with Chris somewhere and I couldn't find Elsie, so I decided to sit on a bench until someone came to take them away.

'Are you all right, Florence?'

It was the handyman. Big talker, little doer. Always appears slightly confused. Wears training shoes, although he doesn't look the type who sees the inside of a gymnasium very often.

'It's Simon,' he said.

Simon. That's it. I would have got there if he'd given me a bit more time.

'It's a bit cold,' he said, 'to be sitting out here on your own.'

'Does it make it any warmer if you sit out here with someone else?' I said.

He didn't answer, although I thought it was a perfectly reasonable question.

'It does old people good to get fresh air,' I said. 'I read about it. In a magazine.'

'I was just worried you were getting a bit too much of it,' he said.

I studied his face. I've never been very good at guessing ages, but I thought he might be about forty. Elsie says I guess the same for everybody, but I've found it suits most people. His face wasn't wrinkled, but his thinking had begun to make lines around his eyes. I sometimes wondered if you were supposed to think more as you got older, and so the lines were there just to make it easier for your face to fall into a thought.

'You need a shave, Simon,' I said.

I didn't know it had come out. Sometimes I think the words stay in my head, but then I look at people's faces and realise my mouth has opened and set them all free. Simon just laughed.

'I think you're probably right,' he said. 'Why don't I walk you back to your flat, and we can have a cup of tea? Warm ourselves up a bit?'

I sat up a little straighter. 'Not with all that cake,' I said.

'Cake?'

'I didn't buy it. Everyone will think it was me, and it wasn't. Even I'm not that mad on marzipan.'

He frowned at me, and so I explained it to him.

'They were supposed to take it away, but no one came. That's why I'm sitting here. To get away from it.'

Simon put his hand on mine, and I let him.

'Why don't I move it for you, Florence? We'll go back together, eh?'

★  ★  ★

I found him an old carrier bag in the back of a drawer.

'There are twenty-three of them,' I said. 'Only one of them is mine. I don't know who the rest belong to.'

He gathered them up and put them in the bag, and tied a little knot in the top. 'Don't you worry about that,' he said. 'We'll let Miss Bissell sort it out.'

'You'll tell her, won't you? You'll tell her they're not mine, or she'll use it against me.'

He nodded and smiled at me, and all the

169

thinking on his face disappeared.

'It looks like they broke your mug when they fell,' he said.

The Princess Diana cup. It lay on the floor in a lake of tea.

'It was my favourite,' I said. 'I'm worried I'll forget about her now.' My voice shook, although I wasn't really sure where the shaking came from. It never used to be there.

'I tell you what,' Simon said. 'I'll soon fix that for you. It's only the handle, you leave it with me, Florence.'

He wrapped the cup in a sheet of newspaper and put it in his coat pocket.

I looked up at him.

'You can call me Flo,' I said. 'If you want to.'

I managed to wait until he'd left before I started crying.

★   ★   ★

I hadn't cried in years. There have been times in my life when I've cried for so long, I completely ran out of tears, but not so much recently, because there hasn't seemed to be much point in it. I thought I'd forgotten how, but as soon as Simon left, I realised it was like riding a bicycle.

It's strange, because you can put up with all manner of nonsense in your life, all sorts of sadness, and you manage to keep everything on board and march through it, then someone is kind to you and it's the kindness that makes you cry. It's the tiny act of goodness that opens a door somewhere and lets all the misery escape.

170

'We'll have to monitor your purchases from now on,' Miss Ambrose said. 'We'll have to be sure you're making sensible choices.'

She said did I want to see a nutritionist? Or the dietician?

I asked her what the difference was, and she just coughed and looked for something in a drawer. I don't know when jobs became so complicated, where all these names come from. I wonder if the names make people feel better about themselves, or perhaps it just makes other people more likely to listen to them. I told her I didn't want to see anybody. I told her the only person I wanted to see was someone who believed me. She didn't even bother to reply.

I'm not even sure Jack and Elsie believed me, although Jack bought me an air freshener. To get rid of the smell of marzipan, he said. Forest Walk, it's called. Sits in a little plastic cube on the draining board. It smells a bit like Jeyes Fluid, but I didn't say anything, because I didn't want to seem ungrateful. The shop sells them. There's Lavender Meadow and Winter Wonderland as well. They all smell like Jeyes Fluid to me. The only difference I can see is the picture on the front. I didn't buy one. The man with the earphones watches me now. He writes down everything I buy in a book under the counter.

I said to him, 'It's like rationing, only it's just me this time,' and I tried to laugh a little bit.

He didn't join in.

\* \* \*

171

When Jack brought the air freshener around, he asked about Beryl again. He tried to hide it in another conversation, but I spotted it straight away because men aren't very good at that kind of thing. He wanted to know what happened to her. How she died. He said we might be able to use it. He said we could play Ronnie at his own game.

It's funny, because I can't tell the difference between those daft air fresheners, but whenever anyone mentions Beryl, all I can smell is the wooden polish of the dance floor and the spilled beer. I can hear the music as well. All those notes, playing in my head. The slide of the trombone and the brush of the piano keys. The tangos and the waltzes and the foxtrots, all spinning around and covering up everything else. I tell him I can't remember. I tell him I walk down all these different paths in my mind, but the only thing I can find are dead ends. Miss Ambrose says everything is up there, I just have to find a way of getting it out.

'It's your retrieval system, Florence,' she says, whenever I forget something. 'You have all these memories stored in drawers in your head, and we just need to find the key to open them up again.' She taps the side of her skull when she says it. Like I don't know where my head is.

If you sit in the day room for long enough, someone comes along with photographs of film stars and prime ministers, and pop singers.

'Come on, Florence,' they say. 'Let's open those little drawers.'

I don't recognise my own face sometimes, so I

172

don't know how I'm supposed to recognise theirs. I just say Winston Churchill to everything, and they go away after a while and pick on someone else.

I tried to explain it to Jack. I tried to explain that sometimes memories don't want to be remembered, that they crouch behind all the other memories in the corner of your mind, trying to be unfound.

'Perhaps there was someone else there, apart from Clara,' he said, 'who might be able to remember?'

I looked over at Elsie. She was sitting in the corner of the room, listening to the conversation with her eyes.

'Cyril was there,' she said. 'Cyril would know.'

'Cyril Sowter?'

'See,' she said. 'You're not as daft as you think you are. You remembered his name. You opened a drawer, Florence.'

★ ★ ★

Cyril Sowter lives on a barge. We'd heard rumour, but we weren't sure whether to believe it or not, because some elderly people have very little else to do apart from exchange nonsense backwards and forwards between themselves to help pass the time. However, on this occasion, it happened to be true.

'Do you think he'll remember the night Beryl died?' Jack said, as we climbed into the car.

'He'll have an opinion on it,' said Elsie. 'If nothing else.'

'He has a full set of marbles, as far as I know,' I said. 'Or at least, as many as he started off with.'

★   ★   ★

Chris pulled into a cramped space by a wooden bench and a litter bin, and we spilled out of the car on to the towpath. I hadn't been here in years. Not since Elsie's mother used to walk up and down the bank, talking to the fresh air, and we would watch from a distance until she'd exhausted herself. In my mind, the water had a strange smell, but now when I took a breath, there was nothing. Just grass and trees, and a faint scent of diesel. What I remembered was probably just a post-war fragrance, when the whole world smelled tired and worn out.

There was a cluster of boats moored further up. A collection of primary colours and gold lettering. They bobbed together against the canal wall like a group of conspirators.

'Which one do you think is his?' said Elsie.

'Cyril's will be the odd one out.' I squinted against the light. 'Whichever one looks like it doesn't belong.'

We left Chris and walked towards the boats. A family of ducks followed alongside for a while, cutting through the water in a line of determination, as though they had a very important meeting to attend.

'You can see the appeal, can't you?' Jack tapped his stick along the towpath. 'Pulling back your curtains in a morning and seeing a view like

174

this, instead of the canteen fire doors.'

'And the whole world slows down,' I said. 'Like someone took out the key to the clock.'

'No one has keys in clocks any more.' Elsie put her arm through mine. 'I think that's the problem.'

\*    \*    \*

Cyril Sowter sat on a deckchair by his barge. I was right: the boat was painted in a canary yellow, and was called *The Narrow Escape*. His name had been written in red underneath. For good measure.

'*Sir* Cyril Sowter?' I said.

'I decided to knight myself. People treat you with a bit more respect when you've got a title in front of your name.' He nodded at the boat. 'I don't see why it should be limited to the Queen; I never voted for her, and it's about time you turned up. I've been waiting all morning.'

'You knew we were coming?' I said.

'You came to me.' He pointed to the empty deckchairs. 'In a premonition. I have them quite often. I told everybody we'd be getting a change of prime minister, and I predicted there'd be a new Tesco on the ring road. I even foresaw Welsh independence.'

'Wales isn't independent,' said Jack.

Cyril tapped the side of his nose and smiled.

'Well you can't have predicted us very well,' I said. 'There are only two spare seats.'

\*    \*    \*

Cyril made a pot of tea and we sat in September sunshine, watching the ducks. Elsie had to make do with a footstool, but it was fine, because she's from a big family. Whilst we listened, Cyril stretched out in his deckchair and gave out the same opinion he'd been generous enough to share with everyone sixty years ago. Another prime minister, different wars in countries with unfamiliar names, a new set of people to blame, but the viewpoint was unchanged. He had just recycled himself for the modern age.

'And that's what's wrong with this country today,' he said. 'Too many do-gooders, clogging up the place with their namby-pamby nonsense.'

'Do-gooders?' Jack said.

'You've only got to look at charity shops.' Cyril paused a mug of tea on the shelf of his stomach. 'Everywhere, they are. Stretched along the high street like bunting.'

'They do a lot of good, Cyril — ' But the end of Jack's sentence was never allowed to make an appearance.

'Not for me, they don't. I never see a penny of it.'

'What about Age Concern?' said Jack.

He snorted. 'No one's concerned about my age. Why should they be?' He tapped the side of his head. 'All in the mind,' he mouthed.

'Is it?' Jack turned in his deckchair. 'How do you mean?'

'Stands to reason.' Cyril placed his mug on the fold-up table with the kind of precision people use when they have what they feel is a very important point to make. 'You expect things to happen, so they do.'

'They do?' said Jack.

'Of course they do.' Cyril moved his mug half an inch to the left. 'You expect to get indigestion after a big meal. You expect to feel cold when it snows. So that's what happens. Same with ageing.'

'Is it?' said Elsie.

'Very powerful organ, the brain. Renews itself every twenty-eight days.'

'I thought that was skin?' Jack said.

'But the brain controls the skin.' Cyril nodded in agreement with himself. 'It controls everything, so if you can fool the brain, Bob's your uncle.'

'Everything slows down as we age, though,' I said. 'Your brain more than anything.'

'Not mine. Faster than it's ever been. I get up to more now than I did sixty years ago. I've got my allotment and my computer class, and I'm learning the trumpet. Stacks of sheet music I've got in there.' He pointed back at the boat with his thumb. 'Hours I spend practising.'

I gave the other boats a small nod of sympathy.

'To say nothing of my enactments. Battle of Edgehill on Saturday, if you fancy it?'

We all found excuses in the backs of our throats.

'Everyone ages, Cyril. Look at us.' Jack used his most reasonable voice. 'We're like different people.'

'On the outside, maybe. But on the inside, I'm the same person I was sixty years ago.' He jabbed at his chest, to show us where his insides were.

'It's just the packaging that's changed.'

Jack shifted in his seat and glanced over at us. 'What kind of person were you sixty years ago then, Cyril?'

Cyril smiled and folded his arms. 'I was the life and soul, wasn't I? Very popular, me. Couldn't walk down a street without being stopped by someone.'

I tried to smile back, but I couldn't quite wring it out.

'Had my pick of the ladies. They couldn't get enough. Spoiled for choice, I was. Like a selection box.'

'So who did you decide on in the end?' Jack said.

'My Eileen, God rest her soul.' He crossed himself. 'Was Everest. You must remember her?'

I felt my mind begin to fidget.

I started to speak and looked at Elsie, but in the end I just said, 'I'll tell you later.'

'Fifty-five years we were married. Never a cross word. Died in her sleep, she did. I just woke up one morning, and she'd left.' Cyril licked his thumb and rubbed at a stain on the side of his mug. 'You'd think, wouldn't you, after all that time, you'd be given a chance to say goodbye.'

I'm not sure if it was because the sun disappeared behind a cloud, but Cyril looked older in those few moments. More fragile. You can see the fracture lines in people sometimes, if you search hard enough. You can see where they've broken and tried to mend themselves.

'My wife died of cancer,' said Jack. 'I think

going in your sleep is a blessing.'

'For them, maybe. I'll be seeing you, Cyril. That's the last thing she ever said to me. I wish there was some kind of sign to tell you it's the last conversation you'll ever have with someone. 'This'll be your lot, mate, so make it a good one.''

We sat in silence, listening to the drift of the boats, and the soft call of a pigeon as it waited for its mate at the water's edge.

'Do you hear of anyone else,' Jack said eventually, 'from the dance?'

'Living it up in the cemetery, most of them. Or else stored away in sheltered accommodation.' He glanced up at us. 'No offence, like.'

'None taken,' I said. 'So you've lost touch with everyone?'

'I hear of a few. The twins moved down Surrey way. Or it might have been Kent. Somewhere far-fetched. Mabel Fogg lives with her grand-daughter and an army of kids. Spends all her time watching cartoons and mopping up Weetabix.' He wrinkled his nose. 'Not my idea of fun.'

'We should count our blessings, though. Some of us didn't make it.' I tiptoed the words towards him. 'Look at Ronnie Butler.'

'Some of us didn't deserve to make it,' he said. 'Nasty business. Although I smelled a rat right from the start.'

I sat up a little straighter. 'You did?'

'He wound so many people up in his time, they would have formed a queue to push him in. And I would have been at the bloody front.'

'He just fell, Cyril. The police decided in the end. He was a drunk.' My throat was so dry, I felt the words try to fasten themselves to the sides. 'Don't be so melodramatic.'

'I saw him on the night of the accident, you know. Talking to whatshername. The girl who died.'

I looked at Elsie.

'Beryl,' I said. 'I think you mean Beryl.'

'That's it. Beryl. Nice girl. Talked too much, but then most of them do, don't they?'

Jack coughed.

'Outside the town hall, they were. Arguing hammer and tongs. I told the police, but no one's ever interested in what I've got to say.'

'What happened then?' said Jack.

'You tell me.' Cyril folded his arms. 'Next thing I heard, they'd found her at the side of the road. Hit and run. Question is, who hit and who ran? No one ever found out, but I know who my money's on.' His whole body was rigid, to match his opinion.

I looked at Elsie. Her expression hadn't changed, but her eyes blinked away at all her thoughts.

'The police must have been suspicious,' said Jack. 'What did they have to say?'

'They kept us in that draughty police station for ruddy hours, asking questions. You must remember that, Florence?' Cyril shook his head. 'Frozen to death, I was. Didn't even have a coat with me.'

It was there. The memory. I felt it, before I even knew it had arrived.

'I remember!' I said. 'There was a frost. When I walked out of the dance, I made clouds of breath with my words, even with a scarf on. All that talking. Afterwards, I was worried she was cold, lying there in the grass all by herself. Waiting to be found.'

Cyril sniffed. 'Proper state she was, by all accounts. The woman who found her said — '

'Ronnie's car!' I could hear myself shouting. 'I remember it driving out of the town-hall car park. I remember him leaving.'

'Of course it was Ronnie.' Cyril dragged air between his teeth. 'We all knew that. It's just that no one could prove it.'

'Not even the police?' said Jack.

Cyril found more air to drag. 'There were no forensic whatnots then. You should know. All a policeman had was a notebook and a sense of duty.'

'It was a long time ago,' Elsie said. 'A different life.'

I felt a memory shift in the corner of my head.

'Was there someone else in Ronnie's car that night?' I said. 'There was, wasn't there?'

I'd found it. The memory. I opened a drawer and saw all the contents and wondered if I should close it again.

Cyril squinted in the September sunshine as it tripped across the canal. 'Of course there was,' he said. 'We all knew that.'

'Who was it, Cyril?' I said.

The question waited in the air.

I realised I was holding my breath.

'We don't know, do we? No one ever came forward.'

'But what do you think?' said Jack.

Cyril picked at a back tooth.

'What I think doesn't really matter, does it? Not after all this time. I said my piece then and no one listened.'

'We're listening now,' said Jack.

Cyril sat back in the deckchair. 'I'd nipped outside,' he said. 'Bit of fresh air. As you do. I saw them arguing, and then she storms off, Beryl does.'

Jack put his tea on the fold-up table. 'Where did she go?'

'She headed across that stretch of waste ground at the back of the town hall. Housing estate now, of course. They couldn't just leave it as it was; they had to start building on it. I used to say to Eileen — '

'So what did Ronnie do?' Jack said.

Cyril coughed away his anecdote. 'He stood there for a minute, smoking his cigarette, staring at where she'd been standing, then he threw the stub on the grass and got in his car.'

'He was alone, then?' I said.

'At that point, yes. But he'd just got to the gates of the car park, and someone stopped him. Banged on the passenger door. He leaned over and they got inside, then the two of them drove off.'

'Did you see who it was?' Elsie and Jack both spoke at the same time.

I could feel the breath in my chest, waiting to leave.

'Not from where I was standing, no. Although I can tell you one thing.' Cyril leaned back in his chair again. 'It was definitely a woman.'

We fired shells of questions at Cyril. 'I don't know,' he said. 'I keep telling you, I wasn't close enough. If you want more than that, you're better asking Mabel.'

'Mabel?' said Jack.

'Mabel Fogg. She was walking to the dance. Said Ronnie nearly ran her over on his way out. She would have got a better look.'

The last admission was blown across his tea, in an attempt to cool it down.

★　★　★

We left, after Cyril had dug around a little more for our motives and found nothing of interest to him. We were just tucking in our scarves and buttoning our coats when Jack turned to him and said, 'I don't suppose you've ever heard of someone called Gabriel Price?'

'Gabriel Price, you say?'

Jack nodded.

Cyril picked a little more at his teeth.

'Can't say as I have.' He examined the fruits of his labour. 'Friend of yours, was he?'

'Someone just mentioned him to us,' Jack said, 'and we can't quite place the name.'

'It does sound familiar, I have to say.' Cyril stared across the canal, as though his memories sat there on the water, waiting for him. 'I knew everyone of course, so it would be most unusual for me not to remember.'

He had another try with his teeth. I wanted to turn him upside down and shake him, until something useful fell out.

'No,' he said. 'Can't place him either.'

But Cyril continued to frown and pick at his teeth, even as we were pushing back the deckchairs.

'Are you sure I can't talk you into a skirmish at the leisure centre car park this weekend?' he said. 'My daughter could soon run you up a costume.'

'Is that what she does for a living?' I said.

'Oh no. Very high up in catering, she is. I couldn't tell you the mouths she's fed.'

'Really?' I said.

He tapped the side of his nose. 'We'll just say Philip and leave it at that.'

\* \* \*

We walked back down the towpath, towards the car. The ducks had vanished, and in their place a breeze brushed at the surface of the water. Winter snaked towards us. You could feel it buried in the grass and hiding in the branches of the trees, waiting to make an appearance. I pulled my coat a little tighter and dug my hands into the pockets.

We were almost at the wooden bench, and Jack had begun to complain about the music we could hear drifting from the car window. Elsie was very quiet. We'd been given back a piece of the past, and I don't think she really knew where to put it. Cyril only just managed

184

to catch us in time.

'I've remembered!' he shouted.

I turned and he was trotting along the towpath, waving a piece of paper at us.

'Here,' he said, through a mouthful of breath. 'I knew it sounded familiar. I was only looking at it last night, and the name stuck in my head. Although it's probably nothing to do with your chap.'

He handed me the paper. It was sheet music. A page full of crotchets and quavers fluttering in the breeze. These things had always evaded me, how dots and tails and ticks could turn themselves into a sound. 'Look.' He jabbed his finger at the top of the page. 'Gabriel Price. Unusual name, isn't it? I knew I'd seen it before.'

There was the name, in copperplate pencil, written above the first line, from an age when we had so few possessions that we claimed ownership of each one, for fear it might become separated from us.

'Gabriel Price (1953),' I said. 'Where did you get it from?'

'My daughter found it on holiday in Whitby. In a charity shop. Great stack of music she got me from there, when I started the trumpet. Couldn't tell you where it came from before that. You can keep it if you want. Never let it be said I haven't still got my uses.' Cyril started to walk back to his boat. 'Leisure centre car park. Nine sharp. If you change your minds,' he shouted.

The three of us walked along the towpath.

'Do you think this Gabriel Price has anything

185

to do with the name Ronnie chose for himself?' said Jack.

'I'm not sure.' I held on to the music as we got back into the car and fastened our seatbelts.

I ran the tip of my finger over the notes. 'It can't just be a coincidence, though. The song.'

'What song is it, anyway?' said Jack from the front seat.

'What song do you think it is?' I said back.

*Midnight, the Stars and You.*

We sang it, all the way back to Cherry Tree. Although none of us really knew why.

# Miss Ambrose

Anthea stared at the computer screen. She had stared for so long, the white of the Word document had begun to shimmer, and the black letters danced and flickered on the page.

The problem with writing a CV was that everything you had ever done, or ever tried to do, looked small and unimportant. Years of effort and misery were condensed into one line, and appeared as if they had taken up just an afternoon of your life. A trivial few hours. It also involved seeing your date of birth nailed to a headline, which led you to peer at that date and wonder whatever happened to yourself. Miss Ambrose leaned back and tried to remember what she might have been doing in 1997. There were vast oceans of space in her life. Spaces she hadn't realised existed, until she tried to explain herself in a single side of A4.

Miss Bissell would try to talk her out of it, of course. She had even tried to talk herself out of it. She had tried to rearrange her existence to make it more appealing. She had wandered around IKEA, and trespassed in make-believe rooms, filled with carefully tousled bedsheets and empty breakfast trays. A little series of worlds, inhabited by absent families, who lived laundered, stainless-steel lives. She had once taken a book from one of the shelves. It was hollow cardboard. Still, she had filled her car boot with potted plants and scatter cushions, to layer over the Cherry Tree beige, but they sat in her apartment and watched her like hostages.

When that didn't work, Miss Ambrose had joined a gym. She had run away from herself on a treadmill and sweated out the very essence of herself on a cross trainer, and then she had walked through department-store beauty halls, past the rows of painted faces, trying to pick which one she might like to become. At one counter, she had been persuaded into an expensive lipstick, in the hope that it might transform her into someone else, but when she put it on, she discovered that she was still only Miss Ambrose, but wearing an expensive lipstick and thirty pounds out of pocket. She had even decided to call herself Ms Ambrose. The only problem was, most of the residents couldn't understand what they were supposed to be saying, and the few who did made her sound like an angry wasp.

The only thing left was her job.

She turned her head, in the hope that her CV might look more attractive from a forty-five-degree angle.

'You want to watch yourself. Sixty-three per cent of people experience neck strain from using a computer.'

'Simon.' Miss Ambrose straightened her neck and tried to click out of the screen, but it was too late. Simon was leaning over her shoulder and pointing.

'What did you do in 1997?' he said.

'I'm not sure.'

188

'You don't want to leave big gaps like that, it makes people nervous.'

'Simon, was there something you wanted?'

He sat in the chair opposite and pulled out his notebook. 'This,' he said. 'I'm not sure what I should be writing in it.'

'Anything you find suspicious.'

'I find most things suspicious, if I stare at them for long enough,' he said.

'Then go with your instinct.' Miss Ambrose gave a small sigh. 'Your gut feelings.'

'I'm not sure my guts have any feelings.' Simon examined his belly. 'I tend to think about something before I make my mind up. For quite a while,' he said. 'Weeks, sometimes.'

'Do you never make quick decisions?'

He shook his head.

'Never?' said Miss Ambrose.

Simon looked down again. 'I went on a day trip once. Caught the first train out of the station without checking where it was going.'

'And?' Miss Ambrose held her breath.

'Ended up in the railway sidings. It was three hours before they found me.'

'Simon . . .'

'I came out in a rash.'

Miss Ambrose tried to find a sentence, but she couldn't decide on all of the words.

'Is that what you're doing now?' He nodded at the computer screen. 'Going with your gut instinct?'

She looked back at the CV. 'I suppose I am,' she said. 'Although I'm not even sure what my gut is telling me either.'

189

'What kind of job do you want?'

'Something interesting,' said Miss Ambrose. 'Something where I can make a difference.'

'Retail can be quite interesting.'

'I want to make a difference, though.' Miss Ambrose twisted the back of her earring.

'Try going into a shop with nothing on the shelves.'

She looked around the office. 'I think I'm in a bit of a rut. I feel exhausted just being me.'

'I was exhausted being in the railway sidings. Perhaps that's the problem.'

'How do you mean?'

'I wasn't being me,' he said. 'I was trying to be someone else.'

'I'm not even sure who I am, Simon. And I don't know where to start looking.' Miss Ambrose studied herself in Times New Roman. 'I used to be so definite about what I wanted. So certain. Now I'm not even sure who Miss Ambrose is any more.'

Simon didn't speak for a while. Instead, he brushed at the fluff on the sleeve of his shirt. When he did reply, he replied softly. 'My granddad always said . . . ' His words tailed off into the distance.

'What? What did your granddad always say?'

Simon coughed. 'My granddad always said, who you are is the difference you make in the world.'

Miss Ambrose frowned at the computer screen.

She was still frowning when she heard Simon cough.

'About this, then?' He held up the notebook. 'What do you think I should do?'

'What does your . . . ' She hesitated for a moment. ' . . . heart tell you, Simon? What do you think is going on?'

Simon took a very large breath. 'I think Florence is frightened,' he said. 'She spends half her time sitting on the benches in the courtyard. She's as white as a sheet. She doesn't even argue with people any more.'

'Old people get frightened. We did it on a course.'

'I haven't done any courses, Miss Ambrose, but even I know she's terrified.' Simon spoke very quietly, which wasn't like Simon at all.

Miss Ambrose sighed. 'She's on probation, you know.'

'What did she do wrong?' Simon said.

'It's a figure of speech, Simon. That's all. I gave her a month to prove she doesn't need to be in Greenbank. It must be well over a week now, and all I've had proved to me is that the situation's getting worse.'

Simon stared at the floor.

Miss Ambrose waited, but he didn't look up at her again.

# 8.15 p.m.

The room smells of haddock.

Friday is haddock. Thursday usually involves some type of pasta, and Saturday is anybody's guess. The smells knit themselves into the walls, and swing from the curtains. You can work out what day it is just by sniffing the air. Even the carpet smells of haddock. The smell seems to have become worse the longer I've been lying here, or perhaps it's because there's nothing else to think about, and so my nose has started making all my decisions for me.

It's not as though I feel hungry, although I should do, by now. I blame the BBC. They need a letter, the BBC, and I've a good mind to send one off. Programmes about food, each time I turn the television on. You fill your eyes with so much of it, it's no wonder your stomach loses interest. I thought the BBC was meant to cater for everybody, and you haven't got much of an appetite when you turn eighty. I read about it. In a magazine. Miss Ambrose was supposed to get me the address. Director General, I said, no point messing about with secretaries. I'm still waiting, of course. Elsie said I shouldn't get myself in a state about it if I don't get a reply, but it's a public service and I'm the public, so they're obliged to. I wouldn't mind, but I don't even like the television. I only switch it on to fill up a room.

If I hadn't turned the television off before I fell, perhaps they'd notice. No one at Cherry Tree makes any noise after ten o'clock, and someone might wonder what I'm up to. There isn't any noise out there now, except the traffic, although I keep thinking I can hear music. My ears must be playing tricks on me. It can't be that late, although the clock's too far away to see, and so all I can do is listen to the ticking. Soothing, a clock ticking. Reassuring. It tells you nothing ever really changes. 'Just listen to the clock,' Elsie would say. 'Don't get yourself in a state, Florence. Someone will be here soon.' She always knows what to say, Elsie does. To make me feel better.

Perhaps it will be Miss Ambrose who finds me. Perhaps she'll come over early for our weekly chat, and she'll worry when I don't answer the door. She'll knock a little harder, to make herself heard over the bypass, and she'll glance over her shoulder at the cars while she waits for me to answer. She'll have to use her keys in the end, but she'll struggle with the lock, and the keys will drop to the floor, because she's rushing so much. When she gets inside, she'll say, 'Florence, whatever have you been doing?' I'll put her mind at ease straight away. 'Don't worry about me, Miss Ambrose,' I'll say. 'I just had a little tumble. I'm as right as rain.' She'll hold my hand whilst we wait for the ambulance. She'll keep looking at the window, for the blue lights. She'll say, 'I hope you haven't been cleaning again, Florence. Cleaning is our department,' and I will tell her about all the nonsense under the sideboard. She'll smile down at me and say how worried everyone will be when they hear what's happened, and I will smile back and say how nice it is to be worried about.

Even though she's busy, she'll come with me to the hospital.

'Nothing is as important as you, Florence. Everything else can wait.'

She will sit with me in a cubicle that smells of hand-sanitiser and other people's despair. When the doctor finally arrives, he will be unshaven and exhausted, and his eyes will be filled with all the other lives who have sat in front of him that day. But he will still care. He will still listen to what I have to say. After he has left, Miss Ambrose will get us cardboard teas from the machine. We will try to sip them without burning our lips, and as we do, I will look over at Miss Ambrose, and I will wonder if I can share my secret with her. I try to imagine the kindness in her eyes. I try to think what she might say. But lying here, choosing the cast to play out the end of my story, I'm not sure even Miss Ambrose would really understand.

# Florence

We were all sitting in the day room when Miss Ambrose told us. I didn't have any desire whatsoever to be over there, but Elsie insisted and I wasn't going to be left on my own staring at four walls. I knew Miss Ambrose had something to say for herself, because I could hear her throat clearing as she walked across the room. Simon was about three feet behind, but he left her to it and leaned against the wall.

'A rather exciting announcement,' she said, when she got to the middle of the carpet.

Not another one, I thought. I could have sworn I kept the words in my head, but I must have said them out loud, because when I looked around, Elsie's gaze was on the ceiling and Jack was hiding his laugh in a chesty cough.

'A rather exciting announcement,' she said again, only she didn't take her eyes off me this time, and said it a bit more quietly. 'I know how you are all very enthusiastic fans of *What's It Worth?*'

A few people glanced up, and even Mrs Honeyman looked interested for once. I've never been very big on it. People raiding their lofts to find out how much money they think they're entitled to and pulling a face when it turns out to be a lot less than they expected. Although it's more entertainment than the food programmes.

'Well,' said Miss Ambrose, 'I'm delighted to announce that the makers of *What's It Worth?*

have decided to set one of their episodes here, at Cherry Tree. They're rather taken with the ambience of the courtyards.'

Even I looked up then.

'Well, that's marvellous,' said Jack. 'There you go, Florence. That will take your mind off things. You're going to be on the telly.'

'Well . . . ' Miss Ambrose stretched out the word whilst her face rounded up some more to add to it. She also did a little bounce in her knees, just for good measure. 'We think, perhaps, it would be best if the residents stayed out of the way. For a bit.'

'For a bit?' said Jack.

'For the whole time, really,' she said. 'In their flats would be ideal. Of course, as soon as the television people have gone, you can all come back out again.'

'Very kind of you,' said Jack.

'It's just that there will be a lot of valuable antiques on the premises. Some very old items. We need to be careful with them. The last thing anyone wants is any of them getting damaged. It would be unforgivable.'

'Of course,' Jack said.

'Some of them might even be priceless.'

'Priceless indeed,' he said.

I saw Simon look at the floor and push at the carpet with the edge of his training shoe.

★ ★ ★

Three days later, they arrived. I opened my curtains and the courtyard was full of people and

196

vans. They were just like the vans you see criminals being taken to prison in, only they didn't have the little bars on the side.

'Would you look,' I said to Elsie. 'All that just for one television programme.'

The courtyard was unrecognisable. Lengths of cable twisted all over the grass and along the footpaths, and people marched up and down with clipboards and boxes, scattering gravel all over the place and treading mud everywhere. By eight o'clock, people had started to queue. There was a whole ribbon of them, stretching around the main building and on to the driveway. They were gripping all manner of things to their chests. Paintings and doll's houses, Toby jugs and candlesticks. There was even a woman carrying something that looked suspiciously like a lavatory seat.

Jack had arrived, and he joined us at the window. 'They're all hoping they had a fortune hiding in the cupboard under the stairs.' He leaned against the radiator with his arms folded.

'I don't even own stairs now,' I said. 'Let alone a cupboard underneath them.'

We stood in silence.

I was going to make us all a cup of tea, to pass the time a bit, but then Jack started talking about the bus that pulls up at the bottom of the drive every quarter to the hour, and how he thought we should all get on it and have a little day out instead.

'Aren't we supposed to tell someone we're going?' I said.

'Florence, they won't even notice we're

missing,' he said. 'They're far too distracted trying to auction off the past.'

And his idea seemed so much more interesting than putting the kettle on.

★ ★ ★

The bus smelled of crisp packets and other people's feet, although we weren't really on it for very long. Elsie made a big fuss of brushing the seat down with her coat sleeve, but she was still in the middle of complaining when the bus tipped us out at the top of the high street.

'Here we are,' said Jack. 'The big city.'

It wasn't a city, and it wasn't really very big, but it was more interesting than staring out of a window all day at the tops of other people's heads.

We started to walk down the pavement, but that was a battle in itself, because of the crowds.

'Where do they all come from?' I said. 'How do all these people have somewhere to go?'

'It's a Saturday.' Elsie looked straight ahead as she spoke, because she said it was far too dangerous to take your eyes from the battlefield. 'Everyone goes shopping on a Saturday. It's what people do.'

There's an unspoken contract to keep up when you're on a busy pavement and we couldn't stick to it. There were too many pushchairs and carrier bags, and people tutting and trying to edge past. Someone attacked Jack's legs with a pram wheel, and so we decided to go into Marks & Spencer to get our breath back.

We walked into the men's department, and it was coathanger quiet. Even though there were lots of people, they were orderly and silent, and rearranged themselves around you very politely on the carpet. People always behave in M&S, don't they? There were different-coloured paths to walk along and mannequins dotted about every so often, and they all had vacant expressions and an absence of eyebrows.

'That one looks like Simon,' I said, as we walked past, but no one took any notice.

Jack bought several pairs of socks and a new pullover (which he said would see him out), and then we drifted into the ladies' department, where Elsie tried on lots of hats, none of which suited her. I kept my thoughts to myself, but I think she picked up on it, because she moved on to scarves without saying a word.

'You don't need a scarf,' I said. 'You've got that lovely one Gwen knitted you.'

She said she hadn't worn that in years. She said she didn't even know where it was. Things go missing, she said. They are left on benches and in cinemas. They fall out of coat pockets. They are lent to people who fail to return them. She plumped for a tartan check in the end. She said it was with it, and I didn't like to shatter her illusions by passing comment.

We travelled up the escalators to the top floor. I've always been a big fan of escalators. I wish they had them in more places, because they don't just get you somewhere, they give you something to look at whilst you're doing it. I wanted to have another go, but Elsie said if we didn't get a move on, the restaurant would fill up, and so I saved it for another time. We chose what we wanted, and took our little melamine trays to a table in the corner and drank coffee out of thick white china. We didn't talk about Ronnie. It was strange, because he didn't even cross my mind once, and for the first time in a long time, I felt like I wanted to think about something else. It was only when we'd left the department store, when we forced our way back into the crowds on the high street and turned the corner at the top of the road that he walked back into my mind. It was the church that did it. It stood at the top of the hill, staring at the town like a watchful parent.

'Beryl's buried in that churchyard,' I said.

\* \* \*

'She's just over there,' Elsie said. 'Behind that sycamore.'

We had walked towards the church gates without even agreeing to do it, and we stood by a little glass cabinet with service times and posters about toddler groups and youth clubs. *St Eligius*, it said, painted in gold along a damp wooden frame.

'I remember the funeral,' I said. 'I remember it as though we've just walked out of the church.'

'You see,' Elsie said. 'It was all there, it just needed to be found again.'

'You don't have to think about it, if you don't want to.' Jack tapped at the pavement with the tip of his walking stick. 'There are some memories better left where they are.'

'No, I want to.' I pushed at the little gate, and it moved away all the leaves on the path for me. 'I have to go back, because it's the only way we're ever going to get any answers.'

★  ★  ★

Ronnie was at Beryl's funeral.

I remembered. He walked up the aisle and took a seat in the front row, and nobody dared stop him. The church was full, but it was full of people who were too young to be there. Elsie and I sat at the back, because I was worried Elsie might need some fresh air. She was pale and tiny, and she was shaking so much, I had to hold on to her hands to stop the hymn book from falling to the floor. I don't remember what we sang. It's the worst time, isn't it, to expect a person to sing? When their throat is filled with so much grief, they can barely find a voice to speak with.

After it was all over, Ronnie walked past us on his way out. That's when it happened. That's when I knew I had to do something. Because he smiled at Elsie. A long, slow, deliberate smile. A smile that said, whatever else might happen in life, he would always win at it. I looked at Elsie. Tiny and frail, and broken, and I knew then that I had to do something. I had to protect her. And I realised in that moment, Beryl dying wasn't the end. It was only the beginning.

★  ★  ★

When I looked up, we were standing right by the church. I glanced back at the path, because I didn't remember walking it, and I wasn't even sure it was there.

Elsie put her hands on the giant wooden doors. All the fancy iron hinges and the black studding, and the way the very top curved into a point.

'Do you want to go inside?' said Jack.

It looked like a magical door. A door into another world.

'No, not again,' I said. 'I think I'd just quite like to go home.'

\* \* \*

The bus dropped us off at the bottom of the drive, and we walked up to Cherry Tree in silence. I didn't look up until we'd almost reached the main buildings, and when I did, I realised most of the television vans had disappeared, but they'd been replaced by a very large police car, and Miss Ambrose standing in the middle of the courtyard with her arms folded. No one gave us a second glance.

We walked past Simon, who was leaning against a wall, chewing gum.

'There's been an incident,' he said. I think he was quite put out, because we walked past without even asking what it was. 'Quite a big one,' he shouted.

'Incident?' said Jack.

Elsie looked back. 'What kind of incident?'

'Something's gone missing,' he said. 'One of

202

the antiques. Miss Ambrose is beside herself.'

I looked across at Miss Ambrose, and I thought it was a fair comment.

'What is it?' said Jack. 'This missing antique?'

Simon did a little more chewing on his gum. 'A watch,' he said. 'I think.'

★ ★ ★

It *was* a watch. I knew it was a watch, because when we got back to my flat it was sitting in the middle of the dining table, waiting for us.

Elsie had unwound her new scarf, which she had chosen to wear even though it wasn't really scarf weather. Jack had hung his cap on the little peg by the front door, and said, 'Are we going to have that kettle on, then?' and I'd followed them both into the sitting room, where we all stood and stared at it.

★ ★ ★

The policeman patted my arm and said, 'Everybody gets confused,' and put away his notebook. He was very understanding, although I would rather, somehow, that he hadn't been. Miss Ambrose, for once, was lost for words. I didn't say anything either. I didn't say we'd been out all day, or it wasn't me, or why don't you ask Ronnie about it, because I knew none of them would listen. I realised I'd run right out of arguing, and so I just kept my eyes on the watch instead.

It was one of those where you can see the

insides. All the little wheels, moving behind the glass, counting each second. I'd never thought about it before, how time works. It's quite beautiful when you see it being made in front of you. All the cogs turned, one against the next, even though some of them seemed so far away from the others, you wondered how it was even possible. Once you'd realised how everything was connected, though, you couldn't help yourself seeing it.

'Why didn't you say something?' Jack closed the front door. 'Why didn't you say we were out all day? No one would have minded that we didn't get permission.'

'Because nobody ever believes me.' I looked at both of them. 'You don't for a start.'

'Of course we do,' said Elsie. 'Neither of us doubts you for a second.'

'I know it wasn't you.' Jack sat in front of me. 'I know with absolute certainty.'

'How can you be so sure?' I said.

'Florence, I've been with you all day. How could it have been?'

'I keep telling you he's breaking in. I keep telling you he's moving things about. No one believes me. All they want to do is sweep me under the carpet in Greenbank.'

Jack stood. He seemed more certain of himself. More definite. 'Well,' he said. 'Two can play at that game.'

'How do you mean?'

'What I mean, Florence, is that we're not going down without a fight. We need to stop him. Before it's too late.'

I could feel all the tears behind my eyes, waiting to happen. 'You can call me Flo, you know,' I said. 'If you like.'

# Miss Ambrose

Anthea Ambrose looked back at the box of Terry's All Gold, which had been watching her all morning from her office shelf. A gift from grateful relatives. Grateful people always gave chocolates, never fruit. They expressed their gratitude in calories and refined sugar, and her waistband strained with appreciation each time she tried to button up her trousers. On this occasion, the gratitude was for two weeks in Lanzarote minus Auntie Ada, who was squeezed into a ground-floor flat for respite, and the size of the box of chocolates suggested how very much they were looking forward to their holiday.

People sent cards, too, and the back wall was a chorus of thank-yous. Each time she closed the office door, they applauded her in the breeze, although some of them were so old she couldn't even picture the resident, let alone their families. But she never threw them away. They made her feel useful. Sometimes, you needed something tangible, something you could hold in your hand, to prove to yourself that your existence wasn't a complete waste of time. She counted them once, and discovered that for each year she'd been at Cherry Tree, she'd been thanked 16.2 times. Although she wasn't sure if this made her feel better, or slightly worse, about herself.

She had just started to count them again,

when Jack tapped on the window with his walking stick.

'Miss Ambrose, I need you to come with me immediately.'

Miss Ambrose swallowed the remains of a Vanilla Flourish. Her favourite. 'You do?'

'It's a matter of the gravest urgency. I do believe we have an intruder.'

'An intruder?' She rubbed at the chocolate in the corners of her mouth. 'It's ten o'clock in the morning. It's a bit of a strange time to be intrusive.'

'I couldn't think of anyone else to tell,' he said. 'No one here is as reliable as you, Miss Ambrose. As reassuring.'

Jack did look rather excitable.

'Well, if you insist.' She considered taking the last Vanilla Flourish for the road, but decided to save it for later. In the unlikely event there was a real intruder and her blood sugars were in need of a boost. 'I'll just get my keys.'

'Oh, there's no time for that.'

She dug around in her pockets. 'It'll only take a second.'

'The last time I saw him, he was heading towards the Japanese Garden.'

Miss Ambrose heard the door of her office yawn open before they'd even reached the end of the corridor.

★ ★ ★

'Well, he isn't in here now.' Miss Ambrose peered over the lacquered bridge, although the only

207

thing it bridged was a collection of flat stones, due to Miss Bissell's paranoia that one of the residents would decide to throw themselves into six inches of water. 'Where exactly did you see him?'

Jack waved towards the bypass. 'Somewhere over there, I think. Or it might have been over there.' He waved in the other direction. 'Of course, it could have been one of the gardeners.'

'What did he look like?'

'Average height. Average build.' Jack kicked at the gravel with his stick. 'I think he might have been wearing overalls of some kind.'

'So he probably was a gardener, wasn't he?'

Jack kicked the gravel a little more. 'Probably,' he said.

It was tempting to imagine Jack had arrived on this earth fully fashioned, grey-haired and stooped, and wearing a flat cap; to imagine all of the residents had jumped from birth to senility in one fatal leap. But just occasionally, very occasionally, she would notice a hint of who they used to be. A look, a laugh, a whisper of mischief, trying to escape from the pages of time, like a prisoner making a bid for freedom.

Miss Ambrose narrowed her eyes. 'There's something fishy going on, Jack.'

'There is?' He wouldn't meet her gaze.

'There is. It involves you and Florence Claybourne amongst others, and mark my words, sooner or later, I'll work out what it is.'

'You will?'

'I will.'

Jack looked down at the stones under the

bridge. 'There are no fish here for you to smell, Miss Ambrose, I can assure you of that.'

And he smiled.

* * *

Miss Ambrose wandered back across the car park to her office. Justin was unloading the accordion from the back of a camper van, and Jack's son sat in a Volvo eating what appeared to be a roasted-vegetable panini. He saluted her with a sliced courgette as she walked past the window.

She eyed her office with deep suspicion, but found it was just as she'd left it. Perhaps she was being overly dramatic. Perhaps she should allow the elderly their small eccentricities. She'd done it. On a course.

*Increasingly peculiar behaviour*, the course brochure had said.

Miss Ambrose continued to count the cards on the wall.

*Can become fixated and paranoid.*

Somewhere in the distance, a door closed, and she turned so quickly, the whole of the room tilted to one side. It was all well and good, but if anyone upset her azaleas, she wouldn't be responsible for her actions. Just the thought of it made her dizzy, and she reached into the box for the last Vanilla Flourish.

But it had disappeared.

# Florence

A copy of the key sat on an armchair, and we all made a fuss of it, Jack, Elsie and me, as though it was a very important house guest.

'Did your Chris not ask any questions?' I said.

'I bribed him with a panini.'

'A what?'

'It's what they call a sandwich when they want to charge you twice as much for it.' Jack picked up the key and held it to the light. 'You did very well to steal the original.'

'I've never stolen anything in my life,' I said. 'We just borrowed it.'

It had gone well. Everyone in the day room was far too busy involving themselves with Alan Titchmarsh to worry what we were up to. The only fly in the ointment was when I decided to help myself to a Terry's All Gold. Elsie was quite adamant I should put it back, but unfortunately, it turned out to be a soft centre. Hopefully, no one was any the wiser.

'Now all we have to do,' said Jack, 'is choose our time to strike.'

'I've no idea if Ronnie ever goes out.' I looked out of the window. 'I don't even know what he gets up to, when he's not prowling around my flat.'

'Every Tuesday. British Legion. Eleven until three,' said Jack.

'Really?' Elsie said. 'How did you find that out?'

Jack tapped the side of his nose. 'Know thine enemy,' he said, and he smiled.

I tapped the side of my nose and smiled back.

★ ★ ★

'It's a bit bare, isn't it?' I said.

We wandered around Ronnie's flat, whispering. I don't know why we found it such a novelty, because all our rooms are the same. Just like a hotel, really, except we live there. He hadn't made any effort to cheer the place up. Not so much as an ornament.

I picked up a cushion. They were the same colour in every flat. Bissell Beige, Elsie called it. I re-covered mine with some leftover material I'd found at the back of a wardrobe, but Ronnie's just stayed as it was. It didn't even look as though anyone had ever leaned on it.

'Perhaps it's the best way. Less clutter,' said Jack, who lived in the most cluttered flat I'd ever set eyes on. His dead wife's clothes still hung in the wardrobe, like a row of silent people, waiting for instructions. Even her hairbrush rested on a shelf in the bathroom, and her coat hung on a peg next to the front door, in case she should ever come back and find she had a use for it.

'There's no harm in an ornament,' I said. 'He hasn't even got a clock on the mantelpiece.'

Jack looked behind the settee and shook his head. 'Perhaps Ronnie Butler travels light,' he said.

I took the sheet music out of my bag. 'Or Gabriel Price,' I said.

211

Jack was in the middle of inspecting a cupboard, but he stopped, and his head reappeared from behind the door. 'Whatever did you bring that for?'

'I'm going to leave it here. I want to rattle him,' I said. 'I want to rattle him as much as he's rattled me.'

'Florence, I really wouldn't.' Elsie sank into an armchair. 'He's dangerous. We don't know what he might do next.'

'I'd give that a miss, if I were you,' Jack said. 'We don't want to rile him.'

Of course Jack and Elsie agreed with each other. They always agreed with each other. But riling Ronnie Butler was just what I wanted. He'd spent the last sixty years riling me, creeping into my mind uninvited, casting a shadow of himself over everything I had — or hadn't — done with my life. Since the night Beryl died, there hadn't been a day when he hadn't wandered into my thoughts. Those were the days when the past felt so nearby, it was as though I could have taken a step and walked through it all over again. So when Jack returned to the cupboard, and Elsie decided to lift up a rug, I slipped the sheet music underneath one of the beige cushions and I left it there. It was my sheet music, and it was up to me what I did with it.

'I really don't think there's anything in here.' Jack stood in the middle of the sitting room and looked around. 'How about we try the bedroom?'

The bland quiet of the sitting room had leaked into the rest of the flat, and the bedroom looked

212

more like the kind of place you'd sleep somewhere off the M6. Snooping around someone else's sideboard had felt strange, but looking around the room they slept in felt even stranger, and we all stood in the doorway, waiting.

'Come on. Let's get it over with,' said Jack. 'I'll check the wardrobes and you look under the bed.'

Elsie took one side and I took the other, and when I knelt down and lifted the eiderdown, I saw her peering back at me from the other side.

'Can you see anything?' I lifted the material a little further.

'Only your face,' she said.

'Nothing in here,' Jack said from inside the wardrobe. 'He hasn't got many clothes.'

'Have you checked all the pockets?' I said. 'People always find things in pockets on the television.'

'Of course.' Jack appeared from behind the wardrobe door and disappeared again.

The bedside drawer only contained a Vicks Sinex Nasal Spray and an old paperback.

'Eighty-odd years and nothing to show for himself,' said Jack. 'It's a bit of a rum do, isn't it?'

We checked the kitchen, although there was nothing in there apart from Miss Bissell's standard collection of saucepans and crockery. Even the fridge was bare.

'Not even a pint of milk,' I said. 'Or half an upside-down orange.'

I pulled open one of the little plastic drawers

213

and Elsie looked inside. It was unoccupied. 'Even with a meal on a wheel,' she said, 'you'd think he'd have something in here.'

'A jar of pickled onions,' I said. 'Or an opened tin of spaghetti hoops.'

'It's disappointing,' said Jack. 'After all that effort.'

Elsie sighed. 'Are you hungry, Florence?'

'A little bit,' I said.

'Had to be done, though.' Jack straightened his cap. 'It needed the once-over.'

'So what now?' I said. 'We've rummaged in every corner of his life, and there's nothing.'

'We need to regroup.' Jack nodded at himself as we passed a mirror. 'We must be missing something.'

We'd reached the hallway (which wasn't a hallway at all, but a square foot of beige carpet between the kitchen and the front door), when Elsie grabbed my arm.

'His shoes. We didn't check his shoes.'

I couldn't understand what she meant at first.

'Don't you remember? Ronnie always used to hide things in his shoes. Matches, money, anything he didn't want someone else to get their hands on.'

'Of course.' Jack was reaching for the front door, but my words made him stop and turn. 'We need to look in his shoes.'

I went back into the bedroom and opened the wardrobe door. A pair of brown lace-ups looked back at me from a quiet darkness. They seemed harmless enough. The toes were a little tarnished and there was a brush of mud on the heels. I reached inside each one and felt around. Nothing; just the smooth, dark feel of leather. Perhaps we'd got it wrong. Perhaps Ronnie had grown out of silly habits, and he no longer hid things in there. As I lifted my hand out of the second one, though, the tips of my fingers felt something strange. The sole seemed to be raised, in the corner. It was just a bump, barely noticeable, but when I lifted it, there was a piece of lined paper, folded many more times than it needed to be, with a smudge of blue ink on the edges.

'Bingo.' I said it so loudly, Jack and Elsie stuck their heads around the door.

\* \* \*

'Come on then, let's get it opened.' Jack put his face very close to the paper, and he squinted.

'Give me a chance,' I said. It was difficult to unfold; the creases were tight and unhelpful, as though it had waited to be opened for a very long time. Eventually, I smoothed it out and placed it on the bedspread.

'It looks like a telephone number,' I said.

'Or a code?' Elsie said.

'I think it's a telephone number as well. It has the right number of digits,' Jack pointed at the piece of paper.

'Let's ring it!' I clapped my hands and Elsie blinked along with each clap.

'Let's just bide our time,' Jack said. 'Copy it down and put the paper back where we found it.'

And so we did, and Jack closed the front door

behind us with a whisper of a click. We followed him along the path. 'Ronnie will never know we've even been in there,' he said, over his shoulder.

'No,' Elsie said. 'He won't.'

Which was fine, if it hadn't been for the sheet music. And all the way back to the flat, and all that night after Jack and Elsie had left, I lay awake and wondered if I'd done the right thing.

★ ★ ★

Mabel Fogg lives at the very top of a house on the very top of a hill. The rest of the house belongs to her daughter and her granddaughter, and three generations of women balance their lives on top of each other, like tiers on a wedding cake.

'I'd quite like to live like that,' said Jack. We twisted along the driveway and rattled our kidneys in all the potholes.

Chris didn't utter a single word.

I was composing a very complicated letter to the Highways Agency, and I decided to compose it out loud, to give other people a chance to chip in. Elsie was sitting next to me and I told her off for yawning.

'Will you please stop,' I said. 'You're making me do it as well.'

'I didn't sleep very well.' She yawned again. 'The music kept me awake.'

'Music?' I said. 'I didn't hear any music.'

'What do you reckon, Chris?' Jack abandoned his walking stick and gripped the dashboard

216

instead. 'How about I move into your loft? I'd only need a bedroom, because I'd be able to sit in your lounge with you every night.'

Chris had been quite cheerful, but all the cheerfulness seemed to disappear back into his face.

Jack looked over the seat and winked at us.

★ ★ ★

We pulled up at the front of the house, and no more than a second afterwards, a small army of chickens shouted past on their way to somewhere else. Unusual birds, chickens. They're quite beautiful if you take the time to study them, but they're like pigeons in that respect. No one ever does. I pointed at them, and started talking about the week I turned into a vegetarian. Miss Bissell nipped it in the bud, which was probably just as well, because mealtimes were becoming something of an ordeal for everyone concerned.

There was a washing line of bedsheets across the lawn, and they snapped and folded in the breeze. It was the kind of house I used to dream I might live in at some point. If things had turned out differently.

'I don't remember Mabel very well, do you?' I said, as we pulled ourselves out of the car.

'I only remember she never stopped talking,' Elsie said.

Mabel, however, remembered us. When I rang the day before, she'd spoken as though we'd all seen each other only the previous week. 'I could tell she was smiling, even over the telephone,' I said. Mabel waited for us on the porch. She was large and reassuring, in the way that a plumpness can sometimes be strangely comforting. Her hair is grey now, of course, but it's a steel grey, and it rested carefully on her shoulders. Wrapped around her legs like two small skin grafts, were tiny children.

She shouted, 'We've been waiting for you,' and when we got closer, the children turned around. They were miniature Mabels. Tiny reflections of a long-ago child. Faces that seemed so familiar, the past was made to look as if it had never really bothered to leave.

★ ★ ★

Mabel's daughter made Chris a sandwich (corned beef, not too much pickle, just a pinch of salt), and we sat with Mabel in a room crowded with sunlight and fresh laundry.

She began by apologising for the mess, but the sentence immediately slid into a discussion about her great-grandchildren. They appeared, one by one, as if summoned by an invisible register. With each child I became more fascinated, until I was openly staring at the sixth one with my mouth wide open.

'Do you not have any children, Florence?' Mabel said.

'I didn't even get as far as a husband.' I watched the final child disappear from the room. 'They're like little pieces of yourself, aren't they? Even when you're gone, they'll still be walking

218

around, carrying on being you. Imagine that!'

Mabel went back to apologising, although to be honest, the room didn't seem a mess at all. Even though light flooded through a stretch of glass, and picked out all the toys and the clothes, and the colouring books, it looked as though everything was exactly where it was meant to be.

We explored pockets of the past. Favourite stories were retold, to make sure they hadn't been forgotten. Scenes were sandpapered down to make them easier to hold. When we talked about the war, we didn't mention the loss and the fear and the misery; we talked about the friendships instead, and the strange solidarity that is always born of making do. There were people missing from our conversation, and others were coloured in and underlined. Those who made life easier were found again, and those who caused problems were disappeared. It's the greatest advantage of reminiscing. The past can be exactly how you wanted it to be the first time around. This meant, of course, that no one mentioned Ronnie Butler, but just as I was trying to think of a way in, Mabel's daughter appeared with a pot of tea, and said it was such a coincidence we'd rung, because her mother came back from the British Legion only last week and said she could have sworn she saw Ronnie Butler on a bus.

There was a piece of fruit cake exactly halfway between the plate and my mouth, and it waited there for a good minute before I remembered I was eating it.

'Ronnie Butler?' I said.

'But of course, it wasn't.' Mabel took another slice of cake. 'It would be impossible.'

'Impossible,' I said.

'Although . . . ' Mabel put the cake down again. 'I really did think it was him for a moment. It was the voice as well, you see, when he spoke to the driver. Exactly the same. Took me right back.'

'It did?' I said.

'And when he walked down the bus, he had a little scar, right in the corner of his mouth.'

She pointed, and we all pointed along with her.

'I said to him, 'You look just like someone I used to know.''

'You spoke to him?' said Jack.

Of course she spoke to him. Mabel speaks to everyone. She'd find someone to speak to in an empty room.

'What did he say?' I leaned forward on the sofa.

'What did you talk about?' said Elsie.

'Nothing much. He said he'd only recently moved, and he didn't really know anyone around here.'

We all exchanged a look across a laundry basket.

'It gave me quite a turn, it did.' Mabel didn't seem like the kind of woman who turns easily, but I would imagine that would almost certainly do the trick. 'Reminded me of the last time I saw him.'

We waited. I was on the absolute edge of speaking. Elsie glanced over again and we had a conversation between us with our eyes. Elsie always says, if you leave someone to use up a silence, they will eventually fill it with far more enthusiasm than they would have done if you had said something. I don't like to admit it, but she's right. Mabel found the story all by herself.

I allowed Elsie a small nod of triumph.

'It was the night Beryl died. I was just turning the corner on the way up to the town hall, when his car came tearing down the road like a bat out of hell. Nearly knocked me off my feet.' Mabel pressed her hand to her chest. 'It could have been me,' she said, and her fingers left little red prints of thinking on her flesh.

'Was Ronnie on his own in that car?' Jack said.

I tried to swallow, but my throat point blank refused to go along with it. I was concerned I'd begin to cough, or have a choking fit, and the more concerned I became, the more likely it seemed it was going to happen. My body has always had a habit of failing to cooperate whenever it's called upon.

'Of course he wasn't. But I've no idea who was with him. Don't think I haven't tried to work it out over the years.'

'Nothing?' said Jack.

Mabel shook her head very slowly. 'All I remember is a flash of red. A scarf, perhaps.'

She stared at us.

'Or a hat?' she said.

One of the children barrelled into the room waving a piece of paper, and everyone reappeared in the present. A strange conversation ensued between Mabel and the child, and I followed every word with my mouth. I held out my hand for the child to come forward, but instead, he helicoptered back into the main part of the house.

'I hope I see him again.' Mabel watched the child disappear.

'Who?' I said.

'The man who looks like Ronnie. Perhaps he's a relative of his?'

'I'd steer well clear, if I were you,' Jack said. 'And of anyone calling themselves Gabriel Price.'

'Who?'

'Just remember the name,' he said. 'And be careful.'

'I'm fine.' She took a mouthful of cake. 'I've got my own resident copper.'

'There's a policeman in the house?' said Elsie.

'Our Sandra married a detective. Retired now, of course, but he still thinks like one. Then there's my Norman.'

'Norman?' I said.

'You must remember Norman from school. We've been married nearly sixty years.'

Norman. Short. Skinny. Can't stand up for himself. 'But I thought he ran away?' I said.

'Ran away?' Mabel frowned at me.

'To London,' I said.

She laughed. 'My Norman's only been to London once in his life, and that was under protest. Do you want to say hello? He's only in the garden.'

I looked through a window to where a man stood on the lawn, hands on hips, surrounded by children and chickens. He *was* skinny and short, but he had that settled, reassuring look that only seems to come from old age and good health.

'We won't trouble him,' I said.

I looked at Elsie. 'We found the long second, didn't we?'

'We did.'

'Perhaps it's time we were on our way,' I said.

She smiled at me. 'It's always later than you think.'

★ ★ ★

As we climbed into the car, and Chris did the little cough he always does before he starts the engine, I looked back at the wedding-cake house, filled with children.

'I would like to have lived somewhere like that,' I said.

Jack peered through the side window. 'In the middle of nowhere?'

I watched a line of grandchildren follow Norman back into the house. 'That's part of it,' I said. 'You always think 'one day', don't you, and then you realise you've reached the point when you've run out of them.'

Elsie turned to me. 'How many more 'one day I'd like to's do you have hidden away?'

'One day I'd like to learn to play the piano,' I said. 'One day I'd like to go whale-watching.'

'Whale-watching?'

'I've always fancied it.'

'You get seasick on a canal boat,' she said.

'One day,' I said, 'I might be the kind of

223

person who doesn't get seasick.'

'I've never fancied it,' she said. 'All that bobbing about.'

'No one's putting a gun to your head, Elsie. No one said you have to come with me. We don't always need to do everything together.'

I saw Chris and Jack give each other side-looks. Elsie pushed herself as far as she could into the seat beside me, and her chin made a home in her coat.

Jack cleared his throat. 'Can you think,' he said, 'who might have been in that car? Who might have been wearing red?'

Elsie shook her head. I could see her face fighting with the past, and the sight of it was so hard to bear, I had to look away again.

'I don't remember,' I said. 'I don't even remember being told Beryl was dead. It's as though I've always known it.'

I rested my forehead against the glass and watched the traffic. So many cars. We're running out of roads, I thought. Soon, it will be a stalemate. An endless line of people looking out over their steering wheels, searching for a destination they'll never reach and stuck on the tarmac forever.

'Some experiences are like that.' I heard Jack from the front seat. 'They affect you so much, you can't remember what life was like before they happened.'

'But I need to remember,' I said. 'We need to find out who it was.'

'You will,' he said. 'You will.'

I leaned further into the glass and closed my

eyes. I'd almost drifted off when I heard Elsie's voice.

'They make wristbands now,' she said, 'for travel sickness. Very effective they are, by all accounts.'

I reached over and squeezed her hand.

⋆ ⋆ ⋆

When we pulled into the grounds of Cherry Tree, Chris said, 'What's all this then?' and put the brakes on so violently, Elsie and I lurched forward in our seats.

'Sorry,' he said.

In the courtyard, there were fire engines — two of them. Fire engines are like cows, in that you don't realise how large they are until they're standing right in front of you. There were people walking around with their hands on their hips, and mixed in with the helmets and the high-visibility jackets, the residents drifted like leaves. Simon appeared to be attempting a head count, but Miss Ambrose had to keep retrieving the heads for him and appealing to their better nature.

'All hands on deck!' said Jack. He unfastened his seatbelt.

I tapped Elsie's arm. 'I thought he was in the army, not the navy.'

'It's interchangeable,' she said, 'in a crisis.'

It was only when Jack marched across the gravel that I realised his stick lay forgotten in the footwell of the car.

'Ah, here you are.' Miss Ambrose spotted us

225

from a distance and made a beeline. She stamped across the courtyard with her arms folded, and pieces of gravel launched themselves into the grass in fear. 'I was wondering when you'd be back.'

'What's happened? What have we missed?' I said.

She looked over at the flats. 'There's been an incident. Quite a serious one, I'm afraid, but no one has been hurt, so we should count our blessings.'

'What kind of incident?' said Jack.

Miss Ambrose bit her lip. 'A fire.'

We all joined in and looked over at the flats. Nothing seemed out of place. 'A fire?' Elsie said.

'Well, more explicitly, a near miss.'

'People should be more careful,' I said. 'Chip pans, gas fires. Everything you put on yourself these days is Chinese and flammable.'

'Where did it start?' said Jack. 'This near miss?'

Miss Ambrose looked at us with a tilted head. 'Well, actually,' she said, 'it was in Florence's front room.'

My mouth became very dry.

I stopped looking at the flats and looked at Miss Ambrose instead. 'My front room? What on earth is there to catch fire in my front room?'

'You left the iron on,' she said. 'It burned a hole in the ironing board. You really should be more careful, it could have been disastrous.'

A fireman walked past. He stared.

I carried on talking, although I wasn't sure anyone was listening any more. 'I don't even use

226

an iron. I've not ironed anything in years.' And then, 'There's been a mistake. Where is Miss Bissell?'

'We need to do some paperwork,' said Miss Ambrose. 'We'll have to fill out an incident form.'

'But I didn't cause the incident. The incident wasn't me.' I knew I was shouting, because Jack put his hand on my arm.

I pulled my arm back. 'I'M NOT AN INCIDENT — '

'And we should all be very grateful to Mr Price,' said Miss Ambrose.

'Mr Price?' The three of us repeated back, in a chorus.

'Yes.' She nodded over to the corner of the courtyard, where Ronnie Butler was shaking hands with a high-visibility jacket. 'He was the one who smelled the burning and alerted us.'

Jack reached for my arm again.

'What was he doing sniffing around my flat?' I said, but Miss Ambrose ignored me and beamed her smile across the gravel.

'He's our Resident of the Month.'

'What's a Resident of the Month?' said Elsie.

'We don't have a Resident of the Month,' I said.

'We do now,' said Miss Ambrose. 'I've made a decision.'

# 8.41 p.m.

That pigeon's back.

Miss Ambrose says they're all the same, but that's only because she doesn't look properly. The shade of their wings, the songs they sing. Each one is quite different. Miss Ambrose just glances over, sees a pigeon and colours the rest in with her mind. This is the evening pigeon. Its tail is darker, and its chest is a beautiful purple-mauve. It's much more softly spoken than the morning pigeon, although they both always have a lot to say for themselves. I pass the time of day with them sometimes. Just for a bit of fun. Of course, I'd never let on, or Miss Ambrose would send me off to the funny farm in the blink of an eye. But it isn't a crime, is it, to speak with a pigeon? In the same way it isn't a crime to climb the stairs one by one? Or to sometimes forget to draw the curtains? People can be so judgemental. The woman from social services, for a start. Round, pale, far too much to say just for one side of A4 paper. The one that set the ball rolling to put me in here.

'You're not coping with your ADLs, Miss Claybourne,' she said. 'Your activities of daily living.'

She didn't know what my activities of daily living were. She didn't daily live with me. She just barged into my front room one morning and accused me of all sorts.

'You can't reach your feet,' she said.

'And what business would I have down there?'

'You can't do up your buttons.'

'Marks & Spencer do a perfectly good range of clothes without a button in sight,' I said.

The clock ticked in the corner of the room, and grew the distance between us. The woman glanced at the clock and glanced away again.

She blinked a few times and then she said, 'That's not the point, Miss Claybourne. We need to make sure you're being looked after. We only want what's best for you.'

'Do we?' I said.

It didn't take them long to undo my life. I had spent eighty years building it, but within weeks, they made it small enough to fit into a manila envelope and take along to meetings. They kidnapped it. They hurried it away from me when I least expected, when I thought I could coat myself in old age and be left to it. A door doesn't sound the same when you close it for the last time, and a room doesn't look the same when you know you'll never see it again.

'I've left something behind,' I said to them. 'I need to go back and get it.'

And so I walked around an empty house for one last goodbye, because I was afraid there might be a day when I'd forget what it looked like, and there would be no one left to remember it except for me.

When I got into the car, they said, 'We've only got a short drive to Cherry Tree — we'll be there before you know it.'

It was the longest journey of my life. When we

229

stopped at a set of traffic lights, I opened the door and tried to leave.

'I've changed my mind,' I said. 'I'm going home.'

They chased me across the high street, and I realised for the first time in my life that I no longer had a mind of my own to change.

★ ★ ★

I have always lived alone, but this was a stairless, hand-railed alone. The rooms smelled of paint and someone else. It took me ages to work out where to put all my things, and even now I keep changing my mind.

Elsie wasn't here then, of course. She moved in a few weeks later. I spotted her walking through the grounds, in a coat that had seen better days, talking to herself and looking up at the sky. I shouted across the courtyard, and she turned to me and waved.

'I didn't know you were here too,' I said. 'When did you arrive?'

'This morning,' she said. 'You can show me the ropes. It's going to be fine, Florence. It'll be just like the good old days. You don't have to worry any more.'

And she was right. I didn't.

# Florence

We'd cornered Simon in the corridor. As soon as we asked him to help, he said, 'Yes.' It threw Jack a bit, because I think he was expecting an argument, and he ended up with all these words and nowhere to put them. Simon took us into the staff room. The staff room! I'd never been in the staff room before, although it was a bit of a disappointment, if I'm honest. Lots of tired furniture and piles of magazines that had clearly never been read.

'We don't know how to cancel the subscription,' Simon said.

He pulled out two chairs. Jack sat on the settee, and Elsie and I settled ourselves down next to a big screen on a desk. It jumped to life the minute Simon pressed a button. He took the piece of paper from me and said, 'Let's have a look on the internet.'

'I've never been on the internet before,' I told him.

'You could soon learn, Flo. I could teach you. We could set up a little class.'

'Sign me up,' shouted Jack from behind one of the magazines.

Simon pressed some buttons and then he turned the screen so we could see properly.

'It's a music shop,' he said.

'A music shop?' I said.

We peered into the computer.

231

'In Whitby,' he said.

'Are you certain?' Elsie moved forward until her face was right in front of the picture.

Simon enlarged the image on the screen. The outside of the music shop was painted shiny black, and its name was written in gold lettering. It was the kind of font you never seemed to see any more, swirled and decorated with the past. The more Simon enlarged the photograph, the more blurred it became, but you could still see instruments in the window. Saxophones and trombones with their Glenn Miller curves, and violins watching from the back, straight and serious, like a row of old ladies. There were lines of silvered flutes and guitars with hourglass figures, and a washing line of sheet music, pegged across the top.

'George Gibson & Son.' I read out the name. 'I've never heard of them before.'

Simon took his hands from the keyboard. 'I thought you said the number was in the back of your address book?'

'It was. I just can't remember why.'

I could tell Simon was suspicious, but I decided if I didn't look at him, it might go away.

Simon wrote the address down for us, on a sticky piece of yellow paper. As he was doing it, Cheryl from the salon walked in. She looked her usual self. Bleached pale and filled up with thinking.

'Hello, Miss Claybourne.' If she was surprised to see us in the staff room, she didn't let on.

'Hello, Cheryl. How are you?'

Cheryl just mumbled something I couldn't hear.

'I'm glad we've seen each other,' I said. 'Because I have something for you. Well, not for you exactly, for your . . . ' I struggled to find the word. ' . . . your assistant.'

I pulled a piece of paper out from my handbag.

'It's about tracing your family tree. I found it. In a magazine. I thought it might help her find the great-grandma from Prestatyn.'

Cheryl took it from me and mumbled something else. 'And how is little Alice?' I nodded at her wrist.

She came out with the strangest jumble of words, and Simon looked up from his writing.

'I met some children recently,' I said. I think she expected me to add something else, but that was really all there was to it, so I asked her how old Alice was instead.

'She . . . ' Cheryl hesitated. I thought it was strange how a mother had to think of her own daughter's age, but people have never stopped surprising me. 'She was born three years ago,' she said, finally.

'And is she a good little girl?' I said.

'The best, Miss Claybourne. The very best. Beautiful blonde curls. The biggest blue eyes you've ever seen. Always smiling.'

She didn't have a photograph with her, but she promised she'd bring one in for me.

'I'd like that,' I said. 'I'd like to see Alice.'

Cheryl went to the sink and started clattering pots around, so I couldn't hear all her words, but she did say, 'Thank you so much for bothering to ask.'

When Simon handed Jack the piece of paper, he gave my shoulder a little squeeze and said, 'You are lovely, Florence, you know,' which I thought was rather nice, when the only thing I'd really done was make conversation.

# 9.02 p.m.

Elsie and I used to complain about how small these rooms are, but right now everything feels very far away. I thought I might be able to reach some of that nonsense under the sideboard. A coin, or whatever's dropped there. Throw it at the window. Get someone's attention, although I don't really know whose. They'll tell me off when they find me, because I should be wearing my medallion. That's what Elsie and I call them, because they're so big. 'I need help' it says on the front. It kept banging on things and getting in the way, and once, I knocked it on the back of the *Radio Times* and Simon barged into the flat with grated cheese all over his chin. I took it off after that. I hung it on the back of the bathroom door.

It's still there now.

I can't even see the bathroom from where I'm lying. I wish that big lamp was on. The dark shrinks your common sense, doesn't it? There's a bulb lit in the hall, but it's one of those energy-saving ones, and you might as well not bother and strike a match instead. It must be getting on for seven, now. The little shop will be closing soon. The man behind the counter will be taking out his earphones and emptying the till. Perhaps he'll think about me as he's counting the coins. Perhaps he'll remember me offering to clean the shelves, and he'll have a bit of a reconsider. He'll lock up and check the door a few times, then he'll wander across and look up at my flat. When he knocks, he'll call out, 'It's only me, Miss Claybourne,' and I'll call back, 'You'll have to let yourself in, I'm afraid.' I'll keep the tone light-hearted. I don't want to alarm him.

He'll come to the hospital with me. He'll insist on it.

'It's the least I can do, Florence.'

We'll talk about the shop and he'll talk to me about what I think he should stock. He'll probably ask if I can pop over and help out from time to time. 'Of course I can,' I'll say. 'And don't even think about paying me. Put it in the charity tin. Give it to the little kiddies instead.'

We'll sit in A&E and people will rush past us. I'll have all these leads attached to me and the wires will travel to a machine that bleeps and counts, and dances with lights, and I will watch it dance, because it's soothing to see all the things that matter about you held together on a screen. Curtains will swish and trolleys will rattle past, and the voices will roll into a giant ball of sound, but all the time when we're in the ambulance, and all the while we wait in A&E for the doctor to see us, the man from the little shop won't feel the need to shout. Not once.

# Florence

I could see all the whites of Miss Ambrose's eyes.

'You want me to organise a coach trip?' she said.

We'd tried to ring the music shop, but no one ever answered the telephone. I thought it might have closed down, but Jack said it was unlikely, being as they were still on the internet; then out of the blue, he suggested we all go up there.

'To Whitby?' I said.

'Yes,' he said. 'Do us all the world of good. When was the last time you saw the sea?'

I tried to think, but my thinking wouldn't cooperate. 'I'm not sure,' I said. 'I didn't think I'd see it again, and I'd just have to lump it.'

'Everyone should see the sea.' He nodded towards the mantelpiece, as though the sea were just the other side of it, waiting for us. 'It does a body good. We're supposed to have trips, you know?'

'Trips?' said Elsie.

'There's a kitty. It's in the small print.' He took a large piece of paper out of his jacket pocket, and stabbed at it with the arm of his spectacles. 'We pay into a 'recreation fund' as part of our annual fee.'

'I can't remember the last time we had any recreation,' I said. 'Unless you count Justin, and recreation isn't really a word I'd associate with a piano accordion.'

'Exactly.' He stabbed at the paper again.

237

* * *

An hour later, we found ourselves standing at Miss Ambrose's desk, with Jack at the front, because he decided before we set off that he was likely to be the most persuasive.

'A coach trip?' she said again.

The three of us nodded.

'Oh, a coach trip is out of the question,' Miss Ambrose said. 'Some of us are still on probation. And it's far too much red tape.'

Red tape. It was an excuse Miss Bissell used all the time. If anyone were to be listening in, they might think the whole of Cherry Tree was decorated with red tape, like tinsel on a Christmas tree, twisting around the doors and the windows, and keeping us all where we were supposed to be.

'Health and safety,' said Miss Ambrose. 'Risk assessment.'

All the excuses fell out of Miss Ambrose's mouth, but we had our hopes pinned. She had to be persuaded.

Jack leaned on the desk. 'All the other nursing homes have trips out,' he said. 'All the other nursing homes . . . ' he glanced at the scissors on her desk, ' . . . manage to cut through the red tape.'

'They do?' Miss Ambrose said.

'Pine Lodge went up the Gherkin.' He paused. 'Cedar House spent a weekend in Marbella. It's a buyer's market, Miss Ambrose.'

Miss Ambrose swallowed rather violently.

'And then there's the kitty,' he said. 'We could

238

always go through the accounts.'

'The accounts?'

He nodded.

'I'll see what I can do,' she said.

★ ★ ★

'Have you taken your Kwells? It's four hours on a motorway,' Elsie said.

I took the packet out of my bag and popped one out of its little silver shell.

'You know your stomach can be a law unto itself.'

Miss Ambrose had been persuaded. It had taken several meetings in Miss Ambrose's office, all of which we'd observed from the day room with held breath. Miss Bissell had done a lot of pacing and throwing her arms around, and Miss Ambrose had pushed her chair as far into the corner as it could possibly go.

After forty-five minutes Miss Bissell's arms weren't moving around quite as much, and Jack said, 'I think she's being won round.'

Handy Simon stepped into the room at one point, and immediately tried to leave again, but he was directed back inside by Miss Bissell's forefinger, and the three of them played out a lengthy discussion behind chequered glass, although none of us could hear what was being said. Eventually Miss Bissell left, but not before she'd stood by the weeping fig for a good five minutes, and stared at us all with her eyebrows.

An hour later, Miss Ambrose pinned a notice to the board, inviting people to sign up for a weekend in Whitby. *Dracula, the West Cliff and Botham's Tea Rooms.* By three o'clock, she needed a second sheet. By four o'clock, I'd started packing.

'We're not going anytime soon.' Elsie watched me roll a pair of socks up and put them inside my spare shoes.

'I'm frightened of forgetting something,' I said.

'I won't let you forget. Don't worry. I'll make sure we have everything.'

She gave me a little hug, and I unrolled the socks and put them back on my feet.

★ ★ ★

It was another week before we went to Whitby. A week of wondering if Ronnie had found the sheet music and what he was going to do about it. I thought he might react straight away, but there was nothing. Not a peep. It was strange, because the quietness seemed worse than anything. Although perhaps it's only in the silence that you're able to hear just how loud your own worrying is. It was a relief when Friday finally came around. I knew I'd still be worrying, but at least I could worry with a different view.

★ ★ ★

I hadn't been on a coach trip for years, and the improvements were very pleasing. There was a small pocket in the back of the seat in front, although when I looked inside, all I could find was a sick bag. 'It's for magazines, as well,' Elsie said, because she knows I can be quite suggestible.

'Decent charabanc, isn't it?' Jack settled himself into the seat across the aisle so he could stretch out his walking stick. He was wearing the same grey anorak he always wears. It's developed a shine on the elbows and one of the buttons is escaping, and Elsie has to keep reminding me not to point it out. 'Quite roomy.' He lifted himself up to see over the back of Mrs Honeyman from number four. 'We could do worse.'

The driver was called Eric. Far more hair on his face than on his head, as if it was trying to make up for it. Poor whistler. Insisted on saying, 'That's the job, then,' every few minutes for no distinguishable reason.

'At Sun Valley Coaches, we pride ourselves on our leg-room,' he said, as he walked past with his clipboard. 'Not one single case of DVT in sixteen years.' He eyed everyone's calves as he moved down the aisle, perhaps looking for a red flag. 'It's all written in the brochure.'

After he'd gone past, I said, 'Why does everything have to have a bro-shoor these days?' and then I whispered to Elsie, 'I'm not sure my bladder can hold on until the Yorkshire Moors.'

'It has an on-board lavatory.' She pointed towards the back of the bus. 'Although you'll have to be on the ball, it seems as though it's going to be quite popular.'

Mrs Honeyman was making her way towards it, and we hadn't even pulled out of the car park.

Ronnie Butler was the last to get on. He walked towards the coach, calm and unhurried, carrying a brown holdall. He was wearing a different trilby. This one had a small feather tucked into the band, and Elsie said it made it look as though he was going hunting. I chose not to comment. He paused when he reached the top of the steps.

'Strange time of year to be going to the seaside.' He spoke to Miss Ambrose and Miss Bissell, who sat together in the front row, looking quite pale, but his gaze fell on us immediately. It stayed there, even as he took off his trilby and found himself a seat.

'It is a little brisk, but we felt Cherry Tree should have a weekend away.' Miss Ambrose turned and joined in with looking at us. 'Like everywhere else does.'

'Any particular reason . . . ' Ronnie sat down and settled his overcoat on his lap. ' . . . you chose Whitby?'

'It's the history, isn't it?' said Jack. 'Nothing more intriguing than the past.' His voice trembled at the edges. He held on to the seat in front, and I watched as his knuckles became pale with determination.

Ronnie turned in his seat and faced the front.

'That's the job, then,' said Eric, and he started the engine. Motorways are very dull. They might get you somewhere more quickly, but there's a very little in the form of entertainment. There's only so much tarmac you can stomach in one day. Elsie dozed off before we'd barely even left the slip road, and Jack was far too busy with his

Sudoku book and a propelling pencil to make conversation. He'd read somewhere that Sudokus prevent you from developing dementia, and he was up to six a day. He tried to involve me in one, but I told him they make me more confused, not less, and if I wanted to waste my time on puzzles, I'd rather plump for a word search. Eric was whistling to himself in the driver's seat, and the back of Ronnie's head hadn't changed position in forty-five minutes. I knew, because I'd been looking at it since we left Cherry Tree. I'm not even sure why. Perhaps I thought if I looked for long enough, I could work out what was going on inside. Although Ronnie was still, everyone else moved around and changed seats. There was a constant parade of people going to the lavatory, supervised by Miss Ambrose. She began to overheat, and about an hour into the journey, she had to start fanning herself down with a sick bag.

Jack closed his puzzle book. 'Our man's very quiet,' he said. 'I bet he's wondering what's going on.'

'Knowing Ronnie, he'll have a plan brewing.' I leaned back to let Mrs Honeyman into her seat.

Elsie woke at the sound of Jack's voice. 'He's always got something up his sleeve,' she said.

'Does he have any connection with Yorkshire, I wonder?' Jack said.

'Not that I know of.' I looked across at Elsie. She had her face against the glass, watching the traffic.

'We used to go on holiday to Whitby,' I said to Jack, 'when we were children, but I don't remember very much about the place. Perhaps it'll all come back to me when we get there.'

It was odd, how that happened. You imagine you forget, but the memories are just sitting there, and it only takes the smallest thing. A smell or the words to a song, or the glimpse of a face in a crowd. The remembrance floods through you as if it had never left. The memories are always waiting, you just need to work out how to find them again.

As it happened, I remembered nothing until we climbed out of Pickering and on to the moors, where the heather rolled out before us, a thick, purple blanket across the landscape. The moor is like no other place. It's scrubbed and scoured, and happy in its lack of decoration. I always find it a comfort, that we can still see beauty in desolation. There were hikers in the distance, all primary-coloured and waterproofed, trying to reclaim a landscape that no one could ever really own.

I tapped Elsie on the sleeve. 'Do you remember,' I said, 'we used to have a competition. The first person to see the sea?'

She wiped her chin and looked out of the window. 'You always won because you were taller,' she said. 'But I've seen it first this time. Look.'

It was there. A sliver of ocean, resting on the horizon. It played hide and seek with us, as the coach turned and twisted on narrow roads until we reached the top and watched the abbey rise from nowhere into the skyline.

'It looks exactly the same,' I said.

'Nothing's changed since we were children.' Elsie sat up a little straighter and watched the horizon.

Miss Ambrose was having a walkabout, and she leaned across and gazed out of the window. 'And it'll be the same long after we've left. We're just passengers really, aren't we?' she said.

'Do you really believe that?' I said. 'Don't you think any of us makes any difference?'

She pointed to the hikers, now pinpricks of red and yellow in the distance. 'We'd all like to think so, but most of us won't even leave a footprint.'

I turned away from the window and closed my eyes. Just as I did, I heard Elsie's voice.

'She's wrong, you know,' she whispered.

* * *

Miss Ambrose had chosen a small hotel on the West Cliff, and the coach pulled up at the Royal Crescent and vomited us out on to the pavement. Elsie and I stayed here before when we were children. Not the same hotel, I don't think, but along the same road. It was impossible to remember which hotel, because they were all identical. A row of guest houses and bed and breakfasts, brushed in creams and yellows, each one named after the sea, and all with little signs in the windows, inviting you to go inside. The whole of the street seemed to consist entirely of hotels. Packets of people, parcelled into rooms, all listening to the snoring of strangers through paper-thin walls. We had no sooner landed on

245

the pavement than our spill of elderly people and walking sticks began to leak away from each other. Handy Simon produced his clipboard, and Miss Ambrose began waving her arms, as if we were all attached to her by invisible string and could be threaded back together again.

'Try to stay put,' she was saying. 'Please don't wander.'

It was too late. Before I knew what I was doing, I was halfway down the promenade, heading for Captain Cook. It was the excitement, I think, of being somewhere I never thought I'd see again.

'Where are you going?' Elsie shouted.

'I'm going to the whalebones,' I called back. 'I want to see if they're still there.'

'Well of course they're still there,' she said.

When I looked back, Miss Ambrose had her face in her hands and Miss Bissell looked as though she had just been given a prize in a competition she had been expecting to win all along.

★   ★   ★

I made it all the way to the whalebones before Elsie caught up with me. I watched people move between them, eating ice cream and pushing buggies, a day's worth of belongings swinging in carrier bags from the handles. People changed their path to pass beneath the arch, as if it was some magical doorway through which they needed to walk.

'They're still here,' I said.

246

'I told you they would be.'

'It's sad, isn't it?' I said. 'For the whale, I mean.'

The sun escaped from behind a cloud, and Elsie shielded her eyes. 'I suppose it's a piece of history. A kind of remembrance.'

We walked to a bench. Across the water, ribbons of people climbed the abbey steps and below them, boats cut a wall of foam through the harbour, on their journey towards the North Sea. Whitby curves around the estuary, its east and west sides facing each other across the water, so as you stare over the bay, you see a reflection of people living an identical life, but on the opposite side of an ocean. As we sat, Cliff Street emptied out its contents. A cast of strangers, stretching across the pavements and littering the grass, sweeping up the remains of autumn before the coastline called time and wound down its shutters for winter. They wandered past, wrapped in conversation, their words catching on a breeze and drifting out towards the sea. No one noticed us. Two old ladies, buttoned into hats and raincoats, watching the rest of the world happen without them.

'They'd never be allowed to do it now,' Elsie said. 'The whales, I mean. Times have changed.'

I loosened my scarf. 'So Miss Ambrose was wrong. Some of us must leave more than a footprint, or everything would always stay the same.'

'Of course she was wrong.'

We'd only been there a matter of minutes, but

already the sea air had pulled away some of the worrying. The colours seemed brighter and other people's laughter was more obvious, and my face fell into a smile so much more easily.

Elsie was watching me. 'You like Whitby,' she said.

'You know I do. It reminds me of holidays gone by. Things I'd forgotten.'

'Do you remember the last time?' she said. 'On the final day, looking for something to buy with our spending money?'

I laughed. 'We always did that. We had to say goodbye to the sea, and take something home with us, just to prove to ourselves we were once here. Even if it was just a pebble from the beach.'

I was still laughing when I felt the past creep inside my head. It stole away the bright colours and the smell of the ocean, and the sound of other people's voices. It's strange how it always does that — appears without notice. It's as though the past and the present shift against each other all the time, and when you're distracted, you can slip through a gap between one and the other, without even realising you're doing it.

'I can hear a child crying,' I said.

I could tell Elsie was trying to listen, over the simmer of conversation as it drifted past, and the shrieking of seagulls in the bay. 'I can't hear it,' she said.

'No,' I said. 'Not now — then. On that last day. There was a child crying.'

'Ah,' she said. 'Yes there was.'

'We walked by, didn't we? Thinking someone

else would help.' Worry stumbled around in my head. 'We didn't do anything.'

'Yes we did.'

'He drowned. Fell from the harbour wall. It was in all the newspapers, don't you remember? I said to you, that's the little boy, that's the little boy we didn't help.'

When I glanced around, people were staring at us.

'Florence, you must calm down. Listen to me.'

'Why didn't we do something?' I began folding the scarf on my lap. 'Why didn't we stop?'

'We did stop. The three of us waited on the steps until his mother came along. We even used up our spending money on ice cream for him.'

I stopped folding. 'We did?'

'We did,' she said. 'His name was Frankie. Don't you remember?'

I shook my head.

'He had really blue eyes. Like this.' She pointed to a colour in my scarf. 'It made us late setting off home. Your mother was furious, but when we told her what had happened, she just kissed the tops of our heads.'

I felt my whole face smile. 'Did she?'

Elsie nodded.

'I still miss her, you know,' I whispered. 'I know I'm not supposed to. Not after all this time.'

'In the end, we were ages getting home anyway, because an hour earlier there'd been a big accident near York.'

She waited to see if my eyes would find the

memory, but sometimes I'm just too tired to search any more.

'Try to remember, Flo. It's important. Really important.'

'Why is it so important?'

She took my hand. 'It just is,' she said.

When we stood to leave, I looked back at the bench. There was a plaque, fixed to the wood.

*In memory of Arthur and Clarice — they loved this place*, it said. They're all over the West Cliff, benches with small brass plates. Lines of people made unforgotten, staring out to sea for the rest of time.

'I think I should quite like a bench,' I said.

'Why on earth would you want one of those?'

'To prove to myself I was once here,' I said.

'Oh, Florence. All you really need to do is remember.' She took my arm and we walked back to the hotel, past the crazy golf and the ice-cream vans, past the conversations and the pushchairs, and the days of other people.

As we walked, I turned to her and said, 'Thank you.'

'Whatever for?'

I smiled. 'You reminded me that my mother kissed the tops of our heads. It was a memory I'd lost, and you found it and you gave it back to me again.'

That was the second thing about Elsie.

She always knew exactly the right thing to say to make me feel better.

★  ★  ★

250

The hotel bedroom was adequate, although the bathroom floor could have done with a going-over and there was a fine layer of dust on the pelmet. I wasn't sure about the carpet, because it involved so many different colours that any stain would have quite happily slid right into it unnoticed. Elsie and I shared a room, because it seemed sensible, and I was worried about getting confused in the middle of the night and not being able to find the lavatory.

I stood in the doorway, the toes of my shoes resting on a little silver line. 'Ronnie can't get in here, can he?' I said. 'It's safe, isn't it?'

'Of course it's safe.' Elsie went over to the window. 'We're on the first floor, and look, you can lock the door from the inside. No one can get in.'

'Where's the lavatory?' I said.

'It's just through here. It's en-suite.'

I hesitated.

'It's just for us,' she said, and we spent the next ten minutes saying how wonderful it all was.

There were twin beds, covered in shiny pink eiderdowns. Comfortable, but not like being at home. The mattress was left wanting. Boxed springs. Saggy in the middle. Vague sensation of static each time you moved. Elsie went for the one nearest the door, because she knew I liked watching the seagulls. Above the writing desk there was a notice telling people not to pinch anything.

I read it out loud. 'Well, I never did,' I said.

I wasn't sure what anyone could find to steal. There was a picture of a zebra above the bed and a pot dog on the windowsill, but in all honesty, I would have paid somebody to take them away. I began unpacking my things. Elsie told me it wasn't worth it, because we were only going to be here for two nights, but I like to turn wherever I am into a home from home.

'It would take more than a tube of Poligrip in a plastic beaker to make me feel that way,' she said, but she let me get on with it.

★　★　★

Miss Ambrose asked us all to be in reception for three o'clock. We walked down the stairs at five past, but half of us was still missing. Ronnie was there, of course, leaning against the telephone table, talking to Mrs Honeyman, and Handy Simon stood on a little velvet stool with his clipboard, but he kept losing count and having to start again. Miss Bissell had gone for a lie-down with one of her stomachs. As soon as I spotted Ronnie, I reached for Elsie's hand. Jack arrived a few minutes after we did, and Miss Ambrose clapped and coughed, and tried her best to lure people away from the television lounge.

'We can watch the television at Cherry Tree, can't we? No need to put ourselves through four hours on a motorway.' She did a little laugh in the middle but no one joined in. We were told what to do if there was a fire or if anyone had a gluten allergy. I did start to ask a question about that, but Elsie put her finger against her lips, and so I decided to save it until later. Miss Ambrose told us what time the front door was locked, and how to request extra pillows, and then she handed us all an itinerary, which Jack used to clean his glasses, and I think I put mine in a plant pot for safekeeping.

'And now we're going on a ghost walk!' Miss Ambrose said.

We all stared at her.

'Ghosts are very popular in Whitby,' she said. 'The place is riddled with them.'

★   ★   ★

Our tour guide was called Barry. He had a bowler hat and very melodramatic arms. In fact, everything about him was melodramatic. He carried a silver-topped cane, which he held aloft as we followed him down the street. Jack copied with his walking stick, until Miss Ambrose told him off outside the Army & Navy. She was right, though. Whitby is full of ghosts. There are crinolined ladies tumbling from cliffs, several runaway coaches, and endless women running down cobbled yards with their hair on fire. We found ourselves standing on a street corner, listening to a story about a screaming cat, but my mind kept wandering. I was trying to keep one eye on Ronnie, but he would insist on moving around and I was always having to turn and check whereabouts he was. I had to ask Barry to repeat what he'd said a few times. Elsie reassured me she'd go through it later, but I said to her, what's the point in going on a ghost walk, if you have to have it all explained to you afterwards?

When we walked on to the main street, Jack

nudged me in the ribs and nodded across the road.

'There's your music shop,' he said.

Barry was being very theatrical about a vampire, and we crossed over unnoticed. It wasn't what I expected. Although we'd seen a picture on a computer screen, it seemed different in real life. It was sandwiched between a charity shop and an estate agent, and it sat there as though someone had lifted it out of the past and forgotten to put it back again. The window was filled with clarinets and trombones, and giant saxophones tilted towards the ceiling. There were polished violin bows, ready to be tightened, and a row of guitars waiting to be tuned. There were instruments I didn't even know the name of.

'Look at all the sheet music,' said Jack.

There was far more than we'd been able to see in the photograph. It stretched across the window. It crept from behind the violin cases and made a lake of crotchets and quavers on the floor. Songs from the past, all waiting to be played again, and right in the middle, looking down at us from a wartime dancehall, was Al Bowlly.

' 'Midnight, the Stars and You',' I said. 'Of course.'

'There he is again.' Jack pointed to the other side of the display. 'Goodnight Sweetheart.'

'My father used to sing that every evening,' I said. '*Goodnight sweetheart, I'll be watching o'er you.*' Then I sang the next line: '*Sleep will banish sorrow.*'

I looked at Elsie. 'If only that were true,' I said.

'Let's go inside.' Jack reached for the door.

'What, now?' I looked over at the ghost walk, which had moved a little down the pavement. Barry was pointing to a church spire, and everyone was looking up with their mouths open.

'Won't they miss us?' said Elsie.

'No time like the present,' Jack said.

I linked my arm through his. 'Isn't there?'

# Handy Simon

Handy Simon had never been big on ghosts. He couldn't understand the point of them. His parents had been firm believers, ever since they'd gone to see a medium in the town hall one Saturday afternoon, and she told them someone called John was trying to speak to them from the other side.

'It must be your granddad's cousin,' said his mother.

'Once removed,' said his father, and no matter how much Simon tried to reason with them, they wouldn't be persuaded on the matter. The medium told them dead people are so keen on making contact, they insist on leaving things for you to find all over the place. Feathers, leaves, very small pebbles.

'They make you hear noises too. Bells ring and music plays,' his mother said, 'and sometimes, you can even smell them.'

Simon sighed. 'Why do they bother?'

'It's their way of communicating.' His mother breathed in very deeply. She had taken to sniffing the air several times a day, just in case there was anyone around who had something to say to her.

'Why?' Simon asked her. 'Why didn't they just communicate when they were alive?'

'It's not that straightforward, Simon. You think you've got all the time in the world to speak up.

It's only when you're dead you realise there was something you forgot to mention.'

'Could it really be that important?' he said.

'To the person left behind it could,' she said. 'It could make all the difference in the world.'

After his mother died, his father saw an empty crisp packet in Sainsbury's car park.

'Cheese and onion,' he said. 'Your mother's favourite.' He pointed to the packet. 'That'll be Barbara, telling us to move on with our lives.'

Simon looked up at the church spire. Barry was saying something about a witch and several people were fanning themselves with their itineraries. Miss Ambrose was looking up too, and biting into her bottom lip.

'Do you believe in ghosts?' he said to her.

She didn't answer, and then after a while she said, 'I'm not entirely sure.'

He told her about the feathers and the pebbles, and the crisp packet.

'It would be nice to think so, wouldn't it?' she said. 'It would be nice to think you could affect things, even from the grave. That your roll of the dice went on for a little longer than you imagined.'

'I suppose.' Simon stopped looking up at the church tower. It was making him light-headed. 'Although I don't think I'm important enough to affect anything when I'm alive, let alone when I'm dead and buried.'

'Are any of us, when you think about it?' They watched a crowd emerge from one of the pubs, and the street filled with a spill of lager and shouting. 'Most of us are just secondary characters. We take up all the space between the few people who manage to make a mark.'

'Like who?'

'I don't know.' The men disappeared into another pub doorway, and for a moment, Simon felt the warmth of a Friday-night bar. 'Politicians? World leaders? The Pope?'

'If we're going to start judging ourselves by the Pope, everyone's going to fall a bit short, aren't they?'

'Your dad, then,' said Miss Ambrose. 'Look at all the lives he saved. He's made a difference.'

'Except he only ever thinks about the life he let go. The one he missed.'

'But that's human nature.' Miss Ambrose tightened the belt on her coat. 'We only ever think about the differences we didn't make, the chances we allowed to drift past, until you start asking yourself, what was the bloody point of it all in the first place?'

And Simon realised she had stopped talking to him and had begun having a conversation with herself. Barry lifted his cane and started to walk up the hill to a set of park gates, where he told them they would be hearing a ghost story so terrifying, no one would be able to sleep that night. He was right, as it happened, but the reason they all lost sleep would be nothing to do with the afterlife.

'Perhaps that's why we like to believe in spirits,' said Miss Ambrose, as she started walking. 'Perhaps it reassures us to think we'll have a second chance at being somebody significant.'

'Or at least send everyone a crisp packet to let them know we're still thinking of them.'

Miss Ambrose turned to him. 'What would you send?' she said.

'How do you mean?'

'What would you send to make someone know absolutely without doubt it was you who was trying to speak to them?'

Handy Simon thought about it all evening. He thought about it for the rest of the ghost walk, and all the way through the drama that unfolded afterwards, and he was even thinking about it as he went to sleep that night, yet he still couldn't come up with a single thing.

# Florence

We walked in, and a little bell above the door signalled our arrival. It was the only noise. For a room filled with the sound of a thousand waiting notes, it was peculiarly silent. I took a breath. The counter was polished, and all around us cabinets shone and glass sparkled, but the shop was still heavy with the scent of dust. It must have been held within the pages of the music and trapped against the frets of the violins, because it smelled as if the past had found a hiding place, safe and sheltered, where no one could be rid of it ever again.

I raised my eyebrows at Jack. 'Bit old-fashioned, isn't it?' I whispered, because it seemed wrong to intrude on the quiet. It felt like a library, but the words were crochets and quavers, and the stories had all jumped ship and written themselves into songs.

We looked up at a wall of photographs, and the past gazed back at us. Black-and-white ballrooms. A hundred foxtrots, captured forever within a lens. Stages crowded with musicians, hardwood floors crowded with dancers. There were band leaders, their batons poised into a smile, and singers leaning their songs into chrome microphones.

'Memorabilia,' I said. 'There are packets of them as well.' I pointed to boxes under the counter, where hundreds of photographs wrapped in cellophane waited to be reclaimed.

'Perhaps we're in there somewhere,' said Elsie.

'I doubt there will be any of us. We weren't fancy enough, I don't think. Despite Gwen's best efforts.'

Jack walked closer to the photographs. 'Al Bowlly again,' he said, and pointed to the top row. 'He gets everywhere, doesn't he?'

'Clacton-on-Sea, 1939.'

The voice appeared from the back of the shop. I gave a little start. When we turned, there was a man standing in the shadows, watching us closely from behind a tuba.

'Britain's first pop star. That's what they called him.' The man walked into the light. Short. Round. A pencil moustache so thin, it made me wonder why he'd bothered in the first place. 'Quite the heart-throb in his day.'

'I remember when he died,' Elsie said. 'We were all quite beside ourselves.'

'The war claimed far too many, far too soon.' The man clasped his hands together in a little prayer. 'Although made even more tragic, given the circumstances.'

Jack turned on his walking stick. 'What happened?'

And so the shopkeeper told us. How Al Bowlly had been reading in bed when the air-raid siren had sounded, and he'd chosen to stay with his book, rather than go to the shelter.

'They found him after the all-clear,' he said. 'Head injury from the blast. Barely a mark on him.'

'It makes you want to go back, doesn't it?' I

261

said. 'Tell him to get to the shelter. Tell him there will be a lifetime of books, if he just changes his mind.'

We all stared at the photograph.

'Small decisions,' Jack said. 'It's always the small decisions that change a life.'

The man coughed and unclasped his hands. 'Was it Al Bowlly you were particularly interested in?'

I looked around the shop. 'Yes,' I said. 'No. To be honest, I'm not even sure.'

The man pursed his lips, and the moustache did a little shimmy across his top lip. 'Not sure?' he said.

Jack stepped forward. 'We're trying to trace someone. Someone called Gabriel Price. We think he might have a connection with this shop. Or Al Bowlly. Or perhaps he might have no connection at all, and we're barking up the wrong tree.'

The man smiled and his moustache straightened itself out again. 'Ah,' he said. 'Gabriel Price. Not the wrong tree at all. In fact, very much the right tree, if you'll allow me.'

# Handy Simon

The park gates were clearly Barry's pièce de résistance. He began telling the story of a severed hand, waving his cane around and putting on different voices, but by this time the wind had got up and Simon found himself wishing he was back at the hotel with a crème de menthe and a bit of central heating. He wasn't the only one, by the look of it. The group was beginning to fray at the edges. A couple of people had stayed behind to look in the window of a shoe shop, and someone else had wandered over the road and was staring at a bus timetable.

'Can we all stay together?' Miss Ambrose shouted down the street, but her words were swallowed up by a pub door. She turned to Simon. 'Do you think we ought to have a head count?'

Simon took a deep breath and pulled the clipboard from his rucksack. He had hoped, in the absence of Miss Bissell, to have a few hours free from counting heads, but he should have known that the influence of Miss Bissell was always far weightier than Miss Bissell herself. Sometimes, it felt easier when she was actually there.

\* \* \*

When he was done Miss Ambrose took the clipboard from him and scanned the names.

263

'Trust Florence to be involved in the mystery.'

'They've probably just been waylaid by a public lavatory,' said Simon. 'Or a charity-shop window. They're probably further down the pavement.'

Miss Ambrose stepped into the road to look.

'Watch out!' Gabriel Price pulled her from the path of a moped, and back to the safety of the kerb. 'You want to be careful, Miss Ambrose. That could have been a nasty accident.'

'Mr Price.' She looked up and tried to steal back her breath. 'I was just checking. We appear to have lost Florence and her friends.'

Gabriel Price picked up Miss Ambrose's bag, which had dropped into the gutter, and he handed it back to her. 'I do believe,' he said, 'you'll find them in the music shop.'

'I didn't know Miss Claybourne was musical,' said Simon.

Gabriel Price smiled. 'I really couldn't comment on that,' he said.

'I do wish they'd all stay together.' Miss Ambrose seemed to have found her breath again. 'I would have expected more from Mrs Honeyman at least. She's not usually so difficult.'

'Mrs Honeyman?'

'Yes. She was with them as well, wasn't she? We can't find her either.'

'Oh I don't think so,' he said. 'I haven't seen Mrs Honeyman since the West Cliff.'

Simon felt his mouth go dry and a ball of unease roll into his stomach.

# Florence

'A musician?' The three of us spoke in a little chorus, and waited in a row for our verdict. Jack gripped the handle of his walking stick, and my hands found the belt of my coat.

'Indeed he was. And a Whitby man, too.' The man with the pencil moustache was buried deep in a drawer of photographs, and his voice trailed up from beneath the counter. 'A travelling musician. Drifted from band to band. There was a lot of it after the war.'

'How do you mean?' Elsie peered down and spoke to the top of his head.

'People were displaced. They felt untethered, I suppose.' The man appeared with a box of cellophaned pictures. 'They wandered from job to job, place to place, trying to find out who they were again.'

'Like modern-day minstrels,' said Jack.

'You could say that.' The man searched through the photographs. 'Only more drums than dulcimer. Although I do believe Gabriel Price was a pianist.'

I stopped twisting. 'I remember watching the pianist at the town hall, seeing his hands on the keyboard. He wore a ring. On his little finger. It was very distinctive, very delicate. Not a ring you'd expect a man to wear at all.' I paused. 'Did Gabriel Price wear a ring?' I was scared to ask. Sometimes, my thoughts can lead me so far up

265

the garden path, it's difficult to find a way back again.

The man pulled a photograph from a sleeve of cellophane and laid it on the counter. 'Let's have a look, shall we?' he said.

# Handy Simon

They covered the whole of the West Cliff. All the way from the whalebones to where a stripe of coastal path disappears its way to Sandsend. There was no sign of Mrs Honeyman. Barry volunteered to keep the rest of the group together, although he'd run out of ghost stories and had to herd them towards the whalebones, where they had a half-hearted sing-along and three verses of the national anthem. Miss Ambrose called Miss Bissell, and Miss Bissell appeared at the side of Captain Cook clutching a Gideon's Bible to her chest.

'I'm sure Mrs Honeyman is around here somewhere,' said Miss Ambrose, although her face didn't look as certain as her words. The veins in her neck beat the same rhythm as Miss Bissell's swearing and Simon could see lines appear on her forehead, even from where he was standing. One of the residents said she remembered seeing Mrs Honeyman go into the public conveniences but didn't recall her coming out again, and it was decided that Simon should investigate just in case a door needed breaking down.

'But they're ladies' toilets.' He stood at the entrance to the building with his arms folded. 'And I'm not a lady.'

In the end, Miss Ambrose agreed to lead the way, and they found themselves staring at three empty stalls, and surrounded by the smell of sand and wet concrete.

'How could she just disappear?' Simon pushed at one of the cubicle doors, even though it was at its maximum pushing. 'People don't just disappear.'

'She was seen going in, but not coming out,' said Miss Ambrose. 'Although being as there's only one exit, it beggars belief where she could have got to.'

They both studied the tiny windows, which were decorated with cobwebs and a collection of specimens that would have made a lepidopterist's chest swell with pride.

Simon put his hands on his hips and took another breath of wet-sand air. 'Two hundred and fifty thousand people go missing each year,' he said. 'Which is the equivalent of the entire population of Plymouth vanishing every twelve months.'

'Simon, I really don't think it's helpful — '

'Seventy-four per cent are found within twenty-four hours.'

'Well, at least that's reassuring.'

'Only one per cent are found dead.'

They listened through the postage-stamp windows, as the North Sea threw itself on to the rocks below.

'Maybe we should call the police,' said Miss Ambrose.

# Florence

We all studied the photograph.

Even though we knew it wouldn't be Ronnie, it was still a shock to see a stranger staring back at us. Gabriel Price was not what I expected. Perhaps I was searching for shades of Ronnie Butler, something I could hold on to and dislike, but the man who looked back at us from the photograph had kind eyes and a soft smile. His hands rested on piano keys, and he looked straight into the camera, as though he'd been waiting for us to arrive. He was a little older than Ronnie. A little thinner, and although I never knew him, I felt as if he was someone who could be trusted.

'It's not Ronnie,' I said.

'No.' Jack sighed. 'But we never really expected it to be, did we?'

'We didn't, but I was hoping they would look like the same person. Isn't it ridiculous,' I said, 'to hope that you might be losing your mind?'

I stared further into the picture.

'He has a ring, though. Look.' I pointed. 'I told you I remembered. I just couldn't think of the person wearing it.'

'It's a very unusual ring, isn't it?' Elsie said. We tried to get closer, but the image blurred into a swarm of dots.

I felt very pleased with myself.

'Perhaps it was his wife's,' said Jack. 'A kind of

keepsake, whilst he was travelling.'

'Oh, I don't think there was a wife.' The man began sorting through the other photographs and putting them back into their box. 'I don't think there was any family. At least none I've ever heard about, and I've done quite a bit of background recently. You're not the first ones to ask about him.'

Jack narrowed his eyes. 'Is that so?' he said.

'Oh, yes. There was a gentleman who rang only a few weeks ago wanting to buy any sheet music Gabriel Price might have owned. He was very interested.'

'I bet he was,' said Jack.

'Not that we had any to sell to him.' His little moustache curved down at its edges.

I heard Elsie sigh.

'This photograph.' Jack tapped on the counter. 'Is it for sale?'

The man's moustache cheered up a bit and did a little dance all the way across his top lip.

* * *

'You drive a hard bargain,' I said as we stepped back on to the pavement. 'I thought he was going to charge us a small fortune.'

'Fifteen pounds isn't cheap.' Jack tucked the paper bag under his arm. 'But it could have been a lot worse, and it might come in useful.'

We stood on the kerb and looked down the street.

'Where the bloody hell have they all gone?' he said.

We walked all the way up to the park gates. We found a hen party and an alternative ghost walk. It confused us for a moment until we realised it was being conducted in Chinese. There was no sign of Barry, or his bowler hat. After Jack consulted an itinerary, it was established that at that precise moment, we should have been enjoying a light supper and cassette music in the residents' lounge. It was on the way back to the hotel, as we walked across the West Cliff and watched the evening sunlight settle itself into the water, that we found Miss Ambrose and Handy Simon outside the ladies' toilets, having a conversation about statistics.

'There you are!' Miss Ambrose shouted, and a family in cagoules turned and looked at us. 'I was wondering when you'd show up.'

Jack's eyes were misted with age. His hands shook with the tremor of a life long lived, but his voice was still steady. 'We are on holiday,' he said, very quietly. 'We were enjoying ourselves.'

'We've been searching all over the place. We have to have rules,' she said, 'regulations. We can't have people just wandering off all over the place.'

Handy Simon was standing behind her, but he turned away.

Jack's gaze didn't leave Miss Ambrose. 'We were enjoying ourselves,' he said again.

Miss Ambrose's face flooded with scarlet. 'We were worried,' she said. 'Especially about Mrs

271

Honeyman.' She peered around Jack's shoulder. 'Where is she?'

Jack frowned. 'Well, she's not with us,' he said. 'Is she not with you?'

Miss Ambrose's face moved from scarlet to white, and Handy Simon began looking on his mobile telephone for the nearest police station.

# 9.46 p.m.

I can't remember the last time I ate anything. I know I didn't eat at the funeral. I can't be doing with little bits of nonsense on a paper plate. I can't remember the last time I drank anything either. You can manage without food for weeks. I read about it. In a magazine. Look at all those poor people in prison, starving themselves because no one listens to them. I'm fairly sure it's just the drinking that matters, though. Simon would know. See! I remembered his name.

Sometimes I remember, and sometimes I don't. Sometimes I say the right thing, and sometimes I don't. Everything makes sense in my head, it's only when I let it go that it gets in a muddle. I can see it in people's eyes when I haven't said the right thing, and I never really know it's happened until I've spoken and looked at them.

Eileen Everest was the wrong thing. We were in the car, on the way back from Cyril's barge.

'Poor little Eileen Everest,' I said. 'I think about her a lot.'

I knew Elsie was staring at me. You can tell sometimes, can't you, without even looking.

'What do you mean,' she said, 'poor little Eileen Everest?'

'Getting run over like that. Never growing up.'
I looked at her eyes. It was the wrong thing.
'In Llandudno,' I said.

'She never went to Llandudno, Florence. If Miss Ambrose catches you talking like that, we'll almost certainly never hear the end of it.'

'So where did she go?' I said.

Elsie looked at me and smiled. 'She went to Whitby, don't you remember?'

I don't remember anything. I just remember standing on the town-hall steps with my mother, and looking up at the clock.

'Did she?' I said.

'You saw the long second, Florence. You told her to go to Whitby. Eileen Everest never went to Llandudno in the end. You stopped her.'

# Florence

The policeman held up his hands. He was clearly an optimist, because it hadn't worked the last three times he'd tried it, so there was really very little chance of it working now.

'If you could all just be quiet for one second,' he said, 'we'll try to establish a system for speaking to everyone individually.'

But the second half of his sentence fell into a shouting match between two residents about whether a chief inspector was higher up than a superintendent.

'Perhaps we could borrow one of the rooms?' said Miss Ambrose.

The woman who owns the hotel was called Gail. Gail with an 'i'. Each time she introduced herself, she explained to us it was spelled with an i, despite no one ever finding the need to write it down. Gail gave a little sniff. 'Another one?' she said. Miss Bissell had experienced a fainting episode next to the whalebones, and had already been taken into the kitchen with a police sergeant and a bottle of brandy.

'Maybe the television room?' said Miss Ambrose.

'That's out of the question. It's Tuesday,' said Gail, rather mysteriously, but she didn't elaborate. 'I suppose I could let you have the staff rest room. Although you'll need to be out by eight, because I've got a new shift coming in and I'll need to change my slacks.'

We sat in a row, waiting our turn. For a rest room, it wasn't very restful. The chairs were wooden and mismatched. Some of them had clearly escaped from the dining room and clung to their usefulness with glue and Sellotape. People appeared and ignored us. They banged locker doors and turned keys, and they put on layers of uniform and turned themselves into someone else. I tapped my feet to pass the time, but Elsie kept glaring at me, and so I tapped my fingers on last night's menu instead.

'Where do you think Ronnie is?' I kept saying. 'Someone should be keeping their eye on him.'

'He'll be outside.' Jack nodded towards the door. 'Along with everyone else. He can't get up to much with all these policemen around.'

'Why don't we play a game?' Elsie said. 'Why don't we try that shelf over there?'

I studied the shelf. 'Clock. Postcards. Dying plant.' I hesitated. 'Candle?'

'Bigger,' she said.

'Candlestick?'

'Wonderful!'

'Professor Plum, in the conservatory.' Then, 'Why did I say that?'

'Because it's a board game,' she said. 'Do you remember? You play it in the day room sometimes, after small amounts of persuasion.'

'Do I? I don't remember. Where do you think Mrs Honeyman has gone?'

Elsie paused. 'Perhaps she just got a little confused. Wandered off. People do from time to time.'

'She'll be back,' said Jack. 'You'll see.'

I wasn't sure if she would, but I didn't say anything. Old people disappear all the time. We allow them a moment of sympathy, and then turn the page of the newspaper. Do we ever know if they're returned to where they belonged? I'm not entirely sure that we do. Elsie started talking about how the plant on the shelf needed watering, and so I clung to that thought instead. Sometimes, you need to hold on to a small worry, to stop you from reaching out for something bigger.

Jack turned around in his seat and looked at the door for the sixth time.

'It's not going to make them move any faster, you know,' Elsie said.

'Being questioned by the police is the most exciting thing that's happened in years,' I said. 'People won't give it up without a fight.'

'I don't know why they need to speak to us anyway.' Jack turned back to us. 'We weren't even there. We were in the music shop.'

I said, 'As long as they don't ask the reason we were in the music shop.'

'Do you think they'll want to know why?' said Elsie.

'It's a free country,' Jack said.

As he spoke, the staff-room door opened and the policeman ushered out the latest interviewee, who was still in the middle of a sentence.

' . . . and that's why I pay my taxes,' he was saying.

The policeman nodded and blocked the way back with his shoulders. Jack struggled to his feet. 'I'm next,' he said.

But Handy Simon walked past us and slipped through.

'Well I never did.' Jack watched the door for a very long time. Even after it had closed.

I squinted at the shelf on the opposite wall. 'I think I'm going to water that plant,' I said.

# Handy Simon

Handy Simon had never been a big fan of policemen. He was stopped by one once for having a tail-light out, and it took him three days to recover. It wasn't so much the uniform, because he was used to his dad's, it was the worry that he might be mistaken for someone else. Simon always thought he looked like the photofits on *Crimewatch*. There was something about his face. Something universal. He could never see it himself, but other people seemed to, so whenever he heard a loud bang, he'd look at the clock and make a mental note of what he was doing, just in case it turned out to be gunfire and he found himself sharing a cell with a tattooist called Daryl.

The policeman smiled at him across the desk, although Simon couldn't decide if it was a smile of reassurance or a smile of sudden recognition.

'We'll just get a few details straight first,' he said, and his pen hovered over the paper.

Simon confirmed his name and address as clearly as he could. He even repeated it a couple of times, just to be on the safe side.

'And you've worked at Cherry Tree for how long?'

'Just over five years. Five years, two months and fifteen days.'

The policeman looked up and smiled again.

The smiling was unexpected and most off-putting.

'Five years? You must enjoy it,' he said.

This was a bit of a curveball. Simon shuffled around in his seat whilst he tried to think of an answer. It was important to be honest, but he didn't want to be too honest, in case it was written down in evidence and later mentioned in court.

'It has its ups and downs,' he said eventually.

The policeman's pen just hovered.

'Aren't you going to write that down?' said Simon. 'In evidence?'

'What?'

'That it has its ups and downs?'

'No. I was just making conversation.' The policeman coughed. 'When was the last time you remember seeing Mrs Honeyman?'

'Are you still making conversation?' said Simon. 'Or is it a question?'

'No, it's a question.'

'I'm not certain. It's difficult to be sure.'

'Difficult to be sure?'

'I mean they all look quite similar, don't they? Unless you're concentrating.'

'And you weren't concentrating?' said the policeman.

Simon sat back. 'Of course I was concentrating. You won't find anyone who concentrates more than I do. Or does as many head counts.' He reached for his backpack, but then he realised his clipboard was already on the desk. 'She was definitely there at the start of the walk, because I counted her.'

280

The policeman looked at the chart. 'But by the time you reached the park gates, she'd disappeared.'

Simon nodded.

The policeman spent the next few minutes writing, and all Simon could hear was the scratch of his pen on the paper.

'So how would you describe Mrs Honeyman, Simon?'

Simon stared at a stain on his jacket. 'I'm not really sure.'

'Why don't we start with what she looks like?'

'Don't you already know?'

'We do, but I want to hear what you have to say about it.'

'Average height. Average build.' Simon continued to stare at the stain in the hope it might offer some inspiration. 'Grey hair.'

'That could describe most people on this trip, couldn't it, though?'

'I suppose.' Simon rubbed at the stain, because it clearly wasn't helping.

'Any distinguishing features?'

Simon looked up. 'How do you mean?'

'Anything that makes her stand out from the others?'

Simon had to think about it for a few minutes before he spoke.

'She's quite good at cribbage,' he said.

★ ★ ★

'Well?' Miss Ambrose stood next to the telephone table in reception.

Simon was afraid to meet her eye, so he spoke to the table instead. 'Nothing, really.'

'I hope you stressed how conscientious we are at Cherry Tree. How resident safety is a priority. You do remember me telling you to say that?'

'Shall I go back?' he said.

He dared to steal a glance and thankfully, she had her eyes closed. He was usually quite good at instructions, at least when they involved moving furniture or unblocking drains, it was just when it was to do with people he found it a bit more tricky.

As he was waiting for Miss Ambrose to finish her deep breathing, a few of the residents appeared in reception and loitered around the foot of the stairs. He knew how they felt. He didn't really know what to do with himself either.

Miss Ambrose studied them. 'And why aren't you talking to the police? I thought Jack was next on the list.'

'I was.' Jack gave Simon a strange look, which he didn't really understand. 'The constable is having a little comfort break, I believe. We've got to go back in fifteen minutes.'

'We should be out there searching,' said Florence. 'Not sitting around here having conversations with policemen.'

'Couldn't agree more.' Jack started buttoning his coat, but Miss Ambrose raised her hand and everyone stopped what they were doing to look at it.

'Don't even think about it,' she said. She left very big gaps between all the words, and the gaps

282

made Jack unbutton his coat again and everyone else gather closer to the stairs and become very quiet.

'At least I managed to get hold of Gloria.' Miss Ambrose turned back to Simon. 'She had a look through Mrs Honeyman's records and managed to fax things over.'

'Any relatives to call?' said Simon.

'No one.' Miss Ambrose checked through the sheets of paper she had in her hands. 'No children. Parents of course, but they're obviously long gone. Not sure of their names.' She turned a page. 'Here we go. Arthur and Clarice.'

The hallway was silent, so there was no doubt about who spoke next. Simon heard all the words very clearly.

'They loved this place!' Florence shouted from the foot of the stairs.

# Florence

'What bench?'

We were back in the staff room. The policeman hadn't yet returned, but still Jack whispered.

'Up near the whalebones.' I waved my arms around a bit in frustration. 'We sat on it this afternoon.'

'Did I? I don't remember sitting on a bench near the whalebones,' Jack said.

'No, not you. It's on a brass plaque: In memory of Arthur and Clarice. They loved this place.' I slipped into shouting again and Elsie was forced to shush me up a bit.

'What are you trying to say, Flo?' She kept gesturing for me to sit, but sitting down and thinking don't always mix very well.

'It's too much of a coincidence. They must be Mrs Honeyman's parents,' I said.

'And if they are?' Jack's eyes were letterbox-narrow.

'They loved this place means they probably came here often. They might have even lived here. Which means she might have done too. And who else has a connection with Whitby? Who was born here?'

Jack shifted in his plastic seat. 'Gabriel Price,' he said.

'So it's a bit of a coincidence, isn't it,' I said, 'that it's Mrs Honeyman and no one else, who

284

has been vanished away?'

'I don't think we should run away with ourselves.' Elsie reached for my arm, as though she might be able to put a stop to any of the running. 'I think it's much more sensible to let the appropriate people deal with this.'

I made sure I took a very deep breath before I spoke. 'I couldn't agree more. Which is why I'm going to tell the policeman.'

★ ★ ★

It is a cliché that policemen look young, but this one really did. His limbs had that uncooperative air only ever seen in adolescents, and looking at the chaos on his top lip, it appeared he was attempting to grow a moustache. I'm afraid he was ahead of his time. I stared quite openly at it as we sat down, and there was nothing Elsie could do to stop me. If people will insist on having facial hair, they've only got themselves to blame if people choose to study it. We were supposed to have our interviews individually, but Elsie and I went in together because she said I was on the verge of hysteria, and no one seemed to mind.

'Try to think before you speak,' she said to me. The room was very small. Judging by the metal shelves and the giant tins of apricot segments, it was some kind of stock room. There was so little air, it felt as though we had to take it in turns to breathe. The policeman was messing around with the window catch, but he smiled at us when he turned back, and I immediately calmed down a little. Policemen always have that effect on me. Policemen and vicars. I suppose one protects me from criminals and the other from fire and brimstone, so it feels as though all the bases are covered.

The policeman asked the usual details. I added my date of birth as well, just for good measure, even though he didn't mention it.

'I'm eighty-four,' I said. 'The same age as Elsie, only I've spent less time in the sun.'

The policeman looked through the many sheets of paper covering the desk. 'The same age as Mrs Honeyman,' he said.

'Are we?' I said.

Elsie sat back. 'I didn't know that.'

The policeman nodded. He asked how well we knew her. He said it with an air of uncertainty, and I didn't want to lose his attention, so I told him we all knew each other extremely well. We didn't, obviously. People have the idea that old people always get along with each other, that everyone swims in the same direction, like a shoal of fish, never finding anything to argue about. I suppose to them, old age must look very much like a battleground, and you all have to fight for the same side, just to survive.

'And how would you describe Mrs Honeyman?' said the policeman.

I held the words in my mouth whilst I had a think.

'Round face. Doesn't speak much. Not very good with stairs,' I said.

'Very quiet,' said Elsie. 'Sleeps a lot. I wonder sometimes if she isn't a little depressed.'

'I wonder if she was depressed as well,' I said. 'She never seems to have anyone to talk to.'

'Really?' The policeman looked at his notes. 'No one else has mentioned that. Has she recently lost someone?'

'Just the person she used to be,' I said, but the policeman chose not to reply.

'So would you describe Mrs Honeyman as vulnerable?' he said.

I thought about it for a moment. 'I suppose so, but aren't we all, if you think about it for long enough?'

The policeman tapped his pen on the desk before he started to write.

After a few minutes, he looked up again and said, 'Anything else?'

'She has a bladder the size of a peanut,' I said.

Elsie tutted. 'I should hardly think the sergeant needs to know about Mrs Honeyman's kidney function, Florence.'

'She disappeared going to the toilet, didn't she?' I tried to raise myself up in my seat, but I'd lost a good couple of inches in the past few years, and I sometimes over-estimate its effect.

'She was seen going into the lavatories.' Elsie turned from me and addressed the policeman.

'Yes,' he said, 'we are aware of that.'

'But that's not the important thing,' I said. 'That's not what I wanted to talk to you about.'

The policeman stopped writing. 'So what do you think might be the important thing, Miss . . . '

'Claybourne,' I said. 'I'm eighty-four.'

'Have you got something you feel you want to

tell the police, Miss Claybourne?'

'We most certainly have,' I said.

'We?'

'Me and Elsie. And Jack of course.'

'Jack?'

'But he's outside.'

'I see.' The policeman folded an arm across his chest, and sighed into his other hand.

'You have someone on that list.' I prodded my finger at the desk. 'Called Ronnie Butler.' I watched the policeman scroll with his pen down the names of the residents. 'But you won't find him.'

He looked up. 'I won't?'

'No, you won't. Because he's not listed as Ronnie Butler, he's listed as Gabriel Price.'

He didn't reply, although his mouth opened very slightly.

'He's masquerading as someone else, Inspector,' I said, 'and he's exceptionally dangerous. He always has been.'

The policeman sat back. 'That's a very serious allegation, Miss Claybourne.'

'Oh, it's not an allegation, it's a well-known fact. He drowned, in 1953, and he's come back from the dead pretending to be someone else. If that isn't dangerous, I don't know what is.'

'It's certainly quite an achievement.'

'But he's still got the scar.' I pointed to the corner of my mouth. 'So it's definitely him.'

'I see.' The policeman tried to lean back a little more, but he'd run out of space to do it in. 'So what exactly does this gentleman have to do with Mrs Honeyman?'

'Well, it's obvious, isn't it?' I said. 'He's done away with her.'

The policeman looked as though he was going to speak, but nothing came out.

'He broke into my flat, did you hear about it?' I said. 'Several times.'

The policeman began to say something, but changed his mind and shook his head instead.

'He's been moving things around. He bought all that cake. No one believes me. Even Miss Ambrose doesn't believe me.'

'Shall I get Miss Ambrose?' the policeman said.

'As a witness?' I gripped the edge of the desk. 'No, I just —'

'He killed Beryl, but none of you could prove it. You'll write it down, won't you, the name? Ronnie Butler,' I said. 'You'll make sure he's arrested?'

The policeman stood, and we copied him. It was the same with doctors and solicitors. The strangest reflex. 'I'll make sure the right people know all about it,' he said.

I held on to the sleeve of his uniform. 'You're the first person who's listened to me,' I said.

I waited for his reply, but there was nothing.

★ ★ ★

It was much later. When Elsie came out of the bathroom, I was leaning against the windowsill and looking out on to the crescent. The interviews took a lot longer than anyone anticipated, and it had grown very dark. It was

289

quite amazing how much everyone had to say about Mrs Honeyman, considering we knew so little about her. The hotel put a light buffet on in the dining room, but no one had much of an appetite. I saw Ronnie Butler eat more than his fair share, and Jack forced down a couple of vol-au-vents, but most of it was returned to the kitchens untouched. Gail with an i sniffed very loudly as she took all the plates back, and said a lot of things about third-world countries which no one could really hear properly, because of all the sniffing.

Elsie joined me at the window. She stood there in her nightdress, silhouetted against a coastal sky, scoops of white hair and frail, worn shoulders, all floodlit by a Yorkshire moon.

'Are you still not hungry?' she said.

'I might be able to manage an Ovaltine.' I didn't turn. 'Except I can't stop thinking about her being out there somewhere. On her own. It doesn't make any sense, Elsie. Does it?'

'No,' she said. 'It doesn't.'

'She wasn't confused. She wouldn't just wander off.'

'It might have been seeing Whitby again after all these years. Perhaps she got muddled. Perhaps she fell into the past and couldn't find her way back.'

In the distance there were lights on the water. Ships, perhaps, sleeping somewhere far across the ocean, and even through the glass, I could hear the tides. The never-ending waves, pulling against the earth, shaping the landscape.

We watched a woman walk by with her dog.

'It never stops, Whitby, does it?' I said. 'No matter what the time is. Most places settle down, but Whitby just keeps moving.'

'I expect it's the sea. A wave travels thousands of miles and finds its way here to make its mark. It must be difficult to sleep when something so amazing is happening.'

I was going to draw the curtains, but something stopped me, and I took one last look through the glass and out towards the ocean.

'I hope she's all right,' I said. 'I hope she can find her way back.'

I held the material in my hand. Never before had it felt so difficult to close a curtain.

# 10.01 p.m.

I don't know when I first started sleeping in that chair.

I only remember staying up one night, because I couldn't stomach the thought of going to bed, and it just happened. I didn't mean it to. I borrowed two pillows from the bedroom and I used the little blanket on the back of the settee. It was quite comfortable, when you got used to it, and if you tucked yourself in, it wasn't that cold. I didn't dare leave the fire on, of course. Not after everything that happened. I kept it plugged in, though, for company, and I watched a red light dance through the imaginary coal and pretend to be a flame.

I would never have been found out, either, if Miss Ambrose hadn't dropped in without any kind of forewarning. I always put the pillows back on the bed, and ruffle up the eiderdown, just for appearances' sake, but she caught me out before I'd had a chance to do it.

'Florence,' she said. 'Have you been sleeping in the chair?'

I chose something to look at.

'Because if you have, I'm going to have to put you on night-time visits.'

I turned to her. 'I don't want someone coming in and putting me to bed, like a toddler.'

'Then can you please go back to sleeping where everyone else sleeps?'

I wanted to tell her I felt better sleeping in the chair, that when I went to bed, all I did was lie there and listen for Ronnie walking around in the flat, that I could never find my sleep, because my mind was too busy trying to think of a reason for all the noises. But how can you talk to somebody when even their eyes aren't listening to you?

'So that's settled then?' she said.

I folded my arms as a reply, and after a few seconds, I heard the front door close to. I did think about carrying on with it, but Miss Bissell has a knack of knowing what you're up to, even if Miss Ambrose rarely has the first clue.

I'd give anything to be in that chair right now.

I can just about see it from where I am, if I turn my head, but it's getting more and more difficult because the longer I lie here, the less my body wants to do what I'm telling it to. It's easier just to look at the nonsense under the sideboard, although I can't make that out at all now. It's so dark.

I keep thinking about Mabel and those little children. I've never really had much of an opinion about children. You don't, really, if you have none of your own. It's not that I ever set out not to have them, life just seems to pick up speed all by itself, and before I knew it, I was having a little retirement party at the factory. Drinks in white plastic cups. People you've never even said hello to before, waving their goodbyes. And you get home, and it's only then you realise you forgot to make a family. It makes you think, though, when you see children close up like that, how they're like tiny versions of yourself, carrying on where you left off.

Mabel said she'd pop in and visit. She hasn't sent word, but people just drop in on you sometimes, don't they? Look at Miss Ambrose. Mabel will be in such a state when she finds me.

'Whatever have you been doing, Florence? How did you manage to get yourself down there?'

She won't move me. You're not supposed to, are you? I read about it. In a magazine. She'll wait for the ambulance men instead. She'll talk to me while we wait, though. About the town hall and the dance, and all those quicksteps we used to do. She'll keep talking in the ambulance, and she'll still be talking when we get to casualty. She'll talk to all the other people in the bay as well, because that's the kind of person Mabel is. She'll be wearing a white top and a skirt full of flowers, and all the flowers will dance when she walks across the room. Her hands will smell of soap, and when I say something to make her happy, her whole face will find the laughter.

She'll talk to the sister when we get to the ward. They'll find something in common, because Mabel always finds something in common with everyone. I'll look over, and the sister will check the watch that's pinned to the front of her uniform, and she'll nod, and Mabel will be allowed to sit with me. There will be lamps on at the nurses' station, but all the other beds will be in darkness, and the rest of the ward will be bathed in a liquid quiet. Mabel will pull her chair closer, so she can whisper. She will brush the hair from my face, and pull the blankets straight, and tell me everything is going to be fine. And it will be. Because sometimes, that's all you need. Someone to be there. Someone to watch over you, as you fall into sleep. Someone to tell you everything is going to be fine.

# Florence

The dining room seemed like a stranger in daylight. We all studied the plates of scrambled egg and the little sachets of brown sauce, as though we couldn't work out what they might be doing there, sitting in front of us. The tables were covered in thick white linen and there were grains of sugar scattered around, where someone had failed to brush them up adequately. I was keen to point this out to the waitress, but after Elsie and I had a discussion, I settled for sweeping them up with my hands instead and dropping them on to the floor very theatrically. The tables were so close together, my elbow occasionally brushed against Miss Ambrose's cardigan sleeve.

'Starving ourselves isn't going to help, is it?' Miss Ambrose shovelled a fried mushroom into her mouth. 'We have to keep our strength up.'

The wallpaper looked very tired. It was the kind of wallpaper that has a texture, as well as a pattern. The kind of wallpaper that makes you want to touch, just to see what it feels like.

'You should really stop that,' Elsie said. 'People are looking.'

I took my hand away. 'But what's the point in putting velvet on the walls, if no one is going to feel it?'

The tea was lukewarm and the toast sat in its letter rack, cold and unwanted. It's odd how worry affects your appetite. Some people completely lose all interest in food, whilst others do absolutely nothing but eat.

'Starve a fever, feed a cold,' I said. 'I wonder if you're supposed to feed a worry as well?'

'Haven't got the stomach for it, I'm afraid.' Jack pushed his plate an inch forward. 'Have you heard anything from the police?'

Miss Ambrose attacked a hash brown with her fork. 'Not yet, but I'm sure they're doing everything they can.'

'I'm sure they are.' He sat back. 'And hopefully, they've listened to all of us very carefully.'

The hash brown disappeared. It left an echo of tomato sauce around Miss Ambrose's lips, and I wiped my own mouth in sympathy. I'd never admit it to Elsie, but Beryl dying made me lose faith in the police force. How they never managed to get Ronnie. How something like that could happen, and no one was ever punished. Sometimes, you go through an experience in life that slices into the very bones of who you are, and two different versions of yourself will always sit either side of it, like bookends.

After she'd pushed the last hash brown around her plate, Miss Ambrose said we should all try our best to carry on as usual, but could we please try to avoid getting lost, and be back at the hotel for six o'clock at the latest. Jack cornered his eyes at us, and Elsie and I cornered ours back, even though neither of us was really sure why we were doing it, and he couldn't really explain it all until we were out on the front step.

'The man who owns the music shop,' he said, buttoning up his coat. 'I think we should ask him to elaborate on that research he said he did.'

I took a deep breath of seaside air, and the three of us walked along the little path towards the whalebones in the first catch of sunlight.

★ ★ ★

There is something special about a coastal morning. The day seems to have so much more potential when there's a seaside attached to it. Perhaps it's the brightness from the water, scrubbing everything clean like a front step, ready for you to start again.

We walked past sleeping ice-cream vans and wet concrete shelters, but the nearer we got to the whalebones, the more people began to appear. Everyone had made an early start, trying to squeeze as many minutes as they could out of their day. They all looked like tourists to me, because they had that air of holiday clothes and bellies full of hotel breakfasts. The traffic seemed local, though. Boy racers, speeding up and down the seafront, squealing their brakes and sending flocks of seagulls escaping into the sky.

As we turned a corner, there was a woman by the side of the road. She had two children, one strapped tightly into a buggy, and the other wandering the pavement, stepping on and off the kerb in some strange little-girl game. One where only she knew the rules. The woman was bending down, pushing hair behind her ears, trying to free one of the wheels of the pushchair, which had jammed against the concrete. The bells of St Mary's rang a Saturday morning out across the harbour.

'Help her, Jack. She's struggling.' I pointed Jack an instruction towards the pushchair, and he rested his walking stick against a bench and bent down. She stood up and looked round for the little girl, taking her hand and pulling her away from the road. Jack freed the wheel. He stood up and the woman was in the middle of thanking him when one of the racer cars tore around the corner, sending a wall of air across the seafront. It nearly knocked Jack off his feet and the woman reached out to steady him.

When he walked back to us, I said, 'There's your good deed for the day,' and Jack said, 'It was nothing.' But there was satisfaction drawn into every line on his face.

★　★　★

'Quite the character, our Gabriel Price.'

The man in the music shop stood behind the glass counter, his hands laced together on his chest, as though he had remained there for the entire night, just waiting for us to return.

We all leaned forward a good inch.

'How do you mean?' said Jack.

'Well.' The man's fingers unlaced and laced back again, like a magic trick. 'I'm not one to gossip when someone isn't here to defend themselves. Heaven forbid that any of our own lives should be open to such scrutiny.'

We all said no, no and of course not, and

made reassuring sounds at the backs of our throats.

'He was a bit of a chancer, by all accounts,' the man said.

'He was?' said Elsie.

'Always dabbling in this and that. Spending his time at the racetrack.'

'Are you sure?' I thought of the soft smile and the gentle eyes.

'Oh, quite sure.' The man rested his fists on the counter. 'He's from Whitby, and it's like any other small town. It never lets you forget. There are still people who remember him, I'm sure, although they will be in their later years, of course.'

He smiled an awkward smile, and we all smiled back and made more noises in our throats.

'Do you know where we might find these people who remember him? Or remember what happened to him?' Jack said.

'That's the mystery.' The man shook his head. 'He just vanished a few years after the war. It happens all the time when you're trying to trace someone from the past. People don't leave a trail like they do nowadays. The next generation will have no such problems chasing any of us.' He straightened some leaflets on the counter, which were clearly in no need of a straighten. It appeared to be some kind of shopkeeper code to signal the end of the conversation.

'You could try the library, of course. Plenty of historical information in there.'

We were at the door, and the little bell was

celebrating our departure, when the man spoke again.

'Of course, you might not find him under Price. It was just his stage name.'

'So what was his real name?' Jack turned back to the man, who still had the leaflets in his hand.

'It's strange, really. His real name sounds more like a stage name than the one he changed it to.'

'So what was it?' I could hear the frustration in Jack's voice, although it clearly went over the top of the man's head, because he was more interested in fussing with the leaflets than answering a perfectly simple question.

Eventually, he looked up. 'Honeyman,' he said. 'Gabriel Honeyman.'

# Handy Simon

Handy Simon waited on a crowded pavement for the bridge to close. He always seemed to catch the bridge at the wrong time, and he wondered if the boats held back until they saw him appear on the horizon and then put their foot down. Simon listened to the slow churn of the diesel engines, pushing through the water. Waiting for them to make their way through took an age, and a collection of people gathered around him. There were holiday teenagers, unfastened from parents, toddlers trying to join them and break away from their pushchairs, and Saturday-morning carrier bags, swinging from sunburned hands. The seagulls, free from the constraints of boats and bridges, watched everything from the harbour wall, and shrieked to themselves in amusement. Simon didn't trust seagulls either. His mother once told him they'd take your eye out given half a chance, and he'd been on his guard ever since. He couldn't see anyone he recognised from Cherry Tree. Miss Bissell had put a strong case forward for keeping everyone at the hotel, but in the end, it was decided confinement might cause more problems than it would solve.

'Just be vigilant,' Miss Bissell told them, which was exactly the kind of vague instruction that made Handy Simon nervous.

He looked over the water to where a mirror of people waited on the west side, and he spotted

Miss Ambrose almost immediately. She was deeply involved in her mobile telephone, but every so often, she glanced up and looked confused by nothing in particular. Miss Ambrose always seemed to find him a little job to do, and he was just trying to work out a way of getting across the bridge without bumping into her when she closed her telephone and darted up an alleyway. This meant they would both be on the same side of the harbour, which made Simon pull the straps on his rucksack a little more tightly, and dig his finger into the collar of his shirt, but it couldn't be helped. He had decided how he was going to spend his morning, and he wasn't going to abandon his plans now.

★   ★   ★

The West Pier is the only part of Whitby that feels like it belongs to the tourists. The rest of the town, visitors just borrow for the summer months, trailing up and down the abbey steps and marching all over the beaches. Whitby really belongs to Yorkshire and to maritime. It belongs to the whalers of centuries past and to the fishermen of now, who slide into their boats in the still black of an early morning. It belongs to Captain Cook and the *Endeavour*, and to all those who sail towards a horizon, not knowing what they might face. Unlike other seaside towns, Whitby has not given itself up to the slot machines and the pink candyfloss. The yards and the snickets, and the alleyways, hold on to the footsteps of our ancestors, and somewhere at the point where the cliffs reach out to the North Sea, the past is valued rather than abandoned, and everyone who visits is given a reminder of their own place in history.

Simon drifted down the West Pier. You couldn't really do anything other than drift, because although it was still early, crowds were beginning to build, and everyone seemed to be walking at a holiday pace. The smell of fried onions mixed with the seaweed green of the harbour, and Simon took a very deep breath. Perhaps if he breathed hard enough, he could hold on to the smell and revisit it whenever he wanted to, when his life returned once more to the aroma of Pot Noodles and guttering. He looked at the row of shops as he walked. Between the hot dogs and the ice cream, there were souvenir stalls. Places which specialised in postcards and sticks of rock, and putting your name on things. When Simon was little, everything he owned had his name on it. Pencils and bookmarks and T-shirts, moneyboxes without money and keyrings without keys. Even the door to his bedroom had his name on it, just in case his parents should get confused and accidentally try to sleep in there overnight. He wasn't even sure why he did it, but every time he saw something with Simon written on it, he had to take it home with him. Perhaps it was the only way he could explain to the world who he was. Perhaps at that age, all he had was his name and an idea of who he might become. Simon kicked his shoes on the sandy pavement. Perhaps he was still waiting to find out.

Beyond the souvenir stalls and the arcades, where the concrete turned to boardwalk and the wind tripped away from the sea and argued with the tourists, Simon found what he was looking for. The tent was only small, perhaps six feet square, and draped in red velvet and fringing. There was a blackboard propped up outside:

*Gypsy Rosa*
*World Famous Clairvoyant and Spiritualist*
*to the Stars*
*Speak with the dead and discover your destiny*

Underneath there was a Post-it note Sellotaped to the velvet:

*Gone to Costa Coffee. Back in 15 minutes.*

Simon looked at the line of black-and-white photographs pinned outside. In all of them, Gypsy Rosa was standing next to someone, and in each one, she was wearing the same headscarf and the same expression. The only thing that altered was her arms, which adopted a variety of poses suggesting she had perhaps conjured up these people by magic. Simon wasn't sure who the people were supposed to be. Perhaps they were the stars mentioned on the blackboard, although he didn't really recognise any of them.

'Don't waste your money, mate!' someone shouted from across the pier. Simon wasn't sure who it was, and he didn't feel as though he wanted to turn around. Instead, he walked over to a little wall and sat next to a poster about a jumble sale, whilst he waited for Gypsy Rosa to return with her latte. If Miss Ambrose should spot him — or even worse, Miss Bissell — he could claim a sudden interest in bric-a-brac.

He studied the seagulls to pass the time. One of them was having a fight with a bin bag, and it hammered and battled with the plastic until it found what it wanted. As the gull disappeared across the harbour with its treasure, the rest of the bag coasted across the walkway, and the breeze began to lift and turn the contents. As he watched, a crisp packet broke free and came to a standstill by his feet.

He stared at it.

It was cheese and onion.

# Florence

For a town filled with history, you would expect Whitby's library to be a building with criss-cross windows and crumbling steps. Instead, it's made of concrete and glass, and there are little turnstiles to prevent you running away with all the books.

I got a bit confused in the turnstiles, and Elsie had to come back and help me, and she got confused as well, and in the end we both had to be set free by a member of staff. Jack wandered over to the encyclopaedias, because I think he wanted to keep a distance between himself and all the commotion. When we finally got ourselves inside, I couldn't believe how big it was. Who knew there were so many stories that needed telling? The shelves stretched as far as you could peer, and above our heads was a whole second floor of adventures.

'Where do we even start?' I said.

'Local history,' said Jack, and he disappeared through a gap between the Iron Age and Elizabethan England.

★　★　★

If you were in the mood for a slice of Captain Cook, you'd found the right place. He was everywhere. He covered all of the tables and waited for you inside glass cabinets, and he was even hung on the wall, looking down on everyone to make sure they didn't forget about him.

'Pleasant-looking chap, isn't he?' Elsie stood in front of the portrait. 'Kind eyes.'

'I thought Gabriel Price had kind eyes,' I said. 'It just shows how deceitful eyes can be.'

'Perhaps,' she said. 'We shouldn't judge a person based entirely upon one aspect of their anatomy, though, should we?'

'I'm not ready to judge him at all yet,' I said. 'Not until we've spoken to someone who really knew what kind of man he was.'

Jack turned to us. 'Captain Cook?'

'No.' I might have tutted a bit too loudly, because a couple of people looked up from their microfiches. 'Gabriel Price.'

'Cook was a pioneer.' Jack walked up to the painting. 'A man of courage. Can you imagine how it must have felt to sail from England's coastline and not know what was ahead of you, to not know if there was anyone else out there?'

'I wonder if he was afraid,' Elsie said, and we both looked into the eyes of the painting, to see if there might be a clue. 'Because to be courageous, you must have fear, surely?'

'No one experiences that now,' said Jack. 'We all know too much. Even astronauts are told where they're going.'

'Except death,' I said.

They both stared at me.

'It's the last voyage into the unknown, isn't it?' I said. 'Like Captain Cook setting sail from a harbour. No idea where we're off to, no idea

308

whether there's anyone else out there.'

'And it takes courage, I suppose. To die,' Jack said.

'Every journey takes courage.' Elsie turned away from the painting. 'Even the ones in which we have no choice.'

★ ★ ★

Captain Cook was all over the shelves as well. It was difficult to find anyone else, to be honest, although we did come up with an Anglo-Saxon poet, an abbess called Hilda, and an odd mention here and there of Harry Potter.

'I'm going to watch that film,' said Jack.

'If you've still not got around to it, I doubt you ever will,' I said.

'I will watch Harry Potter before I die,' Jack put the book back on its shelf. 'It's a promise.'

Gabriel Price was nowhere to be found. I checked each shelf and ran my finger along the smooth, polished wood. From time to time, I was held up by an interesting spine, and Elsie had to jolly me along.

'Is there something I can help you with?'

A young man stood in front of us. Tall. Beautiful smile, and his white shirt looked so flawless, it could have just slid out of a cellophane packet and straight on to his body.

'We're looking for someone.' The tip of my finger still rested on one of the shelves.

'He was a musician, called Gabriel Price,' said Jack. 'Disappeared after the Second World War.'

Jack explained. I felt the need to add bits in

from time to time and the man's smile seemed a bit more of a challenge for his face, but eventually, I think we managed to get the point across.

'Oh, that's vintage,' said the man, and he pointed to an iPad.

We sat with the man at a polished wooden table, and I took in a bit of the library. I did it without moving, because I was worried an inch or two either way might bring me in contact with his left thigh. History stretched itself out on the shelves. I tried to find the seams, the places where one piece of time had been stitched to the next, but they were invisible.

'Any luck?' said Jack.

The man laced his hands on the top of his head. 'Nothing.'

'So there isn't anything on your machine about a musician from Whitby called Gabriel Price?' said Jack. 'Or Gabriel Honeyman?'

The man shrugged. 'I can offer you an Anglo-Saxon poet?'

Jack shook his head and we stood to leave.

'How about St Hilda?' the man said.

I pushed the chairs back under the table, because I'd never quite recovered from school, and we made our way to the turnstiles.

'The man who invented the crow's nest,' the man shouted, but Jack just waved with the back of his hand.

We were about to have another go at the turnstiles, and Jack was looking back and being encouraging with his free arm, when I realised there was a man standing there. He was a bit younger than us, I think, but not by much. His clothes had seen better days, and his shoes were all tired and scuffed. He stood very still. I wondered if we were expected to speak first, because sometimes I'm not sure, but then he said, 'I couldn't help but overhear.' He pointed back to where he'd done his overhearing. 'You were asking about Gabriel Price?'

I nodded.

'Do you know him?' I said.

'My mother will have done. My mother knows everything about Whitby history.'

'Your mother?' I said.

'She's in her nineties now. But she's still the full ticket, and she loves any excuse to talk about the past.' He gave us an address. 'Just tell her Francis sent you.'

I watched as he shuffled back to his seat. 'He had very blue eyes, didn't he?'

'He did,' Elsie said.

She looked down at my scarf, and she smiled.

We left all the concrete and the glass, and as we walked back towards the town, herringbone clouds rolled across the sky and the seagulls caught a river of air, plunging and swooping across the harbour. I looked up at the seagulls. I could never make up my mind if they were servants of the air, or the masters of it.

As we walked, I looked down every side street. I checked doorways and alleyways, and stared into shops.

'Whatever are you looking for?' Elsie said.

'Ronnie.' I peered into another side street. 'He's here somewhere, isn't he? He's up to

311

something, and none of us are going to know what it is until it's too late.'

# Handy Simon

When Gypsy Rosa finally returned to her tent, she was balancing a brown paper bag on top of a cardboard coffee and chatting to someone on her mobile telephone. It wasn't an image that sat comfortably alongside a fringed headscarf, but Simon supposed he shouldn't be passing judgement.

When she saw him stand up from his seat on the little wall, she said, 'Got to go,' into the mobile telephone, and she looked at him. It was the same expression as the one in all the black-and-white photographs, and Simon wondered in the absence of Costa Coffee, perhaps he would have been treated to the hand poses as well.

'Are you looking for your fortune?' she asked, over the top of the paper bag.

Simon coughed and shuffled his feet, and checked the coast was clear. He said he supposed he was.

'Ten pounds for fifteen minutes, fifteen for the full half-hour,' said Rosa.

Seeing into the future was definitely more profitable than clearing U-bends.

Rosa asked him his name and arched an over-plucked brow. 'Well, it depends on how interested you are in your destiny, Simon, doesn't it?' she said.

Simon handed over his fifteen pounds, and

Rosa unclipped the clothes peg from the tent and turned the little sign to 'engaged'. Like a toilet, Simon thought. It was so dark and small inside, the first thing he did was crash into a table. He just managed to catch the crystal ball in time, although Rosa said it was fine, because it wasn't breakable and anyway, she'd got a spare in her holdall.

'I always carry an extra. You never know what's going to happen, do you?' she said.

Simon's mouth fell open very slightly.

'It was a joke,' she said. 'Even fortune tellers are allowed to make jokes.' And she took another gulp of her coffee.

Simon sat on the opposite side of the little table. There wasn't enough room for his legs, so they had to go in the gap between Rosa's holdall and an extra deckchair. It smelled musty. A mixture of damp clothing and fish.

'You'll have to excuse the smell,' she said.

He felt a brush of unease.

'It's the velvet. Lets everything in. I was going to opt for tarpaulin, but it's not as ambient, is it?'

Simon shook his head.

'You should smell it when the wind gets up. Some days, it gets so bad, I'm forced into a can of Glade.'

He coughed and tried to very discreetly check his watch.

When he looked up again, Rosa had her hands on the crystal ball, and her eyes tipped back into her head. Her face did a little grimace and she started to sway very slightly in her seat. This went on for quite some time and Simon tried to

314

work out different ways he might be able to check his watch without being spotted, just in case Rosa's eyes happened to tip forward again as he was doing it.

'I see a long journey,' she said eventually. 'Of many miles.'

Simon started to tell her about the M1, but she held her hand up.

'I can't hear the spirits, Simon. You have to let them speak.'

He sat back and chewed at his bottom lip. It took at least ten minutes before Rosa spoke again, if you didn't count the mumbling, and Simon began to wonder whether he was so dull, even the afterlife didn't want to have a conversation with him. But just when he was on the verge of throwing in the towel, she spoke up again.

'Do you,' she swayed with a little more violence, 'know anyone by the name of Ben?'

He shook his head.

Rosa opened one eye. 'Well, do you?' she said.

'I was letting the spirits speak.' Simon shifted in his seat. 'No, I don't think I do.'

'It might be Bob,' said Rosa.

He shook his head again, and then said, 'No,' in a loud voice.

'Something beginning with B.' She cupped her hand to her ear. 'What's that? I can't hear you.'

'I didn't say anything.'

'Not you, Simon. The spirits. The longer someone has been dead, the softer their spirit voice.'

'Like they're further away from you?' he said.

Rosa took a large breath and nodded very energetically. 'Do you know or have you ever known, at any point in your life, anyone whose name starts with the letter B?'

'My mum was called Barbara.'

'That's it!' She said this so loudly, Simon jumped and his leg became tangled in the deckchair. 'It's your mother. It's definitely your mother.'

Simon peered into the darkness. He wondered where his mother might be. Perhaps behind Rosa, although there wasn't a great deal of space, and she was quite a large woman, to be fair. Maybe she was sitting in the spare deckchair. He moved his leg.

'Your mother wants you to know how very much she loves you.'

'She does?' His mother had never found it easy to say she loved anyone when she was alive, although perhaps being dead made you a bit more outspoken.

'Oh, yes. She wants you to know she loves you, and not to worry about anything, because everything is going to work out just fine.'

The character transformation his mother had undertaken was quite extraordinary. Before her death she'd spent most of her time combing through people's lives looking for potential hazards, and if she was unable to find anything, she would invent one just to be on the safe side. The afterlife clearly suited her. Simon frowned. Perhaps she was talking about Mrs Honeyman. Perhaps heaven gave her a view that no one else could see.

316

'Does she say what, exactly, will work out just fine? Can she be a bit more specific?'

'Ah, Simon.' Rosa shook her head. 'We cannot ask of the spirits. We can only take what they're willing to offer.'

'Not even a little bit?' he said.

She opened an eye again. 'No,' she said. 'Although . . .'

Simon leaned forward.

' . . . she keeps saying something about a dog barking. Listen to that dog barking, she's saying.'

'A dog?' said Simon. 'We didn't have a dog.'

'Oh. A cat, perhaps?'

Simon shook his head. His mother didn't like pets. She said they set off her chest.

'And she's gone.' Rosa looked towards the ceiling of the tent. Simon looked too, and thought of a small finger wave, but decided against it.

The stopwatch rang out an alarm on Rosa's iPhone and she took another mouthful of coffee. Simon picked up his rucksack.

'Could I ask you something,' he said. 'Before I go?'

She narrowed her eyes and nodded at the peg. 'As long as it's quick. I don't want to open that flap and find a queue.'

'Dead people. Do they ever leave things for you to find? Little signs, you know? Something to show you they're around?'

'Oh, all the time.' Rosa took an egg and tomato sandwich out of the paper bag. 'Feathers. Keys. Coins. If you haven't found anything, it's only because you're looking in the wrong place.'

'Why do they do it? What are they trying to say?'

'Times of stress, Simon.' She took a bite of the sandwich and a small collection of tomato seeds hurried on to her chin. 'Whenever you're worried or frightened, they'll leave something for you, to show you that you're not alone.'

'I wonder what I'd leave,' he said. 'To show people.'

'Only you can work that one out.' She reached into the bag. 'Oh damn it, they've given me the wrong sodding flavour. I hate these. Do you want them?'

She pulled out a packet of crisps. They were cheese and onion.

★ ★ ★

Simon walked out of the tent and blinked into the sunlight. It felt as if he'd escaped from a parallel universe and it seemed unthinkable that the rest of the world had continued in his absence. His eyes slowly became used to the brightness, and when they finally began to focus he found himself face to face with Miss Ambrose.

'What are you doing here?' he said.

Miss Ambrose studied the jumble sale poster. 'I was thinking of having a look through the bric-a-brac,' she said.

# Miss Ambrose

Anthea Ambrose had spent the morning walking around Whitby's streets. It gave her the chance to search for Mrs Honeyman, or at least feel as though she was doing something constructive.

She had never lost anyone before. There was a small scare a few months ago, when one of the residents inadvertently locked themselves in a cupboard with the hoover, but no one had ever been gone for more than forty-five minutes. Mrs Honeyman was pushing twenty-four hours. To begin with, she thought she'd spotted her quite a few times. It was a mistake, of course. A flash of grey hair, a stopped figure. Someone else. Miss Ambrose never realised just how many old people there were, until she was trying to locate one. The world seemed to be swarming with them. She'd walked all the way around the east side (although she'd drawn the line at climbing up to the abbey), across the bridge, and once more around the West Cliff. She was just about to cross over again, and at least have a peer up the abbey steps, when Miss Bissell rang her mobile telephone and insisted Miss Ambrose gave the Co-op a once-over, because Mrs Honeyman had previous for getting confused in a supermarket. It would have been a perfect little job for Handy Simon, but he seemed to have vanished as well, so she'd spent the next hour walking between canned vegetables and cold meats, until the store manager asked if there was anything they could help her with.

'Not unless you sell old people,' she'd said, and burst into tears.

It was all too much. She felt responsible. The previous evening, Miss Bissell hadn't helped matters by saying she had 'no words', and then spending the next hour and a half managing to find a whole dictionary full of them.

They'd put her in the staff room with a weak tea and a shelf-stacker called Chelsea, who said her mum swore by the medium on the West Pier.

'They bring them in, don't they?' said Chelsea. 'When someone's missing. They're on telly all the time. They give them an item of clothing, and they can smell the missing person and work out where they are.'

'I thought that was German shepherds?' said Miss Ambrose.

But she had still found herself wandering down the boardwalk with Mrs Honeyman's spare cardigan and a packet of Co-op tissues, which is where she finally found Handy Simon holding a bag of cheese and onion crisps.

She glanced at the poster for a coffee morning. 'I was thinking of having a look through the bric-a-brac,' she said. 'What are you doing here?'

Handy Simon looked back at the tent. 'Thought I'd have a laugh, you know.' He tried to laugh, as evidence, but it didn't quite make it.

Miss Ambrose held on to Mrs Honeyman's cardigan. 'Is she any good, do you think?'

Simon looked back at the tent. 'I can't quite make up my mind. She said I shouldn't worry.'

'Are you worried?'

'Perhaps more than I was before someone told me I shouldn't be,' said Simon. 'Are you?'

Miss Ambrose could feel the packet of tissues in her coat pocket. 'I am, Simon. I keep telling people I'm not, but we're supposed to be heading back to Cherry Tree tomorrow. What if she's still missing? We can't just leave her here.'

'I could stay behind. If you think it would help?'

Simon's offer, along with his shabby rucksack and his cheese and onion crisps, somehow made things worse, and Miss Ambrose felt her eyes begin to fill.

'That's very kind of you, Simon.' She took a tissue out of the packet. 'But I don't see how it would help.'

'Are you all right, Miss Ambrose?'

'It's the sea air. All the salt,' she said, blowing her nose. 'It gets me every time.'

Simon offered his arm, and they walked together up the twist of white steps to the crescent and back to the hotel. Past the unfamiliar faces and the crowds of families, all present and unmissing, and slotted neatly into their lives.

# Florence

'It's that one. Right on the end.' Jack pointed, with his finger this time, because the taxi couldn't cope with his walking stick. 'The one with a cat in the window.'

We'd crawled our way along Church Street. It was a tangle of vehicles and tourists. The traffic came to a standstill outside holiday cottages, where visitors loaded and unloaded their lives and wandered into the road as if they had been gifted with some strange kind of holiday immortality, weaving around cars and annoying the seagulls. People stretched out their afternoons on the wooden benches outside pubs, and spent ice-cream hours sitting on walls, watching the boats, because being away from home means you can let go of the clock. You can eat when you're hungry. You can sit because your legs are holiday-tired. You can stare at the view, because there isn't anybody to tell you there are other things to do.

We'd usually stretch out our afternoons as well, but it felt like less of a holiday and more of a game, and I had this funny feeling we were on our last roll of the dice. All through the taxi ride, I could hear Jack breathing through his mouth and Elsie talking to herself. When we finally pulled up outside the address I'm sure the taxi driver felt as relieved as we did.

The house was flat and silent. I could have

sworn there was no one at home. It's odd how you know a house is empty, just by looking at the outside. If there are people in there, it seems to warm a building up. All the laughter and the conversation seems to leak into the bricks. I was wrong, though, because the noise of Jack's walking stick on the front door had only just stopped ringing in my ears, when there was movement behind the bubbled glass, and the sound of someone turning a key.

★　★　★

'Local history?' The woman was so wrinkled, it looked as if her face was trying to fold itself up and disappear. 'Who exactly are you trying to trace?'

She only opened the door a fraction. I would have been the same, mind you. Three strangers standing on your front step with the most unlikely reason for being there.

Jack explained to her. 'We'd be so grateful for anything you can tell us,' he said.

I could see Jack's charm finding its way into the house. It was a gentle charm. A harmless one. You could imagine what he had been like as a young man. A boy whose eyes creased when he smiled, with slightly stooped shoulders and a good heart. A boy who wasn't as symmetrical, as obvious, as the others, but a boy who women would remember in years to come, when their lives became ironed out with middle age. A boy they'd wish they had given a chance to.

'Francis sent us,' I said. 'He has very blue eyes.'

The woman's grip on the door relaxed just a little bit.

'I suppose you'd better come in, then,' she said. 'But don't be thinking you can con me out of anything. I might be old, but I'm not an idiot.'

Jack smiled. 'I wouldn't, dear lady, imagine that for one second.'

And for the first time, she smiled back. 'You can call me Agnes,' she said.

★   ★   ★

The cat was still on the windowsill. It watched us with pencil-point eyes, as we shuffled ourselves around the lounge. It was a fisherman's cottage and the room was very small. Perhaps because people had smaller lives in those days, and they filled their space up with thoughts and conversation, rather than with sideboards and coffee tables. Agnes didn't offer us a drink. She told us that in exactly fifteen minutes, her television programme was starting and she had absolutely no intention of missing it, even if the Queen of England happened to knock on the door. She sat in a dining chair, and refused to be swapped, even when Jack stood up and made a big fuss of pointing out the settee.

'So, who is this man you're trying to trace?'

We told her what we knew. We left Ronnie out, because he always complicated everything, and there didn't seem a reason to bring him into it. I did think about it at one stage, but Elsie shot me a look from the other side of the room and it made me change my mind.

'And why are you so keen to find him?' As Agnes spoke, the cat leaped from the windowsill and landed on her lap. They're so clever, cats. They always seem to know exactly where they want to go, and the easiest way to get there.

'Well?' said Agnes.

Even Jack's charm was thrown. 'We just wanted a chat with him.' The words stumbled out of his mouth. 'There's something we think he could help us with.'

'Is it about money?'

'Oh, gracious no. Nothing like that,' he said.

'Because if it is, I want no part in it.'

I couldn't say for definite, but I thought I heard the cat hiss at the back of its throat.

'I can assure you it's nothing to do with money.' Jack cleared his throat. 'It's more of a personal matter.'

'Because there are plenty of people who'd want a word with Gabriel Honeyman about money,' said Agnes.

'So you knew him?' I said.

'You couldn't live in Whitby in those days and not know him. Especially around the racetracks.'

'He was a gambler?' said Jack.

'The biggest gambler I've ever known.' Agnes stroked the cat's head, and it started to knead its claws into her skirt. 'All the money he made playing that piano, he threw at the horses.'

'So he was poor?' I leaned forward. I was in the kind of armchair that seemed to have straw for stuffing, and it felt a bit like sitting on an upholstered hay bale.

'Perhaps he made a killing and no one knew,' said Jack.

'Win big, lose big. Although whenever Gabriel did win, he'd give it away. He gave money to people he didn't even know, just because they told him some sob story. He'd write all his money-making schemes down on the back of his sheet music. He was famous for it. There were more ideas on there than words to the song. I heard tell one of his investments finally paid up recently. Just a pity he's not around to reap the benefits.'

Jack looked over at us. 'The music shop,' he said. 'That's why Ronnie was so interested. He wanted to check Gabriel hadn't written anything useful on the back of one of his songs.'

I could tell Agnes was taking all this in. She followed the conversation, back and forth, but she didn't comment. 'He was always giving money to strangers and their hare-brained schemes,' she said. 'They won him over so easily. He was one of those people who seemed to walk around advertising what a soft touch they were.'

'He saw the long second.'

Agnes just frowned at me. 'He was a mug,' she said, 'but you couldn't help but like him.'

I was right about Gabriel's eyes being kind, and I spent a good few minutes looking quite smug about it.

'Did he have any brothers?' said Jack. 'Cousins?'

Agnes looked up from the cat. 'Not that I know of. Why?'

'It's just . . . ' Jack hesitated. He looked across at Elsie and me, and we nodded him on. 'There's a Mrs Honeyman. Somewhere.' He picked out his words slowly. 'A little bit younger. And we can't quite work out how they're related.'

Agnes kissed the top of the cat's head. She lifted him up and put him on the floor before she answered.

'That'll just be his wife,' she said.

# Miss Ambrose

'Do you ever hear voices?'

Anthea Ambrose put down her magazine. She hadn't really been reading it, just glancing at the fashion pictures and trying to distract herself. It had worked, because for the last five minutes, she'd found herself seriously considering a jumpsuit.

'Do I ever what?' she said.

'Hear voices. You know. Inside your head.'

They had been sitting together in silence for the past hour. The last time she'd glanced up, Handy Simon was studying the ceiling, but there was clearly more going on in the far corner of the residents' lounge than she had first imagined.

'Are you trying to tell me something, Simon?'

'Oh, no. Not me. I don't hear anything.' He did a little sigh. 'Well, apart from my own voice. But your own voice doesn't count, does it?'

'I don't suppose so. Although I think it would depend very largely on what you happen to be saying to yourself.'

'I was thinking of Gypsy Rosa,' he said. 'Hearing the spirits.'

'If she actually does.'

'She reckoned she could hear my mam. Said she was talking about a dog barking.'

'Did you have a dog?' Miss Ambrose thought about using a head-tilt, but Simon didn't seem upset, just slightly confused. Although, to be fair, Simon's natural expression always looked more than a little bewildered.

'No,' he said. 'They always brought out her chest.'

'Well there you are then. The fortune teller is probably inventing things, just to get your fifteen pounds.' Miss Ambrose cleared her throat. 'Or whatever she charges.'

She reached for her magazine again, but left it just a moment too late.

'Imagine if you did, though. Hear voices, I mean, or see dead people. I wonder what would happen?'

'They'd put you on a section and prescribe antipsychotics, I would imagine.'

'Joan of Arc saw visions of angels,' Simon said. He was on a roll now, she could tell. 'They told her to drive the English out of France.'

'Now there's a surprise.'

'If that happened today, I wonder if they'd give her diazepam and schedule an outpatient's appointment?'

'Religious visions are different though, aren't they? History is filled with people who saw God and angels, and whatnot. They weren't psychotic, they were just devout.'

'What's the difference, though?' Handy Simon shifted his gaze from the ceiling and looked straight at her. 'When does somebody stop being religious or psychic, and start being mentally ill?'

'Simon, you ask the strangest questions. I have absolutely no idea.' Miss Ambrose picked up her magazine, but she didn't read it. Instead, she

329

stared out of the window and tried to find an opinion for herself.

# Florence

'He had a wife?' Jack's voice was a bit louder, and this time I really did hear the cat hiss.

'Only briefly,' said Agnes. 'And only by necessity. He got her in the family way before they were wed, by all accounts. The whole marriage was kept under wraps. Those days were very different.'

'We're not that much younger than you,' Jack said.

'When you get older, the years become heavier, though, don't you think?' The cat prowled and twisted its tail around her ankles. 'Some decades weigh more than others.'

Jack thought for a moment and then agreed with her.

'She was a bit of a one, his wife. Liked a drink. Liked a party.'

'That doesn't sound like Mrs Honeyman,' I said.

'It doesn't sound like any of us,' said Elsie. 'Although it must have been some of us. At one point.'

'Miss Ambrose told us Mrs Honeyman didn't have any family,' I said. 'Don't you remember?'

I was quite proud of myself, and when I looked over at Elsie, her eyebrows were filled with surprise.

'Our Mrs Honeyman doesn't have any children,' Jack explained, 'so it can't be her.'

331

'In the end, Gabriel's wife didn't either. She lost it. Fell on the abbey steps.' Agnes watched the street through lace curtains. 'Dreadful business. They had a little memorial service at Saltwick Bay. Very unusual in those days. They normally wrapped the baby in brown paper and took it away. I don't think she ever recovered. In her mind, you know?'

Mrs Honeyman. The woman from number four. Round face. Never speaks. Not very good with stairs. For a few minutes, none of us spoke.

'So what happened to Gabriel?' said Jack.

Agnes sat back and her gaze returned to the window. 'Vanished,' she said. 'Not long after they were married. She lost the baby, and he just disappeared on one of his tours. Never came back.'

'What happened?' said Elsie.

'Did he never come back?' I thought of the man with the gentle eyes. 'No one ever heard from him again?'

'He never came back,' she said. 'People thought he must have had a big win on the horses, or met another girl in another town.'

'And what do you think?' said Jack.

'Gabriel Honeyman might have been a fool and a gambler, but he wasn't a bad man. He may have disappeared, but I don't for one second think he had any choice in the matter.'

The room waited for us in silence, but no one spoke. The only sound was the cat, washing at its paws. I looked at Jack, but he didn't look back.

'What did the police say?' I was getting quite

good at ignoring silences, but I couldn't stand this one.

'That he was a grown man,' said Agnes. 'That it was his decision.'

'I wonder,' Jack said, but his wondering didn't find itself any words.

Agnes looked at each of us in turn. 'Is there some other part of the puzzle I've yet to hear?'

'Nothing we can prove. Some things sit so far back in time, it's impossible to see them clearly any more.' Jack picked up his cap and his walking stick. 'I don't suppose you've ever heard of a Ronnie Butler?'

Agnes said the name back and shook her head. 'No. I can't say as I have.'

'Just a shot in the dark.' Jack moved towards the door, although the room was so small, he didn't really have to move very far. 'We'd probably better leave you in peace to your television programme.'

I stood up as well, but I must have done it a bit too quickly because I felt the room sway to one side, and all the blood rush from my head. I reached out for the back of a chair.

'Are you all right, Florence?' said Jack.

'Sit down again,' Agnes said. 'Before you fall.'

I said that I was fine, absolutely fine. I let go of the chair, but I knew I was as pale as paper, even without looking at myself. 'I just stood too quickly,' I said. 'And I can't stop thinking about Mrs Honeyman losing her baby. I can't imagine anything more awful.'

Agnes shook her head. 'I don't think there can be,' she said. 'My Frankie went missing when he was little, and it was the worst few hours of my life. Thank God someone kept him safe until I found him again.'

I looked back at the room. The photographs on the mantelpiece. Weddings, grandchildren, holidays. All those moments of happiness, held behind glass, like treasure. Elsie seemed to know I was looking because she turned back when she got to the door. And we smiled at each other, over the ticking of a mantelpiece clock.

# Handy Simon

'I'm not sure this is a good idea.' Handy Simon looked through the box of cassettes. They were all people he'd never heard of. *Sing-Along-a-Wartime*, one of them said. *Twenty Songs That Made Britain Great*. 'It feels too much like a celebration.'

'It's not a celebration.' Anthea Ambrose was up a stepladder with a string of bunting. 'It's called carrying on as normal. Old people like routine. It makes them feel safe.' She wobbled on the ladder and held on to a pelmet for support. 'I did it. On a course.'

Handy Simon didn't say anything, because he was certain he'd ended up in Miss Ambrose's notebook over the Joan of Arc conversation, but he wasn't entirely sure what normal was any more. He didn't think it would ever be possible to feel homesick for Cherry Tree, but he felt as though he actually wanted to be back there in the staff room with his Pot Noodle, and not a glimpse of a seagull in sight.

'Does Miss Bissell think it's a good idea?' said Simon.

Miss Ambrose drove a drawing pin very violently into the wallpaper. 'The hotel always has a dance on a Saturday night, so we might as well make the most of it. Who knows, Simon, you might actually enjoy yourself.'

It was something his mother always used to

335

say to him when he was younger. 'Who knows, Simon, you might like it if you give it a try.' He didn't, usually. Like it. He'd tried lots of things. Spanish guitar. Judo. Chess. Once, he spent a whole afternoon trying to get on a horse, but the horse was having none of it. His father suggested rugby, but just being in the changing room made him clammy. 'Bell-ringing?' said his mother, but Simon just shook his head. Nothing he had a go at seemed to fit. Life sometimes felt like trying on the entire contents of a shoe shop, but all of them pinched your toes.

'Perhaps I'm just not good at anything,' he said to his mother. 'Perhaps I'm not a hobby person.'

'Nonsense. Everyone is good at something. You just haven't found yourself yet.'

She died whilst he was still searching.

Simon put the cassette back.

'Unless . . . ' He sniffled the air and did a little finger wave at the ceiling.

'Did you say something, Simon?' Miss Ambrose looked down from her stepladder. 'Only if you didn't, make yourself useful and pass me the end of that Union Jack.'

★   ★   ★

The room looked quite pleasant when it was finished. Someone had pushed all the furniture back to make a dance floor, and there was a drinks table set up at the far end. Miss Ambrose's bunting stretched all the way around the room, except for a small gap in the corner due to an oversize painting of the Princess of Wales. Simon and Miss Ambrose both stood with their hands on their hips, admiring their efforts.

'Shame about Diana.' Miss Ambrose looked over at the corner.

'I could get the Sellotape,' said Simon.

Miss Ambrose stared at him. 'I meant passing away so young.'

'Oh. Right. Yes. Although.' Simon hesitated, but once he'd grown a thought, he felt it was wrong to let it go to waste. 'There isn't really a good age to die, is there?'

Miss Ambrose folded her arms. 'I'm not sure,' she said. 'I think I'll be ready for it, when I'm old.'

'But when you're old, you probably won't agree. You'll probably feel just like you do now.'

Simon wondered if he should have shared that particular thought, because he saw fear sail through Miss Ambrose's eyes.

'You might not, though,' he said. 'You might be completely up for it.'

An edge of bunting escaped from its drawing pin and floated on to the windowsill.

'Pin that back up,' said Miss Ambrose. 'I'm going for a snowball and a lie-down.'

\* \* \*

Simon tested the stepladder. You could never be too careful, especially on holiday. After he'd pushed it a few times for good measure, he made his way to the top and reached over for the

337

bunting. That's when he saw them. Sitting on one of the benches on the promenade, looking out across the sand. They were having some kind of animated discussion and every so often, Jack waved his arms about and pointed towards the North Sea.

Simon tried to remember where he'd put his notebook.

# Florence

'Terrible way to die. Drowning,' Elsie said.

I looked at her.

'I would imagine it's terrible,' she added. 'Although I suppose it might be quite peaceful. Once you've accepted it.'

'Every death is peaceful, according to the local newspaper.' I tightened the belt on my coat. I had to listen very hard to hear Elsie's voice, because the wind skated across the water and stole it away. 'But I don't see how any death can be peaceful. Although I don't suppose you really know until you get there. It's not as though we've got anyone to ask.'

Elsie sighed. 'Perhaps that's just as well.'

'It must have been Gabriel Price who drowned and not Ronnie. Yet I was so certain.' My scarf was wound tight around my chin, and when I spoke, I could feel all the warm air fall back into my face. When I looked up, Elsie was staring at me. 'We all were,' I said.

Jack had gone to get us a takeaway tea from one of the kiosks. I'd watched him walk across the grass. I wasn't sure if it was the light, or if it was the visit to the fisherman's cottage, but he'd looked smaller somehow. Not as significant. As though he was taking up so much less space in the world.

'I'd quite like to go in my sleep,' I said. 'The woman from number sixteen died in her

339

sleep. She did very well.'

'You make it sound as though she should be awarded some kind of certificate.'

'Just to close your eyes, to do what you do every night, but the next time you open them, it's all done and dusted. I think that's what I'd plump for.'

'It's not a travel agent's, Florence. We're not choosing a holiday.'

We sat in silence for a while, and watched the sea. The tide had gone out, and it left behind fresh sand, smooth and unspoiled. It always amazed me to see that happen. How a wash of the ocean took away a day's worth of footsteps and conversations, and arguments. How it made everything new again. When I was a child, I liked to walk the unmarked sand with Seth. He would bark his lopsided bark at the waves and we would make the first footprints on the beach, but then I would look behind and feel sad that I had broken it, but my father would laugh at me and say, 'How do you think sand is made in the first place?' I wondered if Seth's footprints were still there, somewhere underneath all those days of other people.

★ ★ ★

The bench was cold and hard, and unkind to old bones. The wind was getting up too, and the waves made knots of white, flickering in the distance as we watched. Below us, a woman walked along the beach with her dog. I tried to think what breed it might be. It was one of those excitable, energetic dogs that crash through the waves with no fear, chasing sticks and finding joy in the unlikeliest of places.

'Try to think, Florence,' Elsie said. 'What kind of dog is it?'

I followed the marks they made in the sand.

'It's not a Labrador,' I said. 'Or a Dalmatian. I can tell you all the things it's not. I just can't decide exactly what it is. Perhaps we could do that and just see what's left?'

'It's a Border collie, Florence. Do you think you can remember that?'

'I think so,' I said. 'You know, the only problem with dying in your sleep is that you die alone.'

'You're never alone, Florence,' she said. 'Just because you can't see someone, doesn't mean they're not there with you.'

I looked at her, but Elsie's gaze rested on the sea.

'Milk, no sugar.' Jack handed me a cardboard cup. It had a little corrugated waistband and a lid.

'Put your hands around it, keep yourself warm.' Jack sat at the end of the bench. This seat wasn't dedicated to anyone. I checked before we choose it. Perhaps they made sure there were spares, in case they thought of someone who needed remembering right at the last moment.

I wrapped my fingers around the cardboard. 'It's strange Mrs Honeyman didn't say anything. About someone turning up with her husband's name.'

'Mrs Honeyman slept through most things,'

341

Jack said. 'And when she wasn't sleeping, she was in a little world of her own.'

Elsie said, 'Best place to be, if you ask me,' and sniffed away the cold air.

'And I don't suppose she'd think anything of it.' Jack swallowed a mouthful of tea. 'Someone turns up with a name your husband used occasionally. A husband who disappeared sixty years ago. In a different place and a different time.'

'Who looked nothing like him,' I said.

The woman and her dog were far in the distance now. Little specks of people, like biscuit crumbs near the pier. I thought I could still spot her, but I might have been wrong.

Jack rested his tea on the arm of the seat. 'What are you thinking about, Florence?'

'Do you think,' I said, 'we could go for a walk on the beach?'

★ ★ ★

Sand is surprisingly difficult to walk on. You wouldn't think so, would you? From a distance, it looks like it would be a piece of cake, but once you're there, your legs become heavy and tired so much more quickly and it doesn't take many minutes before each step feels like an enormous achievement.

Jack didn't last very long before he found a rock to lean on.

'I think I'll stay here for a bit.' He waved his stick about. 'You carry on, if you want to.'

I was a little ahead of Elsie. I made slow,

342

deliberate footprints, and every few minutes, I looked behind me and checked on them, and made sure she was still following.

'Whatever are you doing?' she shouted, but the sea stole her words again and carried them away. As I walked, I watched the waves. The tide had changed and it pulled at the beach, as if the water was trying to persuade the sand to go along with something. Each time a little closer, a little more successful. It must be an instinct that makes us always stare at the ocean. Perhaps because we realise how important it is, and so we need to keep an eye on it to make sure it hasn't left.

I stopped to look at my footprints again, and Elsie caught up.

'Aren't you tired?' she said, but I said, no, no, I'm fine. I want to keep walking, I told her. To make more footprints.

She asked why, but I carried on further up the beach, and she shouted, 'Why do you keep marching off, Flo? What's got into you?'

If we'd stopped to think when we were younger, that one day we would be back here, stooped and grey, if we'd given a moment to think how we would struggle against the wind to stay upright, and how our feet would feel afraid and uncertain; perhaps, then, we would have taken a little more time over things. We would have enjoyed the soft, easy days of childhood a little more. Arms and legs full of confidence and energy. Minds free from hesitation. Perhaps we would have danced through our youth a little more slowly.

It was cold on the sand, much more so than on the cliff-top, and I fastened the top button of my coat. Elsie saw me do it. 'It's freezing, Florence,' she called out. 'We need to go back.'

'You should have worn your scarf,' I shouted back. 'The one Gwen knitted for you. The red one.'

I slowed down.

I could feel a memory making a path from the back of my mind, trying to find its way. I wasn't even sure what it was at first, but I knew it was important. It was like waking in the morning knowing a terrible thing happened the day before, but at first, you can't quite reach the thought and work out what it is. I knew it would only be a moment before it arrived. Before everything was changed.

When it did, I realised I had stopped walking and I was staring at the sand. I turned to look at Elsie; we were both still. Just the breeze, catching the edge of a coat, a strand of hair.

She moved towards me.

I said nothing. I pushed my hands into my pockets and looked for clues on her face, because when the memory appeared, it brought all the others along with it.

'It was you,' I said.

She didn't reply.

'It was you,' I said again. 'You were in the car with Ronnie that night. The red. The red that Mabel saw. It was your scarf.'

'Yes, it was my scarf,' she said.

The air was cruel and salted. It made my eyes and my lips smart. It buried itself into my skin, and filled my mouth with the taste of nothing else.

'Why didn't you admit it? Why didn't you say anything?'

'We said everything we had to say back then. We talked about nothing else for days.'

'Did we? I don't remember. I don't remember any of this.'

'You've just forgotten, Florence, that's all.'

'Remind me, then. Help me to remember, like you always do.'

She hesitated and her face searched for an explanation.

'My mother,' she said eventually. 'Ronnie threatened to report her. Don't you remember?'

I shook my head.

'He said he'd shop her to the authorities if anyone went to the police. Get her sent to an asylum if we ever whispered a word about how Beryl died. We decided, the two of us,' she said. 'No one could help Beryl any more, so we protected my mother instead. She wouldn't have lasted a minute locked away. It would have ended her.'

I looked at her across the sand, trying to find the words I needed. 'He wouldn't have been able to do that. How could Ronnie have got your mother committed?'

'Florence, everyone knew she'd lost her mind. Everyone. But people turned a blind eye. If Ronnie reported her for the assault, and made it official, they would have had to do something. The people at the hospital were suspicious enough already with the injuries he had.'

345

'But you let him get away with it,' I said. 'He should have been punished.'

'Our word against his, you mean? You know what kind of places asylums were then. Filled with stink and misery. It was the right decision. It kept her with us, it kept her safe.'

'How could you watch your own sister killed and keep quiet about it? How could you?'

'I couldn't lose them both,' she shouted. 'If I'd opened my mouth, I would have sacrificed my mother as well.'

We stood in silence, and the wind disappeared across the water, leaving us in a pocket of quiet.

'I need you to find a forgiveness,' she said. 'And when you do, I need you to hold on to it, no matter what happens.'

'I can't remember any of this. Why do I always need you to remind me who I was?'

She started to answer, but the words disappeared back into her throat. Instead, she said, 'What do you remember?'

'I remember being at the dance,' I said. 'I remember the music, but we stopped listening to it.'

'Why? Why did we stop?'

I tried to find my way back. 'Because we were watching Beryl and Ronnie. They were arguing in the car park, and we were trying to listen through the glass.'

'And?'

'She stormed off. Beryl. Didn't she? Off into the night.'

She nodded.

I turned to Elsie. 'And I decided to go after her.'

'I tried to stop you. I said it wasn't your place to go.'

'We were in the cloakroom. You said I'd freeze to death out there, but I wrapped myself up and I told you I'd be fine.'

'You did.' Elsie's voice was a whisper, and it slipped into the sound of the sea and disappeared.

'I can't remember any more,' I said. 'You must have got into his car whilst I was out looking for her. You must have been the one who hammered on the car window and persuaded Ronnie to let you inside, thinking you'd find Beryl more quickly if you got Ronnie to take you.'

Elsie creased her eyes against the salt and the wind.

'He would have had a drink, wouldn't he?' I said. 'Careless, angry. Fast. Casual hands resting too lightly on the wheel. Eyes on the argument instead of the road. You would have said, 'Watch what you're doing, you'll get us both killed,' but he'd have been too busy spitting out hate to take any notice. When you looked up and saw Beryl standing in the road, you'd have reached for the steering wheel. I know you'd have tried to swerve the car, because Ronnie hadn't even seen her. I know you tried to save her, Elsie. I know you did.'

The words made me shake and I didn't really know why.

'The noise,' I said. 'It was the noise you couldn't forget. I remember you telling me.'

'You do?' she said.

'Afterwards,' I said. 'All of us in your kitchen. You, me and Ronnie, building the story between us, piece by piece. We were at the table, trying to work out what to do.' I looked at her. 'The scarf was there too, sitting in the middle. I could see where Gwen had dropped a stitch and rescued it again. Row after row of flawless work. You could only spot the mistakes if you knew where to look, but once you knew, it felt as though you would never be able to see anything else.'

'You don't have to remember, Florence. Some things are better left still.'

'Oh, but I do.' The memories were tumbling around, and I tried to catch them, before they all disappeared again. 'You told me Ronnie stopped the car further up the road, he ran back to where Beryl lay on the verge. You stayed in the car. You couldn't face it. It was fine, though, to stay in the car. It doesn't make you any less of a person, does it?'

'No, Florence. No it doesn't,' Elsie said.

'The road was straight and measured. When you looked back, Ronnie was in the distance, caught in a smear of light from a winter moon. She's gone. She's definitely gone. That's what Ronnie said, when he got back in the car. You would have found a phone box, otherwise. You would never have let her down if there was still a chance. You would have called an ambulance. The police.'

'Ronnie never would have allowed that,' Elsie said.

'And when Ronnie got back to the car, the

348

lights of another vehicle stopped in the distance. Beryl had been found, and you both watched from the back window as someone crouched by the side of the road.

'And Ronnie took off the handbrake and moved away. He didn't switch on the engine. He didn't turn on the lights.

'I knew then,' I said. 'I knew he had no intention of telling anyone. No matter what we did.'

'You fought him, Florence. You put up a good fight.'

'How do you know?'

Elsie watched me across the sand. 'Because I can still see the battle on your face,' she said.

'It wasn't too late. Even then, when we sat in your kitchen, we could have told the police. Explained to them. They would have understood it was the shock. No one did anything because of the shock.'

'And that's when Ronnie threatened us. He said he'd make sure my mother was locked away forever.' Elsie turned away and watched the ocean. 'I remember looking at the ceiling when he said it. My mother was fixated on the idea that people were listening to her through the walls, that there were microphones and cameras hidden all around the house, and she had pulled away at the plaster with her bare hands to try and prove it to us. Do you remember?'

I nodded.

'How easy it would have been to let her go and be free again. How very simple it would have been to walk through the door Ronnie had just opened. It was so obvious, so easy, but I couldn't bring myself to do it.'

'No,' I said.

We looked at each other, and I knew it was exactly the same way we'd looked at each other before, sixty years earlier. As if the person you thought you were had fallen away right in front of your eyes. We'd agreed then, never to talk of it. To tissue-paper it away in the past and never take it out. Yet here they were, exactly the same words, waiting in the air for sixty years, waiting for the chance to be spoken again.

The sun had fallen towards the horizon as we talked, and the day disappeared from the sky, and was out of reach. The light was so frail, so weak, I could barely see Elsie's face as I spoke.

'You mustn't blame yourself,' I said. 'It wasn't your fault. You did what you thought was right.'

'You forgive me?' she said.

'Of course I do. I will always forgive you.'

She reached out her hand, and I reached back, and it felt as though we'd been carrying around a piece of the past for all this time, and we'd finally found a place to put it.

'I just wish I could find the rest of the memories,' I said. 'It still feels as though things are missing.'

'If you ever do . . . ' Elsie hesitated. 'Just remember you forgave me.' Her voice knitted into the wind. 'Remember you said I wasn't to blame.'

'What do you mean?'

She waited before she spoke, and when she finally did, I could barely hear her. 'If you ever open a drawer, Florence. If you ever open a drawer and find something there you weren't expecting, just remember there is so very much more to us than the worst thing we have ever done. Remember that, Florence. Please remember, even when I'm not here to remind you.'

We stood together in the silence, and all I could hear was my breathing. It seemed an age. A lifetime. An eternity before we began to walk back, hand in hand. Our hands were older now. The skin was livered and loosened, and the bones pressed into our flesh, but her hand still fitted into mine, just like it always did. I could feel its strength, and I squeezed, to make sure that she could feel it too.

'You'll be fine,' Elsie said. 'You'll be just fine.'

# Handy Simon

Handy Simon looked up at the glitter ball. It was quite hypnotic once you started staring at it. Soothing, almost. As if looking at the world through all its little mirrors made everything seem small and less important.

'Are you going to watch that all evening?'

Miss Ambrose had returned from her nap and was marching between the kitchens and the buffet table with a wide selection of finger food. She had marks on her cheek where the pillow had pressed itself into her thoughts.

'And if you wouldn't mind troubling yourself, there's a Black Forest thawing out on the side.'

Simon went through to the kitchen. Gail with an i was standing by a stainless-steel surface with a face like thunder.

'I'm not used to all this to-ing and fro-ing,' she said. 'I hope your hands are clean — we don't want environmental health back again.'

'Again?' said Simon.

'We're all trying to move on,' said Gail. 'And watch what you're doing with that cake slice.'

Simon wiped his hands on the front of his trousers. When he got back to the ballroom, the entertainment had arrived. His name was Lionel, and his shirt had its own set of ruffles, which ran from the knot in his velvet bow tie all the way down in parallel lines, until they disappeared themselves into his cummerbund.

'Welcome, welcome,' said Lionel.

Simon balanced the gateau on a trestle table. 'Oh no,' he said. 'I'm only staff.'

'No one is 'only' anything, young man.' Lionel's eyes opened very wide. 'Do you not dance?'

'No. I don't think so. I don't know.' Simon looked up at the tiny mirrors in the glitter ball.

'Everyone can dance. Everyone. You just need to find the right song.' Lionel waved a little baton through the air in a figure of eight.

Simon watched the baton. 'Is there an orchestra?'

'Cassettes, young man, cassettes.' Lionel made the word sound interesting and Italian.

'Tapes,' said Miss Ambrose, as she walked past.

'But even cassettes need a leader.' Lionel did another flourish. 'And dancers need to know when to whisk and when to chassé.'

'To what?' said Simon.

'Watch me.' Lionel pointed at his shoes, which shone with such enthusiasm, the entire world appeared to be reflected back in them. He did a little manoeuvre across the floor and then pointed at Simon. 'Now you try it,' he said.

Simon did. It was surprisingly easy.

'Now this one,' said Lionel. 'Now, put them both together.'

It was odd, but Simon felt as though his feet knew exactly what they should be doing. Usually, his limbs waited for instructions from his brain, and his brain could very rarely make up its mind about things, but for some reason, a whisk and a chassé made complete sense to him.

'See,' said Lionel, clapping his hands. 'You're a natural.'

Simon grinned at him, and realised he was still holding the cake slice.

'If you wouldn't mind,' said Miss Ambrose, taking it from his hand, 'there are some Ritz crackers over there just shouting out for a tube of Primula.'

# Florence

We got back to the hotel, and after the central heating had warmed up our faces, Elsie and I got ready for the dance just like we used to. We held clothes up to choose, and lent each other jewellery, and did everything we could to make a space between ourselves and the conversation on the beach. When we closed the bedroom door, Jack was waiting for us on the landing.

'I thought we'd go down together,' he said, and offered his arm. 'Ladies should never enter a ballroom unaccompanied.'

I put my arm through his, and the three of us slipped into the room with the music and a glitter ball, back into a world so far in the past, we had almost forgotten it existed.

★　★　★

There is a certain magic about a dance floor, even if no one is dancing. Perhaps it's the smell of polished wood, or the beat of an orchestra, or perhaps it's the remembrance of dances past. The memory of circling a room in shoes that pinched our toes but made us happy. Listening to music that wrapped itself around buried thoughts and made us feel less alone.

'There's a food table,' said Elsie. 'And free drinks. We never had that at the town hall.'

I looked over to where Miss Ambrose was supervising a tray of egg sandwiches. They were crustless, because sometimes in life, it's better to anticipate problems and address them head-on, rather than wait for them to appear. Next to the sandwiches and Miss Ambrose, and shrouded in the darkness of a corner, Ronnie Butler stood with his hands behind his back, watching the rest of the room walk past.

'Why now?' Jack said, his words under cover of the music. 'Why risk a lifetime of hiding to come back now?'

I stood beneath a spotlight. I was certain Ronnie could see me, but I'd reached a point where it didn't seem to matter any more. I lost him occasionally, as the room began to fill with people and couples made their way to the dance floor, but he was always there, behind the crowd. Staring across the years.

'It must have been that young man saving him from being mugged. He hid away for all those years, and then out of the blue, he was on the front page of all the newspapers,' I said. 'He must have been afraid someone would recognise him for who he really was, and the past would catch up with him. So he thought he'd catch up with us first.'

'I think that's what you call a grave mistake,' said Jack.

★   ★   ★

We found a seat at the other side of the room and watched with plates of sandwiches on our knees as the world circled by in tangos and waltzes.

'I remember all the steps,' said Elsie. 'Do you remember them, Florence?'

I did. It was strange how some things are never forgotten. Even though my feet had walked tens of thousands of miles, pulling me through the last eighty-odd years of my life. Even though they had become slower and more measured, and they faltered as time passed by, my feet hadn't ever forgotten who I used to be. Even if my mind sometimes did.

There were people I didn't recognise on the dance floor, strangers from other hotels who had jumped ship for an evening, locals who came just for the dancing, and mixed amongst them were all the residents of Cherry Tree, waltzing their way back to a life once lived. Handy Simon was in the thick of it, promenading and side-by-siding like a natural. Men were in short supply as it was, let alone young men, and no sooner had he finished one dance than he was being whisked away by someone else for the next.

'Are you not dancing, Florence?' Miss Ambrose crouched beside us. She always believed getting on the same level as other people was important, although in reality, it just gave everyone else a panoramic view of her cleavage.

'I'd take you round the dance floor, but I'm afraid those days are long gone.' Jack tapped his stick very gently on the floor.

'I could always recruit Billy bloody Elliot over there.' Miss Ambrose nodded at Handy Simon.

357

'It looks as though he's finally found something he enjoys doing.'

'I'm fine as I am, thank you.' I held on to the plate of egg sandwiches. 'It's important in life to know when to sit a dance out.'

Elsie was looking at me. I could tell by the angle of her head, although I refused to turn round. When Miss Ambrose had disappeared to crouch in front of someone else, and Jack had gone to refill his plate, she whispered in my ear.

'Will you dance with me, Florence? For old times' sake? For all we know, this may be our very last chance.'

As she spoke, the little man on the stage waved his baton at the cassette player, and the first few bars of a song drifted into the room.

'See!' said Elsie. 'It's Al Bowlly. It's fate. Just one more dance, Florence. One more foxtrot.'

We hadn't danced together since Beryl died. We lost each other somehow after that, and things were never the same. I danced with other people, of course, but it wasn't like dancing with Elsie. Now we were together again, it felt as though the orchestra had only paused for a moment before starting the next song. As though the whole of the rest of our lives had been spirited away.

Her shoulders felt more frail. I could feel the bones of her, pressing into flesh, and she was lighter, less sturdy. The slightest breeze could have stolen her away. But as we danced, these things seemed to become less important. She was familiar. Constant. She was Elsie. The person she had always been.

358

We shuffled around the floor, rather than danced. I'm not sure if it was Elsie or if it was me, but perhaps neither of us moved with the same amount of certainty. Elsie sang as she danced, and I sang, too.

*I'll be remembering you, whatever else I do,*
*Midnight, with the stars and you.*

Because sometimes, you need to sing and dance. Even if you are eighty-four. Even if your bones push into your flesh, and the slightest breeze could steal you away.

The other dancers seemed to move back, and when Al Bowlly's voice finally drifted into the distance, Elsie and I were standing alone in the middle of the floor. I could see Miss Bissell and Miss Ambrose staring at us; Handy Simon, too. And Jack, who had risen from his seat and was looking right into my eyes. I didn't care. I didn't care how strange it might look that two women were dancing together, and I didn't care that we sang as we danced. I was about to tell everyone who was passing judgement on us how very much I didn't care, when the double doors opened at the bottom of the room, and a woman stood in front of us looking confused and dishevelled, and ever so slightly bewildered.

It was Mrs Honeyman.

# Handy Simon

'She hasn't said a word.' Miss Ambrose had a telephone in one hand and the side of her head in the other. 'Not a word. The police think she's in shock.'

Handy Simon peeped through the gap in the door. Mrs Honeyman was sitting on a giant armchair in the staff room. Or perhaps the armchair wasn't giant at all, but Mrs Honeyman had shrunk at some point during the last twenty-four hours.

'Where has she been?' Simon peeped a little more. 'What's she been doing?'

'No one knows, Simon.' Miss Ambrose gave him the kind of look usually conjured up by Miss Bissell. 'That's the whole point. Each time we ask her, she just stares at us in silence.'

'Should we ring for a doctor?'

Miss Ambrose pointed at the telephone and blew out her cheeks.

To avoid any further eyebrow-lifting and cheek-blowing, Simon wandered towards the noticeboard and read about checking-out times and spare pillows. He was never very good in a crisis. Perhaps because his father was usually there, and he appeared to have a natural affinity for it. Simon usually hung around at the edges, swinging his arms slightly and occasionally bending his knees, to distinguish himself from the furniture.

360

Despite being told to remain in the ballroom, a small group of Cherry Tree escapees appeared in reception, led (of course) by Florence Claybourne, and they gathered around Miss Ambrose in a pool of curiosity.

'I don't know any more than you do,' he could hear Miss Ambrose shout over their heads. 'She is, but she isn't saying anything.' And 'No, you can't go in there.'

'But she must have given you some clue?' Florence's voice rose above the rest, as they followed Miss Ambrose and her telephone around the hall. 'She must have said something?'

'Nothing. Now if you'll excuse me, I'm just trying to get hold of a — yes, hello!'

Miss Ambrose faced into the flocked wallpaper, and the group turned their attentions to Simon, like cheetahs on the Serengeti.

'Don't look at me,' he said. 'I probably know even less than you do.'

★　★　★

When the doctor arrived he was ushered into the room with the giant armchair. Simon tried to walk in behind him, but Miss Bissell shut the door with such a thud, it sent Simon three steps backwards and straight into Miss Ambrose, who appeared to be attempting the same tactic.

'It's just a precaution,' said Miss Ambrose, after she'd restored her balance. 'She looks absolutely fine to me.'

'Absolutely fine,' repeated Simon, although according to his father, his mother had also

361

looked absolutely fine until just before her heart attack. She'd even made her selection from the drinks trolley and inflated a neck cushion.

'We'll wait here. Best not to overwhelm her.' Miss Ambrose took over looking at the spare-pillows notice, and Simon had to find something else to occupy his eyes. In the end, he settled on the kitchen door. Panelled. Scuffed around the edges. Looked through every few minutes by the woman who owned the hotel.

'Will your party be requiring anything else?' Gail said. 'Light refreshments? The rest of the Yorkshire Constabulary? Armed bodyguards, perhaps?'

Miss Ambrose shook her head and Simon stared at the floor. There was a constant parade of Cherry Tree residents up and down the stairs, on the pretext of picking up a leaflet from the reception desk, or making sure they knew how to order spare pillows. Miss Claybourne had been down at least four times and from where he sat, Simon could see Jack waiting for her on the landing. After what seemed like a lifetime, the doctor finally left, and Miss Ambrose stood in reception with her hands on her hips. They were taking Mrs Honeyman to the cottage hospital for a few days. Just as a precaution. Although she still hadn't told anyone where she'd been. Miss Bissell declared herself officially at the end of her tether and went off in search of a lie-down and a small bottle of brandy.

'Perhaps we should all try and get some rest,' said Miss Ambrose. 'We're back to Cherry Tree tomorrow evening, and it won't be an easy journey.'

Simon agreed by standing up. He tried to find some words, but so many had been thrown around during the course of the evening, he didn't seem to have any left. Perhaps it wasn't only Mrs Honeyman who had been shocked into silence. As he started to climb the stairs, Simon looked up at the landing. He couldn't be certain, but he was fairly sure he spotted Miss Claybourne's lace-ups and the edge of a walking stick just disappearing out of view.

# Florence

'Where's the cottage hospital?'

We sat opposite Jack and two scrambled eggs. He'd been pushing them around his plate for the last half an hour.

'Near the library,' said Jack. 'I spotted it yesterday when we were getting in the taxi.'

'Do you think they'll let us in?' I said. 'Perhaps she'll have a policeman sitting outside her room.'

'She's not a criminal,' said Elsie. 'Or a pop star.'

'If she wants to see us,' said Jack. He gave up on the eggs and edged the plate away.

I looked over to where Ronnie sat in the corner of the dining room. He wasn't eating breakfast, either. Instead, he watched us all over a pot of coffee. There was a smile hidden in his eyes, a flicker of victory. I was in a mind for going over there, but Elsie made me sit down again.

'Don't aggravate things, Florence.' Elsie pulled at my arm. 'Just ignore him.'

'I want to give him a piece of my mind.' I was in the middle of pouring more tea, and I realised my hand was shaking. 'Tell him how much misery he's caused everyone.'

I didn't mean to shout. I only realised I was doing it when people turned around and Miss Ambrose peered at us from the other side of the room. 'Try to use your indoor voice,' my mother used to say. Only there were certain times in life when your indoor voice just wasn't quite adequate.

'Let's just stay calm and see what Mrs Honeyman has to say.' Jack stood up.

'If Mrs Honeyman has anything to say at all,' said Elsie, and we followed him out into the sunshine, amongst the holiday clatter and the ribbons of cars, and the scream of the seagulls, all the way along the West Cliff, until the town swallowed us up into the rush of a Sunday morning.

★ ★ ★

Depressing places, hospitals. I've never enjoyed visiting them, because each time I have, the experience has been knitted with misery. My mother. My father. Various friends over the years whose lives have stumbled and faltered long before mine.

'I detest hospitals,' said Elsie, as if she could read my mind.

We walked along a main corridor, behind a belted blue uniform who had deliberated for a good fifteen minutes before she decided to allow us inside. Even Jack and his charm struggled to win her over.

'It's most unusual,' she said. 'Visiting at this hour on a Sunday.'

We were eventually allowed ten minutes, and after we left the corridor, we arrived at a side room, which was washed in early-morning sunlight and smelled vaguely of soap. Mrs

Honeyman lay in a bed, with the same expression she'd been wearing the previous evening, only perhaps looking slightly less tired.

'She's fine, physically,' said the nurse. 'But her mind might not have fared so well. The only problem is, we don't know her baseline.'

'Baseline?' said Jack.

'What she's like normally?' It was presented as a question, and I realised for the first time that I hadn't had a conversation with Mrs Honeyman for the entire time I'd been at Cherry Tree.

'She's usually very quiet,' I said.

'But presumably not as quiet as this?' The nurse smoothed down a sheet and pulled the curtain back a little more.

'No,' I said, 'not as quiet as this.'

'She sleeps a lot,' said Jack.

'Why?' said the nurse.

We looked at Mrs Honeyman and looked back at the nurse. No one replied.

'Because she's old?' I said, eventually.

'Forgive me,' said the nurse. 'I think you are all around the same age?' We nodded. 'Do you sleep a lot?'

'Not especially,' I said.

'I think then, perhaps, we need to look further than someone's age to explain why they behave the way they do.'

We all agreed with her, and I found a watery smile.

'Ten minutes.' This was not presented as a question, but as a starched, blue statement, and the nurse left us alone with Mrs Honeyman in the room washed with soap and sunlight.

Mrs Honeyman. I realised I didn't know her first name, and I looked up at the felt-tipped board above the bed. Ruth Honeyman. Ruth.

'Ruth?' I said. There was not a flicker of acknowledgement, her eyes finding something no one else could see, her hands curled into fists on the bedsheets.

'Ruth, it's Florence. From Cherry Tree.'

Nothing.

'We came to see if you were all right? If you needed anything?'

I heard Jack take a breath out of the silence. Everything was quiet, except a clock in the corner of the room, tutting away at the seconds.

'Ruth, we need to talk to you.' I drew a chair up to the side of the bed and tried to take one of her fisted hands. 'We haven't got long and we need to talk to you about Gabriel.'

Now she looked at me, eyes wide and white, busy with anxiety. 'He's not *my* Gabriel.'

'We know he isn't,' I said.

'But we can't tell anyone,' she whispered, and uncurled a finger to hold against her lips.

'Try not to worry,' I said.

'The police are going to come asking, he said, and when they do, we're to say it's him.'

The fear stretched across her face.

'What did he say to you? Whatever did he do to make you disappear like that?' I said.

Mrs Honeyman lost herself in the distance again. I could hear her breathing. Soft, damp breaths held by a heart that had outstayed its time.

'It wasn't my fault.' Mrs Honeyman wasn't

speaking to us any more. I wasn't even sure if she was speaking to anyone at all, to be honest, because I know that sometimes words just need to be let go of, and it doesn't really matter where they land. 'I hadn't been drinking. I just fell. Gabriel didn't leave me because I murdered my own child. He just . . . ' She searched for a word. ' . . . disappeared,' she said eventually.

Her eyes met mine. For someone who was usually so noiseless and absent, her eyes were sharp. Quick. It felt as though they'd seen everything.

'I missed my footing,' she said. 'Didn't judge it properly. I reached out to save myself, but there was nothing there.'

Looking back, I think that was the moment I started to remember what happened with Ronnie, when the pieces stitched together and finally made sense.

'He didn't leave you, Ruth,' I said.

'He didn't?'

'No. He really didn't. I can't explain right now, because I'm only beginning to understand it myself,' I said. 'You'll have to just believe me. He didn't leave you. He never left you.'

I reached for her hand, and when she reached back, something fell from her fingers. It was a fossil. An ammonite. A spiral of the past; proof of a time long since gone, a reminder of something that once existed. I picked it up.

'I know where she's been,' I said.

★   ★   ★

368

I held on to the ammonite in my pocket as we walked along polished corridors and out of the hospital. Mrs Honeyman wouldn't take it back. Perhaps it had served its purpose for her, or perhaps she gave it to me for safekeeping. Either way, I couldn't let it go. We walked slowly, finding our thoughts in careful steps, and when we finally got outside, the wall of bright sunlight and the smell of the morning made it feel as though we'd been on a very long journey.

★ ★ ★

We sat in the hotel dining room, still in our coats, staring at a blank table stripped of everything except a thick white cloth. I put the ammonite in front of us. It looked so insignificant. So small. It was strange to think something so unremarkable held thousands of years of history inside itself.

Handy Simon walked past and backtracked when he saw what was in front of us.

'A fossil,' he said, rather unnecessarily. He peered down at it. 'Fascinating things, fossils.'

'They are,' I said.

'Sometimes, they're the only evidence we have to prove something once existed.'

'Do you really think that's true?' I said.

Simon straightened up and folded his arms. '*Geographical Scientist* magazine thinks it's true.'

'But what about you, Simon? What do you think? What's your own opinion?'

Simon swallowed a little air to help him digest the question. 'I don't rightly know,' he said after a while. 'I've never really thought about it.'

'Well, why don't you think about it now?' Jack asked.

Simon shifted his weight and took a large breath. 'I suppose,' he said, 'you don't have to be able to see something for it to be significant.'

'Go on,' I said.

'Before this fossil was found' — he had another little peer for good measure — 'it was still influential, wasn't it? It still changed the universe in some way. We just don't know how.'

Jack gestured for him to go on.

'And everything it influenced,' Simon said, 'all those things will change the universe in some way, too. I don't suppose we'll ever know the impact it made.'

'I don't suppose we will,' I said.

Simon stood back, as though the realisation that such a small thing had such a large consequence meant that he should allow it a little more space in the world.

I picked up the ammonite and held it in the palm of my hand. 'No matter how long or how short a time you are here, the world is ever so slightly different because you existed. Although I'm not sure how anyone can ever prove it.'

'Perhaps we don't have to,' said Simon. 'Perhaps just knowing that is enough.'

★ ★ ★

After Simon and his new viewpoint on life had left the room, the three of us sat in silence around the table.

'What now?' I said, because it seemed like no one else was going to speak.

'Perhaps,' said Jack, 'perhaps we should just let Ronnie disappear again.'

'How can you say such a thing?' It was the closest Elsie ever got to a shout.

'That's not like you, Jack.' I frowned at him. 'Where's your fighting spirit?'

'All fought out,' he said, and he tried to smile. 'The police obviously don't believe us, Ronnie's managed to terrify anyone who could identify him, and who's going to listen to what we've got to say anyway?'

'We can't just let him win.' I looked at the ammonite. 'We can't just let him alter the world as he pleases.'

'But how can we stop him?' Jack stood and held on to the back of a chair. 'The bus leaves in a couple of hours, Florence. I think I'm going for a lie-down.'

We watched him shuffle out of the dining room, worn down by all the years and all the thinking. Perhaps it was the sea air. It made a body tired somehow, as though the salt pulled away all your energy. I looked at Elsie.

'So, are you going for a lie-down as well?' I said.

'Of course not. You've gone and forgotten, haven't you?'

'Forgotten what?'

She winked at me. 'We've got to say goodbye to the sea.'

\* \* \*

371

We walked past the stalls selling Whitby fudge
and thick sticks of rock, past the shells and the
beads, and the rows of postcards, towards the
abbey steps, where the shops lay hidden on
cobbled streets, waiting to be found.

'Do you remember,' said Elsie, 'we used to
spend hours trying to choose what to take home
with us?'

'Nothing much has changed, then.' I looked at
my watch. 'We have to be back soon, or Miss
Ambrose will have a coronary.'

Elsie gazed in the window of a gallery.

'Perhaps I'll buy a painting,' she said, 'of the
harbour. Or perhaps a picture of some beach
huts.'

I thought about the skip outside number
twelve and the crash of glass against metal. 'I
don't think so,' I said.

'Why ever not? Who doesn't love a row of
beach huts? They look just like a smile.'

'Perhaps a tin of biscuits,' I said. 'More
practical.'

'Holidays aren't the time to be practical,
Florence. You can save practical for all the other
weeks of the year.'

We walked a little further, to a window filled
with Whitby jet, smooth and dark, with a
reflection that felt almost like a mirror. There
were rings and necklaces, bracelets and earrings,
all shining back at us from their trays.

'It's a beautiful stone, isn't it?' said Elsie.
'Whitby jet.'

I stared into the window. 'It's a fossil,' I said.
'Is it?'

'Well, fossilised wood. Thousands of years' worth of existence, carved into a shape we can recognise.'

'How do you know that?' said Elsie.

'I read about it,' I said. 'In a magazine. The Victorians wore it as part of bereavement. As a remembrance of their loss.' I pointed to a brooch in the far corner of the display. 'Although how something so beautiful can be associated with sadness is a little bit beyond me.'

'Perhaps it helped them to accept the loss, knowing something from so long ago still had a place in the world.'

'Perhaps,' I said.

The brooch watched us through the shop window. It was a perfect circle, flawless and shining and inky black. Surrounding it was a silver rope, which held it forever in a polished frame.

'Why don't you treat yourself,' said Elsie. 'Something to look back on.'

'I don't think so.'

'Why not? You obviously love that brooch.'

'It's a gift you'd buy for someone you love, isn't it? Not something you buy for yourself. Anyway, I don't wear jewellery.'

'Perhaps you should start?' said Elsie, but I had already moved along the street.

'Shortbread,' I said. 'I'll buy a box of shortbread, and if I don't get around to eating it, Miss Ambrose can have it for the raffle.'

In the end, we both decided on a box of shortbread, and while Elsie disappeared to the toilets, I listened to the church bells and bought

373

us both an ice cream, and we made it last all the way back to the hotel.

'There you are.' Miss Ambrose and her clipboard were waiting on the pavement. 'I was right on the verge of worrying.'

'No need to worry about us, Miss Ambrose.' I beamed at Eric as I climbed on board. 'We've just been saying goodbye to the sea.'

Miss Ambrose started to speak, but she changed her mind and shook her head at Handy Simon instead. Eric started the engine and said, 'That's the job, then,' and we all made our way back to Cherry Tree. Everyone except Mrs Honeyman, of course. We never did see her again. I sometimes worried she'd been sent to Greenbank, but I preferred to think she stayed in the room filled with sunshine and the smell of soap, and the weightlessness of self-forgiving that can only ever be found in time.

\* \* \*

'I don't understand why I have to go.'

I'd been pacing the room for the last twenty minutes. I'm not usually a pacer; Elsie's the one who walks out her anxiety. I'm more of a hand-wringer, a fidget, but on this occasion I had decided to pace, and nothing Elsie said or did could make me stop. We'd been back at Cherry Tree less than twenty-four hours, and my pacing had to take into account my suitcase, which still sat in a corner of the room, waiting to be unpacked.

'I failed, didn't I?' I said. 'I failed my

probation period, and now they're trying to get rid of me.'

'I'm sure it's just a precaution,' Elsie said. 'They'll be sending everyone in their turn. It won't be anything personal.'

I stopped pacing. 'Then why do I have to go first? Why haven't they sent for you before me? This is it, Elsie. This is the beginning of my last goodbye.'

'We'll go together,' she said. 'You don't have to do it alone. No one will mind if I'm there as well.'

I slowed down. 'What if I don't pass the test?' I stopped altogether. 'What if they send me to Greenbank?'

'Of course you'll pass the test. Just think of it as a chat. Just a doctor asking a lot of ridiculous questions. You'll run rings around him.'

'Do you think so?'

'Of course.' Elsie didn't look at me as she spoke, but pointed through the window instead. 'And look how beautiful it is out there. How could anything bad happen on a day like this?'

She was right. It was the kind of October day when the weather forgets who it is, and tiny clouds whisper at the edges of a perfect blue sky. Sunlight warmed all the colours and mopped up yesterday's rain, and everything was so bright and so happy, it looked as though someone had given God a new set of felt tips.

★ ☆ ★

One of Miss Bissell's helping hands went in the taxi with us. Her name appeared to be Natasha,

375

although she didn't introduce herself. Purple tabard. Obsessed with telephone signals. Smelled of chewing gum. I have no idea what the taxi driver's name was, because he didn't utter a single word between Cherry Tree and the hospital, preferring instead to hum along with Radio 2 and tap his fingers on the steering wheel. Elsie sat next to me in the back, and I spent the entire journey swallowing and wondering who I'd become.

'It will be fine. It's all going to be fine,' Elsie said every few minutes, as though she were reciting the words to a lullaby. 'We'll be out of there in no time, and we'll go to the League of Friends and have a custard tart.'

I looked at the sky. Somewhere between Cherry Tree carpark and the bypass, it had changed. It's strange how that happens. You look away for a moment, and when you glance back, everything is different. The rain drew lines across the glass and made the whole world look disappointed.

'Or an Eccles cake. You like Eccles cakes,' Elsie said.

'I've fallen out with currants.' My gaze didn't leave the heavens. 'They're far too complicated.'

No one spoke again until we arrived at the hospital. The taxi driver pulled into the dropping-off zone and we struggled out of the car on to those strange, hatched yellow lines, which were wet with an October downpour.

'This is it, then,' I said. 'I haven't taken a test since I was at school. I thought I'd finished with being tested.'

'Don't think of it as a test, think of it as a conversation,' Elsie said. 'A chat.'

Natasha walked behind us, thrusting her mobile telephone towards the rooftops. 'If I lose you, I'm for the high jump,' she said.

We walked along painted lines in a corridor. 'When you get old, it sometimes feels as if your whole life is just one long exam,' I said.

★ ★ ★

The waiting room was crowded, yet strangely silent, and each time a door opened everyone turned, hoping it would be a doctor or a nurse, or some reassurance that the queue was moving forward. It was a holding point for many different clinics, and we fought our way past walking frames and pushchairs, and outposts of small children, to find a seat in the corner. Natasha immediately gravitated to a window, where she held her telephone up to the ceiling and frowned.

'I could really do with a cup of tea. Is there no tea?' I said. 'Like there is at the hairdresser's?'

There was a machine against the far wall, but it had a sign taped to the front suggesting we all went to A&E.

'I've probably got a Mint Imperial in the bottom of my bag somewhere,' Elsie said.

I shook my head. 'I only wanted it to take my mind off things,' I said. 'Sometimes that's what a cup of tea is for.'

I looked at the criss-cross of walking sticks around the waiting room and all the people, drawn in grey and beige, with whispers of white where their hair used to be and shoes too big for their feet. My father always said distraction was the best way to address anxiety, but the magazines all appeared to have been disembowelled and divorced from their staples, so I picked up a leaflet instead.

*Living With Dementia*, it said.

It was filled with statistics. Handy Simon would have had a field day. See, I remembered his name! It told you how likely you were to get dementia, and how old you might be when you first welcomed it into your life. There were lots of photographs of elderly people with full heads of hair and rosy cheeks, and relatives overflowing with patience and understanding. On the second page, there was a list of symptoms written in bold, and held within a box.

Elsie fought around in the bowels of her handbag for a pair of glasses, but she gave up. 'What does it say?'

'Problems with reasoning,' I said. 'Although that's never been one of my strongest suits.'

'Anything else?'

'Communication problems,' I said.

'You never have any trouble communicating.'

'Quite the reverse,' I said.

'What's the third thing?'

I looked at the little box. 'Mood swings.'

Elsie started to laugh, and I laughed along with her. We laughed so much, Natasha was forced to put down her mobile telephone for a moment and ask if we were all right.

'Perfectly fine, thank you. Do you ever have

mood swings, Natasha? Do you find yourself struggling to reason?' I looked at the mobile telephone. 'Do you have problems communicating with other human beings?'

Natasha frowned and decamped to the far corner. She was still staring at us over the top of the screen when a nurse appeared from one of the rooms and waved us inside.

'This is us then,' I said, and gave a very big sigh.

* * *

The room was quite pleasant, considering it had a doctor inside of it. There were flowers on the windowsill, although I strongly suspected they were of the pretend variety, and a display of the same leaflets I'd been reading just a moment before, only they were arranged in a little fan on the coffee table, like after-dinner mints. Instead of hard plastic seats, there were armchairs. There was even a cushion, although I put it straight on the floor, because cushions always play havoc with Elsie's lumbar region.

The doctor smiled at us. He sat in the armchair opposite, with a pile of notes and a stethoscope swaying from his shirt.

'Are they listening to my heart as well?' I said.

'I don't think so.' Elsie frowned at the stethoscope. 'I think it's just to make sure everyone knows who they're supposed to be.'

The doctor smiled again and asked for our details, and I answered for both of us, because Elsie said I needed the practice.

'And you?' I said.

The doctor stared at us.

'Hello My Name Is?' I said. 'I've watched *Holby City*, I know the rules.'

His name was Dr Andrews, and when he'd washed his hands and rolled his sleeves above his elbows, he told us he was going to ask a series of questions.

'Is there a time limit?' I said. 'For us to answer?'

Dr Andrews glanced at the clock above our heads and said that it was quite a busy clinic.

'The mini mental-state examination doesn't usually take long,' he said.

'Mini?' I frowned at him.

He told us there were thirty questions, which didn't sound very mini to me. The world of medicine appears to be littered with understatements — small scratch, slight discomfort, minor abrasion. I offered him a selection of examples I'd experienced, although I didn't venture into my bowels, or we'd have been there all day.

'Shall we begin?' said Dr Andrews, and Elsie and I sat up a little straighter.

★   ★   ★

It's strange how easily you can become flustered when someone is watching you. If they were casual questions, asked at a bus stop or in a supermarket queue, I'm sure the answers would come to us easily, but when Dr Andrews is staring down at you with his pen waiting over a piece of paper, you begin to doubt even your own name. He started out by asking the day of the week. Of course, I knew it was Tuesday, but going to Whitby threw me off and I plumped for Thursday before either of us had even really thought about it. Elsie said she was going to choose Tuesday, but she waited for me to answer first, because she wanted to know what I'd say. We were so confused by the days of the week, by the time he got to the month and the year, we just blurted out the first thing we thought of. Of course it wasn't 1997. 1997 was the year Diana died. I told Dr Andrews, and asked if we could have an extra point for knowing it, but he shook his head.

'There isn't a box for the Princess of Wales,' he said.

Neither of us could remember the name of the hospital, either. It's not something you notice, is it? And Natasha pressed the button in the lift, so how could we know what floor we were on? I told him Natasha would fill him in, and should I go and get her, but Dr Andrews just moved on to the next question.

'Take seven away from a hundred,' he said. 'And keep taking seven away, until I tell you to stop.'

I looked at his clipboard across the coffee table.

'You have the answers.' I pointed. 'Printed at the side.'

Dr Andrews curled his arm around the sheet of paper, like a child in a classroom. 'You shouldn't worry about what I know,' he said.

'But of course I should worry about what you

know. You're the person deciding which one of us is going to be sent to Greenbank.' I craned my neck. 'Spell WORLD backwards. D-L-R — '

Dr Andrews sprang from his seat like a jack-in-a-box and conducted the rest of the test from the far corner of the room, next to the window. Elsie struggled to hear what he was saying, because it's her bad side, and I had to repeat everything to make sure she understood. The last thing he did was hold up a piece of paper. It said, *Close Your Eyes* on it.

'Why would we want to do that?' I said.

'Because I'm asking you to.' Dr Andrews held the instructions a little closer.

'Is it a surprise?' I said.

I heard Dr Andrews sigh. 'Do you not usually do as someone asks?'

I frowned. 'Not if I can help it.'

When we'd finished the test, we watched Dr Andrews fill out an entire side of A4. We buttoned ourselves into our coats and I turned to him and asked what we'd got.

He said he would be forwarding on the results to Cherry Tree in due course. He still didn't look up. Not even when I said, 'They're our scores, though, aren't they? Shouldn't someone tell us first?'

The nurse herded us back into the care of Natasha and her mobile telephone, and we were marched through the hospital — past the League of Friends — and shuffled on to the back seat of a taxi. I looked out of the window.

'I didn't really enjoy that little chat very much, Elsie,' I said.

When the taxi pulled in at Cherry Tree, it struggled to do a three-point turn, because there was a police car sitting right in the middle of the car park.

Natasha looked up from her mobile telephone for the first time in twenty minutes and stared. It's strange how we always stare at emergency vehicles. Whenever there's a siren, everyone appears at their windows to watch it whip past, even though no one has the first clue where it might be going. Perhaps it's reassuring to hear the sound of an alarm disappear into the distance and away from our own lives. Although the police car at Cherry Tree was silent, it was parked at a peculiar angle, in the way only police cars seem to be able to get away with.

Of course, Elsie and I headed straight for the residents' lounge, to watch through the glass. Jack had already taken up his position on the sofa, and nodded at us when we walked in.

'Something's afoot,' he said. 'Although no one is saying what.'

There were two policemen in Miss Ambrose's office, and their uniforms seemed to take up all the space. Miss Ambrose was crowded into the corner, squeezed up against her desk, watching them lift everything out of the filing cabinets.

'Fraud, do you think?' Jack said. 'Has someone been cooking the books?'

'Miss Ambrose doesn't look the type, does she?' I said. 'She buys all her clothes from Marks & Spencer.'

Jack wandered over to the noticeboard and lingered by the door.

'Does shopping at Marks & Spencer offer some kind of indemnity?' Elsie said. 'Because if that's the case, half of Cherry Tree must be sainted.'

Jack wandered back. 'Can't hear a bloody word,' he said.

We sat in a row on the sofa. After a few minutes, Handy Simon appeared through the double doors with a clipboard, but as soon as he saw the policemen, he took three steps backwards and disappeared again.

'Do you think they're after the handyman?' I said. 'It's usually the handyman, isn't it? Or someone in the background, someone you've not noticed very much.'

Elsie stared at me. 'Life isn't an episode of *Columbo*.'

'Sometimes it is,' I said.

The policemen left ten minutes later, with a selection of envelopes and their hats back on. Miss Ambrose watched us for a while through the chequered glass. There was a moment when I thought I saw her smile, but perhaps I was mistaken. When she finally left the office, Jack opened his eyes and shouted, 'What was all that about, then?' and Miss Ambrose said, 'You tell me and we'll both know,' which confused me for a good fifteen minutes.

'At least it's taken our minds off the hospital,' I said.

Jack turned from watching Miss Ambrose disappear along the corridor. 'And how did that go?'

'You can only do your best,' I said. 'Can't you?'

Jack looked at me, and his eyes held my words for a moment. 'You look after yourself, Florence, won't you? We all need help from time to time. All you have to do is reach out and ask for it.'

'I don't think I deserve any,' I said.

'Of course you do. Everyone does. What on earth makes you say that?'

The words came out before I had a chance to go through them first.

'I was so sure it was Ronnie who drowned, not Gabriel Price. I would have put my life on it.'

I watched him hesitate. 'How can you be so certain, Flo?' he said.

I looked him straight in the eye. 'Because I was the one who pushed him in.'

# 10.13 p.m.

I remembered in Whitby, I think, but I'd put it in one of the drawers in my mind and tried not to think about it too much.

After Beryl died, neither of us went to the dance again. We couldn't face it. The night Ronnie drowned, I poked my head around the door of the town hall, but the colours were too bright and the music was too loud, and the whole thing seemed almost obscene. I was just about to leave when I spotted Ronnie. Standing by the bar. Talking to some girl I'd never seen before. Whispering in her ear, a fraction too close, a moment too long. And he was laughing. He was laughing as though the whole board had been wiped clean and he could start all over again.

I don't remember leaving. I don't remember turning around or closing the door, or finding my way down the steps. The next time I even knew where I might be, I was marching into Elsie's kitchen, looking for someone to join in with my anger.

The house was silent. Everyone was in bed. I paced around the empty room for a few minutes, and then I stood at the bottom of the stairs and listened. You could usually hear Elsie's mother walking around, no matter what time of the night it was, but even she was still. I remember the clock ticking in the hall and the silent floorboards, and I remember thinking the whole house must have found its sleep. Then I heard it. The crying. At first I thought it was a child somewhere, but it was too complicated for a child and it wasn't crying that asked for anything. It didn't even want to be heard. And then it hit me. It was Elsie.

I wanted to go to her. I even put my foot on the first step. Something stopped me, though; something held me back. It wasn't because it was late, or because it felt awkward to find someone else crying. It was Elsie, and nothing had ever felt awkward with Elsie. It was because I knew that whatever I said, my words would never be able to make a difference. No matter how much I cared for her, and no matter how much I wanted to, I would never be able to help her through it. And so the thing that stopped me, really stopped me, from going to her that night, was the fact that it meant facing up to my own inadequacy.

I was shaking when I got back into the kitchen. I'm not sure if it was anger or frustration, or a cold November night, but I can remember poking at the fire and looking straight into the flames until it made my eyes smart. I must have decided right then, as I watched the coal burn, that I needed to do something. If I couldn't find the right words, perhaps I could fill all the spaces up between them, and if no one else was going to face up to Ronnie Butler, then perhaps it was down to me.

I left Elsie's house full of breath. I slammed the kitchen door behind me, and the sound seemed to fill the whole street. But I didn't turn around. Instead, I headed straight back to the town hall. Of course, everyone had left by that time. Through the windows the evening lay abandoned. The empty stage and a wooden floor littered with streamers, and the pattern of glasses on silent tables. There were no people. They had all disappeared back into the warmth of a kitchen or the softness of a bed. Even the streets were empty. But I still searched. I knew Ronnie was out there somewhere, and I couldn't face Elsie until I'd found him.

I don't know how long I walked for. An hour. Perhaps more. I checked all the pubs, because I knew the musicians often found themselves in back rooms, drawing out their evening behind a locked door, and I wondered if Ronnie might have talked his way in there. I walked all the way to his flat, on the other side of the river, but the windows were still and dark. I'd done two circuits of the town, and I was just about to start a third, when I spotted him. At the top of the road, almost at the place I had started to look an hour before. He stumbled on the pavement, and leaned into a wall to steady himself.

I had no idea where he'd been. Perhaps he'd found a conversation in a bar that suited him, or a woman who didn't look too closely, or maybe he'd just wandered the streets, as I'd done, trying to find a path home. I took a breath to shout, but my voice stayed in my throat. I'm not sure if I was afraid, or it might have been because I'd searched for him for so long, I just wanted to enjoy the satisfaction of finding him at last. He moved up the street, weaving a path between lampposts and fences, and I followed, at a distance, wishing my feet weren't so loud, and that the breath wouldn't cloud from my mouth. Ronnie didn't turn. He was too busy concentrating, and so I edged a little closer, watching from the shadows of the street.

The river slices through the town, cutting a path between the old and the new. The alms-houses and workmen's cottages on one side, where Elsie and I lived, which peered over the curve of a bridge to the factories and flats, and guest houses on the other. Ronnie lived on the new side. He lived where the streets were wider and the people were unfamiliar. Strangers, drifting through a town and never pausing long enough to be recognised. He could have taken the bridge. He could have spent a little longer getting home, but instead, he decided to follow the river. He made a choice, but I hesitated. The water was fast and wide. It raced through the town, pulled by the tides in the estuary, and my father had always made me promise never to walk there in the dark. 'Too dangerous,' he said. 'Too many opportunities to slip.' But this was different. This was something I had to do, because I couldn't lose Ronnie now. Not when it had taken me so long to find him.

The moon was fat and settled in the sky, but every so often, tangles of black traced across its surface, and I lost the figure in front of me. He was a sketch in the distance. A slight movement against the black. I tried to be sure of my feet, to trail my hand through the weeds and grass on

389

my left, but all I could hear was the river, waiting for me to fall. And so I did what I'd always done when I was nervous, even as a child. I counted. I started by counting my breaths, but they were too fast, and I couldn't find one from another, so I counted my steps instead. I tried to match them to Ronnie's. Listening for his boots in the distance. The only problem was, I was so busy counting, I didn't notice he'd slowed down, and before I knew it, he was so close, I could almost touch him. I could smell the beer and the leather of his boots, and the sound of his breathing seemed to fill my whole head. He was leaning forward, his hands on his legs, vomiting on to the riverbank.

When he'd finished, he stood and wiped his mouth on the sleeve of his coat. He was off guard. Disorientated. Light-headed perhaps. It was right at that moment, just as he lifted his head, that I pushed him. It's strange, because there are some things you do in life, and they don't seem to have any thought fastened to them at all. It was only at that moment, I decided to do it. I only followed Ronnie to give him a piece of my mind, to tell him exactly what I thought of him, but as I stood on the riverbank, it felt as though pushing him in was all I was ever meant to do. There are some moments in life that just seem to happen. The falling was slow at first, like a plate finding the edge of a table or a child beginning to walk. I could have reached out to him then, in the darkness. I could have stopped it, but there was an inevitability. A certainty. The feeling that this was all meant to happen, and to try to stop it would have been pointless. I whispered. I whispered to him, as he fell. 'Don't think I'm going to help you.' And then I shouted it. I shouted it with all the breath I could find in my lungs.

'Don't think I'm going to help you!'

I heard him. I heard him cry out as he hit the water, and I heard the river open its arms. It was the silence, though, the silence after he'd disappeared that was the loudest. I waited in the space where he had stood only a moment before, and I listened. I stood there for a few minutes, being sure, and then I ran. I ran along the side of the water and back to the bridge, and however I managed it without falling in myself, I'll never know. Luck. God. Destiny. All of the things we thank when we have nowhere else to put our gratitude. When I reached the road, I held on to the walls of the bridge, and wondered if I would ever be able to find my breath again. The town felt as if it had been waiting for me to return from wherever I had just been. I could even hear people in the distance. Laughter and goodbyes, and conversation. Someone from the dance, perhaps. Someone who hadn't just stood on a riverbank and watched a man drown.

I could have found the voices. I could have shouted for help. I could have hammered on the first door I came to. I could have done any of these things, but I chose not to. I've spent the last sixty years trying to find the path I took to arrive at that choice, and I don't suppose, lying here in the dark, I will ever find it now. But it has never stopped me from looking. It has never stopped me from remembering the person I thought I was, and trying to bring her back again.

# Florence

They didn't say anything as I was telling the story. Jack just closed his eyes, as though he needed everything else to go away, so he could concentrate on the words.

'I was so sure it was Ronnie,' I said.

Jack reached out. His hand was knotted with age. 'We all act in the heat of the moment,' he said. 'No one is blameless.'

'I took someone's life,' I said. 'I killed Gabriel Price.'

'But you thought it was Ronnie.' Elsie looked across at me.

'It doesn't make it any better, though, does it? That it wasn't the life I meant to take?'

Jack still rested his hand on mine. 'It could happen to any one of us, Florence, given a set of circumstances.'

'But no one deserves to die, do they?' I said.

'Did you mean to kill him?'

'No,' I said. 'Of course I didn't. I just wanted to hurt him, like he'd hurt Elsie.' I looked over at her. 'Like he'd hurt all of us.'

'Then there is your answer,' he said.

'You've got to find forgiveness, Florence,' said Elsie. 'You find it so easily for other people, why do you struggle so much to find it for yourself?'

'But I should tell someone. I should tell the police. I'm a bad person. I'm flawed. Damaged.'

'Of course you are.'

I looked at him.

'We all are. Every one of us is damaged. We need the faults, the breaks, the fracture lines.'

'We do?' I said.

'Of course we do. However else would all the light get in?'

I could see Elsie smiling at us.

'You can't define yourself by a single moment.' Jack held my hand very tightly. I could feel him shaking. 'That moment doesn't make you who you are.'

'Then what does?' I said.

'Oh, Florence. Everything else,' he said. 'Everything else.'

# Miss Ambrose

Anthea Ambrose sat in the Japanese Garden, staring at her fingernails. They'd been much longer before her weekend in Whitby. Miss Ambrose had always imagined she'd have a job where there would be room for nice fingernails, where she would write with a fountain pen, instead of a crushed Biro. Where she would have an office made entirely of glass and chrome, and where she'd keep a spare pair of heels in the bottom drawer of the filing cabinet. The interview she'd missed was for a job like that. Perhaps she should call them. Perhaps they might have another vacancy right now.

'Vacancy for what?' said Jack.

She hadn't realised Jack was standing right in front of her, and she hadn't realised the words had come out.

'A job,' she said. 'I missed an interview a few years ago, because of an incident here, and I was just thinking it might not be too late to try again.'

He sat on the bench next to her. 'Do you want to try again? Perhaps you missed it for a reason.'

'Do you really believe in all that fate nonsense?'

'I believe in long seconds,' he said. 'Perhaps whoever stopped you from going to that interview was just helping you to write your story.'

Her confusion seemed to amuse him. 'It's something Florence believes in,' he said. 'A long second is when the clock hesitates, just for a moment. Just long enough to give you the extra time you need to make the right decision.'

'Have you seen these long seconds?' she said.

Jack sat back in the seat. His coat was worn at the sleeves and she could see a thread on one of the buttons. She must speak to Chris. Sort him out a new one. Old people didn't always realise they needed these things. She'd done it. On a course.

'There was a long second,' he said. 'During the war. I watched a soldier once, leaving the battlefield. Older man who'd reached the end of his tether. He turned and started walking, and he just didn't stop.'

'He was a deserter?'

'There was a lot of it. More than people think. Men suffocated by fear. It's hard to imagine terror like that, unless you've lived alongside it.'

'So what did you do?'

'I followed. Ran until I caught up with him.'

'Did you report him?'

'No,' said Jack. 'I talked to him instead. He was terrified. The exhaustion and the lack of food, weather beating down on you. Killing everywhere. You couldn't find a place to look where there wasn't death in your eye-line. He missed his children. He called them his piano keyboard, although I've no idea why.'

'What happened?'

'I persuaded him to return. You wouldn't think I'd have managed it, a young whipper-snapper like me, but eventually we both walked back together, and neither of us ever said another word about it.'

Miss Ambrose shook her head. 'You were lucky to make it home,' she said.

'I nearly didn't. There was one night . . . '

He hesitated and Miss Ambrose looked away to build him an escape route, but after a moment, he carried on.

' . . . one night, we'd been under fire for hours. We didn't think it would ever end. It was the noise, more than anything. There was no space. No silence. We thought we could just stay put. Sit it out. But then we had instructions to move.'

'What happened?'

'We had to do it, of course. No choice. But it was the landmines, the place was rife with them. Imagine walking across a field, not knowing if the next step you took would be your last, and all you can hear is the sound of your own breath and the shells rattling down on you. We were almost at the other side, nearly made it, when the chap to my left pushed me to one side. He must have seen it coming.'

'And?'

'It got him,' Jack said. 'Blew him to pieces. He just vanished, Miss Ambrose. He just disappeared right there in front of me. It was as though he'd never existed.'

Neither of them spoke. Miss Ambrose watched a robin feeding on the bird table. Soft brown feathers with a brush of red. Eyes like coal. She wasn't even sure how long she watched it for, and afterwards, when she thought back, she wasn't entirely sure she hadn't just imagined it.

'That must have been your long second, then?' she said eventually.

Jack shook his head. 'Oh no, it was when I persuaded the deserter to come back.'

'Surely not? Surely the long second would be the man who saved your life?'

Jack smiled. 'And who do you think that was?' he said.

Miss Ambrose felt her throat tighten.

'Don't worry,' he said. 'This is the best place to do your remembering, when you need to.'

'The Japanese Garden? I thought no one ever bothered with it?'

'Oh, you'd be surprised. Mrs Honeyman used to visit all the time, and Florence loves it in here. She likes watching the birds, and walking backwards and forwards across that fancy little bridge. You did a fine job, Miss Ambrose.'

Miss Ambrose's throat tightened a little more. 'Jack?' she said.

'Hmm?'

'What time is it?'

He patted her arm. 'Time I was gone.' He smiled, and you couldn't help but smile back, even though his smile was soft and unsure, and it trembled at the edges.

She watched him shuffle down the path, tapping his walking stick at the gravel, in a coat worn at the sleeves. Although perhaps she wouldn't have a word with Chris after all. On second thoughts, perhaps Jack was completely fine just as he was.

# Florence

We sat in the day room, in front of a television programme. I said I'd stay, as long as it wasn't anything to do with cookery, and so they found me something to watch where people were trying to push little counters over an edge and win money. My gaze wandered all over the room, although it wasn't as bad as when it sits in the middle distance doing nothing.

'Isn't it exciting?' Elsie pointed. 'The postwoman from Leighton Buzzard is on the verge of winning a hundred and fifty pounds.'

'I'm not really interested,' I said.

Jack reached down the side of the settee, and pulled out a carrier bag. 'In that case, I have just the thing to cheer us all up.'

I glanced over. 'What have you got there?'

'Miss Ambrose bought them for me from the jumble sale in Whitby. Don't say I never keep my promises. Now, which one shall we watch?'

It was a stack of Harry Potter DVDs. The covers were shiny and filled with swirls and swords, and a boy in glasses who grew older with each progressive image.

'I think we should perhaps see them in order.' I began sorting through, trying to guess the boy's age on each one.

'That's so typical of you,' Elsie said. 'Life always has to have rules.'

Jack picked up the one on the top of the pile.

'I think there comes an age,' he said, 'when you have to worry less about following the rules, and more about living in the moment.'

And so we found Handy Simon, who put a disc in the little slot and sorted out the television, and we all watched the film together. Even Simon, who leaned against the wall for a while, before giving in to himself and sitting on one of the armchairs. Even Miss Ambrose came out of her office. She didn't tell Simon off, but sat alongside him instead and opened a box of Terry's All Gold. We escaped from the day room and from Cherry Tree, and into a world of wizards and broomsticks, and ordinary people who were not ordinary, but who were people who turned out, in the end, to be quite extraordinary after all. Because sometimes you need to run away. You need to believe in something without looking for proof. You need to enjoy a thing without finding a need to measure its value. You need to run away from a familiar life, into something quite unfamiliar. Even if you are so old, the only running away you will ever do again is in your mind.

I watched the film from the corner of the room. My eyes following the story, and my mouth following the words. I could remember a time when our whole lives felt like that. Unread chapters. Waiting stories. I didn't want the film to end. I wanted it to keep on running, because I knew as soon as the credits began to roll, all my thoughts would return to Ronnie, and if I could just hold us all in this room forever, we could unremember everything that lay waiting for us on the other side of the door.

★  ★  ★

They found Jack the following morning. I was with Elsie when they told me. Simon said he looked really quite peaceful, and Miss Ambrose said dying in your sleep was the very best way to go.

'But I never got a chance to say cheerio.' I sat in Miss Ambrose's office with a glass of water. 'He never said goodbye.'

Although when I thought about it, perhaps he had. I just didn't manage to hear it.

I looked for Jack over the next few days. I listened for the tap of his walking stick and the sound of his voice, interfering in other people's conversations. It felt as though there had been a terrible mistake and someone would come running up to me and say it hadn't really happened and it was all just a false alarm. The world seemed so incomplete without him there. So unlikely. I think the hardest part of losing anyone is that you still have to live with the same scenery. It's just that the person you are used to isn't a part of it any more, and all you notice are the gaps where they used to be. It feels as though, if you concentrated hard enough, you could find them again in those empty spaces. Waiting for you.

★  ★  ★

I thought the funeral might help us accept Jack had gone, but it all passed by in a moment. Elsie and I sat right at the back, because Elsie was worried I might need some fresh air. Miss Ambrose and Miss Bissell took it in turns to look over their shoulders at us, and when Chris left the church, he stopped and squeezed my arm.

We stood at the graveside afterwards, Elsie and me. The minibus waited in the car park, and for once, Miss Ambrose didn't try and hurry us along.

I could smell the earth, resting against the October air, and the rain, gathered into pools on the plastic. It was the kind of cemetery where everything was tidy and careful. All the flowers were in vases and the edge of the grass was clipped. Even the dead waited in neat lines, as if even the afterlife required you to form some kind of orderly queue and take your turn.

After a while of silence, we walked along the path towards the car park, past rows of unremembered people, carved into stone and left behind.

'Do you believe in life after death?' I said.

Elsie answered without even looking at me. 'Of course,' she said.

'How can you be so certain?'

She smiled. 'Doesn't it make so much more sense, Florence?'

★ ★ ★

At least Ronnie had the decency not to show his face. We didn't see him on the morning of the

402

funeral, or even at the tea Gloria put on in the residents' lounge afterwards. I didn't have much of an appetite, and I stood in the corner for most of it, watching people move through the space where Jack used to be.

'Are you sure we can't tempt you?' said Miss Ambrose. 'A small plate of something?'

I shook my head. 'I think I might go back to the flat,' I said. 'I think I'll just go and find Elsie.'

Miss Ambrose took my hand. 'Stay here for a while longer,' she said. 'Just until I'm sure you'll be all right.'

\* \* \*

After everyone had eaten, they drifted into the day room and sat around a television, searching each other for clues as to how they should behave. Miss Ambrose decided the best approach was to take our minds off it all. I heard her use those words to Simon, when she asked him to get the Activity Box down from the cupboard in the day room.

'Give them something else to think about,' she said. As though any thought in our minds could be taken out and immediately replaced with another.

I saw Simon frown, but he didn't say anything.

Scrabble, they decided on, in the end. Elsie wasn't there, and I don't think for one second she'd be particularly disappointed to have missed out. There were four of us, people I didn't know or had never spoken to, all sitting round the big table, staring at letters spread out in front of us on a little rack. Simon and Miss Ambrose and Gloria all walked around the table, leaning over our shoulders and rearranging the letters and making suggestions. I didn't know why they couldn't just play the game themselves, and let us go back to staring into a television set.

They had arguments about which words were allowed and which weren't, and when the woman from number seven asked why some letters were worth more than others, it led to a debate that went on for fifteen minutes. I just looked across at the chair Jack used to sit in. No one had used it since. It felt like trespassing, even though we all knew he'd never sit there again. I suppose when someone finally did, it would be the end of a chapter, because it would mean we'd all moved on, and he had been left behind in the past.

'You've got some good letters there, Florence.' Simon looked over my shoulder. 'Have you found any words, yet?'

I hadn't even looked at the tiles.

'Car, star, acts,' he said.

He reached over and moved all the tiles around. 'You've got a six, look: tiaras.'

Simon seemed very pleased with himself.

'Oh, I think we can do even better than that, young man.'

It was Ronnie. I could feel his breath on the back of my neck. I wanted to turn around, but I couldn't, because if I did, he'd see the fear in my eyes and then he'd know straight away that the game was over.

'I can't see a seven,' said Simon. 'Is there a seven?'

I could hear Ronnie smiling. 'There is, but I think it's best if we let Florence find it for herself, don't you?'

I felt Ronnie's hand rest on my shoulder.

'Don't think I'm going to help you,' he said.

'What?' I spoke without turning. 'What did you just say?'

'I said,' his breath was a little closer, his voice just short of a whisper, 'don't think I'm going to help you.'

The room felt very far away. Miss Ambrose talking to someone, and the scream of the television set in the corner, and Jack's empty chair, waiting to be used again. It was as if I was watching it from the ceiling, or the next room, or somewhere in the future. A tangle of colour and light, and confusion, that didn't seem to belong to me any more, and so I stood.

'I don't want to play this game now,' I said. 'I've changed my mind.'

'But you've only just started,' I heard Ronnie say. 'Don't give up before it's over.'

'Sit down, Flo.' Simon straightened the tiles. 'You're doing really well.'

'I don't have to play. I can do whatever I want, and I want to leave now.' When I turned, I caught the edge of the board, and all the letters scattered to the floor.

'Now look what you've done.' Simon crouched down and started collecting them up. 'They've gone everywhere.'

When I looked up, I was staring right into Ronnie's eyes.

'It was you,' I said. 'Wasn't it?'

He didn't reply.

'I knew it was. I knew it was you.' I think I was shouting, because Simon stood and frowned at us both.

'You're right, Florence. It was me,' Ronnie said. He glanced at Simon, who was frowning at us even more. 'I caught the edge of the table, I was the one who upset the board.'

'Right.' Simon put the tiles back on to the table. 'I see. Although I think you'll find it was actually Florence.'

'It might look that way.' Ronnie reached out and patted my shoulder. 'But it's just a case of mistaken identity,' he said. 'Isn't it, Florence?'

★ ★ ★

'I really wish you'd stay, Florence.' Miss Ambrose had picked up the last of the tiles from the carpet. 'I'd feel much more comfortable if you were over here, with us.'

'I want to go back. I don't want to be in this place any more.' I pulled the coat around my shoulders. 'I've had enough.'

'I can't force you,' she said. 'But we're all here, if you change your mind.'

I wasn't going to change my mind. I'd had a bellyful of small conversations and side plates, and games of Scrabble. I looked for Elsie on my way out, but she was nowhere to be seen, and so I left Miss Ambrose and the sound of people carrying on with their lives, and I started walking down the corridor towards the courtyard.

I knew he was behind me.

I knew before I even looked.

'Haven't you got time for one more game?' he shouted.

I stopped. I turned. I walked back until I was so close to him, I couldn't take even one step more.

'It was you, wasn't it?' I said. 'All of it.'

He smiled, and the scar at the corner of his mouth disappeared. 'Was it?'

'The binoculars. The Battenberg. Even ordering the pizzas and the taxis. All of it was you.'

'Don't forget the elephant, Florence. Imagine the irony of forgetting an elephant.'

'You killed Gabriel Price, didn't you? You were the one who pushed him in the water.'

'You were the last person I expected to see on that riverbank, Florence. I was waiting for Gabriel. I had it all planned. I needed an identity to borrow, a name I could steal without too much fuss being made.' His expression never changed, even as he said the words. 'Things were getting a little too complicated.'

'You were waiting for him?'

'I knew he'd take a shortcut back to his digs. Then you popped up. Perfect timing, Florence. Strangely enough, because of you, becoming someone else was so very much simpler. If anyone would have kicked up a fuss and dug around, it would have been you. But you were hardly going to say anything under the circumstances, were you? You just underestimated how easy I found it

407

to swim back to the bank and carry on with the job I'd set out to do in the first place.'

'And the police didn't suspect anything.'

'I became a missing person. A few weeks later, a body washes up. Similar build, similar age. I knew it might happen, but by then Gabriel was unrecognisable. None of this DNA identification nonsense in those days, the police just used their powers of deduction. Lucky for me they managed to deduce incorrectly.'

'And no one missed Gabriel. No one thought it might be him?'

'Of course not. He was a traveller. A nomad. People just assumed he'd moved on to the next town. Being missing generally relies on someone bothering to notice you're not there any more.'

'And you just took his place. You stole his ID card and became a whole new person.'

Ronnie simply smiled.

'I'm going to tell them,' I said. 'I'm going to tell them everything. Right from the beginning.'

'And do you really think they'll listen?'

'People have always listened to me. My whole life. No one has ever doubted anything I've said.'

'Florence.' He leaned forward and the words tiptoed into my ear. 'When are you going to face up to it? You stopped being the person you used to be a long time ago.'

I could still feel the breath of his words on my face, even as I walked away.

★   ★   ★

When I got back to the flat, Elsie was sitting at the table, waiting for me.

'Where did you get to?' I knew I shouldn't have shouted. 'Why weren't you there?'

'Whatever's happened, Flo?' She shrank back in her seat and made herself very small. 'You look like you've seen a ghost.'

'It's Ronnie,' I went over to the window and drew the curtains. 'He pushed Gabriel Price in the water. He waited for him by the river, and he killed him. He confessed it to me, just now, when we were playing Scrabble.'

'Scrabble?'

'He swam to the side and got out. He was down there waiting, planning to drown Gabriel Price. He said me coming along just made it easier for him, because it meant I wouldn't stir up trouble.'

When I turned back, she had gone.

'Where are you now?' I said. 'Where have you got to?'

'I'm in here. You've had a shock, I'm making you a sugary tea.'

I went into the kitchen and put the milk back in the fridge. 'I don't want any sugary tea. I just want you to listen to me.'

By the time I'd closed the refrigerator door, she was back at the table with a piece of paper.

I snatched it from her hands. 'Will you just keep still and stop moving around. I can't keep track of you.'

Elsie became very quiet, and she watched me from the corner of the room. 'I'm not sure what

409

I'm supposed to do,' she said eventually. 'Tell me what to do.'

'I just need you to listen. He confessed it to me, now I need you to help me decide what's best. Jack would know. If Jack was here, he'd have a plan.'

'He isn't, though, is he?' she said. 'It's just you and me, and all those secrets. Who will ever believe us?'

'Someone has to, surely? For Ruth Honeyman? For Beryl?'

She didn't reply.

'I don't understand why you're here,' I said. 'If you're not going to help me.'

'I've helped you already. I helped you to find out the truth. That's exactly why I was here,' she said. 'Haven't you been listening?'

When I looked down, I realised my hands were shaking, and I had ripped the paper into tiny pieces.

'I think you need to lie down, Florence. Just for half an hour. Give your mind a rest.'

★ ★ ★

I didn't remember getting into bed. But I found myself lying there somehow, in curtained light, thinking about Ronnie.

I stood on the bridge for a while after he'd fallen. Instead of finding help, I decided to find Elsie. She was the only one who would understand. The only person I could tell. Not my father, who was too forgiving. Not Gwen, who would fashion an excuse for me, but Elsie.

410

Elsie was my best friend.

She was the only person who would have the right words.

Because Elsie always knew the right thing to say to make me feel better.

I started to run back to Elsie's house, along the pavements and the cobbles and the dark streets. I'm not sure what I noticed first, but I think it was the smell. I couldn't understand why I'd started to cough, why I found it more difficult to breathe, but as I grew closer, it was everywhere. Black smoke. Filling the streets. Twisting and winding its way through the night. Then I heard it. The crack of the flames. The whip of orange and red against the sky. I knew. I knew before I'd even turned the corner. I knew, because I remembered looking into the coals and losing my judgement in a fireplace full of thinking. I didn't put the guard back across. I poked at the fire and left it to smoulder, and a spark must have caught the carpet. Elsie's house was burning to the ground, and it was all my fault.

The fireman saved almost all of them. Almost a whole family.

All of them except one.

★   ★   ★

I never usually slept in the middle of the day, let alone fully dressed, and when I woke, the sheets were twisted and unhappy and there was a lacquer of sweat on my forehead. Elsie had gone. I knew straight away, because the flat felt empty of her.

'Are you there?' I shouted, just in case. 'I'm going to tell everything to Miss Ambrose.'

My voice fell into the silence.

'I need you to come with me.'

When I got out of bed, I tripped over the bedspread on the floor and I felt the pain shoot up my leg. It didn't seem to matter, though. The only thing I could think about was finding Elsie. I went outside into the courtyard and looked at all the flats. I wanted to knock on Elsie's door, but I couldn't decide which one was hers. She always came to visit me. She said my window had the better view. My eyes tried to find their way inside each house, through the glass and past the curtains, but all I could see was myself reflected back, potted plants on windowsills and bottles of washing-up liquid, and other people's empty lives. Jack would know which door to knock at, and I had to keep telling myself that he wasn't there to ask. My mind couldn't find its way out of sleeping, and each thought I had needed to be pulled through the slurry in my mind.

Perhaps Elsie had gone ahead. Perhaps she had thought for herself for once, and was already with Miss Ambrose, waiting for me.

# Handy Simon

Simon had never seen anyone arrested before. It wasn't like the television. There were no hand-cuffs, and he didn't hear anyone use the word 'nicked'. It was the same policemen from the other day, but this time, they didn't remove their hats.

Ronald David Butler.

He didn't look like a Ronald Butler. Although, to be fair, he didn't really look like a Gabriel Price any more either.

'Surely there's been some mistake?' said Miss Ambrose, when her jaw had recovered.

Gabriel Price (or perhaps Ronnie Butler) didn't say anything. He almost looked as though he'd been expecting it, but of course, he couldn't have been. No one else had. Simon and Miss Ambrose had been clearing away the funeral plates. They were all helping, to be fair. Even Cheryl. Every time he turned around, she seemed to be there, and when he was stacking all the cups and saucers, she'd come right up to him and they'd had a long conversation about how sad it was and what a shame you didn't realise how interesting someone's life was until the vicar read it all out from a pulpit. He was just going to move on to the side plates, when she asked him what he was doing that weekend.

'Nothing much,' he said, because she'd caught him off guard.

'Are you going to the cinema at all?' she said.

He told her he hadn't been planning to, and she just laughed and shook her head. 'Well I'd like to,' she said, 'if you fancied it?'

He said he would. Very quickly, before she changed her mind.

'You seem brighter than usual,' he said. 'What's put a smile on your face?'

She thought for a moment, and then she looked at him and said, 'It was Florence, actually.'

'Florence?'

'Yes,' she said. 'Florence. She asked about Alice. No one ever asks about Alice.'

Simon hesitated. 'We don't know what to say, Cheryl. None of us. We don't want to make you upset, we just can't find the right words.'

'That's because there aren't any,' she said. 'There never will be. And sometimes, even if you don't have the right words, it's better to use the ones you've already got, rather than say nothing at all. It upsets me more not to talk about her, because it pushes her further and further into the past.'

Simon wondered how someone so small could carry around so much grief all by themselves. 'You can talk to me about Alice any time you want,' he said. 'I'd love to hear about her.'

Cheryl reached up and kissed his cheek. 'There's so much more to you than first meets the eye, Simon.'

★ ★ ★

Simon was clearing away the last of the plates, and thinking about Cheryl, and trying to hold on

414

to the feeling of kindness on his face, when Gloria looked out of the window and said, 'The Old Bill are here,' because she watched too many television dramas. Simon tried to head for the kitchens with an armful of crockery, but he was intercepted by Gloria and forced to sweep crumbs from a tablecloth instead. He decided the best course of action was to focus the whole of his attention on the crumbs, but when the police asked for Gabriel Price, he turned around and stared. He couldn't help himself.

'Gabriel Price?' said Miss Ambrose. 'Our Gabriel Price?' As though there was an entire squadron of them somewhere, waiting to be called upon.

The policeman nodded.

Miss Ambrose sent Gloria to go and get him, and everyone looked at each other. Simon resorted to handpicking the crumbs from the carpet, and Miss Ambrose read a notice she'd written herself only ten minutes earlier. The policemen just waited. They were obviously used to silence, and didn't feel the need to fill it up with polystyrene words.

When Gabriel Price (or perhaps Ronnie Butler) finally appeared, the police said they were charging him with an arson attack.

'The ironing board in Miss Claybourne's front room?' said Miss Ambrose, which led to a ten-minute conversation with the policemen and a lot of confusion about health and safety.

No, no, they said. This was an incident dating from 1953. A house fire. Someone was killed.

Simon's mouth opened very slightly.

Ronnie Butler didn't even skip a beat. He simply straightened his trilby and smiled. He was just about to leave when Miss Claybourne burst through the double doors, spilling over with shouting and hysteria, and carrying what looked like pieces of torn sheet music.

'Finally,' she said. 'Finally someone listened.'

'Miss Claybourne. Florence . . . ' Miss Ambrose's words did nothing to alter the situation, and the first policeman shepherded Ronnie Butler out of the room and into the car park, because it looked as though Florence might launch herself towards him at any moment.

'He pushed him in,' she shouted after them. 'HE PUSHED HIM IN.'

'No one pushed anyone anywhere.' Miss Ambrose lowered Florence into a seat and crouched beside her. 'This is to do with a fire, although I don't know any more details.'

'A fire?' Florence became very still. 'Which fire?'

Miss Ambrose looked up at the second policeman, who looked at his colleague disappearing from the room and coughed.

'From a long time ago, from the *1950s*. The fire brigade got everybody out, except one.'

Simon started to say something, but changed his mind.

'How can you possibly connect someone with it after all this time?' said Miss Ambrose.

'Oh, Ronnie Butler was a suspect back then. The accelerant was found at his property.'

'Accelerant?' said Miss Ambrose.

'Petrol.' Simon shuffled his feet. 'That's what

416

people usually use. Although it would have still been rationed in 1953.'

The policeman looked over at him. He didn't look away for quite a long time.

'I do a lot of reading,' said Simon. 'It's one of my hobbies.'

'Witnesses also placed Ronnie Butler at the scene.'

Simon watched Florence. She looked as though someone had pressed a pause button. The hysteria was still there, it just seemed to be held in the moment, somewhere behind her eyes and in the lines that gathered around her mouth.

'Ronnie started the fire?' she said. 'It was Ronnie, not me?'

The policeman frowned at her.

'So why on earth wasn't he arrested sixty years ago?' said Miss Ambrose.

The policeman coughed again and looked at his notebook. 'Because,' he said, 'for all intents and purposes, he was dead.'

'Dead?'

'Drowned,' said the policeman. 'Or at least, that's what we were led to believe.'

'Washed up on Langley Beach,' Florence whispered. 'The fish ate most of him. My Fred would have been so proud.'

Miss Ambrose glanced at Florence and looked back at the policeman. 'So how did you trace him here, and why is he calling himself Gabriel Price?'

'He came to our attention after he was mugged, and we noticed the name Gabriel Price was still on the Missing Persons Register. We questioned him, and something just didn't feel right.'

'No,' said Miss Ambrose. 'It didn't feel right here either.'

'We've had a number of phone calls, including one from a retired detective. Perhaps individually they wouldn't have meant much, but put together . . . plus, there was some interesting information put forward by North Yorkshire Police. He had a motive, too. He's still a suspect in a hit and run.'

'A hit and run?' Miss Ambrose saucered her eyes.

The policeman looked at his notes again. 'Also from the 1950s. A young woman was killed by a car, and no one was ever charged. Big investigation. Lots of hearsay, but unfortunately nothing could be proved.'

'But you think Gabri — Ronnie Butler is responsible?'

'Almost certainly,' said the policeman. 'That's why he made the arson attack a short while afterwards. He believed there were witnesses in the house.'

'Belt and braces,' said Florence. 'He knew I always stayed over at Elsie's after the dance. It was me he was trying to get rid of, just in case they eventually caught up with him after all.'

The policeman frowned again, but he didn't say anything and returned to Miss Ambrose's questions. 'We thought we could prove that one.'

'But he wasn't charged, because you presumed he'd drowned?'

'Exactly. A body we believed was him washed

up a few weeks later. No formal identification of course, not in those days, but the height, build and age matched, and when we traced back along the estuary, we found Ronnie's ID card on the river bank. With no one else reported missing, we assumed the body was his and the case against him drifted into nothing.'

'Did no one think the body might be Gabriel Price's?' said Miss Ambrose.

'Gabriel's wife didn't go to the police for some months, because she just assumed her husband was still on the road. When she finally did try to file a report, up in Yorkshire, there was no reason to connect him with a body washed up all the way down here.'

'Until Ronnie was mugged,' said Florence. 'And a small act of kindness put Gabriel Price's name on the front page of all the newspapers.'

'Which is why he came looking for anyone who might be able to identify him. He wanted to frighten them off. Discredit them.' The policeman closed his notebook.

'But you can prove it's him now?' said Miss Ambrose.

'We think we've got a good chance. Especially with the dental records.'

'Dental records?' said Miss Ambrose.

The policeman nodded at the filing cabinet. 'He had a set taken in his twenties as well. Got into a fight.' He did a little policeman laugh. 'Fortunately for us.'

'He needs an X-ray and stitches. My father will take him,' Florence said, although Simon wasn't sure who she was talking to.

He looked at Miss Ambrose. She had her hand to her mouth.

Everyone watched from the door as Ronnie walked across the car park. At first, it was strange to think of him as Ronnie and not Gabriel, but it was amazing how quickly you got used to it. Perhaps a name didn't really mean much at all, Simon thought. Perhaps it was just another thing to carry around, like your date of birth and your national insurance number. Perhaps what really made you you, was where you were now, where you wanted to be, and how you decided to get there.

It was whisper-quiet as Ronnie got into the car. He didn't seem to be bothered about being arrested, which Simon found very strange. Ronnie even started whistling, although it wasn't a tune that Simon recognised.

★　★　★

'Ronnie started the fire. Ronnie.'

It was all Florence had said since the police drove away. She couldn't be tempted on to any other subject, no matter how much everyone tried. Miss Ambrose got her a glass of water, and then a small sherry, but none of it made any difference.

'He was worried I'd change my mind, and tell the police,' she said. 'He knew I stayed over at Elsie's every Saturday night, and he wanted me gone.'

'She's making no sense,' said Miss Ambrose. 'What does she mean, 'tell the police'?'

Simon shrugged and knelt on the floor. 'That's a nasty bruise you've got on your ankle, Florence. Did you have a bit of a stumble? It needs a compress, that does.'

He nodded at Gloria, who disappeared into the kitchens.

Florence leaned forward. 'Ronnie started the fire,' she said. 'All these years, I thought it was my fault, and it was him all along.'

'I know he did, Flo. But it's nothing to do with you. Nothing to worry about.' Simon held on to her hand.

'I need to let Elsie know. I need to tell her.'

Miss Ambrose looked at Simon, and she gave a small shrug.

'What have you done with her? Where is she?' Florence tried to stand up, but she seemed to change her mind. 'You've sent her to Greenbank, haven't you? Whilst my back was turned?'

Simon looked at Miss Ambrose, and tried to find some guidance in her face.

'No one has sent anyone to Greenbank.' Miss Ambrose knelt down as well. 'Try to stay calm, Flo.'

'Then where is she? Where's Elsie? She can't cope for very long without me, she gets confused.'

Gloria returned with the compress, and it distracted Florence for a moment. She stared at Gloria.

'You have very kind eyes, Gloria. You remind me of someone, but I can't think who. Have you ever been to Llandudno?' she said. 'Have you ever ridden on a tram?'

421

Gloria shook her head.

Florence looked at them all. 'Elsie would know. If Elsie was here, she'd know straight away. What have you done with her? Where is she? Elsie's my best friend. There are three things you should know about her, and that's the first one.'

'And what's the second thing we should know about her, Flo?' Simon took the compress from Gloria, and wrapped it very gently around Florence's ankle.

'That she always knows what to say. To make me feel better.'

Simon took the edge of the bandage and started to fasten it. 'And the third?'

Florence looked at him. 'I don't know,' she said. 'I've forgotten.'

'Well then,' he said. 'Perhaps the third thing wasn't that important after all. Perhaps it didn't make much of a difference in the end.'

'But I need to find her.' Florence tried to stand. 'I need to make sure she's all right.'

Simon took Florence's hands and looked into all the panic. 'Elsie isn't here right now, but it's nothing for you to worry about. I think the best thing to do is try and get some rest. It's been a long, strange, very sad day. My granddad always used to say everything looks better after a sleep. I think maybe he was right.'

Florence stared at him. 'You didn't do it.'

'Didn't do what?'

'You didn't talk to me like a child in the whole of that little speech you just gave.'

'No,' Simon said. 'Because that would have

been a bit patronising, wouldn't it?'

Florence sat back in her chair, and she smiled.

* * *

'I've left her with Natasha,' said Miss Ambrose. 'She'll stay until Florence has calmed down a bit. She said she'd leave her with the television on. She likes the news, Florence. It gives her an opportunity to fall out with people.'

Simon had just about finished clearing the plates away.

'I didn't know what to say.' Simon drew the curtain a little further to. 'When she was asking about Elsie.'

'None of us do. I know Jack tried to tackle it a few times, but it's so difficult. You did very well.'

Praise wasn't something Simon was particularly used to, and he held the words in his ears for a little while, before he allowed them to leave.

'Who was this Elsie, anyway?' he said.

'No one really knows.' Miss Ambrose reached into a cupboard in her office and took out a bottle of brandy. 'We tried to find out when Florence first came to live here, because we thought we might be able to trace her, but it turns out she died years ago. When they were in their twenties, I think. She's buried in the churchyard in town. Just by the chancel, in the corner.'

'She talks to her all the time.'

'I know.' Miss Ambrose poured them both a drink in little plastic beakers. 'It seems to give her some comfort, though, and it does no one any harm. There are times when I think Elsie is

423

just a little piece of Florence. The only part of her left that hasn't become confused. We've all just got used to it.'

'How strange it must be, to believe something with such certainty, and then to find it was just your mind playing tricks on you.'

'Dr Andrews said she did nothing but talk to Elsie during the whole of her assessment, and look at her dancing all alone when we were in Whitby. Dementia is a terrible thing.' Miss Ambrose looked at him over her beaker. 'You were very kind to her. With the ankle and everything.'

'It's funny.' Simon hesitated, because he didn't know if Miss Ambrose would want to hear, but he decided to go ahead anyway. 'A twisted ankle is how my mum first met my dad.'

'Really?'

'On a bus. Someone gave up their seat for her, or they never would have found each other. What are the chances?'

'And if they hadn't, you wouldn't even exist,' said Miss Ambrose.

'I'm not sure that would be such a bad thing,' Simon said.

'Nonsense. In fact,' Miss Ambrose poured another inch of brandy, 'I think you should consider retraining.'

Simon thought of his U-bends. 'As what?'

'A support worker. Care of the elderly. You have a kindness about you. I think you'd be brilliant at it.'

'Would I? I've just signed up for ballroom-dancing lessons. It would have to fit in around my hobbies.'

Miss Ambrose said, 'Oh, I think that can be arranged In fact, 1 think we should make quite a few new arrangements.'

'How do you mean?'

'Tai chi,' she said. 'For the residents. And ballroom-dancing lessons.'

'I was thinking of computer classes,' said Simon.

'Excellent idea. And I think we should plant some cherry trees. A whole group of them, at the front.'

'You won't be here to see them grow, though, will you?' Simon sniffed at the brandy, and decided he'd perhaps had enough. 'What with your CV and everything.'

Miss Ambrose clearly had no such reservations, because she poured herself another inch. 'I've had a change of heart,' she said. 'Although it's perhaps not a change. More of a revisit.'

'So you're staying?'

'I am. I just needed to find my long second.'

Simon decided not to ask, because Miss Ambrose looked at least ten years younger and he didn't want to spoil it.

'Anything else?' he said.

'Oh, plenty.' Miss Ambrose smiled. 'Gardening, for a start.'

'Jack used to say planting seeds at his age was an act of optimism.'

'I think that might be the best reason of all for doing it,' said Miss Ambrose.

# 10.54 p.m.

It's too late, now. All the people I thought might find me have disappeared back into their own lives.

Jack won't, of course. Somehow, I don't think Elsie will, either. Elsie was my best friend. That's the first thing you should know about her. The second thing is that she always knew what to say to make me feel better. There was a third thing, I'm sure of it, but it's slipped my mind for now, so it can't be all that important in the grand scheme of things.

'There is so very much more to us than the worst thing we have ever done.'

She said that to me on the beach. Elsie always knew the right thing to say. I can't imagine how I would have coped without her all these years. She said exactly the same thing to me the night Beryl died as well.

The last time I saw Beryl, Elsie and I were pressing our faces into the window of the town hall. We looked out into the darkness, cupping our hands against the glass to block out the lights, and we watched Beryl and Ronnie arguing in the car park and tried to hear what they were saying. Beryl and Ronnie falling out was nothing new, of course, but it was something else to look at when we got tired of other people's feet. Although it was Beryl doing all the arguing; Ronnie just watched her in silence.

'Do you see anything?' I pressed my hands more tightly against the window. 'Can you hear what they're saying?'

Elsie shook her head.

'What if he hits her, Elsie? What will we do?'

'Cyril's out there, too.' Elsie breathed into the glass and her words clouded the view. 'He won't hit her, not in front of someone else.'

We watched Beryl pace out her anger across the tarmac. Backwards and forwards, throwing her arms in the air, shouting in his face. I saw the tip of his cigarette glow brighter in the darkness as he drew in lungfuls of smoke. After a few minutes, Beryl stopped screaming. Her eyes were inches from his, but just when I thought he might raise his fist after all, she turned on her heel and marched off towards the fields.

'He can't just let her go like that,' I said. 'It's pitch black out there. She has no coat.'

'She'll come back. She won't get very far,' Elsie said, although she kept her eyes on the window.

The three of us waited. Elsie and I watching through the glass, and Ronnie out there in the car park, watching the darkness.

She didn't come back.

'I'm going after her,' I said.

Elsie followed me into the cloakroom. 'Don't be ridiculous, Florence. If anyone goes, it should be me.'

'No,' I said. 'You'll only end up arguing with her as well. I'll go. I'll bring her back for you.'

I pulled on my coat, and my arms argued with the sleeves in a rush to leave.

'Why do you care so much, Florence? Why?'

I stopped fighting with the material, and I looked right into Elsie's eyes, past all the questions. 'Because I can't bear anything to hurt you. Because whatever upsets you, I need to make it stop.'

I could hear my own breathing. It was the only thing I can remember about that moment, and when I look back to us standing there, just the two of us, it's all I can hear.

'You'll freeze to death,' she said.

I reached across to one of the pegs and took something. Something that wasn't mine to take. 'I'll have this with me, I'll be fine,' I said. 'Just fine.'

And I wrapped her red scarf around my neck and went out into the night.

# Handy Simon

The brandy had warmed Simon's bones, but when he walked into the courtyard, the evening air rushed inside and cooled them all down again. September had clicked into October when no one was looking, and Simon thought it was always the biggest leap. Other months blended nicely together, but those two were always a bit of a jump, and everyone seemed to panic and start wearing big coats. He thought about calling into the staff room and borrowing something for the walk home, but he'd probably be fine once he got going.

Cherry Tree was in darkness. Ten o'clock and everyone was in bed. His boots ate their way across the gravel, and the world was as silent as a Christmas morning. He was halfway across the car park, and considering the idea that he might never have existed at all, when he heard it. A dog. Barking with such urgency, it stopped Simon in his tracks. It was an unusual bark, too. A bit lopsided, and he couldn't make his mind up if it was a very long way from him, or almost at his side. No one at Cherry Tree had a dog. No pets allowed, that's what Miss Bissell had decided. Even though there had once been a very heated debate about a goldfish.

He tried to follow the lopsided barking, and the dog seemed to know, because it became more urgent. He followed the path and turned the corner, where he found himself looking up at Miss Claybourne's flat. There was a light. Just a faint one, in the hallway, leaking a yellow-orange on to the footpath. The barking stopped. He walked up to the front door and the whole of the courtyard was filled with the bright sparkle of the security lights. Natasha must have left hours ago.

'Miss Claybourne?' He knocked very lightly on the glass. 'Florence? It's Simon. Is everything all right in there?'

# 11.12 p.m.

If I were to look back on my life and find the most important moments, I'm not sure I'd know how to choose. I've had plenty of time to think about it, lying here, but I still can't decide which ones they were.

Perhaps it was when I got into a car with Ronnie Butler. I remember it now. How the seats smelled of beer, how I held on to the dashboard and begged him to slow down. I reached out. I tried to steer him away from her. I did everything I could. I know I did.

'You've got to find forgiveness,' Elsie said; I just didn't realise she meant I had to find it for myself. Perhaps that's the most important moment. Not the moment of the mistake itself, but the moment in which you finally forgive yourself for making it.

'When you thought I was the one in the car, you found forgiveness, Florence. So why can't you find it for yourself?'

I can hear her saying it. Even though she's not here any more. It's strange, because sometimes it feels as though she's never even left my side.

Perhaps the most important moments of all turn out to be the ones we walk through without thinking, the ones we mark down as just another day. Just another day we have to get through before something more interesting comes along. We benchmark our lives with birthdays and

431

Christmases and holidays, but perhaps we should think more about the ordinary days. The days that pass by and we don't even notice. Elsie once said that you can't tell how big a moment is until you turn back and look at it, and I think, perhaps, that she was right.

I think this may be the last of all my moments. I think my forever must have finally arrived. I didn't imagine this is how it would happen. Lying all alone on the floor, waiting for someone who never arrived. I thought Simon might have been the one to find me. He'll be clearing away the funeral tea now with Miss Ambrose, stacking plates and sweeping up crumbs. He'll talk whilst he's doing it, because that's just how Simon is. He'll probably talk to Cheryl more than anyone. I think she's sweet on him, although he's as daft as a brush and he hasn't even noticed. Perhaps he'll have a drop of brandy before he goes home, to take the edge off the chill, and then he'll cross the courtyard and his boots will crunch at the gravel in the silence. He'll be wondering about borrowing a coat before he starts walking, but then he'll think about me for some reason and he'll decide to call and check I'm all right. You get these feelings sometimes, don't you? There's no sense behind it, but for some reason, you know you need to do a thing and you've no idea why.

He'll notice there's a light on in the hall, and so he'll knock on the door, and he'll shout, 'Miss Claybourne? Florence? It's Simon. Is everything all right in there?'

He'll keep saying it.

'Florence?'

Over and over again.

I open my eyes. Someone has triggered the security system, and the room is filled with light. It hurts my eyes at first, and I close them against the glare. When I open them again, everything is back. The furniture and the curtains and the television. All the life I left a few hours ago before I fell. But the first thing I see, washed with light, is the mess underneath the sideboard. The pens and the coins, and everything that fell without me noticing. It takes me a moment for my eyes to find it, but it's there. Right at the back. Resting against the skirting board.

'Florence?'

A brooch.

A brooch with a smooth, dark stone, and a reflection almost like a mirror. A fossil. A piece of Whitby jet. It's a perfect circle, flawless and shining with an inky black. Surrounding it is a silver rope, which holds it forever in a polished frame.

'Florence?'

Something you would buy for someone you love. Not something you would buy for yourself.

'Miss Claybourne? Florence? It's Simon. Is everything all right in there?'

* * *

I stared at the brooch.

'I'm fine, Simon. Everything is fine.'

The strength to shout came from somewhere. From a place I didn't know existed.

'Are you sure? Is there anything you need?'

The brooch stared back at me. Elsie found me again after all. I stopped myself from reaching out, but then I realised I really didn't have to any more.

'No,' I said. 'I don't need anything. Everything I need is right here.'

I heard him turn to leave, his shoes on the footpath outside. 'I'll say goodnight, then,' he shouted.

I waited just a fraction too long. I knew he wouldn't hear, but I still shouted back. 'I'll be seeing you, Simon,' I said. 'I'll be seeing you.'

The light clicked and the room fell into black again. It was strange, because it felt more of a comfort now. More of a friend. I waited in the quietness for the music to return. For Al Bowlly. For a dancehall filled with who we used to be, circling a room, in shoes that pinched our toes but made us happy. Listening to music that wrapped itself around buried thoughts and made us feel less alone. A time we never wanted to leave.

I never did tell anyone my secret. It's strange, because I told them everything else. I even told them about Ronnie in the end. I just couldn't tell this. In those days, you couldn't say a word, and then it became too late. Elsie had found her Albert, and I had to use up the remnants of other people's lives to decorate my own. I didn't mind so much, as long as we could be friends. As long as she didn't leave me. It's strange, isn't it? How love paper-aeroplanes where it pleases. I have found that it settles in the most unlikely of places, and once it has, you are left with the burden of where it has landed for the rest of your life.

The music is very loud now. I can't imagine where it's coming from, although I think a part of me is beginning to realise. There was a point when I thought Simon had come back, when I thought I heard him knock at the door again, but the tap was too light, too gentle, and I knew it couldn't have been him.

I know I won't have to wait long.

I'm not sure I have enough time to remember it all again, from the beginning, because there's so much to fit in.

I have never done anything remarkable. I've never climbed a mountain or won a medal, and I have never stood on a stage and been listened to, or crossed a finishing line before anyone else.

I have led a quite extraordinary life.

# Acknowledgements

I honestly believe that every person we meet alters us in some way. From the smallest encounter, to a life-long friendship, we are always changed by those who pass through our lives, even if they only walk with us for a short time.

With that in mind, it's almost impossible to write acknowledgements. There are many people to whom I owe a huge debt of gratitude. My amazing agent, Sue Armstrong, and all the team at C&W, especially Emma, Jake, Alexandra and Alexander. My fabulous editor Suzie Dooré, and an entire army of brilliant people at HarperCollins (especially Kate, Holly, Charlotte, Hannah, Tom and Fran). The truly wonderful and indispensable Ann Bissell, trusted keeper of my sanity and so much more than a publicist. I feel privileged to have the opportunity to work with you all.

Over the past few years of writing, I have been fortunate enough to meet very many generous people — fellow authors, booksellers, readers and reviewers. An enormous thank you to everyone who took the time to read my words, especially to Simon Savidge, Hannah Beckerman, Leilah Skelton, John Fish, Nina Pottell and Anne Cater. Your kindness will never be forgotten.

This story is also, in part, a love letter to

Whitby. Accompanied by my parents (who deserve endless acknowledgement), I spent my childhood holidays climbing the Abbey steps, wandering around Woolworths, and terrifying myself on ghost walks (run by Harry, who — unlike Barry — told the very best stories). From Botham's Tea Rooms to the arch of the whalebones, it will always be my very favourite place on earth.

As always, though, this book would never have been written without the patients. In Tamworth, Derby, Chesterfield and Burton, I was lucky enough to not only work with incredible teams of people, but also spend time with patients I will remember forever. My life was definitely changed by meeting you and my writing and thinking will always be guided by the short time we walked together.

We do hope that you have enjoyed reading
this large print book.

Did you know that all of our titles
are available for purchase?

We publish a wide range of high quality
large print books including:
**Romances, Mysteries, Classics**
**General Fiction**
**Non Fiction and Westerns**

Special interest titles available in
large print are:
**The Little Oxford Dictionary**
**Music Book**
**Song Book**
**Hymn Book**
**Service Book**

Also available from us courtesy of
Oxford University Press:
**Young Readers' Dictionary**
**(large print edition)**
**Young Readers' Thesaurus**
**(large print edition)**

For further information or a free
brochure, please contact us at:
**Ulverscroft Large Print Books Ltd.,**
**The Green, Bradgate Road, Anstey,**
**Leicester, LE7 7FU, England.**
**Tel:** (00 44) **0116 236 4325**
**Fax:** (00 44) **0116 234 0205**

## THE TROUBLE WITH GOATS AND SHEEP

### Joanna Cannon

England, 1976: A town somewhere in the East Midlands. An avenue within that town. The hottest summer that anyone can remember. Mrs Creasy has disappeared — vanished into thin air, even leaving her shoes behind. Her husband wanders the street, waiting for her to return, convinced that she will be home in time for their wedding anniversary. But ten-year-olds Grace and Tilly are determined to find her. As the summer shimmers endlessly on, doors and mouths begin to open, the cul-de-sac gives up its secrets — and the amateur detectives will learn more than they could ever have imagined . . .

# DALILA

## Jason Donald

Irene Dalila Mwathi comes from Kenya with a brutally violent personal history. Once she wanted to be a journalist, but now all she wants is to be safe. When she finally arrives, bewildered, in London, she is attacked by the very people paid to protect her, and she has no choice but to step out on her own into this strange new world. Through a dizzying array of interviews, lawyer's meetings, regulations and detention centres, she realises that what she faces may be no less dangerous than the violence she has fled . . .